THIS WASN'T AN ORDINARY DELIVERY . . .

No one would have guessed that the benign figure dressed in a red and green pizza delivery uniform was a killer—unless they looked in his eyes. A fire burned there, but not a blaze that would lend any warmth. He was intense, a man with a mission, holding the keys to life and death. And tonight he chose death.

This wasn't his first time. He had done it before, and would again. He glanced at his watch. In exactly ten minutes.

The killer entered the building, pizza box balanced on his right shoulder. With his left hand, he felt inside his jacket for his weapon of choice. His fingers closed around it, and he was surprised at his own calmness. He wasn't even shaking, his head was clear, his resolve intact. He was getting better every time.

He glanced at his watch. "You've got about two and a half minutes to live," he told the man in the apartment above. "Two and a half minutes and counting."

* * *

Sonja Massie has lived in New York, Toronto, and Los Angeles, and has travelled extensively in Ireland. She is the bestselling author of *Far and Away, Dream Carver,* and *Carousel,* as well as the critically acclaimed novel *Moon Song.*

THE DARK MIRROR

Sonja Massie

ZEBRA BOOKS
KENSINGTON PUBLISHING CORP.

To the loving father
Who can make any hurt "all better" with a hug,
To the little boy
Who coaxed the child in me to come out
and play again—
after so many years,
To the man
Who is my lover, my best friend, my husband,

To Rob
Who is all three to me . . . and so much more.

One

"No! Don't! Oh, God . . ." The young woman's breath came in harsh gasps and she made whimpering, gagging sounds as she pleaded with her attacker. "Please, don't!"

She sat on a thick Persian carpet, curled into a fetal position, her arms wrapped tightly around her body. Her peach silk camisole hung from only one thin strap, ripped down the front, revealing dark red welts across her throat and breasts. The remainder of her clothing lay strewn across the hunter green chintz sofa, the antique cocktail table, and the polished marble floor. A room of refinement, style, and good taste. A room whose ambiance belied the brutality of the act which had just taken place within its mahogany wainscoted walls.

Illuminated by the blazing logs in the fireplace and the soft glow of a Tiffany lamp, the woman's pretty face contorted with pain. Tears flowed down her bruised cheeks and blood trickled from several cuts on her lips.

Her entire body shook violently, as she stared up at the middle-aged man who towered over her. His chest was bare—his shirt lying beside her torn blouse on the sofa—and his linen slacks were unzipped. He reached one hand toward her, palm outstretched, in a conciliatory gesture. His hand trembled as much as hers.

She cowered and threw up her arms to shield herself from another blow. "No! Don't!"

For a moment he stared down at her as though shocked by her reaction. He glanced briefly around the room, noting the torn clothing, and appeared nonplussed to find himself in this circumstance.

His naked chest glistened in the firelight, slick with sweat. He, too, fought for breath as he watched the young woman, at least twenty years his junior, concern registering on his darkly handsome face.

"Tina, I . . . I mean, are you . . . ?"

Again he held his hand out to her, but she slapped it away and sobbed even harder. "Just get out of here! Leave!" she said, strangling on her words.

His concern evaporated, and in seconds his expression had changed from that of a confused, anxious friend offering assistance, to the enraged, callous rapist he had been only moments before.

Grabbing her by the wrist, he twisted her arm behind her and gave it a vicious jerk. She screamed and rolled onto her side, her face buried in the carpet. A sick smile lit his eyes. "Don't you *ever* hit me again. Understand?" He squeezed harder. She moaned her compliance and nodded weakly. Tossing her hand aside, he added, "And stop your blubbering before I give you something to cry about."

Turning his back on her, he zipped his slacks, walked over to the sofa and retrieved his shirt. She sat up and watched him, her eyes burning with hate and suppressed fury. Her fingers clutched at the torn edges of her camisole; she grabbed a handful of the silk and squeezed until her fists turned white. "You son of a . . . ," she muttered through clenched jaws. Closing her eyes tightly, she began to cry again.

As he slipped on his shirt and buttoned the front he said, "Come on, Tina. Don't tell me you didn't enjoy that, too."

Once again he walked over to her and knelt beside her on the carpet. She shuddered as he glided his fingers from her bare shoulder to her elbow. "You wanted it. That's why you invited me over here when your parents were in Europe."

She rolled away from him, gathering her shredded silk around her. "You were . . . supposed to . . . tutor me," she said between chattering teeth.

He smiled, but the expression held no humor. Lifting a lock of her hair from her shoulder, he fondled it, twisting it around his forefinger. "And I did, huh? You learned a thing or two."

"I said *no*. But you did it anyway. You raped me!"

His expression darkened and he yanked her hair. She raised one fist as though to strike him, looked into his eyes, and lowered her hand. " 'Atta girl," he said. "You're learning."

He walked over to the cocktail table, lifted a half-empty bottle of Dom Perignon, and filled a crystal champagne flute. The glass's mate lay shattered, glittering shards on the marble. "Rape is an ugly word, Tina. Be careful how you use it."

He took a long drink and emptied the glass, then handed the flute and the bottle to her. When she refused it, he set both beside her on the hearth. "I'm your professor; you're my protegé. I'd never do anything to hurt you."

Lifting his tweed jacket from the floor, he meticulously picked a few imaginary bits of dust from the sleeve. "You invited me over when you were all alone. You offered me champagne. What was I supposed to think?"

He smiled at her, his eyes caressing her bare limbs. "You wanted passionate romance. You got it."

She grabbed one of the satin pillows stacked beside the fireplace and clasped it in front of her to shield her breasts from his view.

"If you tell anyone, who do you think they'll believe, an accomplished professor, or a snot-nosed student? With my help you'll be a world-renowned concert pianist someday. Don't screw it up." He pulled a golden pocket watch from his jacket, opened it, then snapped it closed. "My, how time flies. We'll have to do this again . . . soon. Tomorrow night, my place."

"No," she said, her face deathly white even in the red glow of the fire. Slowly, all fear receded from her eyes, to be replaced by fury. "Not again. Never!"

He chuckled. "You'll be there. Because if you aren't, I'll have to come back here. And I won't be very happy about it, either."

Bending over her, he gently stroked her cheek, then trailed his fingertips over the welts on her neck and down to the swell of her breast. "Seven-thirty, Tina. My house. Be there."

Their eyes locked. His shone with the grim satisfaction of the conqueror, the intoxicant of having total control over another, the narcotic of omnipotence. Hers blazed with a hotter flame, that of outrage which had gone beyond insult or offense. An assault on the body might lacerate the soul, but in her case, it hadn't killed her spirit.

He broke eye contact first and moved away from her. Squatting to retrieve his keys and wallet from under the table, he didn't notice as her hand closed around the neck of the champagne bottle. With a choked scream of rage she rose onto her knees and swung. The bottle struck his temple and cheek—a dull, liquid thud. Groaning, he dropped to the floor.

In a second she was standing over him. Again she lifted the heavy green bottle over her head and brought it down. Again . . . and again . . . and again. Champagne sprayed over them both, glistening golden droplets in the firelight.

Eventually, her strength and emotions spent, she backed away from him. Stunned, she looked at the blood-smeared bottle in her hand. She threw it to the floor. The bottle broke in half and the neck rolled across the marble to the hearth where it clanked with a note of finality. In the heavy silence that followed the only sounds were those of her harsh, ragged breathing and the crackle of the fire.

"Professor . . . ?"

She reached out one hand as though to touch the body, but withdrew it. She waited. And waited. He didn't move.

Slowly, woodenly, she staggered over to the table with the Tiffany lamp and picked up a French enameled telephone. She dialed three numbers.

"Yes, this is an emergency," she said, her voice steady now, calm. "Please hurry. I think I've killed my professor."

* * *

A moment later, the image of the young student and the firelit room faded from the screen, to be replaced by another woman. As this lady glided across the sparse studio set, her shoulder-length blue-black hair glittered even more than the black, beaded couture gown she wore. With a fluid wave of one hand, she indicated a large oval mirror to her right, the only prop on the white stage. Set in an ornate, gilded frame, the full-length glass reflected the room in the scene before, the young woman speaking on the telephone, her attacker lying dead before the fireplace.

"Ladies and gentlemen," the woman in black said, her voice sonorous, husky but distinctly feminine, "I challenge you to look into the Dark Mirror, that shadowy reflection of the human soul . . . in this case, the soul of a murderer. And I dare you to ask yourself the question, 'Under the right . . . or wrong . . . circumstances could *I* take the life of another human being?' "

The camera moved closer, until the woman's face filled the screen. Her black hair and high cheekbones spoke of shades of a Native American heritage, but her eyes were as light as her hair was dark, the palest blue, rimmed with black lashes. The feminine line of her full lips contrasted with her strong chin and its dimple.

But it was her expression, not her beauty that arrested the eye. When Elizabeth Knight looked into the camera, her television audience could feel her gazing into their souls. And the secret to her success was her ability to make them uncomfortable, while fascinated, by what she revealed.

"How many of you would commit that most heinous of crimes, murder, if you were in the same circumstance as this young woman? How can any of us know . . . unless we've been there?" She drew a deep breath and smiled mysteriously. "How can anyone know the heart of a murderer?"

The camera moved to the mirror where the image reflected was that of dozens of faces, male and female, young and old, common and aristocrat. Faces that betrayed the spectrum of human emotion: love, hate, fear, and happiness. In the center Elizabeth's face appeared.

"Until next week, this is Elizabeth Knight wishing you many interesting revelations in your own . . . Dark Mirror. Good night."

The woman who sat in the small, posh theater, staring at the fading image, bore little resemblance to the dark beauty on the screen. The silky black hair was pulled back into a ponytail, the svelte body covered by an oversized, red sweatshirt which bore the logo "Toronto Skydome—Where the World Comes to Play." The graceful, regal bearing had disappeared. She sat with her arms wrapped around her knees, her sneakers propped on the top edge of the seat in front of her. Only the eyes were the same—piercing blue lasers that constantly calculated, evaluated.

"Hate it, don't cha?" said a twangy southern voice, reminiscent of female country singers who extol the virtues of "standing by your man."

Elizabeth turned to the older woman sitting beside her. "It stinks. Of course I hate it. And Brody knew I would. That's why he managed to avoid letting me see the final cut until the last minute."

She rose from her seat and stomped down the aisle toward the back door, her friend in pursuit. "What are you gonna do?" Silver coins strung on leather fringes jangled on the woman's jacket as she hurried after Elizabeth. In spite of the handicap of two-sizes-too-small jeans and five-inch stiletto heels, she caught her at the door and grabbed the sleeve of her sweatshirt. "Whoa, hold on there. You're not going to give ol' Brody hell, now are ya?"

Momentarily curbing her irritation, Elizabeth donned a "patient" look. "Cass, you know I love you dearly . . ."

"But . . . ?"

"Butt out."

Cassandra Wilson nodded, her bleached, frosted, and thrice-highlighted blond curls bobbing. "O-kay. You handle it your own way. Just don't get your fanny canned."

"Not bloody likely." Elizabeth slapped Cass's fringed shoulder companionably. "Meet me in my office in fifteen minutes. We'll go out for a beer. It's Corona night at Donohue's."

Cass grinned as Elizabeth strode down the carpeted hall toward the network president's office. "Five minutes," she said with a grin. "As mad as she is, it won't take her long to give Brody a snoot full."

As Elizabeth traced a crooked path through the maze of hallways, past recording stage doors, cutting rooms, and more than one hundred offices, she recalled the first time she had walked this route. Her pulse had pounded in her temples, her face flushed, her knees shaky. Just like now. Only then, her symptoms had been brought on by nervousness, not fury. She had been going to meet Mr. Brody Yarborough. The big man himself had asked for an interview. More accurately, he had demanded an appearance.

After paying her dues, living in a cold, drafty, Manhattan apartment, writing more screenplays than she cared to remember and working for minimum wage as a waitress in a nearby pub, her agent had placed her latest idea for a series in the right hands. And the proposal had been shuffled upward through the Yarborough Broadcasting hierarchy to *the* Mr. Yarborough. She had left his office that day with a contract in her hands, her head in the upper stratosphere, and a sinking feeling in the pit of her stomach—the uneasy premonition that she was going to have trouble with this guy.

Listen to your gut more often, she told herself as she flung open the door to his reception area and marched inside.

"I'll tell Mr. Yarborough you're here," said the buxom blonde secretary behind the desk as she reached for the phone.

Elizabeth had decided long ago that Yarborough's two basic

requirements for a secretary were blonde hair and a breast augmentation. Office skills seemed less important.

"That's okay, Bambi. He's expecting me," Elizabeth said as she crossed the posh reception area with its Berber carpeting, limited edition lithographs, and contemporary white leather seating clusters. Yarborough Broadcasting System hired only the best decorators. Visitors *must* be impressed at any cost.

But the evidence of good taste ended the moment she threw open the door to Brody Yarborough's private office. Yarborough was a "manly" sort of guy . . . at least in his own estimation. The ivory carpeting ceased at the threshold, to be replaced with a brilliant scarlet which raised the blood pressure ten points.

Exotic animal heads lined the walls, testimonies to Yarborough's skill with a gun—or at least to his ability to hire safari guides who possessed that expertise. Antelope, gazelle, a buffalo, and a grizzly bear snarled down on visitors. More than once upon entering this room, Elizabeth had wondered how the taxidermist had managed to get a gazelle to snarl.

In a prominent place directly over Yarborough's desk hung his prize trophy, a full-maned African lion . . . the symbol of Yarborough Broadcasting System. The perfect trademark for a manly sort of network. Snarling, of course.

Tall, well-built in a Nautilus-five-times-a-week sort of way, in his late forties or early fifties, Brody was an impressive physical specimen. He stood before an enormous gun cabinet which displayed an arsenal of antique and contemporary weaponry. It contained everything from a pair of Napoleonic dueling pistols to the latest assault rifle with laser scope. As she strode into the room, slamming the door behind her, he replaced the gun he had been fondling and slowly locked the cabinet door, carefully ignoring her entrance. She waited, her anger building, as he sauntered over to his desk and sat down.

With great ceremony he propped his snakeskin cowboy boots on the desk beside a bronze figurine of a steer in an indelicate squatting position. Beneath the animal's rump was a pile of manure and an engraved caption which read, "No bullshit!"

He pushed back his oversized cowboy hat and flashed her a broad smile, as though noticing her for the first time. No one at the network could remember seeing Yarborough without his hat, and some said it was surgically attached. But Cass, who had known Brody since their wild days in Texas years ago, had confided to Elizabeth that Brody's affection for his Stetson lay in the fact that it covered a head which was almost completely bald.

"Hi there, sugar. What a nice surprise," he said, waving a hand toward a leopard-print velvet chair. "Take a load off."

"I saw the final cut of this week's show," she said, ignoring his invitation to relax.

"And aren't you proud? You sure were lookin' pretty in that black gown. I don't mind tellin' you, certain parts of my anatomy sure stood up and took notice."

"Your friendly taxidermist can stuff your . . . anatomy . . . and hang it on the wall for all I care."

He shook his head and clucked his tongue. "Now, now, 'Lizbeth, when are you going to start talking like a lady?"

"When I find myself speaking to a gentleman."

With a sigh he crossed his arms over his chest. He dropped the "good ol' boy" facade and assumed a poker expression. "So, you didn't like the show. What did we do wrong *now?*"

Elizabeth noted, not for the first time, the absence of his Texas drawl when talking business. And she remembered why she hadn't liked him when they had met three years before. Her "don't trust this guy" alarm had gone off with high decibels when she had shook his hand and looked into those cold, gray eyes. She had searched for a soul and found only calculating intellect.

Oh, he could be quite charming when it served him. Building an empire from scratch required a certain amount of charisma. But she couldn't honestly say that in the years she had known him and worked with him, she had ever seen him demonstrate genuine kindness or sentiment toward anyone.

She swallowed her anger and forced her voice to sound calm as she leaned both hands on his desk and fixed him with her blue lasers. "You know damned well what I don't like. When I wrote that script and handed it to you, it was a straightforward story about date rape. A middle-class music student, her small-town professor."

"So, we spiced it up a bit."

"You sensationalized a simple story by accentuating the wealth, the nudity, and the violence."

"Money, sex, and murder—my dear—are the staples of the American television diet."

"Because it's all that's being dished up by network executives like you. That is *not* what we agreed 'The Dark Mirror' would be about. In the beginning we had a clear understanding, but every week, you're pushing it further and further. The exploitive violence, the tits-and-ass routine."

"What have you got against tits and ass as long as it ups your ratings?"

"There's more to life, Brody. What do *you* have against entertainment aimed at the adults in the audience rather than the over-aged adolescents?"

She walked over to the window which looked out over a bustling midtown Manhattan. Seventeen floors below, a group of demonstrators braved a cold winter downpour to carry their placards, complaining about the "sin" portrayed by the network . . . specifically the program, "The Dark Mirror."

She knew what they said—

"Sex and violence, anti-family, anti-God."

"Y.B.S. must be accountable before the Lord."

"Elizabeth Knight brings murder and fornication into our living rooms."

Every morning and every evening, Elizabeth had those signs thrust into her face when she arrived or left the studios. In the beginning she had merely been irritated by their self-righteous attitudes. But lately . . .

"I'm not so sure they're wrong about us anymore," she said, staring down at the drenched pickets. "You're giving them more ammunition with every episode."

Brody rose and walked over to the window to stand beside her. He laid one hand on her shoulder. She glanced down at the hand coldly and he removed it.

" 'Lizbeth, why don't you just write your great scripts, look gorgeous every week in your prologue and epilogue, and leave the rest to me? We've got a golden goose here. Let's don't kill it with all this bickering."

Elizabeth looked down at the picketers as the rain fell even harder, the dark clouds turning the city a drab, wet monotone gray. Many of them had no umbrellas. She had to admire their dedication and stamina.

"It isn't a matter of money or ratings," she said, suddenly feeling drained. As usual, her temper had flared and burned out more quickly than she had intended. "It's a matter of honor. I had a special reason for bringing this show into the world and . . ."

"I know," he said. "You're a lady of high moral purpose and I love ya to pieces for it. But you're giving me another ulcer with all this complaining crap."

"Yeah? Well, my masseuse says that *you* are the pain in my ass that she has to rub out every Wednesday."

She walked to the door where she paused, looking back at him over her shoulder. "I'm not kidding, Brody. 'The Dark Mirror' was created to inform and enlighten . . . not titillate. If it ceases to do that, you'll be shopping for another writer/hostess. And I don't mean to sound conceited, but you'd have a hell of a time replacing me. I'm good."

Brody smiled warmly. "Of course you are, darlin'. I'm your number one fan."

The moment she left, closing the door behind her, the smile fell away from Yarborough's face. He walked to his desk, picked up the phone and punched in some numbers.

"Elizabeth was just in my office, giving me shit," he said, landing a solid kick to the side of his desk. The toe of his boot left a dint in the polished ebony surface. "I told you not to let her see the show before it aired." He paused, pulled a cigarette from the front pocket of his western shirt and lit up. "I don't give a damn if she insisted. I told you *not* to show it to her."

He took a long draw from the cigarette and released the smoke through his nose. "Yeah, well, you're fired. Get the hell out of my studio. Now!"

After slamming the phone down, he picked it up again and buzzed his secretary. "Tell security that if Norman Paulson hasn't left the building in three minutes, have the cops arrest him for trespassing. Then call bookkeeping and tell them to 'lose' his check for a couple of months."

Sitting at his desk, he picked up an eight-by-ten glossy of Elizabeth, the latest in a series of promo shots. "Hoity-toity bitch," he said, staring at the photo, "you need to be taken down a notch or two."

Two

"You'll never get promoted until you get rid of that decrepit coat and that mangy, flea-infested mascot."

Nick O'Connor glanced down at his battered bomber jacket and then at the British bulldog who trotted along behind him at the end of a sturdy leash. As Nick and his best friend, Peter MacDonald, picked their way around the mud puddles that dotted the sidewalk on a rain-slick Lexington Avenue, a light cold mist fell, encircling each traffic light with a red, green, or gold halo. Holiday tinsel of the same colors glimmered in shop windows.

Although it was almost nine o'clock, the street still teemed with pedestrians, taxis, and vendors who hawked their "genuine" Rolex and Gucci watches for $9.99. Christmas gifts for the discriminating of taste and frugal of pocketbook.

"Hey, Hercules, did you hear that?" Nick asked the brindle and white bull, who looked up and cocked one ear quizzically. "Pete called you mangy. Bite his ass. Take a nice juicy chunk out and then I won't have to feed you supper."

Peter MacDonald laughed and punched Nick in the shoulder. Nick absorbed the jab without flinching or grimacing. Hercules growled at Peter, and Nick reached down to pat the broad head.

"That's okay, boy," he said. "Thanks for the offer, but I can take care of ol' Pete by myself."

Half a second later Nick threw the obligatory retaliation punch. Peter didn't flinch either.

Both Nick and Pete had been raised as street kids in a less than prestigious section of the Village. In their circles physical violence had been the only acceptable way for one male to show affection to another.

Twenty years and two N.Y.P.D. badges later, the code remained the same: If it hurt, you swallowed it. Whether your buddy punched you, or your superior chewed you out and made you feel like shit, if your woman told you she didn't want to be your lover anymore because she wasn't getting what she needed from the relationship, or when you scraped some kid up off the street because the parent was too stupid and careless to buckle them up. If it hurt, you swallowed it.

Words to live by, Nick thought as he tried to ignore the ache in his shoulder. His only consolation was that smart-ass Pete's was hurting worse. *Decrepit jacket, mangy mascot.* Served him right.

As the two strolled through the fog-misted darkness, they couldn't have been a more mismatched pair. Nick still looked the part of street kid, aging black bomber jacket and jeans that had seen better days—in the early eighties. His thick blond hair reached his collar, an unruly mane that distinctly had a will of its own. The humidity was causing it to wave in several directions.

On the other hand, Peter presented the picture of an up-and-coming executive in his London Fog trench coat and brightly polished Italian loafers. His thinning brown hair was carefully combed, making full use of each remaining strand.

Nick looked his friend up and down scornfully. "You look like a damned Fed in that outfit. With your wardrobe you may get promoted, but I'll bet you don't get laid very often."

"I've enjoyed the company of some delectable, sophisticated ladies recently. And I'll have you know—"

"Where did you find them? Forty-second or Times Square?" Nick laughed and ignored Peter's glare. "Get yourself some leather and denim and you won't have to pay for it."

"Quite the stud, aren't we?"

Nick dropped the act and grinned self-consciously. "To be

honest, I haven't had time for the . . . softer . . . pleasures of life in a long time. They keep me pretty busy at the station."

Peter pulled a monogrammed handkerchief from his pocket and blew his nose. "To be perfectly truthful, it's the same for me. Right now I'd enjoy ruminating on a nice dinner with a human being who doesn't shave."

Nick grimaced at the vocabulary and rasped his palm across his three-day-old stubble. "Well, *I* haven't been shaving much lately. If you're paying we could—"

"No thanks, that wasn't exactly what I had in mind."

They paused at a corner and waited while a fleet of taxis raced by, jostling for space, making five lanes out of three. Steam rose from the grating, warming the spot where they stood by a few degrees. A woman wearing a full-length mink passed them, walking her Shih Tzu and holding the handle of a poop scoop daintily between thumb and forefinger. Nick tightened his hold on Hercules's leash. The bulldog was particularly fond of gnawing on the hind legs of walking dustmops.

The lady in fur passed a couple of street people, an elderly man and woman trying to absorb every degree of warmth possible from a steaming grate near a laundry. The dichotomy of New York City. The filthy rich; the just plain filthy and poor. Even though Nick had been born and raised here, he had never quite gotten over it.

The light turned, and the tide of bodies surged into the street. Those who were in a hurry, still caught up in the New York City hustle, impatiently scooted around those, like Nick and Peter, who were in the process of winding down for the evening.

Nick breathed in the rain-fresh air, scented with exhaust fumes and roasting chestnuts. Already he could smell the enticing aroma of his mother's Italian deli a block away. Tomato sauce and garlic—the smell of his childhood. The savory bouquet always gave him a warm feeling inside, a friendly beacon to welcome him home.

"Why don't you come inside and have one of Mama's famous meatball sandwiches?" he said.

Peter gave him a mischievous sideways glance. "That depends . . . how old is that younger female sibling of yours now?"

Again, a blow flew fast and hard to the shoulder. This time Peter winced, code or not.

"Nina's seventeen . . . a baby, you old pervert."

They had arrived at the deli and stood under the brown and white striped awning that leaked in several places. The steamy windows were plastered with signs, advertising the day's specials. Peter peered between the banners. A pretty girl with long, dark hair and big eyes shoved a sandwich across the counter to a customer.

"Hey, not bad!" he said. "When will she be eighteen?"

"Up yours, buddy," Nick replied. "You just lost out on a hell of a sandwich."

"Oh, well, I have to get going anyway. Have to put in some extra time if you're going to make lieutenant. Takes consecration to ascend the ranks."

The hard lines of Nick's face softened as he looked into his friend's eyes. Peter was changing. And Nick didn't want him to. They had been friends for twenty-five years, but, lately, Nick missed the kid who had played football with him, jumping over piles of rubbish in empty lots. Where was the teenager who had painted graffiti with him on the subways, gotten busted and served weeks of community service scrubbing off the same scrawlings?

Who was this stranger in the trench coat who used monogrammed handkerchiefs and words like "ruminate?" Nick couldn't bring himself to tell Pete that, rather than impressing people, he was mangling the English language. Nick salved his conscience by convincing himself that he couldn't bear to hurt Pete's feelings. But, in fact, he enjoyed watching his status-hungry buddy make an ass of himself. At times, he found it more gratifying than downing a cold beer and watching the Macy's fireworks display from a rooftop on the Fourth of July. Pete was always worrying about who was trying to make a fool of him. He needed no help; he did a fine job all by himself.

But Nick liked him. He wasn't sure why anymore. Maybe it was just a habit. Maybe they had simply drifted apart over the years and needed to spend more time together, like they used to in the old days.

"Don't be such a stranger," he said. "Hercules misses you."

Peter bent over and scratched behind the dog's ear. The animal closed his eyes in ecstasy and leaned his considerable weight against Peter's leg. "Yeah, well, maybe I'll saunter over in a few days for that sandwich. Tell Nina 'hi' for me; she's a sweet kid."

He slapped Nick across the cheek. "It's back to work for me, old chap."

Pete tugged his tie into place, turned and marched away, back ramrod straight. These days Pete made the Marines look like slouchers. "Pete MacDonald's on patrol," Nick said with a smirk. "The world's a safer place."

He watched, a pensive expression on his craggy features until his friend disappeared around a corner. Yeah, Pete would make lieutenant, all right. Hell, he'd probably be chief of police someday.

Doesn't matter, Nick thought as he turned and opened the door to the deli, ushering Hercules inside. *If push came to shove, I could still whip his ass.*

He grinned at his own immaturity. His mama was right, boys never really grew up, they just got bigger. And her good Italian food had done the trick; he was six-four and a fine example of Italian/Irish breeding. He had inherited his father's blond hair and green eyes. Only the deep gold of his skin indicated his Mediterranean heritage.

On the other hand, his sister had come up all Italian when the genetic dice had been thrown. She frequently teased him about being Irish, and as a result, they hurled a string of "mick, wop" insults back and forth.

He saw that she was waiting on one of her least favorite customers, Alfredo Marino, an elderly gentleman who came in every night for his hot pastrami on rye. Inevitably, he appeared one minute before closing time, entertaining the mistaken notion that he would receive a discount since it was the end of the day and presumably, the food was stale. He hadn't gotten a break in fifteen years, but it didn't stop him from trying.

"Ah . . . this pastrami looks a little a'bit dry," he said, closely examining the sandwich in its styrofoam container.

Nina rolled her eyes upward with that high degree of contempt which only a teenager can achieve.

"That will be four-seventy-five, Señor Marino," she said, ignoring his complaint and the face which Nick was making at her over the pasta display. Hercules started to trot around the counter, eager for a tidbit, but Nick softly called him back. "Lay low, boy," he whispered to the dog, motioning for him to sit at his feet. "There's gonna be trouble."

Marino handed her a five dollar bill, then snapped to attention, a delayed reaction to her words. "Hey, wait one a'minute. That's ten a'cents more than I paid last night."

She deposited his five in the register, grabbed a quarter and slammed the drawer closed. "I know. New policy. We're charging a dime for the container."

"Since a'when?"

"Since my mama decided to start making a profit in this joint." She slapped the quarter down on the counter beside his sandwich, her dark eyes flashing with irritation.

"What is this?" he shouted, his face turning a spectacular shade of purple, veins protruding from his forehead. "I come in here every night for years and in return you rob me? You try to take the money right out of my pocket with me watching?"

"Señor Marino . . ." she said with feigned patience. Nick watched her tighten her jaw, and he stifled a giggle. He knew his sister. Any minute now she was going to blow. "From now on," she continued, "your dinner is going to cost you ten cents more. If you don't feel it's worth it, there are three other delis on this block. But that's the way it's going to be. A dime for the container."

Marino brought his fist down on the counter, rattling the cans of biscotti near the register. "I can notta *eat* the container, and I'm a notta gonna *pay* for the container."

That did it; she blew.

"You don't think you can eat the container?" she shouted, grabbing the styrofoam and shoving it at his face. "Well, you *can* eat the container. I'm gonna show you!" She started to climb over the counter. "You *will* eat the container! Right here, right now!"

This had gone far enough. Nick hurried around the pasta and grabbed her just before she vaulted over. Señor Marino stood, staring at them both, his purple complexion nearly white. Hercules forgot the admonition to sit and scurried after his master, barking joyously. This was too exciting to sit out behind a pasta display.

"Nina, Nina," Nick said, squeezing her arm when she tried to wrench it away. "Surely we can work this out. Señor Marino is an old friend. Maybe we can make an exception this time . . . ?"

The fire in her dark eyes caused Nick to reconsider.

"Tell you what," he said, digging in his jeans pocket. "Why don't you let *me* buy the container for you, Señor Marino. It would be my honor." He pressed the dime into Nina's hand, ignoring her glare.

"Well, I don't think *you* should. . . ." The old man's confused expression showed the internal battle between honor and thrift.

"No, really," Nick said, laying one hand on the man's shoulder. "Let *me* buy your containers for a few weeks, and you treat me to a beer sometime."

Marino smiled broadly. "That's a'good of you, Nicholas. You're a nice a'boy." He gave Nina a look of righteous indignation. "You tell your mama, I say she's got a nice a'boy."

Nina scarcely waited for the door to slam behind Marino when she exploded again. "That old coot! Who does he think he is, coming in here every night a minute before nine and keeping me after for ten minutes, cutting his pastrami just so! And then he complains about a stinking *dime!*"

"Ah, Ninuzza . . ." Nick playfully tweaked one of her long

curls. ". . . I've been looking forward to seeing my two favorite girls all day. Don't let a stingy old man ruin it. Give your big brother a kiss."

The affectionate diminutive version of her name never failed to win her over. She rose on tiptoe, he bent his head and she gave him a peck on the cheek.

Then, briskly snapping into business gear, she hurried to lock the door and turn over the Open/Closed sign. After pausing for only a second to pat Hercules's head, she began putting the food away with a vengeance.

"What's the hurry?" Nick asked, though he had a theory. Without a doubt it had something to do with a boy.

"Got a hot date," she said with a teasing grin. Predictably he raised one eyebrow in big brotherly fashion. "Bobby's coming by to get me at 9:30. We're going to a movie."

"Bobby who?"

"Bobby, the guy you scared the crap out of when you gave him the third degree last week. Flashing your gun and everything . . . God, I was so-o-o-o humiliated."

"Oh, yeah . . . him. I don't like him. He's a punk."

"You think all my boyfriends are punks."

He threw his jacket onto a nearby stool, grabbed a cloth and began wiping down the faded red linoleum counter. "Look, I know how young punks are; I used to be one. All they want is to boff your bones. They can't help themselves."

"I'll keep that in mind."

He watched as she scooped the lasagna from the heating tray into a large plastic bucket. In a few minutes a volunteer would collect it at the back door and take it to a homeless shelter. Mama O'Connor didn't believe in throwing anything away that could help another human being.

Nick glanced at his watch. "Hey, it's 9:15. Don't you need to change clothes and do that silly girl shit with your hair and face?"

"Well, yes . . . but . . ." She waved a hand at the unfinished work.

"I'll do it. Get out of here."

She brightened. "Really?"

"Yeah, tell Mama I'll be up to see her in a few minutes."

"Gee, thanks!" She peeled off her apron and threw it into a bin with other soiled linens. As she walked toward the door leading to the upstairs apartments, she paused. "Really, Nicky . . . I mean . . . you know . . . thanks."

"Yeah, yeah. Just come down and say goodbye before you leave."

"Oh, no," she said with a sigh, "the big brother, predate speech. I knew there was a catch."

Fifteen minutes later, she bounded back down the stairs, transformed from a sullen deli attendant to a juvenile sex goddess. Nick took a quick visual sweep of the black leather mini-skirt, high heels, black hose, and tiger-print silk shirt. And her hair—he was always astonished at how "big" she could make it on these occasions.

"Okay, that does it," he said, tossing a bit of pastrami to Hercules who sat at his feet, watching the exchange with intelligent curiosity. "Get back upstairs and change. You look entirely too good."

She giggled and struck a pose. "O-o-oh, thank you."

He retrieved her dirty apron from the bin. "Well, here, at least put this on over it."

She shook her head, curls bouncing. "I don't think so."

"Then take Herc with you."

The dog heard his name and the corkscrew tail began to wag furiously.

"No way, you've been feeding him pastrami and he's got awful breath."

"All right then, looking like that and without a canine chaperon, you definitely get the big brother speech." He stopped to draw a deep breath. Mistake. She took advantage and jumped in before him.

"I know, I know. Watch yourself at all times, stay in the neighborhood on well-lit streets, purse close to the ribs, no drinking, no smoking, no dope, and especially . . . no sex. In other words, don't do anything fun that *you* used to do when you were my age."

"You're damned right." He walked over to her and pressed a packet of condoms into her palm, all teasing gone from his face. "I know you're a good girl, Ninuzza, but if you decide you don't wanna be tonight, use these."

"I understand," she said, grinning up at him coquettishly. Nick thought it no wonder his father had fallen hopelessly in love with his mother if she had been even half this pretty. "Don't worry so much, Nicky. I'm a big girl now."

He glanced at her ample cleavage, peeking above the vee in her silk shirt. "I know. That's why I'm worried."

"Gotta go," she said, giving him a kiss on the cheek. "Bobby's waiting out back."

As she hurried toward the door, Nick shouted after her, "And you tell that punk boyfriend of yours that if he even French kisses you, he'd better have one of those things on his tongue!"

No one would have guessed that the benign figure dressed in a red and green pizza delivery uniform, riding a bicycle up Fifth Avenue, was a killer. Unless they looked into his eyes. A fire burned there, but not a blaze that would lend any warmth. He was intense, a man with a mission—empowered, holding the keys to life and death. And tonight he chose death.

He had chosen who, and where, and when, and how. Each selection made with infinite care. He had covered all bases, attended to each detail with precision planning.

In spite of the careful preparation, he experienced the occasional niggling doubt. What if he went to all this trouble, risked everything and still didn't accomplish his goal? What if it all backfired on him? What if he were caught?

He consoled himself with the thought that not everyone had the courage to commit murder, or the cunning to get away with it.

But he had.

This wasn't his first time. He had done it before, and he would again. He glanced at his watch. In ten minutes.

With less skill than would be expected of a professional delivery person, he guided the bicycle through the traffic, passing Forty-Ninth Street and heading uptown. He swerved to miss a rain-filled, garbage-choked gutter and nearly rammed the side of a taxi. The driver sounded a long, irritated honk. The bicyclist flipped him his middle finger and once again nearly lost control of his bike.

Only a few blocks from his destination, he mentally inventoried the items he had stowed in the pockets inside his bulky jacket. Yes, he had everything.

He stopped before an old brownstone and chained his bicycle to the iron railing which led up the stone steps. Glancing up at a third-story window, he saw a feeble light glowing. A greenish, sickly, flickering light. The guy was watching television.

A thought occurred to him and he grinned . . . his first smile of the day. Wouldn't it be ironic if the soon-to-be-dead man were watching *that* particular show? That would just be too much.

He reached into the black garbage bag he had tied to the back of the bike and pulled out a flat, square cardboard box. Tucking it under his arm, he strode up the steps, scanned the directory and punched the appropriate button with a gloved finger.

"Whadda ya want?" a surly voice crackled over the speaker.

"Pizza delivery. A giant combo with extra sausage."

"You got the wrong apartment. I didn't order any pizza."

"Aren't you number 369?"

"Yeah."

"Well, this is your combo, buddy. Paid for and everything, but if you don't want it. . . ."

"Paid for?" The voice perked up.

"That's what it says here on the slip, but—"

A loud buzzer sounded and the lock on the door clicked.

"Bring it on up."

The killer entered the building, pizza box balanced on his right shoulder. With his left hand he felt inside his jacket for his weapon of choice. His fingers closed around it, and he was surprised at his own calmness. He wasn't even shaking, his head clear, his resolve intact. He was getting better at this every time.

He glanced again at his watch. "You've got about two and a half more minutes to live," he told the man in the apartment above. "Two and a half and counting."

Three

"You've been a good papa to your little sister, Nicky," Mama O'Connor said as she lay back on her bed, punctuating the statement with a heavy sigh of fatigue.

Nick grabbed a pillow which was adorned with his mother's embroidery, the edges trimmed with his Grandmother O'Connor's Irish lace, and fluffed it thoroughly. Carefully, he slid it beneath her swollen feet.

Sitting on an old ladder-backed chair beside her bed, he took her hand in his. Her skin was soft and fragile, freckled with age spots. He thought of all the people she had fed with those hands, his family, his friends, his police buddies, neighbors, and the homeless. If ever anyone had accumulated brownie points in heaven, this woman had.

Rosemarie O'Connor's eyes were still as large and luminous as her daughter's, her hair as full and curly. In two months she would celebrate her sixtieth birthday, but she still turned plenty of male heads when she served her customers downstairs. "I heard some of what you said to her tonight," she continued with a weary sigh as her eyelids fluttered closed.

Nick thought of the smart-aleck comments about the condoms. He glanced up at the crucifix hanging over the bed and cleared his throat. "Yes, well . . ."

"It's okay. I understand. You both . . . sensible kids. I only wish your papa had lived to see how fine his children grew up. He would be so proud."

"I know you miss him. So do I."

Nick thought of his handsome father, a towering, blond, green-eyed Irish cop. Every morning he had shaken Nick awake, looking smart in his patrolman's uniform, smelling of Old Spice cologne and toothpaste.

But fifteen years ago, when Nick was seventeen and Nina only two, his father's partner had knocked on the downstairs door in the middle of the night and given them the news that had shattered their world. A liquor store burglar, a chase down a dark alley, and one bullet had ended it all. Ryan O'Connor, his soft Irish brogue, his clean smell and warm embrace were all things of the past.

"You know what I miss most, Nicky?" his mother said.

Nick knew the answer well; this was a ritual they had played over the years. He looked into her tired face which, despite the years of work and sorrow, bore more laugh lines than frown. Something told him he wouldn't have her with him much longer. She missed her old love too much, and her heart was no longer content to live in the present. This ritual was becoming more and more common lately.

"No, Mama, what do you miss most?"

"I miss when he used to read to me. Every night he read Yeats to me. I can still hear his pretty voice, so soft on the ears."

Nick reached for the well-worn Yeats collection which lay on the nightstand beside the silver framed photo of Rosemarie and Ryan on their wedding day. They stood in front of Ryan's 1955 Ford, his foot propped jauntily on the shining chrome bumper, a cocky grin on his face. Rosemarie wore a simple dress with a full skirt and tightly cinched waist which accented her hourglass figure, and a pillbox hat and gloves. Their faces glowed with the light and optimism of youthful romance.

Nick sighed inwardly as he studied the photo again for the thousandth time. The older he got, the younger they looked in that picture. He had always hoped that someday he would feel as happy and in love as they seemed at that frozen moment of time. After almost twenty years of dating, pursuing and being pursued by the opposite sex, he was becoming cynical. Maybe that sort of romance didn't exist anymore. Perhaps he was being idealistic to even entertain the hope that he could find it.

"I don't have Papa's Irish lilt," he said, picking up his mother's not-so-subtle cue, "but I could read to you a bit, if you like."

She grinned broadly. "I like."

He picked up the book, turned to one of her favorite passages and began to read.

The gentle drone of his deep voice, the ticking of the bedside clock, and the creaks and groans of the old radiator, soothed her, and her breathing became slow and steady. He continued to read until he was certain she was sound asleep.

Closing the book, he glanced at the clock. Midnight. Downstairs, he heard Nina coming home from her date. He returned the book to its place beside the photo, tucked the quilt around his mother and kissed her cheek. "Sleep well," he said, "and dream of Papa."

He left the apartment and crossed the hall to his own modest four rooms: a living room, bedroom, kitchen—which he never used—and bath. The "bear's den" Nina called it. Okay, so it would never grace the cover of *Bachelor Pad Beautiful,* but it served his purpose. The futon functioned as sofa or bed when a visitor became too drunk to go home, or when one of the cops at the station got kicked out by his wife.

The rest of the furniture consisted mainly of stacks of books. Books lined the walls, covered most horizontal surfaces, and even provided a fourth leg for a wobbly table. Mysteries, science fiction, techno-thrillers, an impressive array of the classics, and a complete collection of Louis L'Amour testified to Nick O'Connor's only passion which surpassed his police work.

If being Italian meant eating good food, drinking fine wine, and enjoying life's hedonistic pleasures to the fullest, being Irish meant an abiding reverence for the written word. Any moment when he wasn't working, spending time with his "favorite girls," walking Hercules, or drinking beer at his favorite pub, he spent curled in his father's old recliner, munching a Macintosh apple, reading and occasionally scratching his dog's head as Hercules lay at his feet.

The guys at the station ribbed him from time to time, suggesting he spend his spare time in more vigorous entertainment. But Nick considered the job of homicide detective on the streets of New York City stimulating enough.

Picking up Dean Koontz's latest from the coffee table, he grabbed an apple and a bottle of beer from the refrigerator and sat down. Obediently, Hercules plopped down in front of him, his chin resting on the toes of Nick's sneakers. In less than two minutes the dog began to snore loudly, dewlaps fluttering.

No sooner had Nick settled into the story than the phone rang.

"Damn!" As he reached for the phone on the table beside him he nearly knocked over his beer. He glanced at the small alarm clock which was buried beneath a stack of paperbacks. Ten minutes after twelve. "O'Connor," he growled, not bothering to hide his irritation.

"Sorry to bother you, Sarge, but—" began Dan McMurtry, a patrolman in his division.

"Yeah, right. What's up?"

"A homicide down here near 54th and Madison. Seems some guy was watching television here in his apartment. Got his brains bashed in. It's pretty messy."

"How long ago?"

"He's fresh."

"Thank God for that," Nick said, remembering a case last week where the corpse was old. Not old enough to be dry and crispy, his definite preference for old corpses, but still in the putrid and juicy stage. He could smell it on his skin and in his hair for days, despite repeated scrubbings. "Scene secured?"

"Sure. Taped off."

"Good boy. And witnesses?"

"We're checking them out now."

"Give me the address." Nick rose and pulled a small black notebook and pen from the inside of his jacket which he had stashed along with his gun and holster on the end of the futon.

He scribbled it down. "All right. Call the coroner and the lab boys. I'll be there in ten."

He hung up the phone and began to strap on his shoulder holster. The previously unconscious bulldog became instantly animated.

"So, Herc," he said, reaching into his jacket pocket and extracting an almond biscotti, "the bad boys are at it again. Wanna play Rin Tin Tin?"

The dog downed the cookie in one gulp and stood, ears perked, crooked teeth revealed in a wide grin, entire rear end wagging furiously.

"Okay, let's go. And this time, don't piss on any of the evidence. It's hard to explain in court."

"What's this? You goin' home already?" Cass scowled across the beer-stained table at Elizabeth who was gathering up her purse, coat, and gloves.

"You've been a real party poop this evening," added Michael Donahue who sat beside her in the booth—the owner, bartender, and all around entertainment chairman of Donahue's Pub and Grill, the favorite hangout of many of the Y.B.S. staff and employees. "First you won't watch your show with us downstairs like you usually do, then—"

"I've already seen it, Mike," she said, trying to push his considerable bulk aside so that she could slide out of the booth. "It didn't bear watching twice."

"Hey, we liked it. You're just too picky about your own stuff."

"Better drop it," Cass told him under her breath. "A touchy subject."

Elizabeth leaned her back against the wall, planted the soles of her sneakers against his bottom and pushed with all her might. "Michael, I want to go home. I have a 12:45 train to catch at Penn, and if I miss it . . . because . . . of you. . . ." Her face was turning red, and she was losing her breath, but he wasn't budging.

Finally, she gave up. "Do you keep all your patrons here against their will?"

He grinned broadly, displaying the famous Donahue smile that had made the pub such a success, generation after generation. "Only the bonny lasses," he said with an affected Irish brogue. "The ones who aren't married and dance a lively jig . . . when they're in the mood that is."

She smiled at him in spite of herself, remembering the evenings filled with raucous laughter, a few too many Coronas, and sprightly Irish dancing. She had whiled away many pleasant hours within these dimly lit, dark green walls, throwing darts, dancing to the Irish folk music, and contributing to the blarney that floated more thickly than the cigarette smoke above the tables. Donahue's down-to-earth atmosphere provided a welcome reality which contrasted with the illusion—and sometimes disillusionment—of show business.

And Michael Donahue was the pub's greatest asset. The epitome of a gentle giant, Michael's passions in life were the latest rugby scores, Makem and Clancy's Irish folk music, lukewarm Guiness, and good storytellers. Since Elizabeth kept up on the game, could sing Tommy Makem's best songs, and spin a great yarn, she was held high in his estimation and dear to his heart. He forgave her for preferring a cold Corona to the room temperature Irish ale. And he always protested when she tried to leave.

She reached over and tweaked his nose affectionately. "Don't pout," she said. "I'll dance with you next time. Now move it, before I have to get rough and hurt ya."

All three laughed. Considering that Mike outweighed her by at least a hundred and fifty pounds, her threat fell a bit short of terrifying.

He sighed. "Then I'll have to settle for a good night kiss." He puckered and closed his eyes.

She planted a quick peck on his cheek. He opened his eyes and sulked. "I was hopin' for a bit more."

"Hope blooms eternal. Now move, before I have to climb over you."

He raised his eyebrows suggestively.

She glowered at him. "Move!"

He did. As he helped her into her Mets jacket he said, "Is everything all right, Liz? You seem a little down tonight."

She looked up at him for a long moment and an unexpected sense of sadness welled up inside her. *What's wrong with me?* she thought. Four times today she had been on the verge of tears. She had her ups and downs like anyone else, but she liked to think she was up more than down, and she didn't usually feel this bad for no apparent reason. Looking up into his kind eyes, she had the overwhelming urge to lay her head against this big teddy bear's chest and cry right here in the middle of the pub.

"I'm all right, Mike," she heard herself saying as she gave him a hug. "Just a bit tired, I guess."

Cass stood and put her arm around Elizabeth's shoulders. "Come on, kid. I'll walk you out."

As they threaded their way through the bodies, tables, and chairs toward the door, more than a dozen patrons wished Elizabeth goodnight. As always, she felt their genuine affection which went beyond star worship. These people had known her when she had been a struggling student. In fact, she had even waited tables here two summers in a row during her junior and senior years at Hunter College. They knew the real Liz, not just Elizabeth Knight, the sophisticated hostess of the hit series.

Near the door sat a man who was clearly not joining in the festivities. He sat with his head bowed over a mug of beer, his fists clenching and releasing, his face sullen.

"Norman . . ." Elizabeth paused beside his table. ". . . I heard what happened. I feel terrible about you losing your job. Brody's an ass, and stupid. You're the finest post-production manager we've ever had."

He stared up at her, obviously very drunk, his eyes striving to focus. "Yeah, thanks," he muttered. "Thanks a lot."

"If there's anything I can do," she said, "help you with contacts, give you a good reference, I—"

"Thanks, Ms. Knight. I think you've done enough already."

She stood there for a moment, looking down on him, feeling helpless and guilty. She realized it was illogical, that Brody was the one who had wronged the man, but she still felt responsible somehow.

"Good luck, Norman. Thanks for everything."

"Sure."

Cass led her away, one hand on her elbow. "It wasn't your fault, kid," she said when they reached the door.

"I know. But it's still a bite in the butt."

Peering into Elizabeth's eyes with maternal scrutiny, Cass wrapped one arm around her waist. "I don't know what's bothering you, babycakes, and I don't think you do either, but if you figure it out and want to talk, give me a ring tonight."

Elizabeth returned her embrace and grinned. "Yes, mom."

"Don't you 'Yes, mom,' me! I'm half your age!"

Turning away, Elizabeth headed for the door. "Only in spirit, my friend," she said enviously. She glanced back over her shoulder. Already one of the lads had grabbed Cass and was spinning her toward the dance floor. "Only in spirit."

She stepped out of the humid warmth of the pub and into the brisk cold of the November night. Blowing a cloud of white fog into the air, she looked up and down Fifth Avenue and smiled. Having been raised in a sleepy California seaside town, she still marveled at the beauty of New York City at night. The buildings that towered over her looked like giant Christmas trees, glittering white, gold, and silver. And even at midnight the traffic roared, a low sensual thrumming punctuated with a cacophony of horns and sirens. This city vibrated with an invigorating power, generated by its inhabitants. New Yorkers, the most energetic people on the face of the earth, pouring their unique vitality into the structures that absorbed it like batteries and radiated that energy back to those walking the sidewalks and driving the streets.

Elizabeth loved this dirty old city. She didn't see the grime, only the glamour, the excitement, the unusual happening around her every moment. Sure, you had to be on your toes, streetsmart, as in any major city. But she felt stronger, younger, sexier, and more alive walking the streets of this town than anywhere else in the world.

Never a dull moment, she thought.

As though materializing out of her thoughts, she turned a corner to see several squad cars parked in front of a brownstone which had been cordoned off with yellow tape. The red and blue flashing lights bounced off the buildings on either side of the street, giving the scene an eery, surrealistic feel.

Ever the curious writer, she paused for a moment, listening to the conversations of those standing nearby. Apparently, they were as curious and uninformed as she.

A black Jeep came to an abrupt stop beside her. The door opened and an enormous white and brindle bulldog bounded out, nearly knocking her off her feet. Her heart thudded as she stared down into the wrinkled face sprouting crooked fangs that curled up over its top lip. Then the dog's tongue lolled out and the gargoylelike mug split into an embarrassed lopsided grin.

Charmed, she dropped to one knee. "Hi there, fella. Why, you're just a big pussycat, aren't you." She patted the broad head and was rewarded by a wagging rearend.

"Sorry about that," said a deep voice. "I hope he didn't scare you."

A pair of exceptionally long legs appeared beside her, muscular legs molded by worn denim. Her eyes travelled upward, taking in the slender hips, the barrel chest, the broad shoulders, the black leather jacket which, like the jeans, had been worn so long that it fit and accented every male contour.

"He's really friendly," the voice continued. "Especially to pretty ladies. He has good taste in women."

She rose and found herself looking up into one of the most captivating faces she had seen in a long time—other than the dog's. By the glow of the streetlamps, the man's thick blond hair glistened, and his eyes were friendly, though intense as he studied her.

She was accustomed to being stared at by fans who recognized her, but she couldn't tell if this man knew her or not. He was making a full evaluation of her, noting each detail of her features and attire in a way that made her wish she were wearing something a bit more glamorous than a Mets jacket and sneakers.

"He didn't scare me," she said. "Well, he did at first, but he seems nice. A really beautiful animal."

Her praise had been genuine, but had it been calculated flattery it wouldn't have garnered a more enthusiastic response. The man flashed her a broad smile that made her catch her breath. He was incredibly handsome, in a rugged, rather bedraggled sort of way, yet something told her he didn't consider himself particularly attractive. Refreshing, in Elizabeth's world of actors and male models who constantly fought her for the makeup artist on the set.

"It takes a special woman to appreciate the beauty of a bulldog," he said, his voice low and slightly sexual. She felt it in the pit of her stomach before it trickled downward into more intimate regions.

She was surprised to feel her knees were a bit weak. *This is silly,* she thought. *You meet a guy on a street with a bulldog and your knickers are a 'twitter.*

Searching for another conversational gambit, she said, "Wonder what's going on here," nodding toward the building where uniformed policemen hurried in and out.

"A homicide," he replied flatly.

A rush of emotion swept over her that had nothing to do with the attractiveness of the hunk standing beside her. This was the sick, bitter feeling that had been slowly building all day.

"A young girl?" she asked. The words sounded strange, inappropriate, even to her.

He looked at her curiously. "No, a man, I believe. I'm on my way right now to find out all about it."

"You're a cop," she said, her voice less friendly than before.

"One of New York's finest," he said with a smirk. "You got something against cops?"

Something against cops? she thought. *Hell, yes.*

"Just catch the killer, would you?" she said with an uncomfortable tightness in her throat, "and lock him away for a long time."

His smile faded and he studied her again with those intense eyes. "I'll do my best, Ms. Knight."

He reached down and snapped a leash onto the dog's choke chain, then hurried up the stone stairs and disappeared inside the building.

So, he had recognized her after all. Strange, he hadn't treated her with the usual, giddy nervousness that she found so unsettling, the avid curiosity, or the hostility shown by the groups that picketed the studio. He had reacted to her as though she were an ordinary citizen, and she found she preferred the feeling of anonymity. No need to prove anything or provide the expected facade.

But he was a cop.

She realized she should get over this prejudice, but her own experience with the police had been less than . . .

Quickly she pulled her mind back from that line of thought. She glanced at her watch. Twenty minutes to get to Penn Station or she would have to wait two hours for the next train.

Walking over to the curb, she held up one hand, hailing the first cab she saw with a lit dome light. Just before she opened the door to get inside, she glanced back at the brownstone. *What an interesting, appealing face,* she thought. As she scrambled into the cab she added quickly, *the bulldog's, that is. Certainly not the cop's.*

Four

Nick stepped into the apartment and scanned the room, trying to take in every detail. The boys from the lab had already arrived. One was snapping pictures of the body which lay, face up, in the middle of the floor, a pool of blood staining the rug around his head. Another was on his hands and knees, vacuuming around the corpse with a small, hand-held, battery operated machine. A woman was making the rounds with a fingerprint kit.

With an effort, Nick pulled his mind away from the other woman, the one on the street. God, she was beautiful! Even more so than on the screen. For a moment he had felt like an adolescent kid—one of the punks he had warned his sister about—with his tongue hanging out and his blood flowing to his crotch. One of his favorite stars, standing there in the glow of the streetlight, looking like a cross between an angel and a black-haired witchy seductress, patting his dog's head.

"You lucky mutt," he told Hercules as he pulled the keys from his pocket and led the bulldog over to the far corner of the room. "Do you know how many males would give their right nut to trade places with you? Only the ones ages eight to eighty." Dropping the key chain onto the dirty pea-green rug, he said, "Herc . . . guard."

Instantly, the dog parked himself beside the keys, an expression of grim self-importance on his face. Nick looked up to see Patrolman Dan McMurtry standing nearby, wearing a sarcastic grin.

"Hey, it keeps him out of trouble, right?" Nick said.

Dan shrugged. "Whatever you say, Sarge." He pushed his hat back on his forehead and took a deep breath, expanding the ample stomach that filled out his patrolman's uniform.

"So, what have we got?" Nick said, turning his attention back to the room. The air stank of dirty laundry, stale human sweat, and old food—probably in the fish category. He promptly decided not to breathe too deeply and adjusted his respiration accordingly. Shallow and through the mouth.

Every semblance of softness, friendliness, or humor disappeared from his face. The easy-going family man was recast as an unemotional investigating officer.

"Just the facts, ma'am," they bantered in Dragnet style at the station. And it was true. You had to go on intellect at a time like this. Invest your heart and you got it broken. Nick had learned that one the hard way. Years ago.

"We left everything as is until you got here. We got one dead guy, over there, whacked on the head . . ." He pointed to the corpse. ". . . and a building full of good citizens who don't give a damn. Apparently, he wasn't one of their favorite tenants."

"Any witnesses?" Nick walked over to the body and dropped to one knee beside it, being careful not to disturb the chalked outline. The victim was fully dressed in a pair of shabby trousers and a shirt that had been in need of laundering. A moot point, considering the blood splattered over it.

"The only one who heard anything is the lady across the hall." Dan pulled out a notebook and flipped it open. "A Mrs. Orton. She came out to get her mail and saw the apartment door ajar. Says this guy is usually locked up tight, for fear of getting the shit beat out of him by his neighbors."

"Why?"

"Don't know. She wouldn't say. Anyway, she pushed the door open, looked inside, and voilà. She ain't exactly broken up about it."

Nick looked around the floor which was littered with several items of expensive feminine lingerie, lacy panties, and a silk camisole which had been ripped down the front.

"Looks like a female was on the scene," Nick commented. "Could it have been Mrs. Orton?"

Dan chuckled. "This ain't her stuff."

"How do you know?"

"You haven't seen her yet. Trust me."

Nick turned his attention from the body to the silk garments. "Have you taken all your shots?" he asked the photographer who was packing his camera and flash into a canvas pack.

"Yep," he replied. "It's all yours. I'm outta here."

Nick picked up the camisole by one tiny strap and examined the label and the thickness of the silk. "Whoever the lady was, she had good taste." He glanced back at the body. "How do you figure a woman of high degree dating someone like this?"

Laying the camisole back on the floor, he studied the glass bottle beside the victim's head, smeared with blood—apparently the murder weapon. The neck of the bottle had broken off and lay several feet away. Something about the color of the bottle and the distinctive shape of the label rang a bell. He looked closer. "Dom Perignon?" Glancing around the dirty room at the decrepit furniture, scattered garbage, and piles of soiled laundry, he said, "I wouldn't have thought he had the budget or the inclination. A little out of character, don't you think?"

Dan looked confused. "Why? Is that expensive stuff?"

"Uh . . . yeah."

Nick looked back at the victim, noting the expression on his face. Surprise more than anything else. The open eyes stared into nothingness, but the brow was slightly furrowed as though considering some distressing puzzle. The splattered shirt was slightly open, revealing a tiny incision in the midriff. "I see that Dr. Rigor Mortis has been here."

"Still is." Dan nodded toward the next room. "He's in there."

Nick walked over to Hercules, who still stood guard over the keys. A patrolman passed too close and was greeted with a deep bass growl.

"Atta boy, anybody touch those keys, you chomp 'em." He

grinned at the young cop who backed away warily. "Don't worry, his growl's worse than his bite."

The patrolman looked down at the numerous, pointed, and crooked teeth that sprouted from under the hanging dewlaps. "Yeah, sure."

Nick walked into the kitchen where he found a short, overweight man rinsing blood off a scalpel at a sink full of dirty dishes. He looked up and peered at Nick through thick bifocals. When Nick came within his field of vision, he grinned and nodded.

"Sergeant O'Connor. This is your case?"

" 'Fraid so." Nick liked Dr. Reggie Morris, fondly called other names behind his back. He was a rather eccentric sort, but then it helped, considering his occupation. More than once Nick had stood beside the examining table as Morris had cut into a skull using a small, hi-powered surgical saw. The doctor had an unsettling habit of holding his breakfast—usually a day-old danish from a nearby bakery—in one hand while sawing with the other. Nick had gingerly brushed away the bone chips from his own leather jacket, and marvelled that the doctor didn't seem to mind the extra calcium accumulating on his pastry.

"Well, you got a weird one on your hands this time." The doctor slung the water from his scalpel and the large thermometer, then deposited them in his traditional black physician's bag. He was the only doctor, coroner or otherwise, who Nick had ever seen use a real "little black bag."

"How's that?" Nick asked, looking around the kitchen for any signs of struggle or evidence that the killer had entered this room. But the filth and clutter seemed uniformly undisturbed.

"Come on and I'll show you."

Nick followed him into the living room where Dr. Morris's deputy coroners were zipping the victim into a plastic bag. "Just a minute there." The doctor hurried over to the body and pulled the bag away from the head. "What do you suppose the murder weapon was?" he asked Nick with a sly grin.

Nick had the feeling he was being set up to look stupid. This was a game the good doctor often played with his fellow law enforcement partners: "I Know Something You Don't Know." But his tactics were without malice. All in good fun.

Nick didn't mind. He figured it was the doc's way of compensating for the fact that he was only five foot, three, weighed over two hundred pounds, and had to wear pop bottle lenses to see. He'd give the man his dues; after all, he was a damned good coroner.

"Well . . ." Nick stalled for time, thinking. ". . . the obvious answer is the champagne bottle. But for some silly reason I have a feeling you're going to tell me it wasn't."

The doctor beamed. "That's right. Look at this."

He lifted the hair on the left side of the victim's head, exposing a deep straight cut, surrounded by a dark bruise. "The bottle's surface is blunt. Whatever cut into his head had a sharp edge to it . . . like a wooden board, or something long but squared, not rounded like a bottle."

"I see," Nick said.

"You do?" The doctor looked surprised and slightly disappointed.

"Kinda."

"That's what I thought." He slipped on a surgical glove, bent down and picked up the bottle. "See the pattern of the blood?"

Nick looked closely, determined to get this one. "I'll be damned," he said, "it isn't splattered, it's smeared. As though they—"

"That's right. Someone wiped the bottle over the wound, picking up the blood. If he had been smacked with it, the pattern would have been an uneven splattering. Very good, sergeant."

"Hey, you've been teaching me well."

"And there's something else. Look here at this rip in the lingerie." He held up the garment for Nick's inspection.

Nick looked it over carefully. "Sorry, I'm afraid I peaked with the bottle."

"The first half inch of the tear . . ." He shoved it under Nick's nose.

"Yeah?"

"It wasn't torn. It was cut. Look, it's too even."

"Are you saying he used scissors or a knife to get the tear going?"

"Sure. The edging here is delicate, but much stronger than it looks. He must have had some trouble ripping it and used a cutting implement to get the tear started."

Nick fingered the fabric, studying the rip in question. "If he'd been removing it from an unwilling lady, it would either be torn or cut all the way down, not a combination of both."

"That's right."

"So, what the hell is going on? Do we have an honest to God crime scene here or some sort of set up?"

"Well . . ." Dr. Morris watched as the crime lab assistants zipped the bag on the victim. ". . . you got a creative killer with an interesting way of arranging his scene. Obviously, he wants you to read something into this that didn't happen."

"Sorta has a make-believe quality . . . except for one thing." Nick watched as they rolled the gurney out the door. "The scene may be staged, but it doesn't matter to that guy. He's still just as dead."

He walked over to Hercules and scooped up his keys. Instantly the dog dropped his Buckingham Palace guard stance and scampered around, tail wagging, tongue lolling. "Come on, Herc," Nick said, slapping the dog's rear. "Let's go find the bad guy." He glanced back at the exquisite, though tattered lingerie on the floor. "And maybe we can find the lady, too."

Elizabeth scanned the multi-colored monitors that lined the walls and ceilings of Penn Station, until she saw her train schedule.

Port Madison. 12:45. Track 11.

Weaving a path through the crowd, she made her way toward the large door bearing the correct number of her departure track. Scores of homeless—drunken derelicts and honest, hard-

working families down on their luck—sat with their backs
against the walls, their meager belongings gathered into shabby
bundles around them. They held placards that begged for any
loose change. Elizabeth reached into her jacket, pulled out some
quarters and dropped them into the bucket of a young woman
with a baby. She kept change in her pockets for that reason; you
didn't open your purse in public in New York City.

Security officers strolled their beats, vigilant in a bored, low-
key sort of way. They congregated beneath the large heaters on
the ceilings, the main source of warmth in the giant maze of
hallways, malls and shops, tunnels and escalators.

Blue-uniformed conductors and assorted trainmen hurried
from track to track, their coin belts jingling. They gathered outside the Dunkin' Donuts and traded bawdy jokes between themselves, usually at the passengers' expense.

Hoards of business people, dressed in their New York finest,
scurried toward their appointed gates, eager to leave the city
behind in favor of the quaint, small-town ambiance to be found
on Long Island.

Elizabeth bounded down the stairs, descending into the depths
of the complex, where rails led into the enormous cavern, then
disappeared out the other side into a labyrinth of black tunnels.
She ran into the train's first open door, nearly upsetting a conductor.

He flashed her a flirtatious smile. "Don't need to run, pretty
lady," he said in a lazy Long Island drawl. "I wouldn't leave
without you."

"Yeah, sure," she said, returning his smile. "You've never
waited for me before." These trains departed on the minute, come
hell, high water, or late passengers.

"That's because you didn't let me know you were coming.
These things take a little time to set up, you know."

"I'll remember that."

She entered the car to find it crowded. The first car always
was. In spite of the fact that she had shoved her hair up into a
baseball cap, wore lightly tinted glasses, and casual attire, several

passengers recognized her and stared. Seeking a bit more privacy, she headed toward the far end of the train.

Four cars back, she found one that was completely empty. What luxury. She settled into a seat which faced backward and propped her feet on the cushion across from her. The stress of the day began to drain away as the hydraulic doors slid closed and the train glided out of the station and into the seemingly endless dark tunnel which led beneath the East River.

Having arrived at a high degree of success, Elizabeth could have chosen to be driven every day from the city to her home in Port Madison, but she loathed the expressways, even if chauffeured, and the trains were faster. Besides, few New Yorkers were ill-mannered enough to approach her, and she found the forty minutes it took to reach her small north shore town was an excellent "down" time.

Though tonight she wasn't enjoying the ride as much as usual. She looked at her reflection in the window next to her. With only blackness on the other side, she could see her face clearly, the dark circles, the pallor.

"What's the matter with you, kid?" she whispered. "Snap out of it."

The reflection didn't respond, but stared back at her with tired, sad eyes.

As they emerged from the tunnel and approached the first stop, Woodside, the train passed through a power station and the lights inside the car went out for a few moments. Her mood lifted momentarily. This was her favorite part of the ride and the reason she always sat backward. The New York City skyline glimmered against the blackness of the winter sky, a sight that made her catch her breath, no matter how many times she saw it. Her eyes sought out the impressive height of the Empire State Building, lit red and green for the upcoming Christmas holidays, and the graceful lines of the Chrysler Building with its elegant, glowing arches.

But her delight in the view was short-lived tonight. In the darkness she felt something . . . something ominous, stealing over her, around her, wrapping her in a strange, suffocating embrace. She closed her eyes for a moment, willing the inexplicable paranoia to leave. But it didn't. The feeling of danger only increased.

And it felt as though it were coming from behind her.

She turned toward the back of the car and found she was no longer alone. A figure stood, silhouetted against the window in the door which led to the next car. She couldn't see the face, or discern anything remarkable about the attire, but she couldn't mistake the foreboding sense of hostility that radiated from him to her.

A dozen courses of action raced through her mind. She thought of the can of pepper spray in her purse, the karate kubatan attached to her key chain. Her hand moved toward her bag.

She glanced down for only a second, to locate the flap and unsnap it, but when she looked up again, the lights flickered on and the figure was gone.

Jumping to her feet, her purse, kubatan, and keys in hand, she ran to the window and peered into the next car. She could see only four people: a young man and woman who sat, facing her, and two other men with their backs to her. One wore a suit and the other a brightly colored red and green jacket.

Now what?

She couldn't exactly charge into the car and ask why someone had been looking at her. What would she say? "You were giving me bad vibes?" Besides, her visitor could have made it through that car by now and into the next.

Slowly, she walked back to her seat, then thought better of it and continued on to the next car where there were several other passengers. Safety in numbers.

She sat down and picked up a newspaper that had been left behind. Her eye caught the date in the upper corner, and her heart skipped a beat. Her throat closed into a tight knot, that allowed her only shallow breath.

November 29.

Now she knew why she had felt so sad and angry all day. It had been ten years ago. Today.

Every year about this time she suffered from a bout of depression. Subconsciously, she avoided thinking about the date. But inevitably it sprang out at her from a calendar, her checkbook, her appointment book . . . or a daily newspaper and grabbed at her heart.

A face passed before her eyes, the face of a teen-aged girl, every feature so like her own. Quickly she closed her eyes, attempting to blot out the image, but the blackness behind her eyelids only clarified the picture, delineating the eyes, nose, and mouth, soft with youth, innocence, and naiveté.

Oh, Martie, she thought. Tears sprang to her eyes and rolled hot down her cheeks. She bit her lower lip to fight them back and tasted the bitter saltiness.

She was aware of several passengers watching her, but for once she didn't care. For tonight her heart ached too much to care about anything.

"I'm glad somebody killed him, the son of a bitch, and I hope he rots in hell."

Nick studied the middle-aged woman across the broken-down formica table where two cups of coffee steamed, the most vile he had ever tasted. But when the only witness in a homicide case invites you in and serves you coffee, while jabbering on about the victim and possible suspects, you don't decline. You just take several antacids afterward.

She wore a faded sweat suit which he suspected, from the shape of her figure, she never used for working out. Her gray hair was hacked off short and a number of large moles covered her neck. Her face reflected the excesses of vice and her expression the lack of kindly virtue.

"Did *you* kill him?" he asked, fixing her with a green-eyed stare that made her squirm in her Eisenhower-era, vinyl and chrome dining chair.

"Nope," she said, sucking a long draw from the cigarette which she held between nicotine-stained fingers. "But I wish I had."

"I'm glad you didn't," he said, his voice softening into the sultry tones he used especially for interrogating females. "I'd hate to have to arrest a nice lady like you."

She melted visibly. Nick chided himself, but only for half a second. He wasn't a fool; he knew he was better-looking than the average guy. And he wasn't above using it to his advantage while on the job. Personal life was a different matter. He tried to keep the lady-killing routine to a minimum. What he lacked in conscience, Mama dutifully supplied, whether he welcomed it or not.

"What did Mr. Jarvis do that made you wish you'd killed him?" He took a sip of the horrible coffee and tried not to grimace.

"He raped a girl—fifteen years old. Lives two flights down with her mama and daddy. And do you want to know the worst thing about it?"

"Absolutely."

She leaned forward, bloodshot eyes squinting through the smoke that rose from the ashtray between them. "She was his *student!* Can you imagine? Him a teacher and all. You should be able to expect better from someone in a position like that."

Nick searched his brain for the details of a story that he had read about in the papers a month or so ago. Something about a gym teacher who had been accused of seducing one of his students. He had been tried for statutory rape, but had been found innocent. The defense attorney had dragged boy after boy into court, having them testify that they had slept with the girl, painting a picture of her as the school slut.

The young lady's family had made death threats against Jarvis after the trial, and police had been called out several times to save the guy's hide. Apparently, they couldn't cover him at all times.

"Tell me about the man you saw at Mr. Jarvis's door tonight," Nick said, making notes in his little black notebook.

"I heard someone knock, and I went to answer it. I looked out the peephole first and saw that it was the door across the hall. Sometimes you can't tell from the sound which door's being knocked on."

Especially if you've consumed a fifth of gin, Nick thought, noticing the empty bottle on the table and the half-empty shot glass. Something about her breath and the glazed look in her eye told him she had consumed it alone.

"And then?" he prompted her.

"And there was this guy standing there, wearing a red and green coat, carrying a pizza."

"Are you sure it was a man?"

"Well, I suppose it could have been a woman. I just saw his back."

"How tall?"

"Couldn't tell."

"Heavy, thin . . . ?"

She shrugged.

"Color of hair?"

"Don't know. It was covered up with a red hat."

Nick scribbled furiously. "What else?"

"Nothin'. Jarvis answered the door and I went back to . . . what I was doin'."

"And what was that?"

She hesitated for a moment, as though deciding whether or not to be truthful. "Drinkin'."

Nick nodded and smiled, grateful for her honesty. "Mrs. Orton, I don't mean to insult you, but were you sober enough to be sure of what you just told me?"

"Sure. Hell, don't take much to see one of them red and green coats."

"Just two more questions. Did Mr. Jarvis order pizza frequently?"

"That ol' tightwad? He lived on tuna fish and macaroni. Stunk up the hall every night with it."

"And do you know of any pizza joints in the area whose delivery people wear those red and green jackets?"

"Sure. Papa Joe's, down the street. Turn right when you leave the building, go three blocks. Can't miss it."

Nick rose, handed his card to the woman and walked toward the door where Hercules waited patiently . . . guarding the keys.

"Thank you, Mrs. Orton. You've been a lot of help. If you think of anything else, be sure to call me," he said.

She smiled broadly, showing teeth as yellowed as her fingers. "Oh, I'll probably think of something."

He groaned inwardly. She'd be calling him three times a day with piddly bits of worthless information; he could just tell already. Maybe the lady-killer approach wasn't such a good idea after all.

He hurried to the door, Hercules in tow.

"Say, sergeant . . . are you married?" she asked coyly. She glanced down at his hand. "I don't see no ring."

"Ten years," he said quickly. "Six kids: three girls, two boys."

Shit! he thought as he rushed down the hall, his butt warming from the heat of her lascivious stare. *Got nervous and screwed up the math. It'll be three times a day for sure.*

Elizabeth hurried up the stone steps to the veranda of a charming gingerbread Victorian house that sat back from the road, hidden in a copse of pine trees. The second she opened the door and stepped inside, she felt a bit better. At least safer.

Usually, she walked the ten minute hike from the train station to her house. But tonight she had treated herself to a cab. The aftertaste of her experience on the train, combined with an anniversary she could never forget, left her drained and glad to be home behind closed doors.

A couple of years ago, when she had first sold the concept for "The Dark Mirror" to Y.B.S., she had bought this old house and decorated it in what she fondly referred to as "Early Bordello." The ivory brocade sofa had curved Victorian lines as did the coffee table with its cobalt blue mirror top. A lamp with glass-beaded fringe cast a soft light onto dusky rose walls trimmed with ornate white molding.

Over the fireplace hung a gilt framed mirror. Tonight, Elizabeth carefully avoided looking at the display of family pictures that lined the mantel.

A small calico cat bounded down the winding staircase to greet her. It purred loudly while tracing a figure eight between her feet. She threw her bag onto the sofa and gathered the cat in her arms.

"Katie Kat, how are you? Were you a good girl today?"

Then she spotted the white teddy bear lying in the center of the floor. Small tufts of fur were scattered across the dark blue oriental rug. She placed the cat on the floor and glared down at her. "Katie! What have you done to Paws?"

She picked up the stuffed animal and shoved it in the cat's face. Katie's big golden eyes shifted from right to left, refusing to focus on the toy.

Elizabeth knelt beside her. "So, you get mad at me for leaving you alone too long, and you take it out on Paws, huh? Bad cat. Ba-a-a-ad cat!"

Rebuffed, Katie slunk away to the kitchen. Elizabeth followed, stowing the bear in his rocking chair between the fireplace and the grandfather clock. In the kitchen she punched the flashing button on her answering machine and walked over to the refrigerator. Pulling out a bottle of cranberry juice, she listened to a message from Cassie, reminding her again that if she needed to talk, she was only a phone call away.

Elizabeth pulled a wine glass from the cupboard and filled it with the red juice. Then she paused, listening to the unfamiliar male voice on the next message.

"Ms. Knight, this is Sam Martinson from the warden's office at Bellingham Men's Correctional Institution. I'm sorry . . . there was this clerical mixup and we should have called you a couple

of weeks ago." The voice faltered. "See . . . ah . . . we just saw
the notation that we were supposed to notify you and . . . well . . .
the point is: David Ferguson was released on parole a couple of
weeks ago. We're all sure that he won't be bothering you or any
member of your family. The prison psychologists all agreed that
he's been rehabilitated and . . ."

Elizabeth's hand began to shake as the emotions she had been
fighting all day came crashing down on her. The grief, the im-
potent rage.

David Ferguson. Released.

Free to resume his life, to walk the streets and feel the sun on
his face and breathe the air. Privileges her younger sister would
never enjoy, because on November 29th, ten years before, Ferguson had wrapped his hands around her throat and squeezed
the life out of her.

The wine glass fell from her hand and shattered, spilling the
crimson fluid across the polished oak floor.

Elizabeth stumbled back into the living room and over to the
fireplace where she picked up Martie's sophomore picture, the
last picture that had been taken of her. One month before . . .

As she reached out and traced the girl's cheek with her fingertip, Elizabeth allowed the tears to fall, not fighting them as
she had on the train.

After a moment she walked over to the sofa, sat down and
picked up the phone from the end table. She dialed a number
and wiped her tears away. "Hello, Cass?" She sniffed. "You said
I could call." She started to cry again, hearing the tender concern
in her friend's voice. "You know . . . what I was upset about. . . ."
She took a deep breath. "My baby sister was murdered ten years
ago today. And it was my fault."

Five

When Cassie charged up the steps from the subway and emerged on Fifty-First Street and Lexington, she was in no mood for foolishness. Not anybody's. The half a fifth of Jack Daniels which she had consumed the night before was still sludging through her veins and pounding in her temples. It was going to take at least three cups of coffee to get her tongue unstuck from the roof of her mouth.

Hell, she could have drunk three times that much ten years ago, spent the rest of the night rolling in the straw with some good-looking cowboy, and still woke up the next morning ready to square dance.

So much for getting older.

She hurried past a newsstand, not taking time to pause, as she usually did, to peruse the colorful assortment of magazines, earrings, and "hair-thing-a-ma-bobs" as she called them. The stand was owned and operated by three generations of the Milano family. As she walked by, grandfather, dad, and son watched with avid male interest, their eyes following the skin tight, red leggings and equally scarlet spike heels. All that square dancing had paid off in nicely rounded calves, and a tiny gold chain with a diamond studded heart accented her shapely ankles.

Cassie grinned. Even on a bad day she could take time to enjoy attention from the opposite sex. After all, it wasn't the age or even the mileage of the vehicle. It was the maintenance. And Cassie saw herself as a meticulously serviced, vintage Rolls Royce.

Her brief ego boost quickly fizzled when she turned the corner and saw the studio. The emotional residue from last evening came rushing over her, reminding her of why she had felt the need to polish off that bottle of Jack Daniels and why she wanted to bash somebody's head this morning. Almost anyone would do. She thought of her telephone conversation with Elizabeth and she wanted to cry.

All this time she had known that something was wrong with her friend. Somewhere, beneath that sophisticated, intelligent, worldly facade, was a deeply wounded little girl. Cassie had never experienced the joy of mothering her own child, but she loved children and saw them everywhere she looked, even though many of them ran around in thirty, forty, fifty-or-more year old bodies. And she couldn't resist doing the "maternal thing."

Last night she had listened for two hours as Elizabeth had told her the dark secret which she had kept bottled up for years. Now Cassie knew the nature of that little girl's pain. The horror, the grief, and the guilt.

Cassie had never experienced anything like Elizabeth's loss, but she had been gifted with a heart that understood and empathized. And this morning she carried part of Elizabeth's sorrow with her. She would carry it for the rest of her life. For Cassie, that was what it meant to be a friend.

Her anger surged as she saw the picketers, standing in a line outside the studio doors. Didn't they ever give up? Of all the shows broadcast every week over the airwaves, couldn't they pick another one to harass, just for variety if nothing else. Spread it around, for Pete's sake. Surely they weren't the only ones polluting the mind and soul of America.

When she saw Elizabeth, fighting her way through the crowd from the opposite direction, Cassie plunged headfirst into the melee. Where were those damned studio security guards anyway?

She elbowed a dozen protesters aside to get to Elizabeth, who had been shoved up against a building and several of the discontents were screaming into her face. Pale and drawn, Elizabeth looked far more vulnerable than usual this morning, and Cassie's maternal instincts roared.

"Leave her alone, you self-righteous hypocrites!" Cassie shouted. "You preach against violence, but look at what you're doing right now!"

"It's okay, Cass," Elizabeth said, reaching for her friend's hand. Cassie was shocked at how cold her fingers were and how badly she was shaking. "They have a right to say what they believe." She fixed the nearest man with a determined look that caused him to glance away. "And *I* have the right to go to work . . . whether you approve of what I do, or not. If you would please step aside. . . ."

She started toward the door but was intercepted by a tall, handsome man in his mid-fifties with an impressive crown of thick, silver hair, wearing an expensive charcoal designer suit and a benevolent smile.

"You'll have to excuse my followers," he said in a rich, bass voice that was thick with a down-homesy Southern accent, "but when it comes to the matters of the Lord, they do get a might zealous." His eyes, the same shade of gray as his suit, locked with Elizabeth's so intensely that Cassie felt more than a passing concern. She moved to step between them, but Elizabeth held up a hand. Cassie knew the look on her face. It meant, "Butt out." She bit back the caustic words she had been about to speak.

"I understand, Reverend Taggerty, isn't it?" Elizabeth said, her voice as smooth and emotionless as her face. The man smiled, obviously flattered that she had recognized him. "We *all* are consumed with zeal for what we feel is right. You and your followers believe that my show is evil. Obviously, I don't, or I wouldn't continue to write it."

"You would if you're the instrument of Satan," he said, his smile belying his words.

"You do me credit, reverend," Elizabeth said. "I'm afraid I don't have any high-powered, supernatural connections. I'm just a writer. And I'm sorry that you don't like what I write. Now please let me pass."

A man to Elizabeth's right moved out of her way, providing a path for her to leave. He was a younger, dark-haired clone of the reverend, though he wasn't dressed as flashy and his expression was more humble. As they passed him, Cassie thought he even seemed apologetic. She wondered what it must be like, having the Reverend Taggerty for a father. Tough break for the kid.

One by one, the pickets moved aside, following his lead and allowing them to pass, until they reached the door. But Taggerty couldn't resist one last shot. As they stepped inside the building they heard him say, "May the wrath of the Lord descend upon the heads of those who defy his decrees."

Cassie couldn't stand it. That was too much. She stepped back outside for a moment and said, "Why don't you just let the Lord speak for Himself. I'm sure He doesn't need bombastic fools like you running around claiming to represent Him."

Elizabeth grabbed her by the arm. "Sh-h-h, that's enough, Cass. Get in here."

Cass resisted long enough for one last shot. "And if you ever attack Ms. Knight like that again, I swear I'll be kickin' some bo-hunkus around here."

Elizabeth yanked her inside and pulled her down the hall to the elevator. Neither woman said a word as they stood, breathing hard and trembling, waiting for the elevator.

Once inside, Cassie ventured a look at Elizabeth, expecting to be met with blue lasers. She had definitely overstepped her boundaries this time. Friend or no friend, Elizabeth placed great importance on public relations.

When her eyes met Elizabeth's she was surprised to see her grinning broadly. "Let me get this straight," Elizabeth said. "You're going to kick . . . *bo-hunkus?*"

Cass smiled back, shrugged and nodded.

"Good God, Cass . . ." Elizabeth shook her head and began to laugh. ". . . you really are a Southern cracker."

"And proud of it," Cass returned. *"Damned* proud of it."

* * *

"So, why did you invite me out here for lunch . . . really?" Peter looked down at the hotdog in his hand, and his nose crinkled with distaste. He dabbed at a bit of mustard on his lower lip with his linen handkerchief. "Surely it wasn't for the gourmet cuisine, delectable as it may be . . . or for the dining ambiance." He shifted on the park bench, carefully scooting the hem of his trenchcoat away from a particularly fresh pigeon deposit beside him.

Nick tried to ignore the criticism, but it hackled him whether he wanted it to or not. What a snob old Pete was becoming these days. There had been a time—over twenty-five years ago—when the two of them had spent their Saturday mornings collecting aluminum cans. They had cashed them in at the local market and then caught the uptown subway to Central Park where they had purchased one hot dog, loaded with relish and sauerkraut, and one orange soda. They had shared the dog, bite for bite, and the soda, sip for sip, then spent the rest of the afternoon throwing a baseball, bemoaning the fact that they didn't have mits, and dreaming of the day they would collect enough cans to pay for train fare and tickets to Shea Stadium in Queens.

Nick hadn't eaten anything for a long time that had tasted as good as those shared meals. He looked across the expansive lawns at some pre-adolescent boys who were throwing a small plastic football. They weren't bad. But they deserved a real ball. They probably blew all their money on hot dogs and sodas, too. Boys and their long-term monetary goals are soon parted.

He and Nick had never made it to Shea.

Nick picked off the corner of his bun and tossed it to Hercules who sat at his feet, patiently waiting for his obligatory tidbit. The bulldog allowed the bread to fall to the ground, where he sniffed it dispiritedly, then licked a couple of times at the mustard and relish. He looked back at Nick, a reproachful scowl wrinkling his forehead.

"All right, all right," Nick said, biting off a bit of the wiener and tossing it to him.

The dog caught it in midair and swallowed it without a chomp. The corkscrew tail wagged and one ear perked.

"Why don't you and I take in a game at Shea sometime?" Nick said.

"It's November." Pete blew his nose on the non-mustard corner of his handkerchief. "It'd be a bit lonely, sitting in those bleachers all alone."

"In April, smart ass."

Pete shrugged. "We'll see. I'm pretty busy these days. The agenda is decidedly engaged." He glanced at his slimline, designer watch. "Speaking of, we're squandering the afternoon. What did you want to talk about?"

Nick stood, took a bedraggled baseball from his jacket pocket, and threw it across the lawn. "Herc, fetch!"

The bulldog bounded over the grass, tiny ears flopping in rhythm with the flapping dewlaps. In seconds he returned and dropped the slobber-drenched ball at Nick's feet. "Good boy," Nick said, scratching behind the dog's ears. He picked up the ball and threw it even harder, sending it nearly out of sight.

A perverse part of him considered challenging Pete to throw. But that was a cheap thrill. Maybe a cheap shot. *He always did throw like a pussy. Why embarrass the old man now?* he told himself with smug satisfaction.

"I wanted to ask you about that weird case you had a couple of weeks ago," he said, not turning to face Pete, who still sat on the bench.

"I've had a lot of eccentric cases. Which one did you have in mind?"

"The guy who got shot in his bed and—"

"That narrows it down."

"The guy . . ." Nick began again, trying to remain patient. God, had he ever really been best friends with this jerk? ". . . with the trophies."

"Oh, yeah. The non-bowling victim who had smashed bowling trophies lying all around the room."

"Did the wife ever own up?"

"No. She admits he beat her regularly once a week, says she wanted to kill him. Had him arrested several times, but the charges never stuck. Swears she doesn't know anything about the shooting—her alibi checked out—and she never saw those trophies before that night."

"What have you got so far?"

"Not much," Pete admitted reluctantly. Nick knew it cost him to confess that the Great American Detective Peter MacDonald didn't always get his man. "The trophies had been donated to a Salvation Army on Thirty-Third. Nothing there. No gun on the scene. Ballistics says it was a 9mm, point blank. Pretty big mess. Other than the wife, no other suspect."

"So this one's going to get away?" Nick couldn't resist.

"Not necessarily. I haven't closed the case yet." Pete straightened his tie and glanced at his watch again. "Why? You got another stiff surrounded by bowling league trophies?"

"No. But I've got a homicide with unusual evidence left at the scene. Stuff that doesn't seem to fit what happened."

"Bowling balls?"

"Expensive ladies' lingerie and Dom Perignon."

"Much nicer."

"Definitely, but as out of place as your trophies. Both scenes looked . . . staged."

Nick reached down for the retrieved ball and noticed that Hercules's tongue was hanging out several inches further than usual. He only had one or two more runs in him. Time to call this meeting, charming as it was, to a halt.

"Oh, well, the evening wasn't a total loss. I got to meet Elizabeth Knight." He glanced over his shoulder at Pete. He had to see the expression on his face. Pete was satisfactorily stunned, impressed, then jealous.

"Is she as sultry in person as on the tube, or is it done with mirrors?"

"She's gorgeous," Nick said, feeling a testosterone rush to even be talking about the lady. "Taller than I'd thought. The deep voice is for real, too. Pretty nice, but I don't think she likes cops."

"Where did you meet her?"

"Outside the apartment where my guy ate it."

"What was she doing there?"

"Hanging out, watching the action like everyone else. The studio's just a few blocks away."

"Interesting." Nick watched as all emotion left Pete's face, to be replaced by that studied, pseudo-intellectual expression that never failed to piss him off. Like Pete could just sit there on that pigeon-shit bench, using his superior I.Q. and figure out his case for him.

Ignoring him, Nick picked up the baseball and gave it one last hurl. Hercules scrambled after it, though with far less energy than before. As the bulldog ran, a movement caught the corner of Nick's eye—the boys' plastic football, sailing right across the dog's path.

"No! Hercules, no!" Nick shouted, but he was too late.

The bulldog leaped and chomped. As he landed a loud pop resounded across the field, his dewlaps fluttered upward, then settled over smiling, crooked teeth. He turned and trotted back to Nick, prancing, proud as a circus horse. The deflated ball hung limply from either side of his mouth.

"Hey, mister!" yelled one of the boys as he ran after the animal. "Your dog wrecked our ball!"

"I know, guys. I'm sorry. He just really likes footballs and . . ." Nick bent over to take the ball from the dog's mouth, but this bounty was too precious to be delivered as obediently as the baseball. Hercules clamped down tightly and growled. ". . . He . . . doesn't . . . like to . . . let go . . . once he's . . . got it." Nick pulled harder as his face grew redder and the growls got louder. "Damn it, Herc, give me that ball or I'll—"

Suddenly the dog released the ball and Nick fell backward on his rear in the grass. The boys and Pete found this highly entertaining. They guffawed shamelessly; even the dog seemed to be laughing.

"All right. Here's your damned ball," Nick said, shoving it into a boy's hand. It lay there like a dead bird, permanently grounded, never to soar again. No dab of glue would fix those rows of jagged punctures.

With a sigh Nick reached into his pocket and pulled out his wallet. He placed several bills in the boy's other hand. "Take this over to F.A.O. Schwartz and buy yourselves a good ball, not a plastic piece of shit like this."

"Wow! Thanks!" the boy said, gripping the money as though afraid Nick would snatch it back.

"Yeah, thanks," the others echoed as they took off across the grass.

Nick watched them, feeling a momentary pang of sadness. He looked back at Pete who hadn't moved from the bench. His "smug" look was firmly in place.

"Sap," Pete said.

"Yeah," Nick replied as he walked away with Hercules, "and your little dog Toto, too."

Six

The last time Elizabeth had driven her 1966 Avanti up the Taconic State Parkway toward the Bellingham Men's Correctional Institution, she had felt much the same as today, her palms clammy as she clutched the steering wheel, a quivering in her stomach that got worse with every pothole that jounced the car. Normally, she would have been concerned about her car's suspension, which she had just paid her mechanic a fortune to rebuild. Classic cars required a lot of upkeep, and this vintage Studebaker was her baby. Next to Katie Kat, of course.

But today she didn't give the road's surface a second thought. Her mind was as turbulent as her stomach as she mentally rehearsed what she would say to the prison psychiatrist when she arrived for her 3:30 afternoon appointment.

She glanced at her watch. 2:15. A sign told her she had only twelve miles to go. Great. She'd arrive with about an hour to kill.

To kill.

She smiled grimly to herself. Fine choice of words.

The last time she had driven this road had been three years ago. She had made an appearance at David Ferguson's first parole hearing to plead the case against giving him his freedom.

He had sat across the room from her, his soft brown eyes begging her to be kind, to forgive . . . to love him. That was all David had ever asked of her. Her love. Her devotion. For her to be as insanely obsessed with him as he was with her. Not much to ask. After all, he had paid the ultimate price to prove his love for her. He had devoted his life to making her his; whether she wanted to be or not didn't seem to matter. He had given up his possessions, his very freedom. He had killed for her. What more could he do?

She shuddered to think what more he might have in mind.

That day he had gazed at her with loving, sick eyes. The parole panel asked, "Have you come to an understanding as to why you committed your crime?"

He nodded, his eyes never leaving her face. "I broke the law of God and man," he said in a remote, sing-song voice, "and I deeply regret my actions."

"And if you were released," the parole board chairman continued, "would you attempt to pursue a relationship with Ms. Knight?"

Tears filled his russet eyes and spilled down his cheeks. His chin quivered as he said, "I can't deny my love for Elizabeth. I'll love her until one of us dies. But she's made it clear she doesn't want me. I guess I'll have to live with that."

In that moment, as he had uttered those last two sentences, Elizabeth had seen it: the hate, the obsession glowing hot in those quiet brown eyes. For a second, he was no longer David Ferguson, the lovesick puppy, but Ferguson the cold-blooded killer.

Fortunately, the board had seen it, too. And his parole had been denied.

Until two weeks ago.

As Elizabeth approached the gates of the prison she felt the quaking in her stomach rise into her throat until she could taste the bile of her own fear . . . or was it anger?

When it came to David Ferguson, she decided, a fine line divided the two. Part of her hoped to God she never saw his face again. Part of her just wanted to be safe.

But like the people she wrote about every week, she could look into the dark mirror of her soul and see another Elizabeth Knight. And this woman wanted to kill the man who had murdered her little sister.

Elizabeth glanced in the rearview mirror and was startled to see that same hot, sick glow in her own eyes. Maybe the lady in the mirror and David Ferguson had more in common than she cared to admit.

"Look, Mr. Ballini, I understand your anger, but you threatened to kill a man, repeatedly, and now he's dead. That makes you a prime suspect." Nick took a deep breath and a tighter rein on his temper. This guy was being uncooperative, but Nick didn't really blame him. If some high school coach had seduced Nina, he'd certainly feed him his teeth, to say the least, without apology. "You can either answer my questions here in your own living room, or we can do it at the station. You pick."

Mr. Ballini settled back on his dilapidated sofa and crossed thigh-sized arms over his belly. The man's dingy tee-shirt had worn through in spots and dark hair sprouted from the holes. The guy was a dock worker, coarse and rough as the lumber he unloaded from freighters every day. But Nick liked him.

He liked him because, a few minutes ago, the man's three children had returned from school, and Nick had watched as Mr. Ballini had kissed each one and given them a warm, welcome home hug, then sent them off to their bedroom to do their homework.

Nick recalled when his own father had worked the graveyard shift and had been at home to greet him after school each day. It had felt good to be enfolded in those big arms and squeezed until you couldn't breathe. Nick had seen the looks on the kids' faces as they had received their hugs. They had looked happy and contented . . . and most of all, safe. Nick remembered the emotion and realized he'd probably never feel that completely safe again.

"It's family business," Mr. Ballini said, his bewhiskered chin set resolutely. "I won't talk about my daughter to you or anyone."

Nick thought about the wounded look in the pretty teenager's eyes when she had passed through the room and he understood the man's reluctance. His daughter had been violated by that creep downstairs, then by the legal system. Obviously, she needed protecting.

"So, we won't talk about her," Nick said, "but you have to tell me where you were last Friday night between 10:00 P.M. and midnight."

The man shrugged. "At work."

"On the docks?"

"Yep. Ask my boss. He'll show you my time card. I was there from 9:30 Friday night until 5:30 Saturday morning. I was working with fifty guys. Shouldn't be hard to prove."

"No, not hard at all," Nick said with mixed emotions. As always, he had hoped this would be a cut and dried case. Wrap it up in a few days and on to the next. He always hoped, but it never turned out to be that easy. Besides, he was glad it wasn't Mr. Ballini. He would have hated to take this loving father out of his home and away from his family, who appeared to be barely making it as it was.

Nick stood and walked over to the door where he paused. "Are you certain that your daughter doesn't know anything? I really should question her."

The man's eyes softened and he dropped the tough guy facade. "She doesn't know anything, Detective O'Connor, really. If she did, she would have told me and I'd tell you. I swear."

"Okay, then I'll spare her for now, on your word. But if I don't catch the perpetrator soon, I may have to come back."

"I understand." Mr. Ballini reached out his hand and shook Nick's so tightly that he almost winced. "Thank you."

Nick walked out the door and headed down the hall. *Naw, he didn't do it,* he thought. If Mr. Ballini had murdered someone, he wouldn't have needed a club.

He flexed his throbbing fingers. No, a weapon wouldn't have been required. Those massive hands would have been deadly enough. Mr. Ballini, family man and outraged father, was off the hook.

Back to square one.

* * *

Psychiatrists were either the salt of the earth—or they were weird as hell: a theory formulated by Elizabeth in her second year of post graduate work at Columbia. There didn't seem to be a middle ground, she had noted, as with plumbers, secretaries, librarians, and automobile mechanics. They were either well-adjusted, worldly wise humanitarians, serving humankind by guiding the lost back to the light of sanity, or they were the blind leading those less blind into a chasm of confusion.

Elizabeth felt she owed her sanity to a doctor of the first ilk. The second type she avoided like poison ivy-scented, feminine hygiene spray. She found them just as irritating.

Dr. Holcomb appeared to be the irksome type. Apparently, he had entered the field to find answers to his own neurosis. It was equally apparent from his nervous twitches and constantly shifting eyes that those answers had eluded him.

"David Ferguson is fine, Miss Knight," the doctor said as he fidgeted with his pen, spinning it like a miniature majorette's baton between his fingers. "Mr. Ferguson was subjected to a battery of the most sophisticated tests and—"

"Is he still fixated on me?"

The pen tangled in his fingers, then dropped to the battered desktop with a dull thud. *Not a good sign,* Elizabeth thought. She grew increasingly uneasy as she watched him glance around the room, avoiding her eyes. For a moment she, too, studied the poster on the wall. A wide-eyed cartoon character peeked over the top of a rock, the caption reading, "It won't help being paranoid. They'll still get you."

Ordinarily, she might have chuckled. Not today.

"Am I still the object of his obsession, doctor?" she asked again. She could hear the stress in her own voice, the fear, the anger. Strange, those two emotions always came hand in hand when she thought of David Ferguson.

"Well, his . . . ah . . . his feelings toward you have definitely changed. I can't tell you too much without breaking a confidence, but—"

"Doctor, I just want to know one thing: Is my life in danger?"

"Oh, no, Miss Knight. Not at all. I would never have released Mr. Ferguson if I had thought there was any chance he would harm you. More than anything else, he just wants your forgiveness. He wants to make amends with you and restore your relationship."

"Our relationship? What relationship? The man murdered my sister. What relationship does he expect to have with me?" Elizabeth stood and began to pace the width of the small office, from the barred window surrounded by sagging bookshelves to the doctor's desk by the door. He shrank back in his chair and crossed both arms over his chest.

"Just out of curiosity, doctor," she said, lowering her voice to a hoarse whisper, "did you read the coroner's report? Do you know what he did to my sister?"

The doctor hesitated, cleared his throat, and looked up at his poster again. "Miss Knight . . . I . . . I know what he did, but I really don't think he'll do it again."

"Are you willing to bet your life on it, Dr. Holcomb?"

He continued to stare at the poster. The pen twirled in his hand.

She walked to the door and jerked it open. "Or is it only *my* life you're willing to gamble with?"

The killer slid down in his seat and watched her through his steering wheel as she left the front gates of the prison and walked across the lot to her car. He wished he were closer, so he could see the expression on her face. Her beautiful, untouchable face. But he hadn't dared park too near. Prisons had guards and cameras everywhere. No point in saying, "Here I am. Take my picture. I'm the guy you're looking for."

Actually, they weren't looking for him yet. Nobody had pieced the murders together. But they would soon. That cop with the ugly dog. He'd do it. He'd even talked to her outside the building that night. Sooner or later, he'd put it all together and then . . .

She walked with her head high, her long legs taking strong, aggressive strides. She was angry. He could feel the power of her rage radiating toward him. He could also feel her fear. Fear and rage, he'd lived with both all his life and he knew them well enough to recognize them in others.

Watching her gave him a sense of power that, for the moment, eased the fear. *He* was in control now. And, day by day, he was gaining more and more control over this woman. It was a strange and wonderful feeling which he had experienced only rarely in his entire life. The purest form of this power came when they begged . . . just before he killed them.

He imagined *her* begging. Pleading, crying, like the others had. But for some reason, the fantasy didn't thrill him like the memories. Not her. She was special. He didn't want *her* to beg. He wanted her to tell him how grateful she was that he had rescued her. From herself. He wanted her to tell him how much she loved him. He wanted her to realize that he had done it all out of love. An undying, sacred love that would live longer than either of them.

She got into the classic sports car—What was it? he wondered. A Studebaker?—and drove out of the parking lot.

As he had on the way here, he followed her through the winding rural roads and onto the expressway. He didn't need to follow too closely. He knew exactly where she was going. He knew everything about her.

He smiled.

Ah, yes . . . he loved being in control.

Seven

The curvaceous blonde crept down the hospital corridor, glancing nervously right and left at each intersecting hallway. She clutched her purse to her side, a sparkling red beaded bag which matched the skimpy red cocktail dress she wore. Walking on her tiptoes, she tried to keep her high heels from clicking on the black and white checkered tiles.

When she reached the door bearing the numbers "310" she took another cautious glance up and down the hall, then scooted inside.

In the center of the room a middle-aged man lay on a bed. Hoses, tubes, needles, and wires protruded from his inert body. He remained motionless, unaware of her presence as she strolled over to his bed, hips undulating, her full red lips set in a woebegone, but pseudo-sexy pout.

"Billy, I can't stand to see you like this," she said, leaning over his bed, pressing her voluptuous chest against his arm. She wriggled a bit more, but the comatose patient didn't stir. "You've just been lying here for months. I know you'd rather go on to a better place."

She sat on the edge of the bed, her short skirt riding even higher on her thighs. Reaching into her bag, she pulled out a syringe, then dropped the purse on the foot of his bed. "I brought something for you, honey. Morphine. It'll take away your pain forever."

She stood and walked around the bed to the I.V. stand. Pulling the plastic bag toward her, she plunged the needle into the top and squeezed until she had emptied the syringe.

"There . . ." she said, running her scarlet nails down his chest, ". . . you're going to be feeling much better soon. Now remember, I did this because I love you. It has nothing to do with the three million dollars you left me in your will. Nothing at all."

A few moments later, the graphs on the machines overhead began to trace jagged seismic tremors in glowing green across the screens.

"Goodbye, Billy," she said, leaning over him and planting a red lipstick kiss on his mouth. "Thanks for everything."

Grabbing her bag from the foot of the bed, she tried to shove the syringe inside, but in her haste she stabbed herself. With a little cry of pain she dropped the needle to the floor. A loud alarm sounded and she jumped, looking around frantically. She started to reach for the needle, then thought better of it and left it where it lay on the floor beside the bed. With heels clicking furiously, she hurried from the room.

"What the hell is going on here?" Elizabeth Knight said as she walked onto the set. "Brody! Where is he?"

The recently deceased corpse sat up in his bed, tubes and wires dangling. "He's in the booth, I think," he said.

"Cut!" yelled Francois, the director, as he left his position behind the camera and joined Elizabeth on set. A good-natured French Canadian, Francois had always been one of Elizabeth's favorite people on the set and off. She hated to interrupt his taping, but this was too much.

He stood before her, his warm brown eyes irritated but patient as he studied her through tortoise shell frames. He twisted his long curly ponytail with one finger and grinned at her knowingly. "Not happy with the script changes?" he asked with a sarcastic tone.

"Brody!" she yelled again.

The crew gathered around to witness the upcoming fireworks, but they were careful to stay out of range, clustering at the edge of the set.

"Yes, 'Lizbeth?" drawled a voice, heavy with reverb, over the house speaker. "You have some suggestions you'd like to share with me?"

She fumed. "Suggestions? Don't tempt me, Brody. This was supposed to be a sensitive story about an elderly couple. What's with the red cocktail dress and the jiggle routine?"

"I happen to like Cindy's jiggle, and I'm sure my male audience will, too."

"So, what are we producing here? The Dark Mirror or Cindy Does General Hospital?"

Snickers and giggles rippled around the set, but Francois held up one hand and they instantly fell silent.

"What woman, about to commit euthanasia on her husband, wears a red beaded cocktail dress?" she said. "Even if taste isn't an issue here, how about logic, for heaven's sake?"

"I believe . . ." said the voice with the celestial reverb, ". . . the issue here is *ratings*."

"You're underrating your audience, Brody," she said. "They may like jiggles, but they aren't stupid. Insulting them with this trash isn't going to up your ratings."

"Now, now, 'Lizbeth, don't get your panties in a wad. You know how hard that is on crew morale."

Elizabeth glanced around the set at the actors and crew. They all seemed to be enjoying the exchange. Too much, in fact. Her temper had reached its peak and was receding . . . once again, too quickly. This wasn't the time or place for this conversation. She'd take it up with Brody later in private.

Turning on her heel, she stomped off the set. As she left the sound stage, she heard the majestic "voice from heaven" speaking to his lowly subjects. "That was perfect, Cindy. See you later, honey. The rest of you can leave. Get a good night's sleep, boys and girls. Tomorrow morning we'll pick up where we left off . . . before our head writer decided to have her little tizzy fit."

Tizzy fit! she thought as she stormed down the hall. Sometimes she considered doing a script where a writer killed off her obnoxious producer. If she portrayed the executive to be exactly like Brody, surely her audience would consider it justifiable homicide.

By the time she reached her office, her blood pressure had dropped several more notches, but she was still red-faced and breathing hard. When she passed by Cass's desk, the older woman eyed her with a mixture of sympathy and amusement.

"He did it again," Elizabeth said as she passed through Cass's office and into her own. Usually, the quiet elegance of the room soothed her. This room, with its antiques, wainscoting, and oriental rugs that glowed from the warm light of stained glass lamps, made her feel like she was at a home-away-from-home, instead of a cold, impersonal network studio. But today, it didn't help. Nothing was going to help, except maybe punching Brody Yarborough in a vulnerable spot. Hard.

"You wouldn't believe what just happened down there," she told Cassie.

Cass sidled into the room and stood beside Elizabeth's roll-top desk, watching her jerk open the drawers, one by one, and slam them closed.

"Yep, I'd believe it," Cass drawled. "Bud just called me up and told me all about it. He says you really told old Brody off this time . . . in front of God and everybody!"

Elizabeth paused for a moment and looked up at Cass, surprised and irritated. "The set manager called to tell you that we had a fight?"

Cass smiled and nodded.

"Good grief. Don't you guys have a life? You call *that* excitement?" She began to rummage through the oak file cabinets.

"Nope. We call it gossip. And when the bosses fight, that's as good as it gets. Unless, of course, you two were boinking each other. Now *that* would be better."

Elizabeth shot her a deadly glance over the file drawer. "Me and Brody! Not on your life! That man makes me so angry sometimes, I don't know if I'm coming or going."

Cass consulted her watch. "At the moment, you're going."

Elizabeth shoved the drawer closed and opened another. "I'm not going anywhere unless I find my—"

Cassie reached over and lifted Elizabeth's satin Mets jacket from a chair. Beneath it lay Elizabeth's purse. She picked it up and shoved it into her hand.

Elizabeth looked at the purse for a moment, then at Cass and grinned sheepishly. "Oh . . . thanks."

Cass pulled a paper from a folder on the desk and handed that to her, as well. "Here's your speech for the awards banquet tomorrow night and—"

"Damn! I forgot to pick up a gown and I don't —"

Cass held up one hand, halting Elizabeth's tirade. She walked over to a set of French doors and opened the full closet. From inside she pulled out three evening gowns. She held them up for Elizabeth's inspection.

"With all that's been going on, I figured you'd forget, so I picked these up from Antoine's. Does one of them suit your fancy?"

Elizabeth passed over the teal satin and white chiffon, choosing the black silk sheath with a silver beaded bodice. "What would I do without you, my friend?" she said.

A moment of silent, affectionate camaraderie passed between the women, then Cass broke the connection by shoving the other two gowns into the closet and zipping Elizabeth's choice into a garment bag.

"That's easy," she said. "Without me you'd never be able to find your purse, your keys, or your speeches, and you'd be running around naked as a jaybird in winter."

Elizabeth took the bag from her. "That would be fine with Brody, I'm sure. Ratings and all that."

Cass glanced at her watch again. "I'm off duty now, and I don't want to hear about Brody."

Elizabeth laid the bag across the chair and donned her coat, baseball cap, and gloves. "This was supposed to be a show about ordinary people in terrible circumstances committing murder. But he's determined to emphasize the sex and violence over the content. Why do I bother to write a decent script if he's just going to butcher it with—"

"Sh-h-h." Cass placed her fingers to her lips. "I mean it. No more Brody! You don't pay me enough to hear about him after hours. Now let's go get drunk and carouse."

Cass grabbed the garment bag and Elizabeth followed her out of the office.

"Is that all you think about . . ." Elizabeth said, turning out the lights, ". . . drinking and carousing?"

"No," Cass replied matter-of-factly as she locked the door. "Most of the time I think about sex."

Oh no, not again, Elizabeth thought when she and Cass stepped outside the building and were greeted with an even larger than usual throng of protestors. *Not tonight.*

Their leader, the silver-headed Rev. Taggerty hurried over to her. Elizabeth held up one hand like an overworked, annoyed traffic cop. "Don't even start with me, Rev. Taggerty," she said. "Believe me, now isn't the time."

"We are here to appeal to your conscience, Miss Knight," he said, smiling down on her with a sweetness that made her nauseous. "Have you no sense of moral decency?"

"Well, you've got no sense at all," Cass said as she stepped between them. "Move aside, buddy, before I pop you upside the head."

One of the reverend's female followers grabbed the fringed sleeve of Cass's leather jacket. "Don't you threaten a man of God like that!"

"Man of God . . . my butt."

"Cassie, please." Elizabeth shot her a warning look. Then she turned her attention to Taggerty. "Reverend, the last thing I want is offend someone of your delicate sensitivity. If you don't like my show, I suggest you change channels. That's why God created remote controls. Now please get out of my way. I've had a hard day, and I want to go home."

Miraculously, Taggerty and his followers did as she asked and parted, leaving them an avenue of escape.

Once they had left the mob behind, Elizabeth paused and turned to Cass. "Maybe I'll take you up on that sinful offer you made before . . . just on principle. Let's go drink and carouse."

"Really!" Cass looked radiantly expectant.

"Naw, but we could have a Corona at Donahue's."

In the rear corner of the pub, far away from the boisterous crowd who had gathered around the television to watch the rugby match, Elizabeth and Cassie shared a companionable drink. Michael Donahue had joined them when they had arrived. But even two attractive, feisty women weren't enough to keep a true son of old Erin from his rugby. Now he sat in the center of the raucous bunch, draining mug after mug of his own stout.

Points were scored, mugs were hoisted, more ale quaffed and cheers echoed from one green wall to another. Elizabeth and Cassie paused, waiting for the clamor to die down before they continued their conversation.

Cass frowned disapprovingly as Elizabeth squeezed a lime into her bottle of Corona. "You aren't going to get very drunk or do much carousing on a sissy drink like beer."

Elizabeth grinned and sucked on her lime before wadding it into her paper napkin. "I *like* beer. I also like New Age jazz and walks on the beach. So . . . ?"

"Aww, that's just because you're one of those creative California types." She ran her fingers through her bleached curls and shook her head seductively. "Now me, I'm just a good ol' girl. Give me Jack Daniels straight, Kenny Rogers and a good roll in the hay."

Elizabeth lifted her bottle of beer in a toast. "Vive la difference."

"Yeah right," Cassie said with a snort. "Cowgirls don't speak French either."

Another roar filled the room. More than a dozen patrons

scrambled for the bar. Michael's lads must have won, Elizabeth surmised as he offered everyone drinks on the house.

She turned to Cassie who, for once, sat quietly sipping her Jack Daniels. Cass wasn't so rough and tumble as she pretended, Elizabeth thought with a surge of warmth toward the older woman who was so much more than an assistant to her. Any time Elizabeth needed a best friend, a sister, or mother, Cass was there, ready to step into the role and play it for as long as Elizabeth needed her.

Elizabeth wished that Cass needed *her* more often. But she always seemed so self-sufficient. Never disturbed or even ruffled by the potholes in life's unpredictable road, Cass didn't appear to need a shoulder to cry on, or a friend to offer advice. Sometimes Elizabeth imagined a scoreboard, not unlike the one for the rugby game on the television, upon which were recorded the "Kindly Advice/Tears on the Shoulder" debits of their relationship. Elizabeth—347. Cassandra—0.

Yet, Cassie wasn't without her foibles, as Elizabeth knew well. She, too, had her weaknesses; though they were more of a fleshly nature than emotional. One vice in particular worried Elizabeth.

"Are you still 'rolling in the hay' with Bud?"

Cass laughed wickedly and several of the patrons turned to look their way. A couple of young women in the opposite corner spotted Elizabeth and began to giggle, chatting excitedly behind their menus.

Accustomed to unsolicited attention, Elizabeth and Cass ignored them and continued their conversation.

"Well, from that lascivious laugh," Elizabeth said, "I'd say the answer to my question is yes."

"You assume right. We're rolling in the hay, behind the sets . . . on your desk."

"On *my desk?*" Elizabeth choked on her beer.

Cass shrugged. "Hey, when the urge strikes you."

Elizabeth laughed, then quickly became more somber. "I'm worried about you, Cassie. Sleeping with a married man and—"

"Then you don't have to worry. Believe me, when Bud and I are together, we aren't sleeping."

"You know what I mean. I'm afraid you're going to invest your heart in something that isn't going to pan out for you. He'll never leave his family. They never do."

"Yeah, well, don't worry about me. Every woman should be suffering like I am." Cass tilted her glass, draining the last drop. *"You* should try it. Misery like this builds character."

At that moment several of the former rugby fans drifted by their booth, eyeing Elizabeth with obvious male interest. She paid less attention to them than to the young women in the other corner. "I don't have time for that stuff right now."

"That stuff is exactly what you need. A beautiful woman like you, the object of millions of men's fantasies. What a waste."

The front door of the pub opened, ushering in a blast of cold air that smelled like impending snow. Two men walked inside, Bud and an attractive man about Elizabeth's age.

"Why, speak of the devil!" Cass exclaimed, standing and holding her arms out to Bud. "There's my lover man now, and just look what he brought with him."

Bud's companion smiled at Elizabeth, wearing that awkward, blind date sort of grin that was far too expectant under the circumstances. Elizabeth felt a prickling of irritation, soothed by the balm of knowing that her friend had her best interests at heart. But . . .

"Damn it, Cass. You set me up again." She stood and grabbed her coat. "I've told you—don't do that! I hate it!"

"Aw, come on. He's a real cutie and he's not even married. Stick around and we'll make it a foursome."

"A foursome with you and Bud? It would kill me." She headed for the door, nodding to Bud's friend, whose awkward smile was changing to acute disappointment.

As she made what she hoped was a graceful dive out the door she could hear Cass calling after her. "Hey, everybody's gotta go sometime. . . ."

* * *

As Nick followed the owner of Papa Joe's Pizza Parlor through the kitchen and into the office in the rear, he made a mental note: *Never, never eat in this place.* In comparison to Mama's sparkling kitchen, this joint was a miserable dump, from the ceiling which was dotted with bits of molding cheese—thrown there, no doubt, by the unruly adolescents who were tossing bits of vegetables at each other as they assembled pizza pies and salads—to the floor which bore a gray patina of grease and grime on linoleum of indistinguishable color.

The office wasn't much better, but at least the clutter was paper, rather than smelly, organic biodegradables.

Papa Joe was a stout, middle-aged man who seemed to be covered with the same basic gray patina as his kitchen floor. His skin, hair, and once-white baker's uniform were coated with a thin layer of grease, mixed with flour and dotted with red sauce.

As Papa cleared a stack of papers from a chair Nick noticed that his hands were shaking. Felt uneasy around cops, huh? Oh well, who didn't?

"Have a seat, Detective O'Connor," he said in a voice that Nick figured was probably half an octave lower—when he wasn't being questioned about a murder.

"Do you know a Gregory Jarvis?" Nick asked, never taking his eyes from the man's face as he cleared a seat for himself.

"Gregory Jarvis . . . let's see . . . that does sound familiar. Oh, yeah. I heard about him. He's the guy who got murdered around the block. Right?"

Nick nodded.

"No, can't say as I did. And I know a lot of people in the neighborhood. You know . . . doing deliveries and all."

"Did your restaurant deliver food to Mr. Jarvis's apartment on Friday night, November 29th?"

"Ah . . . I can't say right off. But I'll check our records if you want."

Nick glanced around the office. Finding records in this dump would be quite a task, but . . .

"Yes, please. That would be very helpful."

Papa rummaged for several minutes, muttering comments about his secretary who had gone off to Atlantic City for a weekend and never returned.

Yeah, right, Nick thought. *If this guy has a secretary, I have a butler and a chauffeur.*

"Here you go," Papa said, shoving a food-splattered notebook into Nick's hand. He pointed to a list of hastily scrawled addresses and phone numbers. "That's where we delivered that night. It goes from about here. . . ." He grabbed a pencil and drew a line above one of the addresses. "To about here." He scratched a mark near the bottom of the page.

"About?"

Papa shrugged and sat down on his chair, fidgeting nervously. "Yeah, well, it's pretty close. As close as I can tell . . . for sure."

"I see." Nick's eyes scanned the list. No such address. Just to make sure, he checked several pages before and after the delineated area. Still nothing.

"Do you ever recall having delivered to this address before?"

"Not that I remember. And I try to keep track of all my customers. The personal touch, you know."

"Yes, of course."

"Are there any other restaurants in the area whose delivery boys wear red and green jackets?"

"Not that I know of. That's *our* trademark," he said proudly. "I keep track of stuff like that."

"I'm sure you do."

"But funny you should ask about the jackets."

Nick glanced up from the notebook, instantly alert. "Why is that?"

"One of the guys had his jacket ripped off. Left it hanging by the back door on a nail, and the next minute—poof, it was gone."

"When?"

"About a week or so ago."

"Do you have any idea who took it?"

"None at all. I mean, I like our jackets and all, but they ain't exactly a fashion statement, you know."

Nick thought it wise not to agree too heartily. He simply nodded and said, "I see your point." He pulled a card from inside his jacket and handed it to the man. "If that jacket shows up, or if you think of anything that might help me, please give me a call."

Papa took the card and gave him a grateful smile. "Sure," he said, "no problem."

He's just relieved I didn't say anything about turning him in to the health board, Nick thought as he walked through the kitchen.

Passing by the toppings bins, he nabbed a couple of slices of sausage. When he had left Hercules in the Jeep outside, he had promised him a piece of pastrami.

Pepperoni would have to do.

Friday night. 10:58 P.M. The killer in the white smock with the stethoscope draped around his neck watched Elizabeth Knight on the small television set anchored on a shelf near the ceiling of the empty room. He had absorbed every detail of the last ten minutes of the show from this room. Room 308. He didn't even blink as he watched her, savoring every graceful gesture, every expression that flitted across that beautiful face. He searched her eyes. Did she know he was out there? Could she feel him, watching, following? Every nerve in his body was acutely tuned to her. How could she not be aware of him, of his intensity, of his yearnings?

The picture faded and a news teaser came on. "Four killed in bloody expressway collision. Film. Coming up in three minutes."

He shook his head in disgust. Such sensationalism. What did they know about death and violence and blood? Not as much as he did, that was for sure. Up close, murder wasn't so mysterious or intriguing. In fact, with each killing, it was becoming more matter-of-fact. The only drama was whether or not he'd get away with it . . . again.

How much longer until they figured it out? After tonight, it would be pretty easy. He'd seen to that. He'd made certain that this murder took place in the same precinct as the last. On that cop's turf. The one with the bulldog. He'd figure it out.

The murderer consulted his watch again. 11:05. The television screen was filled with the gory images of the accident, the camera zooming in on dismembered body parts by the side of the road. A second later the reporter rammed a microphone under the nose of the hysterical relative standing nearby and asked for a reaction. He got one. More hysteria.

The killer reached up and switched the set off. *Some people,* he thought indignantly. *Didn't they have any class at all?*

Turning his attention to more pressing matters, he reached into his pocket and checked the contents. A syringe filled with morphine—*that* had been hard to find—and a tube of scarlet lipstick. He smiled, remembering how he had obtained that. He pulled a pair of surgical gloves from his pocket and slipped them on.

Ready? he asked himself. *Set, go!*

He walked over to the door and opened it a crack. Listening carefully, he heard only the clatter of a mop and pail far down the hall. He felt a momentary surge of pride that he was developing such keen instincts. He was getting damned good at this. Too bad, nobody knew it. Yet.

On the balls of his feet he crept into the hallway. Three steps took him to the next room. 310. Carefully he eased open the door and looked inside. The patient, an elderly man, lay in the bed, hooked to miscellaneous tubes and beeping, flashing apparatuses.

For a moment—only a short moment—he felt a wave of sympathy toward the old soul. With his silver hair and withered face he reminded him of his own grandfather, long gone.

Then he shook off the feeling. Now wasn't the time for sentimentality.

With a purposeful stride he walked over to the I.V. and pulled out his syringe. The old man's eyes opened briefly and he stared at him, startled, then mollified by the white smock and stethoscope. The killer gave him what he hoped was a physician's warmest bedside manner smile.

Sticking the syringe into the top of the I.V., he released the drug into the glucose solution. After draining the syringe, he dropped it to the floor and gave it a careful nudge with his foot, until it rolled under the bed. In only a few seconds the beeping machines changed tone and frequency. Flat line.

The killer reached into his pocket and extracted the tube of lipstick. Leaning over the corpse, he hastily smeared some on the old man's lips. He tucked the lipstick back into his pocket and headed for the door.

The hallway was clear, though he could hear the scuffing of nurse shoes and excited chattering coming from an intersecting hall.

They were on their way.

He headed for the stairwell and made it inside before they rounded the corner.

He had done it! Again! And soon the world would know. *He* would be the one on the eleven o'clock news.

Or at least the tales of his exploits. Hopefully, not *him*, himself.

But if he were caught, he would pay the price. It would be worth it. He thought of Elizabeth's blue eyes and shining black hair.

Ah, yes, he thought. She was definitely worth it.

Eight

The moment Elizabeth stepped inside her house and saw the blue envelope lying on the floor, her heart started to pound. Katie Kat came running to meet her, but stopped to sniff the letter suspiciously.

"Yeah, that's what I thought, too," Elizabeth said, lifting the envelope by its corner, reluctant to even touch it. Somehow she knew she didn't want any connection with the writer of this letter, not even by touching something he had handled.

After glancing uneasily around the living room and up the staircase, she walked into the kitchen and took a knife from the drawer. Her hand shook as she slit the top of the envelope and looked inside. It contained a letter on matching paper.

Well, at least he's color coordinated, Elizabeth thought with a wry chuckle.

How do you know it's a "he?" she asked herself. She knew why. Because she could feel him. And the feeling brought goose-flesh to her arms.

Laying the knife on the countertop, she took a deep breath and reached inside. She pulled out the letter, unfolded it, and read.

Dear Elizabeth,

I hope you will understand that everything I've done, I've done for you. You are such a special person. I know you don't feel the same way about me as I do about you. How could you? But someday you'll understand that it was for the best. I did it out of love, so that we can be together forever.

"Oh, God," she said, throwing the letter onto the counter and backing away from it. "He's started again."

She pulled a small red telephone book from a drawer, hurried to the living room and picked up the phone. After punching in some numbers, she sank onto the sofa. Her legs were trembling too much to hold her.

"Dr. Holcomb," said a lazy voice on the other end.

"Yes, doctor. This is Elizabeth Knight. I just received a letter from David Ferguson. I think you should hear it."

She read the letter, while the psychiatrist listened silently.

"Well, does that sound like a man who has been rehabilitated, who no longer obsesses over me?" she asked, her voice bitter with sarcasm and fear.

"Did he sign the letter?" the doctor asked.

"No, but—"

"Do you recognize his handwriting?"

"Well, no. It's typed."

"Then how can you be certain that it's from Mr. Ferguson?"

A wave of anger swept over her. Suddenly, it all came back: the fury, the frustration, the futile calls to the authorities, begging for assistance. She had been told, time after time, "Sorry, but we can't do anything until he commits a crime."

"Are you serious?" she asked. "Who else would write something like that?"

"You're a celebrity, Ms. Knight. I'm sure that many of your fans would write you a letter."

"This was shoved under my door. He knows where I live!"

"Really, Ms. Knight, I think you're overreacting. Even if he *did* write it, there's nothing threatening in the letter."

Elizabeth sat, clutching the phone, too angry to speak. The doctor was as nuts as Ferguson if he believed she wasn't in danger. No one could be that stupid.

"You know damned well that there's an implied threat in that wording," she said. "You're just too stubborn to admit that you might have let a dangerous killer out on the streets again. Well, I'll tell you one thing, Dr. Holcomb. If I even *see* David Ferguson's face again, I'll kill the bastard. Do you hear me?"

"Now, now, Ms. Knight. Don't even say such a thing. I know you don't mean it and—"

She slammed the phone down, cutting him off. The fool. She wouldn't get anywhere with him, so why waste her time and energy? She had to decide how she was going to handle this.

A dozen possibilities ran through her mind and, as she considered each one, the intellectual exercise began to calm her emotions. Call the local police? No, she had learned long ago how pointless that was. They would say the same thing they had said ten years before.

Hire a bodyguard? She hated to have her privacy violated to that degree. Maybe later, if it became absolutely necessary.

Should she try to contact Ferguson himself and—?

And what? Would she really kill him if she ever saw his face again, as she had said?

Elizabeth thought about The Dark Mirror, reflecting the faces of ordinary people in terrible circumstances, tempted to take the life of another human being.

Could she do it?

She sat, stroking the cat who had climbed into her lap and was licking her cheek with wet, sandpaper kisses of concern.

She didn't know if she could or not. How could anyone know, unless they had been there? And she wasn't there. At least, not yet.

"So, if you hate me, why don't you just make me walk a beat in Port Authority instead of working me to death? A nice quick slashing by some transient and it would all be over." Nick tossed the folder which his superior had just handed him on top of the stack of paperwork that hid the surface of his desk.

Captain Bob Ryerson picked up the discarded folder, opened

it and shoved it under Nick's nose. "There's a connection between this hospital case and your teacher who got bashed with the champagne bottle."

"Wasn't a bottle. The coroner found slivers of wood in his head. He thinks it was just your ordinary wooden club, probably drilled out and filled with lead."

Nick sighed and ran his fingers through his hair. *Greasy as hell,* he thought. He hadn't showered in two days, hadn't slept in three. After following up on every lead he could think of . . . twice . . . he had come up with exactly zero. This case was really starting to get to him. Now the captain wanted him to take on another?

He couldn't resist glancing down at the folder. "Okay, I'll bite. What's the connection?" He knew he'd regret asking but . . .

"They're both weird."

"Oh, well, that's a hot lead. I can certainly run with that one."

"And they both happened on Friday night."

"Along with half the other murders in this precinct."

"Between eleven o'clock and midnight."

Nick cocked one eyebrow and took the folder from him. "Yeah? Let me see that."

Ryerson grinned, self-satisfied. Nick saw the smirk, but chose to ignore it. He and the captain had expressed their differences in the past; some of their verbal altercations were legendary among the ranks. The thin walls that separated the offices from the bullpen did little to filter the obscenities, insults, and not-so-veiled threats.

But in the end, they respected each other. Maybe even liked each other, though neither would have admitted it even to themselves, let alone to anyone else.

Ryerson sat in the one threadbare swivel chair beside Nick's desk and propped his ankle on his knee. He pulled a pack of cigarettes from his pocket and lit one.

Nick glanced up as he blew a puff across the desk. "Filthy habit," he muttered. "Your lungs will rot and fall out."

Ryerson grinned. "How long's it been?"

Nick glanced at the calendar on the wall which bore several rows of squares marked with red stars. "Three weeks, four days . . ." He looked at his watch. ". . . seven hours, and ten minutes."

"But who's counting."

"Exactly. I've passed the critical point and am now a non-smoker." Ryerson exhaled another cloud and Nick breathed deeply. "When you're in my office, could you do Marlboros? I'm discriminating about my second-hand smoke."

Ryerson laughed, then nodded at the folder. "An old fellow, not an enemy in the world. He was fighting it out in the hospital after bypass surgery, doing pretty good, when somebody gave him an overdose of morphine through his I.V."

"Wife?"

"Nice lady. She's devastated."

"Heirs?"

"A couple of grown kids. Equally nice. No property of any value to leave behind."

"Business associates?"

"Ran a corner newsstand. Retired twenty years."

"Anything else?"

Ryerson picked up the folder and thumbed through it. He handed Nick a photo.

Nick studied the picture. At first, he wasn't sure what he was seeing. Obviously it was a coroner's shot of the man's face, but there was something red smeared across his mouth. It looked like—

"Lipstick?"

"Yep. Ruby red."

"His wife's?"

"Nope. She doesn't wear makeup. Neither do the daughters."

Nick glanced over the report. "He's a little old to be getting it on with the nurses."

"With *his* ticker? Not a chance. And there's something else. The syringe that the killer used to inject the morphine . . . it was lying beside the bed, clear as day."

"Fingerprints?"

"Naw. He wasn't that stupid."

"And we aren't that lucky." Nick glanced through the other photos and skimmed the preliminary report. "You're right. It's weird. Elements that don't seem to belong at the scene."

"It kinda looks . . . staged. Isn't that what you said about your champagne murder?"

"Yeah." Nick mulled it over for a while. "And they were both Friday night."

"Coroner says about 11:15 for both of them."

Nick sighed and picked up the folder. He threw it in his back-pack with the rest of his homework. "Okay. I'll read them over and get back to you."

Ryerson smiled broadly. It occurred to Nick that the captain was quite a pleasant fellow . . . as long as he got his way.

"That's my boy." Ryerson rose and headed for the door. With his hand on the knob he paused. "Why don't you come home with me and have some pizza. The kids'll have somebody else to beat at Nintendo, and my old lady thinks you're cute."

Feeling guilty, huh? He wasn't letting him off that easy.

"Thanks, but I'll pass. My mom and little sister requested my presence tonight to watch T.V. I haven't seen either one of them since I took this case."

Ryerson shrugged. "Suit yourself."

"Besides," Nick added mischievously, "I already spent the afternoon with your old lady, and she wore me out."

"Screw you, O'Connor."

"Yes, she did. And very nicely, I might add."

Ryerson jerked the door open and Nick chuckled. The captain was more than a little insecure about his pretty wife—strawberry blonde, curvaceous, and fifteen years his junior. His Achilles tendon was just too convenient a target. Nick couldn't resist one parting shot. "Tell her I think she's cute, too."

It had been years since Nick had attended Sunday morning mass with his mother and Nina, a family tradition long abandoned. But one ritual was sacred above all else: Sunday evening biscotti and espresso, served with a favorite television show. For years it had been Lawrence Welk, his father's favorite. Then they had graduated to Bonanza. Now with the advent of the V.C.R., choices abounded. Usually, Nina chose and he and Mama resigned themselves to her selection. Nick didn't care what was on the tube; he simply enjoyed spending time with his "girls." Sitting in this small but cozy room, surrounded by the seldom dusted bric-a-brac and memorabilia of his childhood, he felt safe, far removed from the violence and cruelty he witnessed every day on the streets.

They say you can't go home, he often thought as he sat in his father's recliner, Hercules at his feet, Mama and Nina curled on either ends of the sofa. Well, maybe they were wrong. Maybe you could . . . sometimes. And maybe, if you were lucky, it felt almost as good as it had all those years ago.

"What are we watching tonight, sweetcakes?" he asked Nina as she set the tray, bearing cups of espresso on the coffee table and opened a tin of chocolate-coated biscotti.

She grimaced. "Mama, he's calling me names again," she said in an adolescent whine. "Make him stop it."

"Nicky, don't pester your sister. Call her by her name, please." Mama repeated the words from rote, not bothering to glance up from her needlepoint.

Nick grinned at Nina, whose pout was fading fast. He called her a lot worse in private, but this was a game they played, giving Mama something "motherly" to do by refereeing their fights. Lately, Nick was noticing that Nina was taking over more and more of Mama O'Connor's duties: brewing the espresso, serving it along with the traditional biscotti. The transference from one generation to the next was natural and inevitable. But he felt a pang of sadness, nevertheless.

Nina walked over to the V.C.R., shoved in a tape, and punched the appropriate buttons. "Well, since you met Elizabeth Knight and she actually petted our dog, I thought we could watch this week's 'Dark Mirror.' How's that?"

Mama nodded her approval while threading her needle, and Nick grunted appreciatively.

Why not? he thought. *More fantasy material.* His social life had been a rather dry desert lately. A television program, featuring a beautiful woman whom he had met, might provide a pleasant oasis, even if it were make-believe.

He watched, mesmerized as Elizabeth delivered her prologue, commenting on the pain and frustration involved in seeing someone you love dying, oh so slowly, before your eyes and being unable to relieve their pain or ease them over into a better world.

As the story unfolded, scene by scene, he couldn't help comparing the busty blonde actress, who starred in the episode, to Elizabeth. He had to admit that he found Elizabeth's feminine grace and elegance far more intriguing than the blonde's generous bustline. He chuckled inwardly. Hell, he must be getting old.

Commercial time: Nina fast-forwarded the tape while Nick refreshed Mama's cup of espresso and added her three spoons of sugar, then slipped a biscotti to Hercules.

"Nicky, you spoil that animal," she softly scolded. "He'll get gallstones or dog diabetes if you don't stop feeding him chocolate."

"Come on, Mama, give the guy a break. We already had his nuts nipped off and—"

"Sh-h-h," she said, putting a finger to her lips and nodding toward Nina who giggled. "Watch your language, Nicholas."

"Besides," Nick muttered under his breath, "you give him chicken livers and that makes him fart like a—"

"That's enough, young man." Her smile belied the stern tone of her voice. "The show's back on."

Nick stroked the dog's ear as he watched the last act of the show. As the blonde made her way carefully down the hospital corridor, Nick had to admit that she had a mean sashay. But he found himself looking forward to the last few minutes of the program—Elizabeth's epilogue.

The woman on the screen arrived at her destination and the camera panned to the number on the door. 310.

A bell went off in Nick's brain. Just a small buzz that lifted his blood pressure slightly and sharpened his attention. When she reached into her red beaded purse and pulled out the syringe of morphine, he sat upright in his chair, ignoring the bulldog that rubbed against his hand. When she injected the morphine into the I.V. bag, gave him a sloppy red lipstick kiss, and dropped the needle to the floor, Nick bolted up from his chair.

"I'll be damned!" he said. "Did you see that? The morphine, the lipstick, room 310! Holy shit!"

"Nicholas!" Mama looked appalled. "I told you to watch your language when you're around your little sister!"

"No, Mama, really! That's it. A case that we're working on, it's—"

He didn't finish his statement because he was rummaging through his backpack, pulling out papers and thumbing through assorted folders. He found the one he was looking for and scanned it. "Room 310. I thought so."

Nina and Mama watched, open-mouthed, as he paced the floor, the folder in his hand. "Okay," he said, thinking aloud, "the room number could be a coincidence. But the lipstick, the morphine, the needle on the floor . . . no way! Somebody set it up to look like the T.V. episode. They staged it, just like . . ."

He threw the folder on the coffee table and charged into the kitchen, Nina following close behind.

"Nick, what is going on?" she said, grabbing at his sleeve. But he ignored her and headed for the broom closet where a stack of newspapers were bundled with twine, ready to be set out for the recyclers. He grabbed the pile and heaved it onto the kitchen table.

Mama entered the room just as he was cutting the twine with his pocket knife. "Son, what are you doing? I had those all bundled up."

He held up one hand. "It's okay, Mama. I'll put them back, I promise. I just want to check one thing." He turned to Nina. "Here, kid, help me find the last few T.V. magazines."

For once, she didn't even object to him calling her "kid." Sensing his excitement, she began sorting through the papers he had pushed her way.

"Here's one," she said, shoving it into his hand.

"Okay, let's see here . . ." He thumbed through the pages. "When is 'The Dark Mirror' on?"

"Friday night," Nina replied. "Ten o'clock."

"Friday?" The ringing in his head sounded like a four alarm fire bell. "Ten o'clock, really?"

Nina nodded. "Why? What's the big deal?"

"Yes, what's this all about?" Mama peered over his shoulder as he slid his finger down the printed columns.

"There it is." He pointed to the entry and read, "Ten o'clock, 'The Dark Mirror.' Elizabeth Knight invites you to examine the trauma of a young woman who is raped by her professor." He paused, his eyes glistening with excitement, his pulse pounding. He loved this moment. This was what he worked for, that instant when it all came together. The bells went off and the lights flashed in his head. Damn, it was fun! It made the exhausting legwork and the hours of boring surveillance worth it all.

"Nina," he said, lowering the paper, "do you watch 'The Dark Mirror' every week?"

"Usually, if I don't have a date with Bobby."

"Did you see this episode, the one with the girl and her professor?"

"Yeah. That was a good one."

"What did she kill him with?"

Time slowed for him as he waited for her answer, the words he knew were coming.

"She whacked him over the head with a champagne bottle."

"Dom Perignon?"

"What?"

"Was the bottle dark green?"

She thought for a moment. "Yeah, I think it was. Why?"

"And after she killed him, were there torn women's clothes scattered around the room?"

"Yeah, how did you know that?"

In reply, he grabbed her by the waist, picked her up, and planted a hearty kiss on her cheek. "Sweetcakes, I owe you one! Big time!"

He gave his mother a similar peck. "Sorry, ladies. I gotta go. See you later, but don't wait up."

Passing through the living room, he scooped up the folder, his backpack, his jacket, and Jeep keys. A second later he was out the door, running toward the garage. He paused just before he got into the car and made a quick mental note. Nina didn't know what Dom Perignon was. He'd definitely have to blow his budget and buy her a bottle on his way home. No point in the kid being a heathen.

Nine

The instant Elizabeth stepped inside the reception area, Cassie shot up from her desk and hurried over to her, earrings jingling, a wide grin on her face.

"Just wait 'til you see what's waiting for you in your office," she said. "He's *gorgeous!*"

"Damn it, Cass. If you're trying to set me up with somebody again, I swear I'll—"

"This ain't exactly a date." She lowered her voice. "He's a cop."

"A cop?"

Several thoughts flashed through Elizabeth's mind, all relating to David Ferguson. Was this guy here to warn her, to guard her, to give her the news that Ferguson couldn't handle his freedom and had jumped off a bridge somewhere?

No such luck, she thought bitterly. *He'll probably tell me not to call and harass poor Dr. Holcomb again.*

"Yeah, he's a cop," Cassie said, nodding her head. Her blonde curls, firmly fixed with hair spray, didn't budge. "He showed me his . . . badge," she breathed and batted her eyelashes. "He's probably got handcuffs, leg irons, and a big, lo-o-ng nightstick."

Elizabeth stared at her for a moment. "Cass, you are one sick individual."

Giggling, Cassie returned to her desk, while Elizabeth gathered her mental fortitude and opened the room to her office. She didn't really like cops, and the last thing she wanted to do this morning was talk to one. About anything.

But when she opened the door and saw him, standing by the window, she nearly dropped her purse as well as her composure. It was him! The guy with the bulldog. More importantly, the guy with the green eyes, the tight jeans, the broad shoulder, the sexy smile, the—

She pulled her mind back to more practical matters. What was a cop doing here, and what did he want with her?

He turned from the window and his eyes met hers. A strange sense of familiarity swept over her, a feeling of casual intimacy that was completely incongruent with the circumstances. She almost felt as though she could walk over to him, put her arms around his neck and . . .

Stop it! she silently scolded herself.

"Yes, how can I help you?" she asked, far more brusquely than she had intended. She wondered if he had picked up on her irritation. The slightly puzzled, but acutely observant look in his eyes told her that he had noticed. Somehow she knew this man didn't miss anything. Especially when he was on the job. And the intensity of his expression and his rigid posture led her to believe this was far from a social call.

"I don't believe we met formally the other night," he said, extending his hand to her. "I'm Detective Nick O'Connor from Midtown Homicide."

"Homicide?"

Her heart skipped a beat. What now? She steeled herself to prepare for the worst. But what could the worst be? That was the trouble with trying to prepare, you never knew what you were preparing for. It was an exercise in futility, she had learned long ago. In the end tragedy always struck when you weren't looking, from some source you couldn't have anticipated. You were never really prepared. There was no such protection available to the human heart.

But having suffered the worst, Elizabeth had learned that, whatever happened, she could handle it. She would carry on somehow. Constantly reminding herself of that fact had allowed her to go on living with a minimal amount of fear. Until now.

Whatever it is, it'll be okay, she told herself.

She waved her hand toward a comfortable wing-backed chair. "Please sit down, Detective O'Connor. Can I get you a cup of coffee?"

"No, thanks," he said, as he sat in the chair.

She considered sitting behind her desk to provide a barrier between herself and this man, between her heart and what he was about to say. Instead, she forced herself to sit in a matching chair across from his.

"So, am I going to be called on the carpet again for misrepresenting law enforcement in my show?" she asked, trying to sound casual and failing miserably.

"No, I like your show. And my younger sister, Nina, is crazy about it," he said with a genuine warmth that touched her. She heard a slight accent, a gentle lilt that was . . . oh, yes, O'Connor. He had Irish heritage. She decided that, despite the intensity in his green eyes, they were kind. There was an undeniable power in the man, but she had the feeling that he wouldn't use it against a person, unless they were on the wrong side of the law.

Maybe he wasn't so bad. For a cop.

"Then what's up?" she asked.

He leaned back in the chair, studying her. "I'm working on a couple of murder cases, and I think you might be able to help me."

"I'll do what I can."

He nodded and pulled a small black notebook and pen from the inside pocket of his leather jacket. For half a second she saw the flash of a leather strap and gun holster. The glint of blue-black metal. She reminded herself what this man with the warm green eyes and the gentle lilt to his voice did for a living.

He flipped open the notebook and clicked his pen. "Can you tell me where you were last Friday night between eleven o'clock and midnight?" he asked without looking up at her.

"Am I a suspect?" she asked.

"A routine question." He glanced up at her and once again

she felt his power. Something told her there was nothing routine about his question or the case he was investigating.

"I was at Donahue's Pub over on Fifty-fifth, spending some time with friends."

"And the same time the week before that?"

She thought carefully. "Same thing. After I left the pub, I ran into you and your bulldog. Despite what my public may think, I lead a rather predictable, unglamorous life."

He chuckled and she couldn't help noticing what a beautiful smile he had. White teeth against golden brown skin. And dimples. God, she was a sucker for dimples.

"I'd rather not tell my younger sister that," he said. "She'd be crushed."

At his mention of his sister, she felt a momentary pang. She swallowed the emotion and smiled, but he had noticed. She saw it in his eyes. This man noticed everything. She had the uncomfortable feeling he could read her thoughts, and, right now, with him sitting so close, wearing those jeans that hugged his masculine contours, she didn't want him to be able to read her mind.

"Why are you asking me these questions?" she asked. "What do your murders have to do with me?"

He reached into his pocket again and pulled out an envelope. Inside were a dozen or so photos. He handed half of them to her and said, "Take a look at these, and then you tell me."

She glanced at the first picture, afraid of what she might see. Her mind couldn't help returning to another stack of coroner's shots. A cop had asked her to look at those too, the bastard.

The shot was predictable. A corpse lying on the floor, blood on his head. Grim, she thought, but not particularly sensational.

"He was a teacher at the local high school," Nick said. "A lot of people believe he sexually abused one of his students." He paused, studying her face. She could feel the penetrating heat of his gaze, and she experienced a twinge of inexplicable guilt, as though she were being accused of something.

"Okay," she said, considering his words. "The guy was a pervert. So what?"

She flipped to the next photo. On the floor, beside the victim lay a champagne bottle. Dom Perignon. Its neck broken off. Blood smeared on the glass.

A hot, red flush burned her cheeks. Her heart pounded, and she felt as though she couldn't breathe.

Quickly, she turned over the next. The torn lingerie arranged so carefully. "Oh, my God," she whispered. "It's like . . . it's like the show."

She glanced up at the detective. He was leaning forward, his elbows on his knees, obviously watching and evaluating her reaction. His green eyes probed hers and again, she felt guilty, accused.

"When was this murder committed?" she asked in a tight, higher than usual voice. She wondered briefly how he would interpret that.

"Two weeks ago. Friday night."

"The night we met. That's the case you were on your way to investigate?"

He nodded. "That's right. And the coroner estimates the time of death at shortly after eleven."

She thought for a moment, and the hot flush drained from her face. "That's right after . . ."

"Yes, it is." He handed her the second stack of photos. "This is my other case. This murder occurred last Friday night. Shortly after eleven."

With fingers that were trembling, she took the photos from him and looked at the first one. Again, a corpse, lying on a hospital bed.

No, God, please, she thought. *Not a hospital bed.* The victim had red lipstick smeared across his mouth.

You're never prepared, she thought in some calm, detached part of her mind. *No matter how much you try, it's always something you hadn't expected.*

The next picture showed a syringe lying on the floor. Her throat closed a little tighter.

"Morphine?" she asked, anticipating the answer.

He nodded. "I'm afraid so."

Next—a close-up of the door and the room number. 310. By now the numbness was spreading through her emotions—the soul's way of cushioning itself from those unexpected blows.

He reached for the pictures and gave her a brief smile that was unexpectedly compassionate. For some reason which she couldn't understand, she nearly burst into tears. She never wept when angry or even afraid. But if someone showed her unanticipated kindness at a moment of high stress, she could lose it.

She choked back the emotions and resisted the strange urge to reach out her arms to this stranger and ask him to hold her. But it had been years since she had relied on anyone else for strength, and this wasn't the time to change old habits.

"Who is doing this?" she asked. "And why?"

"I wish I knew, Ms. Knight. That's why I'm here. I was hoping you could help me."

She pushed down the last vestige of panic and fear—wryly noting that she was getting very good at this—and allowed her intellect to take over. "I want to help you, Detective O'Connor. What can I do?"

At that moment the phone rang. She stood and walked over to the desk. Cass reminded her of several appointments she had scheduled for the morning. "Yes, Cassie, I know. They'll have to wait. Hold all my calls."

She sat down. "Okay, where were we?" she asked, feeling the unnatural calm sweep over her. Thank God for automatic pilot in times like these. She would fall apart later. At home. Where it was safe.

He glanced down one of the pages of his little black notebook. "Did you know either of the victims, Gregory Jarvis or Herbert Wilcox?"

"No."

"Do you know anyone who is upset with you, with the studio . . . other than the picketers outside. They were pretty obvious when I came in."

"Are you asking if we have any enemies who would wish us

harm?" She thought of David Ferguson . . . and so many others. "Of course we do. Dozens. I wouldn't know where to start."

The phone rang again. Elizabeth jumped. The pretense of calm vanished momentarily.

She grabbed it and said, "Cassie, I told you to—"

"I know," Cass replied. "But it's Brody. When I wouldn't put him through, he said he was coming up. Sorry."

"It's all right. Thanks."

She hung up the phone and grabbed her jacket. "Come on," she said. "Let's get out of here before we get interrupted again."

"We could go down to the station, if you prefer," he said, standing and following her to the back door of her office.

"Oh . . . we can do better than that."

He smiled and, once again, she had the urge to put her arms around him and bury her face against his chest. Long ago, she had come to the realization that no person, male or female, could make everything right in your world. That was fairy-tale crap and she wasn't interested in playing Cinderella. But it would be nice at times like these to have a male friend, a mate with strong arms to enfold you and give you at least the illusion of safety. To not be so alone all the time.

"How do you feel about lukewarm Guinness and rugby?" she asked.

"The name's O'Connor, remember?"

"Oh, yeah."

The killer watched from the edge of the crowd as Elizabeth Knight and the guy in the black leather jacket made their way through the throng of picketers.

So, he thought, *the cop's put it all together.*

And now she knows.

He looked at the protestors with their signs, their slogans, their passionate faces glowing with zeal and purpose. Soon they would know, too. And they would have even more to protest about.

Violence in the media *did* perpetuate violence in society. His actions had proven that.

And he wasn't finished yet.

His self-satisfied smile turned to a scowl as he watched the cop put his arm around Elizabeth's waist and guide her through the crowd. They had just met! He had a lot of nerve, touching her like that.

For the first time it occurred to him that maybe Elizabeth was a woman who invited men's touches. Maybe a lot of men had put their hands on her. What if she wasn't as sweet and wonderful as he had always imagined her to be?

As she and the cop left the crowd behind and hurried down the street, the killer saw them look at each other. It was just a quick glance, but even a glimpse could tell a lot.

There was something going on between them. Already. They had just met and he could tell, even now, that they had a thing for each other.

She liked that damned cop.

And, of course, he liked her. What male wouldn't?

It was just a matter of time until the cop would be in bed with her, doing all the things that *he* had done to her, so many times . . . in so many ways . . . in so many fantasies.

He waited until they were a block away before he followed them. Now that they knew, he had to be even more careful than before.

As he watched them walking together, talking, the cop leaning his head down to hers and taking her elbow as they crossed the street, the killer's irritation and anger grew.

He wouldn't allow it. It wasn't going to happen. Not Elizabeth. Not with that guy. She was *his*. Whether she knew it or not.

He didn't want to hurt her. But he would if she forced him to. After all, he thought as he watched them round a corner and disappear, it was for her own good. Everything he did . . . it was all for her.

Ten

Elizabeth Knight's favorite hangout wasn't exactly what Nick had expected. Somehow, he had thought a star of her celebrity and wealth would have chosen a more pretentious spot. Donahue's was anything but showy. In fact, it reminded him of a pub near his mom's deli where his father had taken him for the occasional bottle of ale. Before.

Nick had been underage, but big for seventeen, and nobody thought it important to card Ryan O'Connor's son. If Ryan said he was old enough, no questions were asked.

The moment he and Elizabeth had walked in together, he realized that they were creating quite a stir. He assumed it was because she was a famous person. Then he understood that it was more than that. These people knew her, and judging from the warm smiles sent her way, they liked her. A lot. They regarded Nick with avid curiosity, then turned to comment to each other. He couldn't help wondering if their reviews were "picks" or "pans."

"Sorry about that," Elizabeth said, a moment later as they slid into a booth near the back of the room. "I should have known better than bring you in here."

"Do you always get this much attention wherever you go?" he said.

"No, it's just that, well, they think we're . . . together."

Together? With this beautiful woman? Him? *Not bloody likely,* he told himself. But he had to admit that even the thought of being here, or anywhere, *with* her, made his pulse pound and his blood flow into the nether regions of his body.

"I see. Friends of yours?" he asked, nodding toward a knot of waitresses huddled around a burly guy who appeared to be the bartender and owner.

"The best," she said. "Michael and the girls knew me before 'The Dark Mirror.' I waited tables here . . . a lifetime ago."

So, she had worked her way up in the world. Her success hadn't been handed to her. Nick found the idea charming. Hell, who was he kidding? He found everything about this woman charming. He was smitten, like a pimple-faced kid. No doubt about it. Just sitting here, watching her wrap those slender, graceful hands around that beer bottle and lift it to those lips . . . it was a deeply spiritual, damn near orgasmic experience.

Yep, he was starstruck.

With a mental slap, he brought his attention to the matter at hand. He was investigating a homicide, and for all he knew, this pretty lady with the beautiful hands, glossy black hair, and pale blue eyes might be his prime suspect.

He watched her closely, trying to observe as a cop, not a love-lorn groupie. Her hands were shaking as she lifted the beer and drank. She gulped the liquid down as though her mouth were dry. For a moment he thought he saw tears in her eyes.

Not too surprising, really. Whether she were involved or not, this would be extremely upsetting. Some idiot was out there, copycatting her fictitious murders. She had to feel responsible somehow. He certainly wouldn't want to be in her shoes.

"These murders . . . who would have thought that someone would . . ." she said. Her lower lip trembled slightly. He watched her bite it and take a deep breath. "I can't believe it's happening. I—"

Her voice broke and the tears welled again. She sniffed and Nick cursed himself for not carrying one of those pansy handkerchiefs that Pete always seemed to have.

"It's a tough break," he said, handing her a paper napkin instead. "There are some pretty crazy people out there."

"One in particular," she said bitterly. She took the napkin and dabbed at her eyes and nose.

Nick perked up instantly. "You know somebody who might be doing this?"

"Yes, I'm afraid so." She placed her hands over her eyes for a moment, and he thought she was going to burst into sobs. He watched as she gained control of her emotions. Obviously, she'd had a lot of practice. He knew the feeling well.

"Tell me," he said softly.

"His name is David Ferguson. He was released from prison about four weeks ago."

Timing's right, he thought. He took out his black book and began to scribble. "Released from where?"

"Bellingham—upstate."

"Yeah, I know. I've sent a few there myself. But who's David Ferguson?"

"He murdered a member of my family, years ago. My younger sister."

Nick felt a deep pain in his gut and a surge of sympathy for her. If anyone ever touched Nina, he'd—

"Has he contacted you?"

She nodded. "I think so. I received an anonymous letter at my home, but I'm pretty sure it was from him."

"Threatening?"

"Not really. He thinks he's in love with me," she said with a wry smile. "Lucky me."

"Not really. Those are the ones you have to look out for." *They'll love you to death,* he added silently. There was no point in upsetting her more than she was already. "I'd like to see that letter."

"Sure, I'll get it to you."

She wiped her eyes again and tried to smile. Nick had the overwhelming urge to reach out and stroke her cheek. Just once. In spite of the fact that she was one of the leading television personalities in the nation, she looked more like a vulnerable little girl than a glamorous star.

"Is there anything else, Detective O'Connor?" she asked. "I want to help you nail this bastard, before he kills anyone else."

"Yes, I need a brief synopsis of your shows that have aired so far this season. And video tapes, if possible."

"They'll be ready for you tomorrow morning, along with the letter. I can have them couriered to your office or—"

"No, that's okay," he said. "I'll drop by."

He wasn't trying to be accommodating, he realized in a moment of self-knowledge. He just wanted the chance to see her again, to talk to her.

"And if you'd make a list for me," he continued, "of anyone and everyone who might be an enemy of yours, the show's, the station's. You said there were quite a few."

She chuckled. "Now *that* will take a while to compile."

He saw her glance sideways at a man who was sitting in a booth alone near the door, sipping a drink, looking morose. He waited for her to comment, but she didn't.

"Who's he?"

"Oh, his name is Norman Paulson. A nice guy, really. But Yarborough fired him a couple of weeks ago for doing me a favor."

Nick scribbled the name in his pad.

"No, not Norman," she said. "He's a bit disgruntled about the whole thing, but he'd never hurt anyone."

"Just keeping my options open, Ms. Knight."

Her blue eyes searched his with an intensity that made *him* uncomfortable for a change. He wasn't accustomed to this kind of scrutiny. Usually he was the one giving, not receiving it.

"I see my name in your little black book. Does that mean that I'm a suspect, too, detective?" she said.

He smiled at her. "Like I said, always keep those options open."

"Who do you think is doing it?"

"Can't tell yet. Besides, I postpone the thinking part of an investigation as long as possible. No point in wasting energy before you've got all the facts."

Again those blue eyes locked with his. "I don't believe that, Detective O'Connor. I think those gears of yours are whirring every minute."

"Naw, that's just my pseudo-intelligent look. It's a required course at cop school. P.I.L. 101."

She laughed and he was pleased with himself for bringing a smile to her pretty face.

"May I ask you something, Ms. Knight?" he said. It wasn't the time or place for a personal question, but he couldn't wait any longer. His curiosity was killing him.

She nodded.

"Why don't you like cops? Is it because, by and large, we're a bunch of assholes, or do you have some reason in particular?"

Instantly, her smile died. She picked up her bottle and drained the last of her beer. He sensed she was steeling herself for her reply.

"I tried to tell you guys," she said, "that David was dangerous. That he was going to hurt somebody. One night he told me he was on his way to my house with a gun to kill me. I called the police, and the officer on duty said, 'Well, let us know when he gets there.' "

Nick winced and cleared his throat. "Thank God the laws are a little better than that now, but not much."

"And the night . . . the night he killed my sister . . ." Her lip began to tremble again, and her eyes flooded with tears. "They questioned me, they accused me, they grilled me for hours. But—"

Her voice broke. She laced her fingers together and squeezed. He watched her knuckles turning white. "But what?"

"But not one of them bothered to say, 'I'm sorry for your loss.' Not one. How could they be so cold, so unfeeling? It's just common decency to offer some expression of sympathy. Don't you think?"

Nick squirmed in his seat, suddenly feeling his face grow hot. How many times had he done the same thing as those insensitive bastards who had handled her case? How many years ago had he stopped feeling, stopped caring? The fact was, he still cared. He just hid behind his meticulously maintained emotional wall and stared out at the rest of the world through a chink in one of the bricks.

He wanted to justify his behavior to her, to provide excuses for his fellow law enforcers. He wanted to tell her what it felt like to watch a young, pregnant mother shot by her jealous, drunken husband, when you were standing only six feet away. To have her blood splatter all over you. To not be able to take the gun away from the guy before he blew his own brains out.

If you allowed yourself to feel, to care, you went nuts. So, you pretended to yourself and others that you didn't care. They weren't murdered people; they were stiffs. They were perps, not some mama's teenaged boy—like your own next door neighbor—gone wrong.

But, looking at Elizabeth Knight across the table, her blue eyes full of sorrow for her murdered sister, he wasn't about to start with the lectures, to lay out the lines of defense. He wasn't going to be just another callous cop who minimized her loss.

"I understand," he said. She lifted her eyes and searched his to see if he meant it. "It must have been hell for you."

"Thank you," she said, and he could tell she meant it. "It was. And now it seems to have started all over again. I felt responsible for my sister's death, and now these people have died. It's as if my show killed them."

He dared to reach over and cover her hands with his. This technique certainly wasn't something he had learned at the academy. Far from it. But it felt like the right thing to do. And once he had touched her, it seemed the most natural thing in the world.

"Your show hasn't killed anyone," he said, "and neither have you. Some warped nut is doing the murders. It's on *his* head, not yours."

She blinked and a couple of tears ran down her cheeks. "Catch him for me, please, Detective O'Connor," she said.

"I'll do my damnedest." He patted her hand and gave her his

best lady-killer smile, designed to instill confidence. "And I'm a very determined sort of guy."

As Nick sat on Mrs. Wilcox's sofa and looked around her living room at the multi-colored crocheted afghan, the rows of family pictures on top of the piano, and the plate of freshly baked chocolate chip cookies on the coffee table before him, he thought she must be the perfect grandmother.

She sat in an old recliner across from him, every silver-blue hair on her head held in place by an almost invisible net, her flowered house-dress not only ironed, but starched. Her brave smile touched his heart, along with the fact that she had taken the time and effort to make cookies for him . . . when her husband had been murdered only four days before.

Looking up at a picture of Jesus knocking at the door of a quaint cottage, she said, "I know we all have to go sometime, but I wanted Herbert to go when the Lord was ready to call him. It hurts so much to lose him this way. It's hard to believe it was really his time, when some wicked soul decided to murder him."

"We're trying to find the killer, Mrs. Wilcox. We can't bring your husband back, but we can make sure that his murderer comes to justice." He sipped from the dainty china cup which held exquisite coffee. For an instant he flashed back on Mrs. Orton's evil brew, and noted the contrast. Both in the ladies and their coffees.

" 'Vengeance is mine,' saith the Lord," she quoted, fingering the gold cross which hung from a chain around her neck. "I won't hate the person who did this. With the help of the Lord, I won't allow myself to."

"Do you know anyone who might have had a grudge against your husband, Mrs. Wilcox?" he said, asking the routine question, but knowing he would receive the expected answer. This murder had nothing to do with Mr. Herbert Wilcox, other than the fact that he had been unfortunate enough to have been placed in room 310, and he had been terminally ill.

"Herbert never had an enemy in his life." She stood and walked over to the piano. Picking up a picture of the deceased from its place on the snowy fringed scarf, she touched one finger to the man's cheek. "He was a good Christian man. The best. He went to church every Sunday of his life, raised a fine family of six children, and loved his grandkids. We have fifteen, you know." She returned the photo and smoothed the scarf. "They're sure going to miss their grandpa."

Nick rose and slipped on his jacket. There was no point in prolonging this interview. Better leave the lady alone with her photographs and her sorrow. He wasn't going to find any more answers here.

"I'll be leaving now," he said, taking a card from his pocket. "If you have any questions, or if you need to talk, feel free to call any time."

As he pressed the card into her hand, he knew that—unlike the repugnant Mrs. Orton—she wouldn't be calling. Her kind never did. Besides, she had all those children and grandchildren to comfort her. She didn't need a cop's sympathy. He turned to walk away, but paused as he remembered something Elizabeth had said.

Turning, he laid one hand on the woman's shoulder. "Mrs. Wilcox," he said, pausing as he searched for the right words.

"Yes, dear?"

He discarded the fancy phrases, the speeches about God's will and how your loved one had found a better place. He decided that the simple words usually meant the most in circumstances like these.

"I'm truly sorry for your loss."

For the first time since he had arrived, tears came to her eyes. She smiled and patted his hand. "Well, thank you, child."

She hurried to the coffee table, scooped up some cookies and handed them to him.

Damn it, he thought as he headed out to the Jeep with his home-baked booty in his hand and a lump in his throat. He was starting to feel again.

That wasn't a good idea. With a serial killer on the loose, this definitely wasn't the time.

"Brody, I have to talk to you, *now!*"

Elizabeth charged into Yarborough's wild animal kingdom office and ignored the fact that Brody was sitting in his leopard-print chair with a disheveled young lady on his lap. Elizabeth recognized her—the actress in the red cocktail dress. Only this time she was wearing a purple tiger-striped jumpsuit. The suit was unzipped down the front and her bedraggled blonde hair looked as though she'd just done the Grizzly Bear Hump on the bearskin rug.

"I'm busy, darlin'," he said smoothly, but his eyes flashed with irritation. "Just wait your turn; ol' Brody'll get to you as soon as he can."

The blonde raised her eyebrows, looking surprised and titillated at this possible gossip.

Elizabeth's temper flared. Brody was forever trying to spread the rumor that they were sleeping together. And, of course, everyone wanted to believe such a juicy tidbit.

"Screw you, Brody," she said.

He chuckled. "Like I said, sweetheart, wait your turn."

"Damn it, I'm not kidding. We have to talk. This is serious." She turned to the actress, who was pushing her voluptuous breasts back into the tight suit and trying to zip it, like an overstuffed suitcase. "Cindy, please leave us alone."

The woman looked at Brody, who nodded curtly. She hurried across the red carpeting, unsteady in her spike heel slides. When she reached the door, Elizabeth put one hand on her arm. "By the way, Cindy. You're very pretty and a not-so-bad actress. You don't have to do this crap with Yarborough or anyone else to get a job."

"But my agent said—"

"It doesn't matter. Leave your name with my assistant, Cassandra, and we'll get you a decent agent."

Cindy smiled an attractive, if slightly dense, smile. "Gee, thanks, Miss Knight."

"You're welcome."

Elizabeth watched her go, then carefully shut the door behind her. Turning to Brody, she ignored the tightness in his jaw, the deep red flush of his skin. So what? After she told him her news, he was going to be in a lot worse mood.

"If you ever do that to me again, Elizabeth, I swear I'll—"

"Oh, can it, Brody. So you lost one. I'm sure you've got dozens more lined up to take her place on your leopard chair."

He smiled broadly, and she shook her head in disgust. The man wasn't smart enough to know when he was being insulted. It took the pleasure out of the sport.

"What's so goddamned important that you had to interrupt my good times?" he said, as he unzipped his jeans and shoved his shirttail inside.

She ignored the gesture which was, undoubtedly, supposed to turn her on. As she walked over to a less offensive, cowhide chair, a wave of nausea hit her. Since she had talked to Detective O'Connor yesterday and learned about the killings, she had been experiencing surge after surge of a sick, helpless sensation that she wanted to deny, but couldn't. The shock was wearing off, and cold reality was setting in.

The wave came crashing over her now, at the anticipation of having to say the words aloud. It was one thing to lie in bed at home and pretend it was all a horrible dream. It was quite another to sit here in Yarborough's office in the light of day and speak the words.

"I had a visit from a homicide detective yesterday," she said.

Instantly, he forgot about his shirttail. He sauntered to his desk and leaned against it, arms crossed over his chest. "Is there somethin' you need to tell me about, sugar? You gone and croaked somebody?"

"Someone has killed two people on the last two Friday nights . . . within an hour of 'The Dark Mirror' broadcast."

"So? People get killed in this town all the time on Friday nights."

She took a deep breath and plunged ahead. "The murderer is killing them in exactly the same manner as the victim was killed on 'The Dark Mirror' that night."

He stared at her, his face blank, for a long moment. "No shit?"

"A pervert was hit over the head with a champagne bottle. Torn lingerie was lying around the scene. An elderly man in hospital room 310 was given an overdose of morphine in his I.V."

Slowly he walked around the desk and sat down with a thud in his chair. "Well, if that ain't a bite in the ass," he said.

Elizabeth searched his eyes for surprise or horror. She saw neither, only acute interest.

He propped his boots on the desk and studied the silver toe tips. "The press know about this yet?"

"I don't think so."

She had been so appalled at the thought of someone copying her work by committing murder that she hadn't considered the implications once the media got wind of this story. The images it brought to mind made her even sicker than before. The whole world was going to know; it was only a matter of time.

"It's going to be hell on earth when those crowds in front of the studio find out about this," she said, rubbing her hands across her eyes as though trying to blot out the mental picture.

"Yeah," he said thoughtfully, "ain't it though."

Suddenly snapping out of his daze, he grabbed a pen and notepad. "What's this guy's name . . . the cop you talked to?"

"Detective Sergeant Nicholas O'Connor. He's with Midtown Homicide."

"Is he sure about this?"

"I saw the crime scene photographs myself." She recalled the poor old man with lipstick smeared on his face and shuddered. "They're far too similar to be coincidental."

"Well, 'Lizbeth, you must be a better writer than we

thought . . . inspiring somebody to go out and whack people like that."

She winced. "Cheap shot, Brody. Even for you."

Leaning back in his chair, he pulled out a cigar and lit up. "I guess this means that some drunk driver's gonna bite the bullet this week."

She thought of this week's plot: a young, grief-crazed father killing the drunk driver who ran over his child and left her to die in the road. Oh, God. It could happen again. He had done it at least twice. There was no reason to think he wouldn't repeat it.

"We'll have to cancel the show this week," she said. "That's all we can do."

He puffed a cloud into the air. "We'll certainly have to take action, that's for sure."

"We can't risk it happening again."

Smiling at her in what she supposed he thought was a paternal manner, he said, "Don't worry your pretty head, little darlin'. Ol' Brody will take care of everything."

If his words were meant to reassure, she wasn't convinced. Something about his nonchalance and the almost-smirk on his face set her on edge.

She glanced at her watch. In ten minutes she was supposed to meet Detective O'Connor again and give him the lists which she and Cass had compiled.

"I have to go," she said, rising and walking to the door. "I mean it, Brody. We have to do something fast. This can't happen again."

"Of course not," he said. "That would be awful."

She left the room feeling more agitated than when she had arrived. She wasn't sure how, but by telling Brody, she had the distinct feeling she had just made everything ten times worse.

Yarborough waited to make sure she wasn't coming back for anything, then he walked over to the window and looked down on the picketers below. He watched for awhile, then a smile curved the corners of his mouth. Not a pleasant smile. More of a Texas-style, shit-eating grin.

Back at his desk, he picked up the phone. "Bambi, get me the news department." He waited, drumming his fingertips impatiently on the desktop. "Yeah, Steve. You boys get up here on the double," he said. "I got a big one for ya. Y'al' get your asses in gear. We gotta make sure this one's ready for the six o'clock news."

Eleven

Elizabeth sat at her desk, staring out the window at the Fifth Avenue traffic that raced by—mostly cab drivers who were practiced at the fine art of timing the lights for a straight run. Occasionally, someone slowed to pick up a passenger and ruined the system. Horns sounded, obscenities were shouted, and even as they sat, waiting for the lights to change, the cabs and their perpetually irate drivers seemed to vibrate with impatience.

But Elizabeth's mind was on another road, another car, and its doomed driver.

Before her, the cursor flashed on her computer monitor, signaling her momentary writer's block. Usually she worked at home, where she could look out her window and watch the sailing skiffs in the Madison Harbor. The serenity of the scene helped her think. There her cursor flew across the screen effortlessly, bringing words and concepts into being which she hoped would entertain and enlighten her audience.

But today Francois needed a scene rewrite, and she had to finish it before she left the office. Ordinarily, she worked well under pressure. Thrived on it. But lately, with so much on her mind, it was becoming more and more difficult to concentrate. To create required a quiet spirit. Today her mind and heart were anything but quiet.

Besides, she didn't know if this story would ever go to air. With the news of the killings, she was determined that no episodes would be broadcast until they had captured the murderer. Brody had told her in a memo to continue writing. They would go ahead as planned, hoping for the best. As long as the episode was "in the can," they could use it, providing—he assured her—the killer was caught.

This show involved a grief-ridden young father who killed the drunken driver who murdered his daughter. Elizabeth had reached the scene where the father caught the man walking out of a bar, reeling from intoxication. In spite of his drunkenness, he crawled behind the wheel of his car and started the engine. The father walked over to the open car window, told the driver who he was and why he was there, then shot him.

But every time Elizabeth put her fingers to the keyboard to write, a picture flashed before her mind. The image of some person, somewhere on Friday night, being killed in the same manner. She felt as though she were signing their death warrant. How could her writing, which had brought her so much joy and success, have caused some sick mind to go out and copy what was supposed to have only been a fantasy? To bring something as horrible as murder out of the screen and into the world of reality . . . what kind of person would do something like that? she wondered.

The phone on her desk rang, startlingly shrill. She jumped and grabbed the receiver.

"Yes?"

"He's h-e-r-e." Elizabeth couldn't help noticing the grin in Cassie's voice and it made her cringe. Not now, for heaven's sake. She hoped Detective O'Connor wasn't standing beside Cassie to see the smirk, but she was certain he was.

"Detective O'Connor?" she asked in what she hoped was her most icy tone. It came out completely soft and mushy. Not good.

" 'Tis himself," Cassie returned in an affected Irish brogue. "In the magnificent flesh."

Elizabeth blushed. Oh, God, had she said that right in front of him? "Thank you, Cassandra. Send him in."

There, now Cass would know she was in trouble. Elizabeth never called her Cassandra unless she was grandly pissed off.

The door swung open and Cassie stood there, wearing the

predictable smile. Elizabeth noticed, with irritation, that she wasn't exactly quaking on her five-inch heels. So much for intimidating the hired help.

Elizabeth quickly forgot Cassie as Detective O'Connor walked into the room. He was wearing the same black leather jacket and a different pair of jeans. These were ripped in the right knee; the others had been torn on the left. His tee shirt bore the slogan: "Just because I'm moody doesn't mean you aren't irritating."

She stood, suddenly conscious of her own clothing. Not because she was underdressed—quite the contrary. She had spent far more time than usual this morning picking the sapphire silk blouse with deep vee neckline and the black leather skirt. Her nearly black stockings and heels accentuated her long legs.

She didn't dare ask herself why she had bothered to dress up today, when she usually wore jeans or leggings to the office. It wouldn't have been because she was expecting a visit from a certain gorgeous hunk of a cop. No, that didn't bear thinking about at all.

In spite of her denial, she felt a rush of female satisfaction when she saw his eyes sweep over her. Not one of those lingering, leering, elevator looks, where a guy checks out each anatomical part and evaluates it. Great, okay, not-so-hot. But one of those quick once-overs that ends with the man's eyes locking with the woman's and an unspoken, "Very nice, indeed."

"Have a seat, detective," she said, trying to appear businesslike while her blood flowed into her cheeks, making them as hot as other areas of her body where the circulation was equally brisk. She picked up a folder from her desk and handed it to him. "Here's the letter I told you about, and the information you asked for. A brief synopsis of all the episodes this season . . . and last. We might as well be thorough."

He took the papers and began to thumb through them. "Thank you, Ms. Knight. We'll check the letter for prints and I'll look over the rest of this stuff. I really appreciate you—"

His words ended abruptly as he stared at one of the papers in the folder.

"What is it?" she asked.

"You had a show about a wife whose husband was a bowling fiend?"

"Yes, it aired three weeks ago. He abused her constantly. One night she had had enough and—"

"And the murder scene was littered with bowling trophies."

"How did you know?"

A dark expression crossed his face. She lowered herself onto a chair next to his, bracing for the worst.

"Don't tell me," she began. "There was another one?"

"Possibly. It was downtown, another precinct. A friend's case."

She wondered why he sounded so bitter when he said the word, "friend." Standing, she walked over to the window and leaned her forehead against the cold pane. "Dear God," she murmured. "Three people. Dead because of . . ."

As she looked down on the pickets, her eyes sought and found one familiar sign. It read: Violence in Media = Violence in Society. She chuckled bitterly. "They don't know how right they are," she said.

Turning, she expected to see O'Connor still sitting in the chair, but he was standing directly behind her, looking down on the crowd. He moved quietly for such a large man, she noted.

"I'm not going to be able to keep this away from the press for very long," he said.

She was surprised when he laid one hand on her shoulder. It was warm and it felt much better than such a simple gesture should. In that moment she realized how little human contact she had, other than the occasional hug from Cassie or Michael Donahue.

"Things are going to be pretty tough for you," he said, brushing back a strand of her hair. "If you need a friend, give me a call. Anytime."

Searching his green eyes, she looked for any sign of ulterior motives. She was all too accustomed to having men hit on her, trying to prove their manhood by sleeping with a celebrity. Was that all he was doing?

Her instincts told her that this man meant what he said and nothing more. He really did want to be her friend. How refreshing.

"Thank you, Nick," she said with a smile. "I appreciate that. More than you might realize." Turning back to the window, she looked down at the crowd and a shudder of premonition went through her. "It *is* going to get really bad, isn't it."

"Why the hell didn't you tell me about 'The Dark Mirror' and your bowling murder?" Nick said, glaring at Pete who had just returned to his office to find Nick rummaging through some papers on his desk.

"Hey, get out of there!" He snatched the folders from Nick's hands and walked behind the desk. "Who the hell do you think you are, nosing through my stuff?"

With a degree of satisfaction Nick noticed that Pete had put the desk between them as quickly as possible. Like that could help him if he decided to take him out. And right now he felt like it. For three weeks this asshole had been holding back information that would have helped them both.

"I thought I was your friend," Nick said. "You know . . . old pals who help each other out whenever possible. Unless, of course, it might give their career a boost to withhold the goodies."

"What are you talking about?" Pete said without meeting his eyes. It occurred to Nick that Pete hadn't looked him square in the eye for a long time.

"Don't play dumb; it just pisses me off more. I read the damned report." Nick jabbed a finger at the paper on the desk. "That's dated three weeks ago. You put your bowling trophy murder together with 'The Dark Mirror' program as soon as it happened. You watch the show all the time. You knew exactly what was going on when I told you about my case in the park that day."

Pete sputtered for a moment, then he donned a righteously indignant expression. "You've got a lot of nerve accusing me of anything. You were the one poking around in my office when I wasn't here and—"

"Oh, shove it, Pete." Nick stood and walked to the door. "There's always been dirty cops who care more about cracking a case and getting a promotion than stopping the bad guys. I just never thought my best friend would turn out to be one of them."

Pete came out from behind the desk, his face flushed with anger, his fists balled at his sides. He rushed up to Nick as though he were going to punch him, but Nick didn't move or even flinch. Pete stopped a foot from his face. "You don't know what it's like because you don't have an ounce of ambition. You never did."

Nick glowered at him, his calm fury a direct contrast to Pete's emotional outburst. "Cram your ambition," he said as he turned to leave the room. "Thanks to you, this guy has killed two more people and there may be others before he's done. I hope you get your damned promotion. It would be a shame if those victims died for nothing."

"What do you mean Brody may not preempt the show? Of course he will, under the circumstances." Elizabeth stopped in the middle of the sidewalk on Fifth Avenue and stared at Cass, hoping she had misunderstood what her friend had just said. "What else could he do?"

The stream of pedestrians parted and flowed around the two women. Several bumped into them and swore, but didn't miss a step.

Cass grabbed Elizabeth's elbow and pulled her along. "Did he tell you he was gonna preempt the show?"

"Well . . . we discussed it and he agreed that something had to be done."

"That's what I thought. Listen, I know Brody better than you do, babycakes," Cass said. "And I believe that the two of you are going to be locking horns on this one. He just ain't gonna see it your way."

"There is no *my way*. It's the only decent thing to do."

Cass chuckled. "Exactly. I think the operative term there is 'decent.' Since when did ol' Brody worry about common decency?"

The momentary lull in Elizabeth's emotional conflict, created by going out for a peaceful lunch with Cassie, evaporated, and her sick feeling returned, even stronger than before. The last few days had a nightmare quality about them, but reality was encroaching, moment by moment, with each chilling realization. This situation was horrible, but she knew it was going to get much worse before it was resolved.

Elizabeth shifted the bags of toys under her arms and considered hailing a cab. But she was only six blocks away from the studio and she couldn't lift a hand anyway without dropping something. She had left Cass at F.A.O. Schwartz, buying toys for her flock of nephews and nieces in Texas. Having been born into a family of seven siblings, Cass never wanted for company during the holidays. Three days before Christmas, the studio closed and everyone left to "go home."

The holidays were difficult for Elizabeth. If it hadn't been for David Ferguson, she might have had a niece or nephew of her own. Her mother might still be alive and there would still be a "home" to go to.

But she didn't allow the holiday blues to get to her, not too deeply anyway. She enjoyed buying several dozen items for the Toys for Tots campaign. The first dozen were in the bags which were constantly shifting and slipping as she jostled them along the crowded sidewalk. She watched her footing, trying to avoid the icy spots which had glazed over the past hour as the temperatures had dropped. New York had enjoyed a mild autumn, but winter was definitely on its way. Time to dig out the earmuffs and insulated gloves from the cedar chest at the foot of her bed.

The moment she rounded the corner and saw the studio entrance, her holiday spirit was dampened by the sight of even larger crowds of protestors, new faces she hadn't seen before. And the news crews. *Good heavens,* she thought, *what do they want?*

Obviously the story had broken, judging by the presence of all three major networks, complete with reporters, camera and sound men, all elbowing their way through the throngs.

This wouldn't do. She wasn't about to try to fight her way through that melee, loaded down with toys like a besieged Santa. Turning around, she tried to make her getaway unseen, but too late. She heard someone shout, "There she is! It's Elizabeth Knight!"

For a second she thought of abandoning the toys in a heap on the sidewalk and fleeing down Fifth Avenue. But she thought of the poster in Dr. Holcomb's office and the little paranoid peering over the rock. It wouldn't help. They'd get her sooner or later.

Drawing a deep breath of resolve, she whirled around to meet them. At first she thought she would be bowled over by the mob that raced toward her, but she braced herself and held her ground as they descended on her. Five microphones were shoved into her face. One struck her cheek. She winced and gritted her teeth.

"Ms. Knight, what do you think of the Mirror Killer?" one of the female reporters asked.

So, they had a name for him already, she thought. Jack the Ripper, the Boston Strangler, the Hillside Strangler, and now . . . the Mirror Killer. The very idea made her feel horribly sick, as though she had somehow personally created this monster.

"His actions are deplorable," she said. "I hope the police find him soon." She thought of Nick and how capable he seemed. A spark of hope. "I know they are working very hard on the case, and we're doing everything we can to help."

A reporter from one of the local religious stations stepped out of the crowd. Elizabeth had seen her before, reporting the news on that station. She was a sweet-faced, blue-eyed blonde with dimples. The all-American girl. Elizabeth couldn't help noticing that she didn't look so demure today as she fought her way through the mob to shove a microphone in Elizabeth's face.

"The violence on your show has inspired some poor, misguided soul out there to commit murder," she said, her blue eyes burning with indignation. "How does it feel to know that you're responsible for something like that?"

A wave of angry voices crescendoed through the crowd, and Elizabeth realized that she was standing in the middle of a throng of people who felt the same way this woman did.

"No one can *cause* someone else to do anything," she replied evenly. "You of all people should know that, with your belief in free will. We all choose our own paths in this world. Apparently, this person has chosen to commit a heinous sin, and that is his responsibility, not mine."

A tall, silver-haired figure stepped from behind the woman, a sickeningly benevolent expression on his handsome face. Elizabeth's heart sank even lower. The Reverend Taggerty, of course. He wouldn't have missed this for the world.

"But your show, and programs like it, are the root of evil in this society, young lady," he said in a condescending tone that made her want to hit him with one of the bags which she had managed to hold onto.

"I believe the Bible says that 'the love of money is the root of all evil,' reverend. I'm surprised you didn't quote your scripture correctly. Besides, I think you're giving my program far too much credit. We can't be polluting the society to that degree. Our ratings simply aren't high enough."

She gripped the bags tightly and held them in front of her as a barrier. "That's all, folks. Now let me through."

Barreling her way forward, she ran headlong into the reverend's son, who stood as always, shamefaced behind his father. He glanced down at the bags and gave her a half-hearted smile, laced with sympathy.

Not a bad kid, she thought. With a glance at the pompous reverend, she added, *must have gotten it from his mother.*

A couple of studio security guards appeared from out of the crowd—better late than never—and hurried forward to clear the way for her. One of them took her bags, while the other grabbed her arm and pulled her through the hoard to the studio doors.

The reporters followed at her heels, shouting questions, while the protestors yelled accusations.

Once inside, she thanked the guards and stood, waiting for the elevator and catching her breath. She thought of Nick, of his comforting words that had been the opposite of what the protestors had said. She thought of the questions he had asked her and how professional he had seemed, how competent.

"Please, Nick," she whispered as she stepped into the elevator, her bags dragging on the floor. "Please catch him. Soon."

Nick looked around the table at the three investigators which he had assembled under Captain Ryerson's watchful eye. The Mirror Killer Task Force.

"I want you to find out everything you can about a David Ferguson, just released on parole from Bellingham."

"What was he in for?" Fred Halley asked around the toothpick that hung perpetually from the right corner of his mouth.

"Murdering Elizabeth Knight's younger sister."

Fred nodded. "Got cha."

"He's from California," Nick continued, looking at his notes. "I need to know his background before the murder. Anything exceptional about his time inside. What he's been doing these past few weeks since he's been out. Right now, he's our number one suspect."

Fred leaned back in his chair, arms over his stomach, looking lazy and bored. But appearances were deceptive. Fred Halley had been Nick's first choice when putting together the team. He was a fifteen-year veteran, thrice wounded and decorated as many times. With graying hair and a spreading paunch, Fred had passed his prime, but he was a particularly gifted investigator. When Fred examined the life of a suspect, he didn't stop until he knew what brand of toothpaste the guy used and the condition of the elastic in his briefs.

"No problem," Fred said, sucking on the toothpick. "When do you need it?"

"Last week."

Fred grinned. "Last week's a little tough. I'll have it for you yesterday."

"Good enough." Nick scribbled on his yellow legal pad. "And you, Ray . . ."

"Yes?"

What Fred lacked in visible enthusiasm, Ray Chawkins supplied. His ruddy face eager, he appeared ready to leap out of his chair and charge for the door, anxious to do Nick's bidding.

"I want you to start with this stuff." Nick tossed him an enormous file of papers which he had collected himself in the course of the investigation. "It's the info I've gathered about the victims. Go over it a few hundred times and see if there's anything there I may have missed."

Ray grabbed the folder and started pouring through it. Six feet, four inches, skinny and red-haired, Ray had worked in records for five years and was a whiz at locating and compiling pertinent data. A few months ago he had helped on a kidnapping case, and had been instrumental in finding the snatched kid— *before* it was too late, for a change. Still basking in the warmth of his success, he had been begging for an opportunity to do some more investigating. When Ray had heard that Nick was assembling a task force, he had come running. Nick figured that anyone so motivated had to be a good choice.

"And you, Stephanie . . . I want you to join the protestors out front of the station," Nick told the pretty brunette at the end of the table. A seemingly gentle, soft-spoken woman, Stephanie Madden had dark brown eyes and a heart-shaped face. Her figure was that of a seventeen-year-old girl—a nice waist, but still hoping the upper portions would fill out a bit. With her demure demeanor, Stephanie could get information out of a close-mouthed brick. People seemed to quickly forget that she was a cop, and they told her the most astonishing things, ranging from juicy gossip to tearful confessions.

"You're a concerned mother, who's upset about the violence being depicted on 'The Dark Mirror,' " Nick continued. "Find out what you can for us about the leader, Rev. Taggerty. Also, watch who comes and goes from the studio. Keep your eyes open for anything unusual. Okay?"

"Sure, Nick," she said.

Nick tried not to notice the slightly hurt edge to her voice and the dewy look in her eyes. Dammit, he had never meant to hurt her. Two years ago, they had been partners on a case involving a string of robberies. They had spent months together, working leads together, eating together, and—yes—sleeping together. Once. The night they cracked the case, they had decided to celebrate.

Bad call.

Nick had known it was a mistake less than five minutes after the fact. He had been depressed. Stephanie had been in love. So much for his rule about not screwing in your own backyard. He had considered himself to be long evolved past the adolescent failing of allowing his hormones to eclipse his common sense. Apparently not. That one lapse in judgment had caused him a lot of regret and guilt. And, considering the look of hurt that still lingered in Stephanie's eyes, it had given her a lot of pain and embarrassment.

He had hoped to make amends by putting her on this task force. The case would be important, a case that would garner nationwide media coverage and build careers. He had done her a favor. Why did she have to sit there, giving him cow-eyes and making him feel guilty all over again? What the hell had he done to deserve this, other than not love her back in the way she had wanted him to.

He thought of all the women he had loved who had told him

in no uncertain terms to shove it. Did they feel guilty now? He sincerely doubted that they gave him a second thought.

"Any questions?" he asked, packing his remaining papers into his backpack.

"Yeah." Fred took the toothpick from his mouth and twirled it between thick, calloused fingers. "Who are *you* gonna be checking out, sarge?"

"I'll be working the studio," he said, zipping up the pack. The zipper caught and he jerked at it impatiently, avoiding eye contact with everyone at the table.

"The studio, huh?" Fred grinned, showing teeth that were uneven and yellowed from twenty-five years of filtering cigarette smoke. "Are we supposed to not notice that you're keeping Elizabeth Knight all to yourself?"

Nick threw the pack onto his back and lifted his jacket from the empty chair beside him. "Notice whatever you damned well want, Halley," he said, carefully not looking at Stephanie. But he could see her in his periphery, and he could feel the waves of sadness and jealousy radiating from her direction.

"See all of you back here tomorrow night," he said, ignoring Fred and Ray's chuckles. "Say, seven?"

They nodded.

He snapped his fingers and Hercules appeared from under the table. The dog squinted at the light and shook his wide head, still half-asleep.

"Nap's over, Herc," Nick said as he pulled a chain from his pocket and fastened it to the dog's collar. "Let's go."

"So, sarge," Fred said, "which are you going to check out first—her legs or her knockers?"

"I think he's more of a leg man," Ray added. "Though she's got a nice pair of both, from what I've seen on the tube."

"You guys are both pigs; you know that?" Stephanie said. "You make me sick."

Nick could hear the tears in her voice as he closed the door and walked down the hall.

Shit.

Never again. Not on the job. Unless, of course, Elizabeth wanted to—

He mentally slapped himself. *No! Never!*

"You did it again, 'Lizbeth! Great job." Brody Yarborough said as he walked up behind her and rested his hands on her shoulders.

From her seat on the stool, Elizabeth studied his reflection in the lighted makeup mirror and continued to wipe the cleansing cream from her face. Considering the circumstances, his broad grin seemed inappropriate, to say the least.

"Thanks," she said without enthusiasm.

He squeezed her shoulders and slowly slid his right hand up to her neck. "Yep, that prologue will be fantasy material for men all over this country when it airs."

She scooped a generous portion of the greasy face cream onto her fingers, leaned back her head and applied a small amount to her throat; the rest she smeared across the back of Brody's hand.

"Oops, sorry," she said with a smirk as she handed him a tissue.

"Yeah, right." He wiped the mess off his hand and tossed the tissue on the vanity in front of her. "You're gorgeous, all right," he drawled. "Too bad you're such a bitch."

She laughed. "Why thank you, Brody. And may I say, I hold you in equally high regard."

For a moment he looked puzzled, then he scowled and turned to walk away.

"Just a minute, Brody," she said, standing and pulling her robe more tightly around her. "I'm curious. Exactly when *is* this episode going to air?"

He hesitated. His eyes held hers with a challenging look that made her uneasy. Surely he didn't intend to . . .

"I'm not quite sure yet, sugar," he said, spreading the drawl on thickly. "I think I'll just leave it up to the programming committee."

A coldness washed over her, a sense of finality that she desperately hoped she had no reason to feel. He was lying through his freshly capped and polished teeth. Brody Yarborough never left anything up to a committee. Elizabeth had long ago come to believe that the only reason he had formed boards in the first place was to have someone to blame when the proverbial shit hit the fan.

"You *aren't* going to air this episode until the killer's been caught," she said. "Please, tell me you wouldn't do that."

"Of course I wouldn't dream of it," he replied. His eyes trailed down to the low vee exposed by the robe. "That would be totally irresponsible of me."

She pulled the front of the robe higher around her neck and gave him a scathing look. Unfortunately, he chose to ignore the visual reprimand and continued to stare.

"I'm glad you agree with me," she said, as she turned her back to him and returned to the vanity.

"Of course," he added, *"I* wouldn't dream of broadcasting it, but you never know what that program committee is gonna do. They're a bunch of wankers. Sometimes I have a half a mind to fire the whole kit and caboodle. . . ."

His voice faded as he walked out of the room, leaving Elizabeth with her sick feeling of inevitability. He was going to do it. Damn his rotten soul, he was going to air that show, knowing that someone might be murdered within the hour afterward.

Suddenly feeling very tired, Elizabeth sank onto her stool and stared at her reflection in the mirror.

"What now, kid?" she whispered to the woman with the pale face who stared back at her. "Whatcha gonna do now?"

But just as she had expected and feared, the woman in the mirror had no answers.

Carefully, he lowered the hood of the Avanti and glanced around the dark parking lot. About a hundred yards away, beneath the overhanging roof of the railway station, three teenaged boys rode their skateboards up and down the handicap access ramp.

Glancing at his watch, he shook his head in disgust. What was the world coming to? People letting their kids roam the streets after midnight. No wonder there was so much crime and mayhem.

He shoved the small spray bottle into his jacket pocket and walked back to his car, which he had parked in the far corner of the lot. Shivering, he slid onto the cheap, leatherette seat and felt the coldness filter through the seat of his pants.

Damn these old cars anyway, he thought, rubbing his hands together and blowing on his palms. *They're always cold as hell.* He grinned, entertained by his own contradiction in terms.

Although he longed to turn on the heater for a few minutes, he didn't dare. The station was patrolled regularly by the city cops; the last thing he wanted was to draw attention to himself with a car that was billowing white exhaust fumes into the frosty night air. No, he'd just have to wait.

He glanced at his watch. Thirty more minutes.

Twelve

Eager to get home to a hot bath and a cold glass of cranberry juice, Elizabeth looked at her watch. Eight-thirty. Ten more minutes. Three more stops.

She watched with amusement as a highly intoxicated businessman, wearing an expensive camel hair coat, carrying an equally classy briefcase, fought to keep his balance as the train pulled to a stop. When the door slid open, he stepped from the train onto the platform, and, as he had for the past five stops, he peered with squinted eyes at his surroundings. Apparently, he hadn't seen any familiar landmarks, because he stumbled back inside, muttering obscenities under his breath.

A conductor ambled down the aisle, wearing a broad grin. "What's the matter, mister?" he asked, placing a steadying hand on the passenger's shoulder as the train took off again. "Don't you like any of our stops?"

"Can't find Great Neck. . . ." he mumbled.

The conductor chuckled. "Well, I'm not surprised, buddy. You're on the wrong train."

"Isn't this the Port Washington line?" He looked like he was about to burst into tears as he grabbed for the nearest support rail.

"Nope. Why don't you have a seat back there in the corner and I'll wake you up when we get back to Penn Station. By then maybe you'll be sober enough to find the right train."

"Oh, yeah . . . thanks." The businessman shuffled to the rear corner of the car and collapsed across three of the seats. Immediately, he began to snore.

Elizabeth smiled up at the conductor as he walked by. "I'd say that's above and beyond the call of ticket collecting," she said. "And they say New Yorkers aren't friendly."

The trainman returned her smile for a moment, then she watched as a change came over his face and the smile turned to guarded anger as he recognized her.

"We do our best, Miss Knight," he said. "God knows, there's enough rottenness out there in the world. Gotta do anything you can to make it better."

Something in his tone conveyed the fact that he thought she wasn't one of those who was improving society. Quite the opposite.

"I hope you don't write anything about train conductors," he added. "Or beauticians. My wife's a beautician. I'd hate to have anything happen to her just because of a stupid television show."

Elizabeth bit back the words that sprang to her lips. She wanted to tell him that it wasn't her fault. There was this bastard out there killing people, yes, but it wasn't her. She was just trying to live her life as best she could, do her job and not hurt anyone.

But the determined look on his face told her that her words would be pointless. His opinion was as set as his square jaw. "I understand," she said.

"Do you?" he replied. "You're rich and famous. You've got it made. How would you know what it's like to be afraid for your loved ones all the time? To go around worrying that some idiot pervert is going to do the same thing to them that he saw that night on the goddamned T.V.?"

He waited for her answer, but Elizabeth couldn't trust herself to speak the words she was thinking. Turning his back to her, the trainman shook his head and walked away.

Finally, Elizabeth found her voice. "I know what you mean," she whispered. "Believe me, I do."

* * *

Flipping on the car's dome light for a second, he checked his watch. Eight thirty-five.

He got out of his car and walked to the phone booth beside the station. His level of irritation rose as he had to check three phones before he found one that worked. From his pocket he took a small piece of paper and unfolded it.

Quickly he made four separate phone calls to the number on the paper. First he used a heavy Southern accent, next a deep bass voice, third, a drunken drawl, and, finally, he barked a brisk, businesslike order.

Then he strolled back to the car, where he watched with grim satisfaction as, one after the other, the cabs began to pull out of the taxi station across the street. All four of them.

A second later, he felt it . . . the rumble in the floorboard beneath his feet. The train was coming. Right on time.

"No, not now. Pl-e-e-ase," Elizabeth muttered as she tried to coax the Avanti to life. But all she heard when she turned the key was a disheartening, dull click, no ignition. "Come on, sweetheart. Be a good girl tonight and I'll give you a tankful of premium tomorrow, I promise."

Sighing, she sank back into the seat and shook her head. Why now, when she was so tired she couldn't see straight? She had just gotten the car out of the shop two days ago. Moisture in the distributor cap again, the mechanic had said, for the fourth time in two weeks. Supposedly, he had replaced the part, so what was wrong now?

She sat, shivering, in the car's frosty interior, and debated the wisdom of owning a classic. She could afford any car she wanted at this point in her career, and, at the moment, a nice new, warranteed Mercedes seemed like a great choice.

"Okay, granny grump," she told the car, slapping its dash. "You've done this to me one too many times. I'm going to buy something else and retire you to summer drives out to Montauk."

Somehow she didn't think her threat upset the old lady. Warm weather cruises to the picturesque point at the end of the island were probably all the Avanti was suited for at this point in its career.

So much for sentimentality, she thought as she climbed out of the car and made her way to the taxi station across the street.

"Sorry, Ms. Knight," the dispatcher told her through the small window that separated the waiting room from the office. "All my boys are out right now. Had a string of calls in a row. You can have a seat if you want and wait."

Elizabeth looked around at the depressing room with its torn and haphazardly taped vinyl seats, tattered magazines and newspapers, and used coffee cups from the dispensing machine in the corner. Somehow, sipping instant coffee or anemic hot chocolate and reading tabloids didn't appeal to her. More than anything else, she wanted to just get home, get warm, and get into bed with Katie curled snugly against her back.

"Thanks anyway," she said. "It's only a ten-minute walk. I could be there before one of your cabs gets back."

"Suit yourself," the dispatcher said with a shrug, turning her attention to the ringing telephone. "Just don't freeze your butt off out there."

Block by block, the fog thickened as Elizabeth neared her house on Bayside Street, giving the sleepy neighborhood a dreamlike quality. The night had been dry and crisp in the city, but here on the north shore of Long Island, only a short distance from the water, the wisps of sea-scented fog floated down the street like so many tormented spirits on an endless quest for peace.

Sometimes Elizabeth felt like that fog, drifting, searching. For what, she wasn't exactly sure.

She had thought she wanted success, financial security, and most of all, to feel she had contributed something to the world. Without a doubt, she had accomplished the first two, and she had taken pride and satisfaction in the thought that she was fulfilling the third. But now, she had to ask herself: Exactly what was she bringing into the world?

She thought of that poor old soul, lying in his hospital bed, fighting for his life, and of his widow, learning to live without a mate for the first time in fifty-three years. What had she brought to them?

Close on the heels of her grief, anger followed. How could anyone kill an innocent person, someone he didn't even know? What kind of sick gratification did he find in the act of murder?

She was afraid she knew the answer—at least part of it. In his mind, the killer wasn't simply murdering his victims, he was killing her, over and over again. By committing these acts, he was destroying Elizabeth Knight, little by little.

In some dark corner of her mind, she found herself wishing that he would just come after her, a face to face battle that would end it, once and for all. The thought terrified her, but the idea of living with this guilt, this conflict, was worse.

An innocent person had died years ago because of her, and that wound had never really healed. Was there anything worse he could have done to her than to repeat that pattern? Nothing she could think of now.

She stared ahead into the ever-thickening fog, trying to visualize this person who despised her so much. Was it the face that first came to mind? Ferguson was the most obvious, but was he the one?

Elizabeth shuddered and pulled her jacket more tightly around her. Try as she might, she couldn't conjure the face, but she didn't need to; she could feel him, the intensity of his emotions, radiating toward her, the sick longing, the frustrated fury. He wanted to destroy her, but he wanted to do it leisurely, enjoying the game as it progressed according to the rules which he set and changed at will.

She passed the dark, silent houses of her neighbors. Here and there an occasional porch bulb burned, but the light was absorbed by the fog before it reached the sidewalk. The golden haloed illumination from the street lamps was diffused as well, making it difficult for Elizabeth to see. She walked carefully along the uneven sidewalk, where the gnarled roots of the oaks that lined the streets burrowed beneath the cement, lifting and cracking it.

Was this street always so dark? she asked herself. Funny, she hadn't noticed before. Perhaps it hadn't been so foggy. Or maybe, she thought, it might have something to do with the fact that there was a murderer out there, one with some sort of grudge against her.

She pushed the thought from her mind, along with a vow to not walk home in the dark alone again until he was caught. To occupy her mind, she concentrated on the sound of her own footsteps and their echo which was muted by the heavy fog.

A dark shape scurried across the path in front of her and she gasped. Her heart gave a jolt, then raced as she stood there, her hand on her chest.

A cat, you dummy, she told herself, leaning on the nearby picket fence for support. *Whoever he is, the killer won't need to murder you if you die of a heart attack over a stupid cat.*

But before she could take comfort from her own admonition, she heard the echo of more footsteps, soft, barely there, behind her. They were tentative, almost stealthy steps, and they were coming closer.

She whirled around and peered into the fog, wishing for a stronger light—perhaps a noonday sun—but she couldn't see anyone. The only movement her eyes could discern was that of the drifting fog.

The steps slowed, then stopped altogether, as though he were waiting for her to go on. A dozen plans of action raced through her head in only a few seconds. She considered calling out, "Who's there?" But the last thing she wanted was for him to reveal himself, here on a dark, deserted street when she was alone.

She could run, but she was afraid he would overtake her long before she could reach her house which was still three blocks away.

And maybe she was being foolish again. Perhaps it was only

one of her neighbors, out for a midnight stroll, who had paused to tie a sneaker shoelace.

Sliding her gloved hands into her pockets, she felt for her keys and the attached kubaton. In the other was her small can of mace. Only slightly reassured, she decided to continue with her walk, as though she were unaware of his presence. Mentally she ran through the drills she had learned in her self defense classes. She could hear the instructor's words, "If he attacks from behind, grabbing you around the neck, turn your face into the crook of his elbow so that he can't cut off your air supply, move your hip to the left and with your right hand jam the kubaton into his groin. Then, run like crazy."

As she neared a corner, she took a right turn away from her house and toward the main street of town which was only two blocks away. If he truly was following her, there was no point in leading him directly to her house. Although, she had a sinking feeling that he already knew where she lived, that he had been there before and had slipped a blue envelope under her door.

Walking briskly, she listened to the footsteps that were continuing to trail her. He seemed to be keeping about half a block or less between the two of them.

Her anxiety rose when she heard him round the corner behind her. Quickening her steps, she heard him match her pace. There was little doubt now that he was following her. This wouldn't be a logical path for anyone to take, she thought as she made another right and listened to his steps that seemed a bit closer.

So, what now, kid? she asked herself. She couldn't walk any faster without breaking into a run, and she had the sinking feeling that running would initiate a full-blown chase. Obviously, she needed help, but from whom? The streets were completely deserted, the shops on Main Street dark and empty.

The deli.

Sometimes the dedicated employees at the Bay View Delicatessen around the corner stayed late to clean and stock shelves. If John or Frank were there, they'd be more than glad to come

to her aid. She was one of their favorite customers who dropped
by for a muffin, bagel, or turkey on rye almost every day.

It was worth a try.

As she headed for the shop, five doors away, she heard the
steps behind her quicken. She ventured a glance over her shoulder and was shocked to find him even closer than she had
thought. He was a featureless bulk, moving through the thick fog
toward her, nothing but a dark silhouette against the surreal mist
and the dim lamplight.

Elizabeth quickly reminded herself that this was no dream. He
was flesh and blood, and his mission wasn't a friendly one. If he
caught her, he would hurt her. Of that, she was certain.

As she neared the delicatessen, she was encouraged by the
sight of light spilling from its front windows onto the sidewalk.
Maybe . . . just maybe.

Yes! Her knees went weak with relief. Looking through the
glass door, she saw him. Big John, as they called him, stood on
a small stepstool, retrieving cereal boxes from a high shelf with
a hooked pole. An easygoing, gentle giant with a knack for making the best turkey sandwich in town, John and his ever-ready
smile were always a welcome sight, but never so much as tonight.

"John, it's Liz. Let me in, please!" she said, pounding on the
door, as he peered at her through the glass.

She looked back to see if her pursuer was near, but the dark
figure had disappeared. The street was quiet, the only sound that
of her own harsh breathing as she gulped in the cold sea air.

The door swung open and the scent of cold cuts and German
potato salad engulfed her, along with a wave of humid warmth.

"Hey, Liz, a little late for a turkey on rye, isn't it?" Big John
asked playfully, smiling down at her. Then he took a closer look
at her face and his smile disappeared. "What's wrong?" he asked.
"What happened?"

"Nothing, thanks to you." She looked back into the shadowed
street and shivered. He was still there. Even if she couldn't see
or hear him, she could feel him. He was watching. And listening.

"Can I come in for a minute?" she asked.

"Oh, yeah. Sure." He grabbed her forearm and yanked her inside. He glanced up and down the street before closing and locking the door. "One of your fans following you home?"

"Someone was following me, but I don't think he was a fan. Thank God you were here. I don't know what I would have done if . . ." Her voice trailed away as the magnitude of her previous situation hit her. The odds were excellent that her stalker had been the murderer himself. And she didn't have to ask herself what he was capable of doing to another human being. She had seen the pictures herself.

Suddenly, her strength drained out of her body and she felt faint.

John's sharp eyes scanned her face from behind gold-rimmed glasses and he wiped his hands on the stained white apron. "You don't look so good. Why don't you sit down back here, and I'll pour you a cup of coffee."

He pushed her onto a stool, then shoved a warm cup into her hand. She took it gratefully.

"So, what are we gonna do about this?" he asked, after giving her a few moments to regroup her physical and emotional defenses. "Do you want me to call the cops or something?"

Elizabeth reached into her jacket pocket, pulled out her wallet and found the card Nick had given her in Donahue's. "Good idea, under the circumstances. Mind if I use your phone to call the city?"

He grinned broadly as he handed her the phone from under the counter. "Naw. You give us enough business to warrant a free call on the house."

As Elizabeth punched in the numbers, she noticed how badly her hands were shaking. Damn that guy anyway. When she found who he was she would . . .

What would she do? she wondered. What *could* she do? Probably not much. Nick, on the other hand, could—

"Hello." The deep voice sounded sleepy. She had woke him. For a split second, the mental image of Nick O'Connor lying in bed flashed through her mind. His blond hair tousled, his muscular chest bare as he sat up to reach the phone. But the vision was quickly followed by the thought that this was no time to entertain fantasies.

"This is Elizabeth Knight," she said. "I'm sorry to call you like this but—"

"No problem. What's up?" The sleepiness was gone; the voice was curt and businesslike.

"A guy followed me from the station tonight."

"He was tailing you? Did you get a license number?"

"No. I was walking and so was he. My car wouldn't start," she added, realizing how foolhardy that sounded.

"I see."

She could tell that he thought her careless to have put herself in that position, but he was considerate enough not to say so.

"Did you get a good look at him?" he asked.

"No. It was dark and it's really foggy here tonight."

"Are you at home now?"

She looked over at John, who was continuing to stock the shelves, while pretending not to be listening.

"No, I ducked into my local deli. One of my friends here will probably give me a ride home." She gave John a questioning look and he nodded vigorously.

"Sit tight," Nick said. "I'm on my way."

"Oh, that's okay. You don't have to come out on the island tonight. I'll be all right."

She held her breath, hoping he wouldn't change his mind, in spite of her courteous protest. His company would be welcome tonight. Most welcome.

"Like I said, I'm on my way. Be there in half an hour or so. Lock your door, don't open it for anyone but me, don't talk to strangers, and *always* dry your hands thoroughly before turning off a lightswitch."

She chuckled. "Yes, sir."

"That's my big brother routine."

"And you do it very well."

"Thank you. Be safe 'til I get there."

"I will."

Hanging up the phone, she turned to John. "Would you mind too much—?"

"Don't be silly," he said, whipping off his apron. "If I treat you right, maybe you'll put me in one of your television shows someday."

"That's a deal. What would you like to be?"

"Anything but a deli clerk. Maybe an oil tycoon, or a secret agent. Something cool like that."

"You got it."

Elizabeth peered out the window of John's new Camaro as they drove slowly down Main Street. As she had expected, there was no sign of her pursuer. He had probably assumed she had called the cops and left the area. At least, she fervently hoped that was the case.

The thought of going home no longer gave her that warm, secure feeling, and a surge of anger washed through her. She had built a haven for herself here in Port Madison, away from the demands of the studio, the fans, and the media. Here, she could be an ordinary person, going to the grocery store for a quart of milk, raking leaves in the fall, eating a sandwich at the park, and watching the swans on a summer evening.

But *he* had come here. He had invaded her sanctuary, and she hated him for it.

As she sat in the warmth and relative safety of Big John's car, listening to a country and western song that played on his tape deck, she realized with a shock the depth of her hate. At first she was alarmed by its intensity and she tried to push it away. She shouldn't hate anyone. It poisoned the soul.

But for the moment, she liked the feeling of power it gave her. Hate and its accompanying anger was preferable to the weakness that fear brought.

"Here we are," John said as he pulled in front of her house.

Realizing that she hadn't said a word to him during the ride, she said, "I'm sorry, John. I guess I'm pretty dull company to-night."

He shook his head. "No, don't worry about that. I'd be spooked, too, if somebody was following me around."

He opened his door to get out, but she stopped him with a hand on his arm. "Hey, you don't need to walk me to my door. Just watch until I get it open."

"Are you sure?"

"Absolutely. You've gone out of your way already for me to-night, and I'm really grateful."

"It was my pleasure, Liz. Anytime."

She leaned over and gave him a kiss on the cheek. "Thanks, John. Take care."

"That's my line."

"Oh, don't worry. I will."

As she got out of his car and walked up the stone steps to her house, she thought how satisfying it was to have a friend like John. He had done this, not because she was a famous person-ality, but because she was someone who bought bagels and turkey sandwiches from him and chatted with him about the latest Mets game.

Glancing into the shrubbery on either side of the walkway, she checked for any signs of an intruder, but all was still and quiet. She pulled her keys from her jacket pocket and unlocked the front door. One quick look inside told her that nothing had been disturbed.

Turning, she gave John the thumbs up and waved goodbye. He flashed his headlights and pulled away.

As she started to pass through the door, a bundle of fur tangled itself around her ankles. "Katie," she murmured leaning down to pet the cat. "How's my pretty little girl?"

Suddenly, she felt a hand close around her elbow and squeeze. She gasped and whirled around.

"David!"

A feeling of inevitability swept over her, the sense that she had known all along that this moment was coming. And it was here.

She was face to face with her sister's murderer. No bars between. No courtroom bailiff or prison guards.

Time seemed to slow as questions raced through her stunned brain. Was he the one who had followed her? Was he the killer who was copying her show?

"Why are you here?" she asked, giving voice to the question that was screaming more loudly than the others.

"I just want to talk to you, Elizabeth. Please, I have to," he said.

He *had* to speak to her. David always *had* to do things. That was the excuse he had given the court. He'd *had* to do it.

Myriad pictures flooded her mind, memories of the night she had come home to find Martie dead: the overturned furniture, the torn clothing, the bloody sheets, the ropes.

And this man—the one standing here on her porch with a sick, sweet smile on his face—had done it all.

Hate eclipsed her fear, and in that moment she knew if she had a gun in her hand, she would kill him. And in the instant she pulled the trigger and saw the destruction it caused to his face, she would enjoy it.

"You aren't welcome here, David," she said in a voice that was far more calm than she had expected. "I'm sure you can understand why."

"Oh, yes, I understand why you don't want to talk to me," he said. "But there's something *you* have to understand, too."

Something in his tone made the edge of her fear even sharper. His expression was benign, but he had been wearing the same look when he had sat in the witness stand and described what he had done to Martie.

"And what is that, David?" she asked, knowing she wouldn't like the answer.

"You have to understand that I still love you. I always will." In a movement so fast that she didn't see it coming, he reached out and grabbed her wrist. His fingers were cold and wet with sweat. "Always," he repeated, lowering his voice to a whisper. "You know . . . like in 'til death do us part."

Thirteen

Elizabeth was dimly aware of her cat scurrying back into the house. She considered trying to do the same, but Ferguson still had hold of her wrist.

"Let go of me," she said, keeping her voice low and calm.

To her surprise, he did as she asked. But she knew he could easily grab her if she tried to bolt inside.

"I've said all I intend to say to you, David," she said. "There's nothing more for us to discuss."

"But you don't have to say anything, just listen." He stepped even closer to her and she could feel his breath warm against her face. She could smell the odor of alcohol and stale tobacco and it made her nauseous.

"I want you to leave, David. I have a friend coming over. He'll be here any time."

"This won't take long. I want to come in . . . just for a minute."

She swallowed hard and shook her head. "No, that isn't possible. After what you've done, I'll never allow you into my home. Not now, not ever."

She wanted to scream at him, to tell him how much she hated him, how much he had taken from her. But her common sense warned her this wasn't the time. Beneath the cool, pseudo-calm exterior, she could feel a peculiar agitation radiating from him, and the last thing she wanted was to excite him further.

For a moment he stared at her, and she could feel his anger building. He was deciding whether or not to force the issue further.

He glanced toward the street, and she could see that he was uneasy. Maybe her ploy about the friend had worked and he was afraid of being interrupted.

"All right," he said at last. "I guess I'll have to say it right here." His face changed again, and he donned an apologetic, pensive expression. As though suddenly shy, he stared down at his sneakers that gleamed white in the light that shown through the open door.

Elizabeth noted that they were new, as were his stiff, dark blue jeans and gray parka. *Oh, yeah,* she thought in a far, detached part of her brain, *they give you a new outfit when they release you from prison.*

"I . . . I just wanted to tell you that I'm sorry for what happened to your sister and . . ."

"It didn't just *happen,* David," she said, unable to control her anger. *"Accidents* happen. You murdered her."

"I know. I know I did. And it was the wrong thing to do. I know that now. But . . ."

But? she thought. There were no buts. No excuses. She wanted to yell at him, but even more she wanted to shoot him or put her hands around his throat and—

No. That was exactly what he had done to Martie. Then she would be no better than he.

"But what?" she asked.

"But I want you to know that, wrong as it was, I did it for you. Because I really do, I mean did, love you."

Who else have you killed out of love for me, David? she thought, but she said nothing.

"I came to ask for your forgiveness." His eyes met hers for the first time since he had begun talking, and once again, she couldn't read the expression there. He seemed . . . empty. "Please, Elizabeth, I need to know that you don't hate me."

Forgiveness? He had to be kidding. Even if it angered him and put her own life in jeopardy, she would never speak those words of absolution. He wasn't going to get off that easily. If it truly did weigh heavily on his conscience—which she sincerely doubted—all the better. She lived in hell, remembering what he had done. Why should he do any less?

"If *I* had killed someone *you* love, would you be able to forgive me?" she asked quietly.

"Of course I would," he said without hesitation. "I've forgiven you for everything."

Inside her coat pocket she clenched her hands into fists. What had she ever done to him that would need forgiving? She hadn't loved him when he had demanded it. That was the extent of her sins against him.

"Thank you, David. Apparently you're a better person than I am," she said, her voice thick with sarcasm.

The thin thread of control she had was beginning to unravel. "I'm going to go into my house now," she said, giving him what she hoped was a non-threatening, but firm, look. "I'm very tired and I need some rest. Goodnight, David."

She paused only a second, and when he didn't respond, she stepped quickly inside the door and closed it behind her. After sliding the dead bolt into place, she flipped on the porch lights and turned off the living room lamp.

Now she could see his silhouette against the oval glass in the door, but he couldn't see inside.

Holding her breath, she watched as he walked down the porch steps and to the sidewalk. From the living room window she saw him disappear down the street.

She sank onto the sofa, her knees trembling violently. Now, she could afford the luxury of falling apart.

Always able to sense when she was upset, Katie crawled into her lap and began to lick her cheeks.

"Wow, Kate," she whispered. "That was a close one."

She glanced out the window again at the empty street. "Hurry, Nick. Please, hurry."

As Nick drove his Jeep through the center of Port Madison, his eyes scanned the darkness and mist for any signs of David

Ferguson or other suspicious figures unknown. But the only activity appeared to be at the Wilted Shamrock Pub and Grill near
the old theater. Several inebriated patrons spilled out the front
door and onto the street as he passed, their raucous laughter out
of character with the quiet dignity of the exclusive, waterfront
town.

This was Nick's first trip to Port Madison, and he felt a tug of
nostalgia as he soaked in the ambiance of the village. Surrounded
by turn-of-the-century buildings, with their ornate marble facades, rustic fishing supply stores, grammar school, complete
with bell tower, and the dock which stretched its glittering length
into the dark waters of the bay, Nick felt himself transported into
one of his favorite childhood books about New England fisher-
men, whaling ships, and treasure hunts.

What a difference from Lexington Avenue, he thought. What
would it be like to live in a quiet, peaceful town like this instead
of a city that never slept? Perhaps, when he was younger, the
prospect might have seemed boring. But Nick had experienced
plenty of excitement in the past ten years—enough for several
lifetimes. He didn't think he would ever be bored again.

He glanced down at the map which was spread across the
passenger's seat. Elizabeth's street must be right about . . . yes,
there it was to his left, leading away from the water. He turned,
heading up the hill, and felt another seismic tremor of culture
shock. The quaint, tree-lined street was flanked by beautiful Victorian homes, obviously single dwellings. Nick didn't know *anyone* who could afford the luxury of having an entire house to
themselves. But then, he reminded himself, he didn't know many
television stars. Only one.

God, he hoped she was all right. She had sounded pretty shaken
on the phone, and she didn't strike him as a woman who was
easily upset.

Again, he searched the street for any sign of her follower. But
the lush shrubbery on either side would have provided effective
cover for a small army.

At first he didn't see her house, then he spotted it, further back from the road, partially hidden by several pine trees. It wasn't the largest house on the block, but with its gingerbread trim and the row of delicate tulip porch lamps that glowed dimly across the veranda, it was the most charming.

He was surprised, though he wasn't sure why. What had he expected? Probably something cold, something gray, black, and white with straight lines and that one-thousand-dollar-an-hour designer touch. He certainly hadn't anticipated a place that would look and feel like a place he wouldn't mind living. A place that felt like home.

He thought of the Elizabeth Knight he had seen on the screen, dressed in glistening black, her makeup perfect, every movement the quintessence of feminine grace. No, that wasn't who lived here. The occupant of this house was the woman who had sat across from him at Donahue's and drank her beer from the bottle, the freckles scattered across her nose as clear as the light of vulnerability shining in her blue eyes.

The thought of anyone hurting that woman—who had already suffered more than her share in this lifetime—made him furious. A protective instinct rose in him that wasn't so far removed from the emotion he experienced toward Nina when she left the apartment for the evening.

Watch it, he warned himself as he climbed out of the Jeep and walked up the sidewalk toward the house. *Don't feel, don't care, and you won't get screwed.*

Yeah, right, he added, when she opened the door and he saw her standing there, looking younger and even more vulnerable than she had at Donahue's. Her back was straight, her shoulders squared, her jaw set with determination. She looked every bit the character of Elizabeth Knight. But the beautiful, courageous woman with the fighting posture wore the expression of a scared little girl. Eyes wide and red from crying, lips tremulous, cheeks tear-stained.

Don't feel, don't care? Nick thought. *Fat chance.*

* * *

When Elizabeth had seen the black Cherokee pull up in front of her house, she had been surprised at the flood of relief she had felt. Nick O'Connor was a trained policeman, yes, and certainly she was safer in his presence. But he was only a man, flesh and blood, as vulnerable in many ways as she was.

The sense of security she experienced had little to do with the fact that he was an armed cop. It just felt so good not to be alone. Until the moment he had walked up her steps and onto her porch, Elizabeth hadn't realized how alone she had really felt these past few years.

And now, seeing him standing there, filling her doorway, his eyes full of concern for her, it seemed the most natural thing in the world to hold out her arms to him.

"Nick, I'm so glad you're here," she said. "Thank you for coming."

He stepped forward and put his arms around her waist, holding her tightly for a moment against his chest. She breathed in the masculine scent of his leather jacket and the faint smell of soap on his cheek as it brushed hers. The stubble of his beard was rough against her skin, but comforting in its maleness.

"Are you okay, kiddo?" he asked, pulling back and studying her face.

"A little shook, I guess, but all right." She stepped inside and opened the door wider. "Come on in. I hope you aren't allergic to cats."

"I don't know if I am or not," he said as he entered, then turned to lock the door behind him. "Hercules has never let one get close enough for me to tell."

She laughed, appreciating his attempt at levity, but she couldn't help noticing how he doublechecked the strength of the deadbolt.

"Well, does it pass inspection?" she asked.

"Yes, but it doesn't do much good, considering that the center of the door is glass."

"That's true, I guess. Hadn't thought of that." She walked over to the Tiffany lamp in the corner and switched it on. Now that he was here, it didn't seem necessary to sit in the dark. "Funny," she said, "there are a lot of things about security that I hadn't considered before. Having a psycho after you changes your perspective on a lot of things."

"Doesn't it, though."

She watched as his sharp eyes took in each detail of the room: the grandfather clock, the antique rocking chair pulled up to the wrought iron fireplace, the curving staircase where Katie peered down at him, curious and shy.

"Nice place," he said. "Cozy."

"I'm glad you like it."

He grinned. "All except the pink walls, of course. Pink's one of those icky girl colors."

"They aren't pink; they're pale mauve . . . with white trim. It's authentically Victorian."

"Mauve . . . pink . . ." he muttered as he walked over to the front window and peered out, ". . . sissy colors."

"I was going to offer you a cup of coffee," she said, "but if you're only here to insult my decorating. . . ."

"I'd love some, thanks. Black and strong enough to jump out of the cup."

He walked from window to window, looking outside and checking the locks, while she set the kettle on to boil and measured a generous amount of Colombian roast into the filter.

She had considered offering him her house specialty, cappuccino. But he seemed like a coffee sort of guy, unlike Cassie, who *loved* her cappuccino.

Moments later, as the rich aroma began to fill the kitchen, Elizabeth started to relax a little. Performing a mindless chore seemed to calm her frazzled nerves. She turned to find Nick watching her quietly in the doorway and she wondered why he hadn't bombarded her with the usual list of detective-type questions. So far, he hadn't said a thing about her intruder.

"Pick a mug from the rack over there," she said, pointing to the collection that hung on the wall.

He walked over to the rack, surveyed the assortment, then gave her a curious look. "Disney mugs? Aren't you a little old for Beauty and the Beast?"

"Never!" She chose the Jungle Book for herself and filled it. "I'm not too grownup for Disney, and neither are you, tough guy. Pick one, or I'll give you Cinderella."

He scowled, then chose Peter Pan. "Because it's blue," he said, as he slid it across the counter to her.

"A 'boy' color, right?"

"Of course."

He followed her back into the living room. As she settled on the sofa, he examined the fireplace. "Would you like a fire?" he asked.

"Sure. But can you build one?" she returned sarcastically.

"Hey, I'll have you know that I was an Eagle Scout, highly decorated for my fire starting ability. Merit badges, the works."

"Really?"

"No. Not really." He pulled the screen aside and began to arrange kindling from the woodbox nearby. "In the neighborhood where I grew up the only fire starting that we kids did was more in the realm of arson."

"Tough childhood?" she asked.

"Not what you'd call privileged, but a lot better than some." He found a box of matches on the mantel and lit the kindling beneath the logs. The orange flame curled, licked, and took hold.

As he replaced the matches, Elizabeth saw him looking at the photograph of Martie.

After a long silence he said, "Is that her?"

"Yeah. That was her sophomore picture."

"A pretty girl," he said sadly. "She looked a lot like you."

"Yes. Apparently David Ferguson thought so, too."

He brushed off his hands and walked over to sit beside her on the sofa. Once again, she was struck by the comfort his nearness imparted.

"Okay, Elizabeth," he said with a sigh. To her surprise he reached over and took her hand in his. "Enough small talk. Tell me about David Ferguson."

"What do you want to know?" she asked. A shiver ran through her despite the warmth of his big hand that was wrapped around hers.

"That's simple," he said, "I want to know everything."

He watched from behind some evergreen bushes in the yard across the street. The silhouettes on the living room curtains said it all. The cop was in there with Elizabeth—*his* Elizabeth—doing God only knew what to her.

And she was letting him.

It was getting harder and harder for him to think of her as a good woman. Maybe he had been wrong about her all along. He had always thought she was decent, a good person. That sexy act she did on television . . . she only did it because the network executives made her. She never would have dressed in that skimpy, tight stuff if she'd been able to choose her clothes herself.

And the makeup. He was sure she wouldn't have put on that much face paint if she hadn't been forced to. She didn't wear it when she left the studio. At home she looked pure, good, innocent, and that was the way he liked her.

Oh, sure . . . his *body* liked her the other way, the way she looked on the screen with her breasts and legs showing. After all, he was only human. But he tried not to think of her that way. Thoughts like that stirred the lust in his body. And when he lusted . . . that was when the trouble started.

Elizabeth was the sort of woman you didn't lust after, not in a dirty way. She was a precious jewel to love and cherish until death—

Maybe he shouldn't think about death either.

Shadows moved on the curtain. Having memorized the lay of the room, he knew they were sitting together on the sofa.

What kind of woman would invite a man into her home when she was all alone? A man she hardly knew?

Not the kind of woman he had thought Elizabeth was. Not a good and decent woman, that was for sure.

He had seen the way she had greeted the cop at the door—like a long-lost lover. And now she was sitting on the sofa with him.

That cop was like any other man, even worse; in no time at all he'd have his hands all over her and then . . .

He wasn't sure what he would do. If he really *knew* they were doing something, he wouldn't be able to stand it. Even thinking that they *might* was driving him crazy.

Rubbing his hands together, he blew on his fingers and tried to concentrate on his physical pain, rather than the pain of betrayal in his heart. He didn't want to feel this way—not about Elizabeth. When he felt this bad, bad things happened. Really bad.

It was one thing to kill a pervert child molester or some old coot who was checking out anyway, but he didn't want to hurt Elizabeth. She was the only really good thing in his world, his only dream, his only goal. If she died, so would he; there could be no other way.

But, he thought as he watched the shadows on the window, *a man can only take so much . . . even a patient, forgiving man with a heart full of love. If they go upstairs . . . if the bedroom light goes on . . . ,* he promised himself, *it's over. They're both dead.*

"I met David at a friend's birthday party," Elizabeth said. "The small town where I lived in California had only one school, and everybody knew everyone. So, most of the kids in town were there."

Elizabeth wrapped her fingers tightly around her coffee mug, drawing from its warmth. She was still shaking and had been since she had heard those first footsteps this evening. The grandfather clock chimed the half hour. She knew all too well what time it was, but she glanced at it anyway. Ten-thirty.

Her eyes met Nick's and she could see her own concern reflected on his face. "The Dark Mirror" was being broadcast. And somewhere, someone was watching . . . and plotting . . . while someone else lived out their last hour on earth.

"What's the episode about tonight?" Nick asked. His voice was gentle, but she could hear the tension just below the surface.

She sensed that he felt a heavy burden of responsibility for the victims, as she did. Inadvertently, she had designed their murders, and he had to catch the bad guy before too many more died. But if she had to carry this weight, she felt better for being able to share the load.

"It's about a drunk driver," she replied, "who's murdered by the father of a child he killed."

"Hm . . . a good night not to drink and drive," he said dryly, glancing at the clock again.

"Exactly what I was thinking." She hesitated, but couldn't resist asking the question that was on her mind. "Do you think he'll do it again?"

"Honestly?"

She nodded.

"Yeah, I'm sorry, but I do. I think he's going to keep doing it until we catch him."

She sighed and took another sip of coffee . . . as though she needed it to stay awake. After seeing Ferguson free and walking the streets of her own town, she didn't think she would ever sleep again.

"If it's David, the murder may happen here, close to home," she said. "He won't have long to get out of the area."

"Actually, he could have taken the 9:55 train to the city, in which case he'd be arriving about now." Nick reached into his jacket pocket and pulled out a Long Island Railroad schedule. "I already checked."

"Hey, you're efficient."

He shrugged. "It's a job. Now, take a deep breath and tell me about Ferguson."

She blushed, realizing he knew she was avoiding the subject. It hurt so much to talk about it, because to talk about it, you had to relive it. And she had told the story so many times to people who didn't really care. Their interest had been solely intellectual. Professionals who only wanted "the facts."

But as she turned and looked at Nick, something in his expression told her that he wanted to hear about Martie, the person, not just the victim, about the heartbreak of losing your only sister to a murderer. That's what he had meant when he had said he wanted to hear it all.

"Like I said," she began, "I met him at a party. I was seventeen. He was a couple of years older. Friends introduced us, and we talked for a while—no more than ten or fifteen minutes. I wasn't interested. To be honest, I thought he was a bit of a nerd. It certainly wasn't love at first sight . . . at least, not for me."

"But he was smitten, huh?"

She nodded. "I'm afraid so."

"I can't really blame him for that," he said. To her surprise, he reached up and touched her hair, just once, very lightly. She was even more surprised that it could feel so nice . . . especially at a time like this.

"You must have been a beautiful seventeen-year-old," he added.

She laughed. "Not really, but thank you for saying so. Truth is, I was in desperate need of braces and painfully skinny. They didn't call me 'ostrich legs' for nothing."

He glanced down at her legs with an appreciative gleam in his eye and started to say something. Then he seemed to think better of it.

"Back to David Ferguson . . ." he gently prompted.

"Oh, yes, good ol' David." She drew a deep breath. "My girlfriend gave him my phone number, and he called me the next day. Three times. The following day it was seven. He followed me to and from school and told everyone we were going steady. He even spied on me when I went out on dates. One night he stormed into the movie theater and challenged the boy I was with to a fight."

"A pretty standard case of obsession," Nick said. "These nuts become fixated on one person, and they just won't take no for an answer. They're actually quite dangerous. They start out just being a nuisance and end up committing acts of violence. Did the cops help you out?"

"Sure," she said with a wry smile. "They told me he was a nut who was fixated on me, and I should watch out because he was probably nuts and potentially dangerous."

Nick cleared his throat and shifted uneasily on the sofa. "Sorry about that. I guess the academies use the same training manuals from coast to coast. I remember that particular quiz; I think it was called 'Pat Answers—The Policeman's Repertoire of Choice Responses.' "

"How did you do?"

"Cinched it. Let me guess what they said next. Could it have been something like, 'We're sorry, but until he's broken a law or proves that he's a threat to himself or society, we can't do anything.' "

"Gee, verbatim. I'm impressed," she said sarcastically.

"If it's any consolation, we hate having to say that shit as much as the public hates to hear it. But, unfortunately, it's the truth."

He raised his arm and laid it across the back of the sofa, his hand on her shoulder. Any other time, Elizabeth might have thought he was trying to make a pass at her. But his touch was completely nonsexual and comforting.

She was especially grateful, because the next part of the story was the hard part.

"I moved to New York the next summer. Partly because I wanted to attend a New York college, but mostly it was to get away from him. Martie was a sophomore that year. She was so excited because she had made the drill team. I still remember her calling me from school right after the try outs and . . ."

A constriction in her throat tightened at the memory. Why was it always the people who were so full of life who seemed to lose it so early?

"Did she know David?" he asked.

"She had seen him around—when he was stalking me, he was

quite visible—and she had talked to him on the phone. But I wouldn't say they knew each other."

"How did it happen?" he asked. His hand tightened on her shoulder.

She looked away, staring into the fire. After a long pause, she continued. "I invited Martie to spend the summer here in New York with me. She had never been to the Big Apple and I thought it would be an interesting experience for her.

"We had a great time. I showed her the town: Rockefeller Center, the Empire State Building, the Fifth Avenue shops, the museums. We got thrown out of F.A.O. Schwartz for chasing each other through the aisles with laser pistols."

Nick stroked her hair again, and it occurred to Elizabeth that it was the same way he had petted his bulldog. "You two were pretty close," he said.

"Yes, we were. She had always been my best friend. I really miss her."

Tears flooded her eyes and spilled down her cheeks. Magically, a tissue appeared in Nick's hand.

"Thanks," she said, taking it from him. His timing was perfect; she was going to need it.

"The night . . . the night it happened, I called her to say that I had to work late at Donahue's. They had a private party going and they needed an extra waitress. It was pay day for me, and I had promised to take her to the Hard Rock Cafe for dinner. I could tell she was really disappointed, but she said she understood. She offered to make dinner and wait until I got home to eat. That's just the way she was. . . ."

Elizabeth paused and dabbed at her eyes and nose with the tissue. As though sensing something was wrong with her mistress, Katie overcame her shyness and ventured downstairs. She crawled into Elizabeth's lap, curled into a ball and started to purr.

"I didn't know . . ." she said, ". . . that David had found out where I was living. I hadn't talked to him for so long. I had no idea that he was even more obsessed than before. He decided that I had abandoned him, that I had probably run away with another man. He had told a number of people that he intended to kill me for my 'unfaithfulness,' but no one took him seriously.

"That night I got off work a little after midnight. When I got home . . . I . . . I found her . . . in my apartment . . . in my bedroom."

"You were the first one on the scene?" Nick asked.

"Yeah."

"Damn, that's tough. I'm really sorry, Lizzie."

She looked into his eyes and was surprised by the depth of compassion she saw there. She had also noted the use of her nickname, which only those who loved her most were allowed to use.

"Thanks," she said. Taking a deep breath, she continued. "He . . . he made her dress in my lingerie, and then he tied her to my bed. He sexually abused her in a number of ways, and he used some utensils from my kitchen to . . ."

"It's okay," Nick said. "I get the idea."

"Later he told a court psychiatrist that he didn't think of it as torture at the time. He was just trying to get her to say she loved him. I guess she finally said it . . . in the end."

"Yes, I suppose she did," Nick said under his breath.

They sat quietly for a long time, both staring into the fire. Eventually, Nick broke the silence.

"How did they nail him?"

"I told them about him stalking me, and they picked him up at the airport as he was boarding a plane back to California. He confessed on the spot—seemed to think they would understand."

"Of course. Everyone knows that if you want to get a woman to love you, you murder her sister. Works every time."

Elizabeth heard the sarcasm in his words, but his tone was gentle and so was his hand that was wrapped around hers. She was glad she had told him about it. Usually she felt terrible afterward, but this time, she felt relieved . . . as though she had released part of the past by sharing it with him.

"I would tell you that I know how you feel," he said, "but my little sister is alive and happy tonight, so I don't. In fact, I don't know what to say, except that I'm so sorry you had to go through that. Both of you."

"All out of 'Pat Answers'?" she asked, smiling at him through her tears.

"Completely dry."

"I'd rather have a hug," she said shyly.

There was nothing shy about the way he gathered her in his arms and held her tightly against him. He pressed his lips against her hair. "Is that what you had in mind?" he asked.

She nodded, soaking in the warmth and strength that radiated from his body into hers. "Feels really good," she whispered as much to herself as to him.

He held her closer, stroking her hair and back. "It's supposed to," he said, "so I must be doing it right. It seems like you've needed this for a long, long time."

"Yes, I have." Her tears flowed freely as she wrapped her arms around his waist and allowed her emotions to spill over their dam. "Nick . . ."

"Yes?"

"I wish you had been there . . . that night, I mean."

"So do I, Lizzie," he said, lightly kissing her forehead. "So do I."

More than anything, he wanted to sneak up onto the porch and look through the window. At least then he would know for sure what was going on in there. But he didn't dare. The porch had squeaked when he had stepped on it before, and he didn't dare risk it happening again with that damned cop inside.

Glancing down at his watch, he swore under his breath. He didn't have all night to stand here, freezing to death, wondering what she and the detective were doing.

He had things to do, places to go, and one particular individual to see.

At the thought of his mission, his anger subsided a little, and a sense of purpose and well-being swept over him.

It didn't matter what Elizabeth was doing in there. Not really. There were much bigger issues at hand. Besides, the most important thing right now was that she know how much he loved her, how completely devoted he was to her.

And after tonight, she would know . . . the cop would know . . . the world would know . . . that he wasn't going to stop. Not until Elizabeth realized that they were meant to be together. Not until she stopped appearing on television and letting other men lust after her beauty. She was his, goddamn it! His alone.

But apparently she hadn't gotten the message yet.

He looked at his watch again. Eleven o'clock. It seemed he was going to have to tell her. Again.

Fourteen

Larry Burtrum wasn't a drunk. Drunks slurred, smelled like stale booze, stumbled when they walked, and, worst of all, they had to go to those damned meetings.

Larry took great pride in the fact that he never displayed any of the classic signs when he had downed a few drinks. He was perfectly articulate no matter how much he had consumed. In fact, a few drinks rendered him quite witty and altogether entertaining . . . in his own estimation.

An impressive assortment of pharmaceutical products guaranteed that he smelled great: cinnamon-scented toothpaste, minty mouthwash, around-the-clock deodorant, aftershave and cologne. Yes, the ladies at the Port Madison bars could smell Larry coming long before he made his appearance. He liked that.

And as far as those damned meetings . . . he had never gone to a single one. Well, except for those court-ordered appearances after the accident. But they didn't count because the judge had hated him on sight and had ordered him to go just to humiliate him.

It wasn't like he was a "real" drunk and needed to go. He didn't drink all that much, and he could stop anytime he wanted.

But he hadn't stopped the night of the accident.

And he hadn't stopped tonight until the bartender at the Wilted Shamrock had cut him off.

The night was still young—only a little after eleven—when he left the bar. He walked several blocks, then turned down the alley where he had stashed his car.

Since the accident all his friends had been on his case for driving without a license. Self-righteous bastards. Like they had never made a mistake in their lives.

So, Larry avoided trouble by leaving the bar on foot and by making sure everyone knew he was "walking" home. He parked down the street in a dark alley for the same reason. Life provided enough hassle on its own without a guy flagging it in.

When he reached the car, he tried several of the keys on his ring without success. Of course, his problem wasn't related to the quantity of alcohol he had drunk tonight; he'd just always had a thing with keys. Swearing under his breath, he tried them all again. This time, one fit.

He slid into the car seat, closed the door, and conscientiously clicked his seatbelt into place. One couldn't be too careful. There were a lot of crazy drivers on the road these days.

Just as he was about to start the engine, he felt a wave of nausea sweep through him. The bit of scotch that surged upward from his stomach into his mouth didn't taste half as nice as it had going down. Not at all.

He rolled down his window and spit onto the ground. It was definitely cinnamon mouthwash time.

As he searched his pockets for a breath mint, he thought he heard a noise at the back of the car. When he turned around, he saw a shadow moving soundlessly along the wall, approaching the rear driver's panel.

In spite of the pleasant haze provided by the scotch, Larry Burtrum experienced a twinge of concern. This wasn't exactly the best place to be alone at night. Port Madison was considered a safe little town, but . . .

The shadow approached his window and stepped into the dim light beside the car. It was a man. One man. And Larry was relieved to see that he was fairly well dressed. He didn't look like a hood or a transient.

"Good evening, Mr. Burtrum," the man said. His voice was quite friendly, but Larry didn't like the fact that someone who was a total stranger to him, knew his name. There had been a lot of local publicity after the accident. Some threatening phone calls, some hate mail from busybodies who had nothing better to do with their time. Those individuals had made it clear that Larry wasn't entirely welcome in their community—to put it mildly.

"Hello," Larry replied cautiously. "Do I know you?" He peered at the man's features which were distorted by the dim light and shadows. Even in the darkness, he knew the answer to his question. He had never met this individual before. Larry Burtrum had a great talent: He never forgot a face. And he'd never seen this one until tonight.

"Of course you do," the man said in a calm, icy tone. "Don't you remember? You ran over my little girl a few months ago. You killed her because you're a drunken fool who doesn't know when to drive and when to take a cab. Because you're stupid, she's dead."

Larry studied the face with its stony expression. Confusion and fear scrambled his brain waves, and he couldn't think. What was this guy talking about?

"You aren't her father," he stammered. "I . . . I saw him every day at the trial. He doesn't look like you at all."

"A mere technicality," the stranger said. "But I have a good imagination, and I'm going to pretend . . . just for a moment."

He reached into his coat pocket and pulled something out. Larry's pulse rate doubled and his mouth went dry when he saw the glint of the gun. He *was* in trouble. Bad trouble. Right here in little Port Madison.

"Look, mister," he said, choking on a bit of the scotch that bubbled up again. "I don't know what you intend to do, but—"

"Well, let me tell you." The stranger pushed the barrel of the gun against Larry's cheek. "We're going to play a little game of make-believe. You know, just like on T.V. I'm going to pretend that I blow your head off, and you're going to pretend to die. Got that?"

Larry tried to swallow, but he had no spit. He could feel a warm wetness spreading across the front of his slacks. He'd never been so scared in his life. A voice deep inside told him that he was about to die. But it was the same voice that had been telling him that he needed to stop drinking, that he needed help. And Larry had grown accustomed to denying that voice's wisdom. "You're . . . you're just going to pretend, right?" he said with hope born of self-serving naiveté.

"Right," said the man. "Just like you pretended to be sober the day you mashed that little girl all over the road."

A second later, Larry saw a bright flash of light and smelled the acrid stench of gunpowder. He felt, rather than heard, a strange liquid popping sound, and he knew that something had changed inside his head.

"Gee, you pretend pretty good," the man said. His voice sounded far away, as though they were at opposite ends of a tunnel that was rapidly getting longer and longer. "You could've fooled me."

Larry slumped forward onto the steering wheel. He tried to lift his hands to his head, but he couldn't move his arms. He couldn't move anything.

He heard the man's footsteps as he walked away, but he felt no relief at his leaving. It didn't matter whether he stayed or not, shot him again or called an ambulance. That quiet voice inside told Larry Burtrum that he was dying. He had only seconds to live.

So, this is what it's like to die, he mused. *I wonder if this is how she felt . . . right after I ran over her.*

That was Larry Burtrum's last cognitive thought. A moment later, his hearing faded along with what was left of his vision. The only sound was that of the quiet inner voice saying, "You're a shithead, Larry. You should have listened. Now it's too late."

Then, even that voice was silent.

"We got another one, Nick," said the voice on the phone. Nick squinted at the radio clock on his nightstand and groaned. Four-thirty. Since it was Saturday morning he was hoping he might get to sleep in . . . say, until five.

"Well, don't sound so damned chipper about it, Ryerson," he said, running his fingers through his tangled hair. God, he hated morning people. "Let me guess," he said. "Some drunk got behind the wheel to drive and our friend blew him away."

"Very good," Ryerson replied. "I see you watch television, too. We've got a convicted drunk driver who killed a little girl last summer, but now he's the stiff. Someone shot him in an alley in Port Madison last night."

"Port Madison!" Nick was instantly awake and alert. Elizabeth had been right . . . almost as though she had had a premonition or something. "David Ferguson was in Port Madison last night," he said, thinking aloud.

"Ferguson was? Are you sure of that?"

"Yeah, he paid a visit to Elizabeth Knight."

"Did he hurt her, threaten her?"

"No, just scared the crap outta her."

"Too bad."

Nick could hear the disappointment in Ryerson's voice, but he couldn't exactly blame the man. Even though you hated seeing someone victimized, sometimes it was a relief to have the suspect finally commit an illegal act. Once he had crossed the line, you could move in on him and possibly remedy the situation.

"So, tell me about Port Madison," Nick said, climbing out of bed. As usual, he nearly stepped on Hercules who lay on the braided rug by the nightstand.

"In the alley behind the theater there on Main Street. You'll want to talk to Patrolman Jimmy Roth. He was the first on the scene. The head investigator will probably be a detective named Petrie."

"Got it. On my way."

"And O'Connor."

"Yeah?"

"We've gotta get this guy."

Nick thought of Elizabeth and the hell she was going through.

He thought of Mrs. Wilcox and her warm cookies, which her husband would never eat again. He thought of the other victims who might die before they caught this guy and put him away . . . or until he just got too old, tired, and feeble to keep it up—a depressing thought.

"I know, captain," he said. "I'm sleeping an average of three hours a night, and I haven't taken time to eat or piss in a week. Got any tips on time management?"

"Sleeping! You're taking time out to *sleep?* The mayor, the chief, and the press are panting down my neck and you're laying around in bed like a lazy whore. This is a career-buster . . . for both of us. Get on it."

Oh yes, the career, Nick thought as he hung up the phone and grabbed his jeans which he could swear were still warm from the night before. Here he was thinking about the victims when the captain's *career* was on the line.

Pete would have thought of it. Pete had his priorities straight. Pete would go far in the ranks.

Maybe I'm just not cut out to be an administrator, he thought as he strapped on his pistol and grabbed his coat.

He couldn't think about his goddamned career right now, or anyone else's, for that matter. He had to think of how he was going to break the news to Elizabeth that it had happened . . . again.

Snow was beginning to fall heavily by the time Nick arrived in Port Madison. Ordinarily, he enjoyed the snowfall . . . even in the city where it made life miserable with filthy slush, icy streets, and slippery sidewalks. So, what was a little added treachery when you were talking about New York City? It certainly wasn't a town that the meek would ever inherit.

And out here on the island, the snow was even more picturesque as the giant flakes drifted slowly to the ground—Charlie Brown snowflakes, his mother called them—and covered the trees, homes, and lawns with a crystalline carpet that glittered blue-white in the early morning light.

Yes, ordinarily Nick would be delighted that it was snowing. But not when he was on his way to a murder scene. An *outdoor* murder scene. Sometimes rain, sleet, snow, and high winds made it that much more difficult to locate and collect evidence. He hoped the officer on the scene had done some preliminary work.

He needn't have worried, he realized when he arrived in the alley. Apparently this had been the first serious crime to occur in Port Madison for some time. Every cop, their dog, their cousins, and their dog's cousins were there. The place looked like Times Square on New Year's Eve.

Nick didn't take long to identify the official in charge. The guy wearing the brown suit and an air of authority had to be the investigator.

Apparently, they had done a good job in securing the scene. They had cordoned off the area and there were only a few footprints on the snow inside the yellow tape. Theirs and one other person's—a woman whom Nick guessed was the coroner.

Nick crawled out of his Jeep and pushed his way through the crowd to the perimeter. "I'm Nick O'Connor," he told the guy in the suit.

"Marvin Petrie," the detective said as he reached over the tape to shake Nick's hand. "I'm afraid this is one of yours." He nodded toward the car with a figure slumped over the wheel.

" 'Dark Mirror' scenario?"

"Yep . . . down to the choice of victim and method of execution."

Nick followed Petrie over to the car and winced when he looked inside. The stench of blood, urine, and feces was overpowering. No matter how many gunshot victims Nick had seen, he had never gotten over the emotional jolt it brought him to see the damage a bullet could do to a human body.

Especially head shots. His dad had been shot in the head, and Nick could never look at a head-shot victim without seeing his father for an instant.

"Who is he?" Nick asked, pushing the emotions aside and switching into "professional" mode. Unplug heart, plug in brain.

"Lawrence Burtrum, insurance salesman, bachelor . . . a bit of a local celebrity," Petrie said with a sarcastic tone.

"What did he do to earn that distinction?"

"He drank too much, got behind the wheel, and killed one of our kids. A little girl, seven years old. He ran her down in the crosswalk right in front of the elementary school."

"Gee, then you won't have any shortage of suspects," Nick said. His eyes scanned the crowd which was gathered around the perimeter, looking for any familiar faces. Sometimes the perpetrator couldn't resist hanging around after the fact and enjoying the excitement, the pain—the fruits of his labor.

"Yeah. We're talking to the kid's parents and other relatives now. But I doubt they did it. As I said, I think this is one of yours."

Nick scanned the ground around the car, but the snow had successfully blanketed the area. "Did you find anything before the snow fell?"

"One casing . . . probably a thirty-five. Some urp on the ground beside the driver's window. Apparently Larry lost some of his booze before the fact."

"Next of kin notified?"

"I've got a guy taking care of that now. He has an elderly mother and an uncle. No wife or kids."

"Thank God for that," Nick replied, thinking of Mr. Wilcox, his wife and children, and all those kids who were missing their grandpa. Something told him that Lawrence Burtrum wouldn't be mourned as much. But that didn't give anyone the right to reduce him or any other human being to a piece of badly damaged, quickly decaying meat.

"You'll get me a copy of the coroner's report as soon as she's finished with the autopsy?" Nick said as he watched the medical examiner tie plastic bags around the victim's hands. In this case, he was sure it was a formality. They weren't going to find any skin or hair under Lawrence Burtrum's fingernails. He had never gotten close enough to his killer to scratch him.

"I'll make sure you get a copy of everything: Patrolman Roth's log, a set of the pictures, my preliminary report. Anything else you need?"

Nick took another long look at the body. He couldn't help thinking that this could have been Elizabeth. David Ferguson had been so close to her last night that he had touched her. If he were the one doing this . . .

"Has anyone told Elizabeth Knight?" he asked. "She needs to know about this."

"Yes, I guess she does," Petrie replied. "After all, she's kinda responsible, don't you think?"

"No, I don't." Nick was surprised at the anger in his own voice.

Petrie glanced away uncomfortably and cleared his throat.

"Ms. Knight is as upset about this as anyone," Nick continued in a calmer tone. "More than most. We just have to find the guy who *is* responsible before anyone else dies."

As Nick turned to walk back to his Jeep, he felt a hot blush creeping up his cheeks. He hadn't exactly played the old cards close to the vest back there. Petrie would have had to be blind and deaf not to know that he was more than a little emotionally involved in this case.

Who was he kidding? His emotional involvement wasn't with the case. It was with Elizabeth Knight. He couldn't stop thinking about the way her black hair had shone in the firelight last night when he had held her. He couldn't forget how good she had felt in his arms. He couldn't help remembering the pain in her beautiful blue eyes and wanting to make it all go away.

"You can't save 'em all, Nick, the mick," he whispered. But the old litany that he used at times like this didn't help as it usually did.

Right now he didn't care if he saved them all or not. He thought of Elizabeth's hand, warm and soft in his.

No, he just wanted to save *this* one.

* * *

Elizabeth was reluctant to open her door to a man she had never seen before, until he showed her his badge through the beveled glass oval. A New York City detective . . . named Peter MacDonald.

The moment she let him into her home, she knew two things: First, there had been another murder. That much was clear from the grim, but darkly excited look on his face. Somehow she got the idea that in some strange, rather sadistic way, he was going to enjoy telling her about it. Which led her to her second conclusion—Detective Peter MacDonald was the kind of cop she hated.

"I regret having to inform you that the Mirror Killer has claimed another victim," he said. "A man from here in Port Madison, a drunk driver . . . an exact facsimile of your broadcast last night."

His news didn't hit her as hard as she had anticipated it would. Maybe there was something to this business of "being prepared" after all, she thought. A second later she silently admitted that she was only fooling herself. Any time now it would strike, like a sickening blow to the stomach. She would think about the victim's family: his mother, father—his older sister—who were left behind to grieve and wonder if they could have done anything to prevent his death.

"I need to query you, concerning a few issues," he said, reaching inside his trench coat and pulling out a small notebook covered in sealskin.

"Do you mean, you want to ask me some questions, Detective MacDonald?" she asked, not bothering to hide her contempt.

"Ah . . . yes."

"This isn't a good time. I'm on my way to work."

MacDonald frowned. "On Saturday?"

"Yes . . . I'm a workaholic. Just like you, I'd guess."

His face turned pink all the way up to his receding hairline.

She guessed he liked her about as much as she did him. Pompous ass.

"I've already spoken to the police," she said. "I'm in close contact with Detective Nick O'Connor from Midtown Homicide."

The lightning that flashed in his eyes told her she had definitely said something wrong. She wasn't sure if it was the mention of Nick's name, or the phrase about "close contact." Maybe both.

"I don't happen to care about your relationship with O'Connor. He isn't the only detective investigating this case," he said with a sniff. He reached inside his coat again, pulled out a linen, monogrammed handkerchief, and wiped his nose roughly, causing it to turn even redder.

"Oh, are you a member of the task force?" she asked.

Again . . . the wrong thing to say. "No, I'm not. But one of the murders occurred within my jurisdiction and—"

"Gee, lucky you," she said under her breath. But he heard it.

"Ms. Knight, I don't like your attitude," he said.

"I can understand that." She shrugged nonchalantly. "I can also live with it."

Waving a hand toward the sofa, she said, "Please, have a seat, detective. And feel free to ask me as many questions as you like." She glanced at her watch. "Hell, I don't have to leave for another three minutes . . . maybe four."

Fifteen

" 'Lizbeth, darlin', have you heard the news?" Brody asked as he followed her into her office.

Elizabeth refused to answer. She didn't want to speak to him. At the moment, she didn't want to even look at him. So much for hoping he would take the weekend off. Unfortunately, like Detective MacDonald and herself, Brody was a workaholic, too. And today he seemed to be enjoying his work far more than she would have thought appropriate under the circumstances.

She slid into her chair, flipped on her computer, and stared at the blue screen, trying to ignore him.

"I did it!" he shouted, shoving a handful of papers under her nose. "By God, I finally did it! I beat them all last night! Look at these ratings!"

He grabbed her chair and spun her around to face him. "And *you* did it for me, little lady! Why, I could just lay a big, sloppy kiss on you, sweetheart!"

"Don't even *think* about it, Brody," she said in a low, deadly calm voice. "Or you'll be sucking your T-bones and Texas fries through a straw for the next six months."

He stepped back, nonplussed. "My, my . . . you've been hangin' around Cassandra too much lately. You're starting to sound just like her."

"Thank you."

Brody plopped down in a chair beside her desk and pushed his Stetson back with his thumb. "Boy, you sure know how to poop in a guy's ice cream, 'Lizbeth. This here is the best day of my life. I've been working years for this."

"Congratulations, Brody," she said half-heartedly. "I'm glad the ratings are up there. I just wish it was for some other reason than because a serial killer is out there murdering people."

"Hey, I'm not gonna bite the hand that feeds me. Ratings are ratings, and I'll take 'em any way I can get 'em."

Elizabeth studied him, only mildly surprised at his callousness. Every time she spoke to Brody Yarborough about business—or anything else for that matter—he only confirmed her previous suspicions that he was an amoral, lecherous, self-serving scumbag. No wonder he had risen to the pinnacle of show business success so quickly.

She glanced over the papers he had tossed onto her desk. He wasn't kidding. Their ratings were through the roof. She supposed that put her on top of that pinnacle with him. Funny, right now it was the last place she wanted to be.

"And have *you* heard the news?" she asked quietly as she stared down at the papers, refusing to look at him.

He perked up like one of his prized hound dogs. "News? What news is that, darlin'?"

"He did it again."

"Really? Our ol' buddy croaked someone else?"

"*Your* buddy, not mine . . ." she said, fixing him with an icy blue stare, ". . . murdered someone. He stuck a gun inside a car window and put a hole in a man's head. It happened about six blocks from my house. So, you'll have to excuse me if I'm not too jazzed about our ratings this morning—considering how we got them."

"Hm-m-m," Brody said, thoughtfully fingering one of the silver studs on his western shirt. "Was the guy who got killed a drunk?"

"I understand he had a previous conviction for vehicular manslaughter."

"So, there you have it. He killed somebody; he got killed himself. The Good Book says, 'An eye for an eye and a tooth for a tooth.' Sounds like he got his comeuppance, just like that child molester who got it first."

Elizabeth sighed. She was rapidly getting tired of this conversation. " 'Vengeance is mine, saith the Lord.' That's in the same book, Brody. No one deserves to have their life taken in that manner, no matter what they've done."

She stood and walked over to the window. It was snowing again. But no amount of pure, heaven-sent whiteness could make the world appear clean to Elizabeth on a day like today. "This killer isn't an emissary of God or society," she said. "He's not a hero who's providing us with great ratings out of the goodness of his heart. He's a cold-blooded murderer who's bringing a lot of pain and fear into the world right now."

Brody sighed and heaved himself out of the chair. "Well, sugar . . . you look at it any way you want. Me? I'm gonna buy myself the biggest steak in town and wash it down with the most expensive bottle of scotch I can get my hands on. If you want to tag along, I'm buyin'."

He offered her his arm, in what she supposed was intended to be a gallant gesture. She shook her head and turned back to the window. "No, thanks, Brody. I think I'll pass."

For a moment he seemed disappointed, then he grinned and nodded toward the computer. "Oh well, I guess you'd best be workin' on that script anyway. Gotta keep this ball rollin', you know."

"I didn't come in to work on a script," she said, still staring out the window. "I'm just going to write some letters, then go home."

She turned to him, took a deep breath, and spoke the words her heart had been aching to say for days. "I'm not going to write any more 'Dark Mirror' scripts, Brody. You might as well know that now. And until this killer is caught, I've decided not to write or do any monologues, either. That's it."

The cocky grin disappeared from his face and he took two steps toward her, his fists clenched at his sides. "You *are* kidding, right?" he asked. She noticed the down-homey Southern accent had vanished along with the smile.

"You know me better than that, Brody. I wouldn't kid about something like that. And I wouldn't make this kind of a decision without a lot of soul-searching. My mind is made up."

"Then you'd just better unmake it real fast," he said. "I fought long and hard to get to this place, and I'll be damned if I'll let some bleeding heart liberal bitch mess it up for me now."

"I can understand why you're angry. But it's a matter of conscience. I couldn't live with myself if I continued to write for the show, knowing people would be dying because of—"

"No!" he shouted. His face flushed a deep red, and Elizabeth could see his pulse pounding in the veins at his temple. "Don't you say another word. It's *not* going to happen! Do you hear me? You *are* going to keep writing, and you *are* going to do those monologues, or I'll—"

"You'll what?" she asked, matching his volume. "You're going to sue me for breach of contract? Go ahead. I'll take my chances with a judge or jury."

In a movement much quicker than she would have thought him capable of, he closed the space between them and grabbed her by the shoulders.

The fear she had felt the night before on her porch when Ferguson had touched her came flooding back. At this moment, Yarborough had the same cold glitter in his eye—maybe even more so. And it occurred to Elizabeth that, while Brody was a multi-millionaire and a network executive, he was also a thug, a street-fighter. There was big money involved here, a fortune. He would do anything to make certain he didn't lose it.

"I don't think you understand, E-liz-a-beth," he said, calling her by her correct name for the first time. "I'm not talking about duking it out in court. I'm not talking about a judge and jury . . . if you know what I mean."

Elizabeth glared defiantly up at him, refusing to flinch as his fingers bit into her shoulders. She couldn't show any weakness or he would eat her alive.

"No, I *don't* know what you mean," she said. "Why don't you just tell me plainly. Are you going to hurt me, break my fingers, my legs, kill me?"

He didn't reply, but she could see in his eyes that was exactly what he had been thinking.

"Smart, Brody," she said. "An intelligent approach. It'll certainly get you what you want."

For a moment his fingers tightened even more and she had the distinct feeling he was considering strangling her.

"Excuse me," said a deep voice behind them. Brody released her immediately. She turned to see Nick standing in the doorway.

He was staring at Brody, and she noticed him slide his hand inside his leather jacket . . . to the spot where she had seen his pistol holster.

"Is everything all right, Elizabeth?" he asked, not taking his eyes off Yarborough.

Elizabeth glanced up at Brody and nodded. She couldn't help feeling relieved and a bit pleased to see the thwarted fury on his face. "Everything is just fine, detective," she said. "Thanks for asking."

"I'd like to speak to you, if this is a good time," Nick said, stepping into the room.

"It's as good a time as any," she said. "Mr. Yarborough was just leaving."

Brody looked from her to Nick and back. "That isn't all I have to say on the subject, Elizabeth." He turned and headed for the door. "We'll finish this discussion later."

"Thanks again," she told Nick when Brody was gone. "Your timing was impeccable."

"So it seemed. What was that all about?"

"I told him I wasn't going to write any more episodes. And considering that we beat all the major networks last night in the ratings, he isn't too happy."

"No, I suppose not."

They stood for a long moment, neither saying anything. Elizabeth couldn't help remembering how nice it had felt to have his arms around her last night. Something told her he was remembering, too.

"I went by your house this morning," he said. "I wanted to be the one to tell you . . . you know, about the latest one."

"I appreciate that. I would have much preferred you to your colleague."

He chuckled. "Yeah, Pete can be a jackass sometimes."

"*Some* times?"

"Okay, most of the time." He walked over to her and placed a hand on her shoulder. She thought how different his touch was from Brody's. Both were powerful men. But one used his power to manipulate and bully, the other to comfort and heal.

"Any results on my blue fan letter?" she asked, dreading the answer.

"Yeah . . . nobody's prints but yours. Sorry."

"Oh well, why should we get a break, right?"

"You look tired," he said, brushing her hair back from her cheek.

"I stayed up too late last night, talking to this guy. . . ."

"I see." He turned around and picked her Mets jacket off a coat tree near the door. "Since you're temporarily unemployed, how about a walk in the park?"

He held the jacket as she slid into it. "Don't mind if I do. After that run-in with Brody, I could use some fresh air."

As they left her office and walked down the hall, she felt his hand on her back. It was a gentle, companionable touch that felt right. All of his touches seemed to feel right.

The thought both pleased and frightened her. She reminded herself that this was an extremely emotional time for her. A time when she was particularly vulnerable and could easily misinterpret a mild professional concern for affection and genuine caring.

They got into the elevator and she punched the appropriate button. Being in a small, enclosed space with him only intensified the feeling.

Finally, he broke the heavy silence. "By the way," he said with exaggerated nonchalance. "Just what kind of guy was he . . . the one you spent most of the night with?"

She thought she could hear a touch of vulnerability behind the teasing tone in his voice.

"Oh, he wasn't too bad. In fact, he was pretty nice," she said, smiling up at him, "you know . . . for a cop."

Nick followed Elizabeth through one of the studio's rear doors, chosen over the front entrance in hopes of avoiding the hoards of protestors.

But a contingency from the first group had gathered there, as well. Nick scanned the crowd, looking for potential problems. The leader of this band seemed to be Reverend Taggerty's son, Christopher. Standing in the center of the troop, juggling an armload of picket signs, he looked uncomfortable with his role as second in command of his father's army of dedicated followers.

"There she is!" one of them shouted.

Christopher snapped to attention and promptly dropped most of the signs. "Ms. Knight," he said, as he bent over to retrieve them from the slush. "Could . . . could we have a word with you, please?"

Nick put his arm around Elizabeth's shoulders, preparing to do the "lineman" routine and clear a path for her to escape. But she paused and held up one hand. "It's okay," she said. "I'll talk to him. For a minute."

Christopher looked extremely pleased. His pale face flushed with embarrassment and he suddenly became tongue-tied. "I . . . uh . . . we, that is . . . would like to ask you to please stop broadcasting the show. Obviously, it's wrong, if it's causing people to get killed."

"A television program can't murder anyone, Christopher," she said calmly. "A *person* is doing this for his own reasons. He's only using the show as an excuse to strike out."

"But if you stop doing the show, he probably won't kill anybody else," said a woman nearby.

Nick recognized the voice and turned to see Stephanie standing behind Taggerty Jr., a picket sign in her hand, a zealous glow on her face. With her hair pulled back into a severe bun and a long, baggy dress and coat hanging from her body, he never would have identified her as the sexy undercover cop who made the perfect prostitute decoy in hot pants and thigh-high boots.

She looked from Nick to Elizabeth, and Nick could see the jealousy in her eyes. He suddenly felt self-conscious for having his arm around Elizabeth's shoulders.

"I *have* stopped doing the show," Elizabeth told her. "I've refused to write or film any more episodes."

A murmur of approval went through the crowd.

"That's wonderful," Christopher said. "I told them you'd see the light and do the right thing."

Nick felt Elizabeth cringe and her chin went up a few notches. "I wouldn't say that I've seen a *light*," she said, obviously struggling to keep her temper under control. "Please don't misunderstand. My decision had nothing to do with your objections to my show. I'm extremely opposed to censorship by groups who want to govern what everyone else watches, hears, or reads. My actions aren't intended to appease my opponents, only to save human lives."

A second later she was fighting her way through the ranks, doing a better job of "lineman" than many pros. Nick had to hurry to keep up with her.

"Well said," he told her when they had cleared the crowd and were heading up Fifth Avenue toward the park. "And to think I was worried about you holding your own."

"With those guys?" She turned to him, surprised. "Ah, they're not that hard to handle. And even though Brody likes to think he's got the world quaking in its boots, he's not so formidable either."

"Then what *does* scare you, Lizzie?" he asked.

"Being called by a pet name," she said after a long pause. "Taking a walk with a man whose company I enjoy. Caring about anyone enough to grieve if I lost them. Things like that."

He knew she was being far more open with him than she was with others. A private person . . . daring to reveal herself to him. Now, *that* was scary.

"The emotional stuff, huh?" he said. "As long as it's in the head, it's okay, but the heart—that's a different story."

"Gee, detective. If I didn't know better, I'd say you know whereof you speak." She gave him a sly sideways glance that made him chuckle.

"Who me? Not a chance."

They had reached the lower edge of the park, where they paused in front of the Plaza Hotel to appreciate the rare sight of virgin snow in New York City. Except for the paths, the blue-white covering was pristine, shimmering pearlescent in the mid-day sun. Horse drawn carriages made the circuit around the park, their harnesses jingling, the coaches decorated with holiday cheer. Their passengers ranged from tired and frazzled shoppers taking a scenic break to boisterous merrymaking tourists.

"I keep trying to remember it's the Christmas season," Elizabeth said as she watched some children begin to roll the lower portion of a snowman.

Nick looked down at her and saw an expression that he recognized in her eyes. It was the sadness of a child who had been shut in too long and needed to come out and play with the other kids.

"Well, it *is* Christmas, Lizzie," he said, grabbing her hand. "And there's brand new snow on the ground. For the next two hours let's forget about 'you-know-who' and have some fun. What do you say?"

She stared up at him, her eyes shining with childlike anticipation. "Really?" she said.

In reply, he pulled her across the street, skirting honking cabs and the piles of steaming horse manure.

She squealed with delight as he scooped her into his arms and headed down the path with her toward an empty clearing.

"Nick, what is this? What are you going to do?" she asked, breathlessly.

He laughed. "Instant snow angel," he said . . . and tossed her, screaming, into the nearest snow bank.

In spite of the holiday season and the newly fallen snow, *he* hadn't forgotten about *them*. He sat on a bench and seethed as he watched them pelt each other with snowballs, roll around on the ground together, and in general, act like a couple of dogs in heat.

The sight disgusted him. When had he ever decided that she was an honorable woman? She looked like someone who would be a good wife to a man, who would be faithful and take care of him and his home. She looked like a woman who could be a loving and devoted mother to a man's children. But, obviously, looks could be deceiving.

It hurt his heart to watch her, wallowing on the ground with that stinking cop, right here in front of everyone. And she didn't even look ashamed. In fact, she looked damned happy about the whole thing.

There was nothing sweeter on earth than a good woman, he thought as he sat there, feeling his stomach acid eating away at his guts. And nothing worse than a bad one.

Sixteen

"Uh . . . I think our two hours are up," Elizabeth said, glancing at her watch. They had begun about noon, and it was four o'clock. Who would have thought it would take so long to find just the right stones and twigs to finish off a snowman? But he was worth it. From their seat on a bench they could see him, grinning broadly at them across the baseball field.

Elizabeth couldn't help noticing with a childish sense of satisfaction that he was bigger and smoother than the ones made by the "other kids."

"Not bad for a couple of old farts," Nick said, nudging her with his shoulder.

"Hey!" She shoved him back. "Watch who you're calling old."

Breathing in the cold, crisp air, she closed her eyes and savored the moment. When she opened them, she caught him looking at her with a strange expression, affection mixed with . . . what was it? Oh, yes . . . plain, old-fashioned lust.

Apparently, the physical contact—the rolling around in the snow, holding hands, and bear hugs—had affected him as much as it had her. It had been a long time since she had felt this way, so long that she couldn't be certain if she ever had.

And she wasn't at all sure this was the appropriate time to feel it.

"Nick, this has been a lot of fun today, and last night was really special, but I'm afraid that—"

"I know," he said. Turning away from her, he reached for the styrofoam cup of coffee he had placed on the bench beside him. "It's not the smartest thing I've ever done. Frolicking in Central Park isn't exactly standard operational procedure in a homicide investigation."

"Especially when the woman you're romping with is one of your primary suspects?" she added with a wry smile.

"You were never a suspect." He took a long drink of his coffee.

She gave him a disbelieving look.

"Well . . ." he said, ". . . not for more than the first five minutes there in your office. The way you looked at those pictures, I knew you'd never been at the murder scenes."

"But it still isn't appropriate for us to be seeing each other," she said, "under the circumstances."

He turned to face her on the bench, and his eyes searched hers. She thought she had never seen that shade of green before . . . a pale, tourmaline green that made her think of the emerald hills of Ireland. His cheeks were red from her rubbing handfuls of snow in his face.

She could feel her own cheeks glowing, from the cold and from the heat that was kindling inside her body. The park and its inhabitants disappeared from her vision, and she was aware of only him, his face, his body, his blatant maleness.

"You're absolutely right," he said solemnly, his eyes following the curve of her lips. "We have to keep this totally professional . . . at all times. Right?"

"Absolutely."

A cold breeze swept down the path toward them, blowing the powdered snow into white whirlwinds at their feet. She shivered and a second later his arms were around her.

"For instance," he said, "it would be a definite mistake for me to hold you . . . like this."

"Oh, yes, *very* bad." Her breath quickened as he pulled her closer. She could feel the warmth of his body radiating through their clothes as his thigh pressed against hers, hard and muscular. She breathed in the faint smell of his aftershave, pleasantly mixed with his own unique masculine scent.

"And if I were a cop worth his salt," he said, slipping off his right glove, "I'd resist the temptation to reach out and touch your cheek . . . say, right about here." His fingertips were rough but warm as they traced her cheekbones, her jawline, and beneath her chin. With his thumb he followed the lipline he had just studied.

"And, of course . . . ," she whispered, ". . . the absolute *worst* thing you could do is kiss me."

"Oh, I can think of worse," he said with mischievous grin. "But if we did *that,* I'd have to arrest us both for lewd conduct in a public place." He laughed, a deep, husky chuckle that turned up the heat in her body. Any man who laughed like that would be fantastic in—

She pushed the thought aside. She was in enough trouble already. His lips were so close and getting closer as he leaned toward her.

"We mustn't, we shouldn't . . . we can't," she said, as she closed her eyes and leaned her head back—waiting.

His lips brushed lightly over hers, and she thought her heart would stop. Quite the contrary, it pounded so hard she was afraid he could feel it against his chest.

"Uh . . . we can't?" he murmured as his mouth brushed hers again. "What exactly is it we can't do?"

"This . . ." She lifted her hands and entwined her fingers in his thick waves. To her delight, his hair was as soft as his body was hard.

"And why is it that . . . that . . . we can't do this?" he asked as he placed small, quick kisses at the corners of her mouth.

"Mm-m-m, at the moment I can't remember."

"Me either. So, to hell with it."

Less than a second later, he was kissing her with more enthusiasm and passion than she had ever experienced. His lips were firm, warm, and insistent against hers, stoking that liquid fire within that was now flowing through her veins and igniting every part of her body.

"Ah, Lizzie," he said, just before he deepened the kiss and

took her breath away. The intensity of her own desire overwhelmed her. Was this what Cass had been talking about? Was this what she had been missing?

Finally, he pulled away and buried his face in her hair. "I wanted so much to do this last night," he said, his breathing harsh and raspy, "but . . ."

"I know. Me, too."

"This is a really difficult time for you, Elizabeth, and I don't want to take advantage of you in any way."

She smiled at him as she slid her hand inside his coat. His chest was warm beneath her palm, and she could feel his heart pounding as hard as hers.

"You should let *me* decide when I'm being taken advantage of," she said in a sultry voice which she usually reserved for the stage.

He growled deep in his throat and nibbled at her bottom lip. "So . . . do you feel you're being exploited at the moment?"

"Absolutely," she said. "Please don't!"

He pulled back, looking confused. "Don't what?" he asked.

"Don't stop!"

"I'm telling you, he was here all night. He went in; he didn't come out. That's it." Fred Halley pulled the shredded toothpick out of his mouth and tossed it onto the floorboard of the old Chevelle.

Nick looked down and saw a pile of discarded picks that was big enough to kindle a Halloween bonfire. Halley and Nick had a bet going on who could last longest on their "smoke-out." The loser had to buy the other a steak dinner. But it wasn't the price of the meal, it was the principle of the thing. The thought of having to listen to the other one gloat about his victory was the best motivation either of them had ever had to quit "the habit" for good. They had started with an agreement to go for one weekend, but stubbornness had kept it going.

"You're going to wear out your dentures, ol' man," Nick said as he watched Fred pull another mint-flavored pick from a box of five hundred on the dash. The box was almost empty.

"Yeah, and I've seen you chewing on some of your dog's biscuits that you carry in your pocket." Fred popped the pick into his mouth and grinned. "So, when this is all said and done, we'll be nonsmokers, but I'll be toothless with splinters in my gums, and you'll bark, chase cars, and piss on fire hydrants, right?"

Nick glanced up at the third-story window and watched the silhouette on the yellowed, ragged blind. "I'm telling you," he said, "our friend got out away from you last night. He was in Port Madison, on Elizabeth Knight's front porch."

Fred snorted and reached for the small notebook that sat on his dash between the toothpick box and air freshener with the sun-faded picture of a bodacious centerfold. Someone had scribbled on a mustache, beard, pubic hair, and an unsightly bristling in her armpits. Nick didn't think the model would be as amused with the alterations as the impromptu artist had been.

Flipping the notebook open, Fred held it up to the light from the street lamp and read, "Seven-fifteen, left the corner grocery store. Bought some bananas and rice, milk of magnesia, and an eight pack of toilet paper . . . double ply." Fred glanced up and smirked around his toothpick. "Must be having a little problem, huh?"

"Your deductive powers never fail to amaze me. What else?"

"He walked home, went in at seven-seventeen. Saw the light come on in his apartment at seven-twenty. It went out at eight-thirty. He was there all night. Popped out this morning, went down to the liquor store where he bought two porn magazines. Came back half an hour later."

"So, he got out some other way last night."

"Couldn't have. The back door opens onto an alley which leads directly out here. To leave he'd have to walk around this side of the building, and if he had, I would have seen him."

"Side doors, fire escapes?"

"Give me a break. I checked it out. Your man was here last night. That's it, that's all."

Nick watched the shadow cross the blind again and he shook his head. "We're overlooking something. Elizabeth saw him; she talked to him. When I got there last night she was scared to death."

Fred fixed him with a scrutinizing look that made him feel like squirming on the Chevelle's old plastic-covered seat. Sometimes Nick thought that half of what Fred came up with on a case was based on intuition. It was almost impossible to hide anything from him.

"Scared to death, huh?" Fred mumbled. "So, did you . . . uh . . . *comfort* . . . her?"

Nick cleared his throat and looked away. "I did what I could," he snapped.

"I'll just bet you did."

"Shove it."

They sat quietly for a few moments, Fred smirking, Nick fuming.

"No kidding, buddy," Fred said at last. "You'd better watch your back. You wouldn't be the first cop who's been lied to by a good-lookin' broad."

"Like I said, Halley, shove it."

Nick opened the door and climbed out of the Chevelle. He had come over here with the intention of questioning Ferguson and making an impression on him. And now that he was pissed, it was as good a time as any.

Nick had been in law enforcement for twenty years, and he still hadn't gotten over the fact that killers never looked like killers. He wasn't exactly sure what a real killer was supposed to look like, but David Ferguson certainly didn't live up to his expectations.

First, he was too small—probably no more than five-eight. After a full dinner he might weigh in at one hundred and forty. And second, he didn't look mean. In fact, he looked pretty damned timid, peeking out of his doorway with the chain still attached.

"Yes?" he asked in a voice that was several notes too high to be ominous. "Can I help you?"

Nick flipped open his badge and held it up for his inspection. "I'm Detective Nicholas O'Connor from Midtown Homicide. I need to talk to you."

He cast a furtive look over his shoulder. Nick noted the move; apparently there was something in the room he didn't want him to see.

"Um . . . now isn't really a good time," he said.

"You don't understand, Mr. Ferguson." Nick placed his palm against the door. "This isn't a request. I'm going to speak to you now, either here in the hall or inside your room. If that isn't acceptable to you, we can go down to the station and have our conversation there."

Just for a second, Nick saw the anger that was hidden below the surface glint in those doe-brown eyes. Then the spark flickered and went out; the submissive, frightened look returned.

"Okay, I . . . um . . . . . you can come in. Just let me take care of . . ."

He closed the door, and after a moment Nick began to wonder if he were bolting out a window.

"Hey!" he said, pounding his fist on the door. "Open up!"

The door swung open and Ferguson stood there, his pale face flushed and wet with sweat. His hands were shaking. He looked like he might burst into tears any minute.

Nick scanned the room, trying to identify whatever it was that he had hidden before he'd opened the door. But he had done a good job. Other than a milk of magnesia bottle, some toilet paper and banana peels on a small table, an empty pizza box—*not* Papa Joe's, Nick noted—an ancient black and white television with aluminum foil hanging from its rabbit ears, and some girlie magazines on the floor, the room was pretty sparse. But then, the guy had just gotten out of prison after ten years. He hadn't really had much time to accumulate worldly possessions.

Mentally, Nick jotted down a reminder to himself to get a search warrant and find whatever he had hidden from view . . . under the blanket on the bed, if that square bulge near the pillow was any indication.

Ferguson saw him looking at it and his face flushed a deeper shade of red. Yep, that was it.

Contrary to his previous expectations after reading hundreds of mystery novels, Nick had discovered that killers weren't necessarily all that smart, either.

"What's this about?" Ferguson asked as he walked over to the edge of the bed and sat down.

Nick strolled to the window, pulled up the blind and looked down on Fred's Chevelle. "Where were you last night, Mr. Ferguson?"

"Last night? Ah . . . right here. I stayed home and . . . ah . . . I read."

Nick turned and glanced pointedly down at the magazines on the floor. "All night?" he asked with a sarcastic tone.

With a nervous giggle, Ferguson said, "Not *all* night. Just until I went to sleep."

"Which was about . . . ?"

"About eight-thirty."

Eight-thirty jibbed with the time Fred had said the lights had gone out, but Nick only saw two magazines on the floor and Fred had seen him buy two this morning. He hadn't had them last night.

Nick studied the rectangle under the blanket from his periphery. A little too large for magazines.

Lie Number Two.

"Why are you asking me these questions?" Ferguson asked. "What do you think I did last night?"

Nick looked into his face and saw something behind the meek facade. Ferguson was nervous, but on some level he was also enjoying this. He thought he had pulled one over on them—in a way, he had—and he was doing his best not to look too self-satisfied.

"Oh, I *know* what you did last night, Mr. Ferguson," Nick replied. "But I have a feeling that you and I are going to have a long and very close relationship, and I want to get to know you better. I was just asking the questions to see how many lies you'd tell me in five minutes."

The anger flared again in those brown eyes and this time it remained. Ferguson jumped up from the bed and walked over to the door.

"Are you going to arrest me for something, Detective O'Connor?" he asked, his hand on the knob.

"Not yet."

"Then I'll ask you to please leave."

Nick didn't move for several seconds, and the silence grew heavy in the already stuffy little room. Finally, he walked to the door where he stopped, his face only inches from Ferguson's.

"Have you known many New York City cops, Mr. Ferguson?" he said.

Ferguson plastered his body against the wall, trying to put some distance between them, but he said nothing.

"I didn't think so," Nick continued. "So, if we're going to be seeing a lot of each other, let me tell you about New York cops." He leaned forward until Ferguson's nose was pointing at his Adam's apple. "You don't want to screw with us. Got that? And you don't want to screw with anybody who's under our protection."

He paused to let his words sink in, then he said, "Elizabeth Knight is under my personal protection. And that means you are not to see her, speak to her, write to her, or even look at her picture on the front of a *T.V. Guide* in the grocery store. Because I would consider any of those things to be screwing around. Do I make myself clear?"

Ferguson's eyes met his for one hate-filled heartbeat, then he looked away and nodded slightly.

"Good."

Nick walked out the door and made sure to slam it hard behind him, pretending the guy's fingers were inside. It never hurt to punctuate a statement . . . just for emphasis.

But as Nick walked down the stair and out of the building, he knew it hadn't worked. He had seen it in the guy's eyes.

Oh, Ferguson had heard his words, all right.

But Elizabeth's problems weren't over yet. He still hadn't gotten the message.

Seventeen

"I'm in the process of getting a restraining order against David," Elizabeth told Nick as she sat at her office desk, staring at the computer monitor in front of her. Her fingers flew over the keyboard as she called up screen after screen of lists, searching for the one she wanted.

"Good move," Nick said, watching her from the winged back chair which he had pulled closer to her. "Once it goes through, I can bust the guy if you even smell him in a down wind."

"I can't believe that staying away from me isn't a condition of his release. I had a long talk with his parole officer this morning, but I might as well have been talking to one of Brody's stuffed safari heads. It wasn't written into his release papers originally, and it can't be changed now."

Nick sighed and shook his head. "That's the sort of crap that made you hate law enforcement in the first place, isn't it?"

"Yes, I'm afraid so." She turned away from the screen for a moment and gave him a half-apologetic smile. "I'll admit that my opinion, like most prejudices, was based on ignorance."

"Are you saying that throwing some snowballs in Central Park changed your mind?"

"Oh, I wouldn't say that I've changed my mind completely. I still think the system lets people down . . . frequently, and when it counts most. But the system also has some really sincere, intelligent people in it who are trying to work within its confines and do a good job."

"Well, thank you," he said in an "aw, shucks, ma'am" tone.

She raised one eyebrow. "I wasn't talking about *you*. Geez, you cops are conceited."

"I walked right into that one," he said, scowling. "How do you know that I—"

"Wait, enough witless banter, I think I've got it. Yes, there it is." She pointed to the screen which contained a list of names and their titles. "That's everyone who has access to the scripts . . . from Brody to the assistant who types them."

"Can you print it out for me?"

"Sure."

She pressed a couple of keys and the laser printer on a table nearby began to purr.

"Whoever he is," Nick said, when she handed him the list, "he has to have access to your story lines ahead of time. He couldn't have waited until he had seen the episodes broadcasted to set up the murders. They were too complicated."

"He would have had to do some research," she added, nodding. "How do you think he's choosing his victims?"

"We're working on that. The task force is combing the files on the victims, trying to find a connection, but I don't think we're going to come up with anything."

"He probably gets them out of the newspaper." She punched a button and printed a copy for herself.

"That's what I figured. But none of the local librarians have noticed anyone with an unusual interest in going through the microfiche. I know, I talked to them all."

Elizabeth scanned the list of her coworkers. "It's a pretty sick feeling, knowing that it may be someone I see everyday, maybe even someone I call my friend."

"It often is," he said.

For the hundredth time that day, she thought of Martie . . . and David. "Yeah, I know. Sometimes I think it would be easier if it were a stranger. There would be less of a feeling of betrayal. I had never really considered David Ferguson a friend, but . . ."

"I understand," Nick said, when she couldn't continue. "It's hard to believe that there could be a really, honest to God killer among us. It's a lot safer to think of them as the bad guys on television. Even the eleven o'clock news seems like fantasy."

"Yes, and that's a dangerous attitude to hold. It lulls a person into a false sense of security. I don't know how many women have thought that their husbands and lovers would never *really* hurt them." She swallowed and bit her lower lip. "I never thought David would really . . . you know."

"Is that why you did 'The Dark Mirror'?"

"Yes . . . but it looks like my plan to enlighten has brought more pain and fear than light."

"That isn't *your* fault, Elizabeth. It's *his*. And we'll find him."

At that moment the door burst open and Brody stomped in. Without acknowledging Nick's presence, he marched over to Elizabeth's desk and slammed a legal document down before her.

"Are you responsible for this?" he shouted.

Elizabeth picked up the paper and read the first few lines at the top. "Why, Brody . . . you're being sued," she said in a honey-dripping Southern accent. Her eyes continued down the page. "And these figures are most impressive. Let me count . . . six, seven . . . no, *eight* figures!" She looked up at him and grinned. "Now that would knock a hole in *anybody's* bank account. Even yours."

"You did this, didn't you?" he yelled, pounding her desk with his fist. Nick rose and took a step toward him. For the first time, Yarborough seemed to notice him, and he backed away a bit.

"Me?" Elizabeth said coyly. "Now, why would you think a thing like that. I mean, just because you're suing me for breech of contract, you think I would be so mean spirited as to get these folks riled up enough to sue your ass off? Brody, you do have a suspicious mind."

Slowly she stood and picked up the paper. While he fumed, too angry to speak, she sauntered over to him and shoved the document inside the front of his western shirt. Then she gave his chest a little pat.

"I'm glad you think I'm so influential," she said. "And I wish I could claim credit for this, but I can't. I'd say that the families of the victims are sufficiently angry and in enough pain that they want to cause you some discomfort. After all, you're making a 'killing' off the deaths of their loved ones. Why shouldn't you pay for the privilege of exploiting their grief?"

"Have I ever told you that you're one smart-mouthed bitch?" Brody asked, his voice quiet but bitter.

Nick moved one step toward him, but Elizabeth held up her hand. "Oh, many many times," she said with a nonchalant shrug. "But coming from a good ol' boy like yourself, I just figured it was a down-home term of endearment."

She dropped the smile and took a step toward him. "It's called karma, Brody," she said, fixing him with an icy blue stare. "You hurt people, they hurt you back. No big mystery."

"If you're making a fool out of me, Elizabeth," he said. "I swear I'll—"

Brody turned and stormed out the room, slamming the door so hard that the windows rattled and one of Elizabeth's prized vases toppled over onto its side.

As she checked it for damage and set it straight, Nick walked over and put his hand on her shoulder. "Liz," he said, turning her to face him. "Listen to me."

"I'm listening," she said, surprised at the grave tone of his voice.

"I know Yarborough makes you furious, and I know you're great with the 'banter' routine, but I'm telling you, you need to watch out for that guy. He's dangerous."

"I know," she said, leaning her forehead against his chest. Suddenly she felt very tired. "Yarborough is dangerous, the crowd outside is dangerous, Ferguson is dangerous . . . and then, there's the Mirror Killer . . . if he isn't one of the above."

She looked up into Nick's green eyes and saw a depth of compassion that gave her strength. "So, it's a dangerous world out there . . . getting worse by the minute. But I'm not ready to roll over and play dead. Not just yet."

"That's my girl," he said, chucking her under the chin.

"Your *woman*," she said before she thought of how it sounded.

"Really?" he asked.

She smiled. "Come on. Let's get back to that list."

Nick looked down the table and saw three of the most tired and bedraggled individuals he had seen in ages. Stephanie, Fred, and Ray looked like he felt . . . and that wasn't good. Until this afternoon, Nick had never seen Stephanie without makeup. Not even when they had slept together. He hadn't realized that her eyebrows and lashes were courtesy of Maybelline.

Ray, usually a meticulous dresser, looked severely rumpled. Nick would have surmised that he had slept in his clothes, but one look at the bags under his eyes contradicted that theory. And Fred . . . well, Fred was always rumpled, but he was generally less surly.

At the far end of the table sat the two V.I.P., Detectives Peter J. MacDonald and Marvin Petrie from Long Island. So far they hadn't contributed squat to the meeting, and Nick didn't have high hopes that they would. Obviously, they had merely come to pick up any leads he and his team might have come up with.

They looked remarkably fresh, rested, and well-fed, bathed, and shaved. Nick hated them on sight.

Stacks of reports lined the center of the old table: autopsy reports, medical histories of the victims, background checks on over two hundred individuals relating to Y.B.S., Reverend Taggerty's followers, and personal enemies of Yarborough and Elizabeth Knight. And, of course, an enormous pile of stats on David Ferguson.

Nick ignored the two at the end and focused on his team. "You three have done a great job. We may not have had a substantial break yet, but it isn't because you haven't tried," he said. "You've been busting your humps out there, and I just want you to know I appreciate it."

Ray's ruddy face beamed. Fred snorted and chomped on his

toothpick. Stephanie stared down at her hands which were folded gracefully on the table top.

"How's it going on the picket lines, Steph? What are you finding out?"

She looked up at him for a moment, then began playing with the turquoise ring on her finger. "I've gotten to know quite a few of the reverend's followers. Most of them are decent, sincere people. They're out there on the line because they feel it's helping their children and society. They adore Taggerty . . . a real case of hero worship. I think they'd do anything he asked, believing it was a direct order from the Almighty."

Nick leaned back in his chair and folded his arms over his chest. He wished he didn't feel so defensive around Stephanie; it interfered with his ability to concentrate on the work at hand. And while the two at the end of the table were probably clueless, one glance at Fred told him that Old Eagle Eye knew what was going on. Sometimes Fred was just too perceptive for comfort.

"And how impressed are *you* with the good reverend?" Nick asked.

She shrugged. "I don't think he's the voice of God, but I'm amazed at the power he wields over his people. I can understand their adoration in a way. He's really quite wise when it comes to personal dilemmas. He gives good advice and appears to care about them. And he's a hell of a motivational speaker. His rallies are something else. He even gets me all fired up and ready to change the world."

"What about it, Ray?" Nick asked. "What have you uncovered on Taggerty?"

"He says he was called into the ministry at the age of four, but Florida authorities have a different story."

Ray pulled out a three-ring binder and opened it on the table. Nick noted with amusement that it was divided into color-coded sections with tabs and pocket folders and the occasional computer-generated graphic. Ray was thorough and painfully organized, no doubt about that.

"What did you get from Florida?" he asked.

"Twenty years ago, when he was in his thirties, Taggerty was involved in a couple of questionable business deals. One having to do with selling some land to a group of senior citizens from New York. They wanted to retire in the sunshine, and he sold them 'lake front' property."

"Swamps?" Nick asked.

"Yep . . . alligators, snakes, bugs, the works. Completely uninhabitable."

"Nice guy," Fred said around his toothpick. "Nothin' like rippin' off the old folks."

"And then there was that mail-order thing in Ohio." Ray grinned, pleased with himself. "The postmaster came down on him for selling worthless, earn-a-living-at-home kits. The basic idea was to sell similar worthless kits—which, of course, you could buy from him—to other people. I guess a lot of elderly folks, the handicapped, and young mothers lost out on that one."

Nick noticed with satisfaction that Pete and Marvin were taking notes frantically. Pete would reach the top someday, but not by walking on other people; he was too big a wimp for that. He'd accomplish his goal by riding on their coattails. Sadly, most of them would never know why their load had seemed so heavy. Nick didn't care anymore . . . just as long as he wasn't among their ranks.

Turning to Stephanie, he said, "I wonder how Taggerty's followers would feel if they knew his history?"

"They wouldn't believe it," she replied. "They'd say it was a lie, a Satanic plot to cast aspersions on a man of God."

"How convenient. Basically, you can do whatever you want, and if anybody complains, it's religious persecution." Nick turned to Ray. "So, how long has he been a minister?"

"About ten years. The protest against media violence is a fairly new thing for him. For the past five, he's been concentrating most of his efforts in the anti-abortion movement."

"Hey, watch it," Fred said. "I'm a pro-lifer myself."

"So am I." Ray's face turned a shade redder. "But I'm talking about a fanatic fringe of the movement. He was associated with a group that's been implicated in clinic bombings, physicians being shot, etc. They're believed to be responsible for five deaths. Not exactly 'pro-life' if you ask me."

"You've spent a lot of time with Taggerty and his group," Nick told Stephanie. "Do you think any of them are capable of this?"

"Anything's possible," she said. "But not really. It isn't Taggerty's style. I think his primary objective is to get as much media coverage as possible, to expand his ranks and, ultimately, his pocketbook. He's pretty upfront about what he does."

"Anybody else?"

"His son, Christopher, is a low-key sort of guy. To be honest, I think he's embarrassed by his father's unorthodox methods. Everyday his dad reminds him that he's grooming him to take over his empire, and in the same breath he lets him know that he's inadequate to run it."

"And is he?"

"Yes, I'm afraid so. He seems like a nice enough guy, but he doesn't have his father's charisma or drive. I think he would have been a lot happier if he'd been born the son of a butcher, baker, or candlestick maker."

Nick turned to Fred. "Anything new on Ferguson?"

"Nope. He just hangs out there at that flea-bag hotel of his and—"

"Except for when he shakes you off and takes a trek to Long Island," Nick interjected.

Fred shot him a dirty look and continued, "As I was saying, he spends almost *all* of his time at the hotel. I talked to the woman who owns it. She says he's a nice, quiet boy who doesn't cause her any trouble. No women, no parties. In fact, she's letting him work off his rent by doing odd jobs around the place."

"Does she know about his record?"

"Says he told her all about it the first time he set foot in the place. She's convinced he's rehabilitated, and she figures it's her civic duty to help him find his way back into society."

"Now *that's* true Christian spirit," Stephanie remarked.

"Yeah, let's just hope it doesn't wind up costing the lady her life."

"How about his prison record, Ray?"

"Got it . . . right here." Promptly, Ray flipped to the blue section of his notebook. Nick was beginning to consider the advantages of organization.

"Model prisoner . . . of course. No trouble at all. Got his clock cleaned a few times, but he wasn't the instigator."

"At least, not overtly," Nick muttered. He was well aware of certain "quiet" types who always managed to be in the center of trouble, but supposedly, did nothing to provoke it. Personally, he found them more of a pain in the ass than the tough guys who were blatant about their involvement.

Pete cleared his throat with an air of importance and flipped his own notebook open. "You might be interested in knowing that Ferguson was gainfully employed at the prison book repository."

Everyone at the table stared at him blankly for a moment, then Ray said, "Thank you, sergeant, but I have that, too." He consulted his notes. "He inventoried books and magazines on Mondays and Fridays from 7:00 A.M. until noon."

Pete lifted his nose a couple of notches. "My team was privy to that information as well."

"We aren't here to discuss your team's outhouses, Pete," Nick said with a completely straight face.

Fred snickered, Stephanie covered her mouth with her hand, and Ray looked from Pete to Nick, confused. A lot of jokes got past Ray, Nick had noticed.

"Did you talk to any of the guards or his cell mates?" Nick asked him.

Ray looked slightly offended. "Of course, I did. They actually liked him. But each of them said one thing in particular that was interesting."

"Which was?"

"All he talked about for the ten years he was in the joint was Elizabeth Knight. From everything he told them, they honestly believed that he had had a steamy love affair with her. And he made no bones about the fact that he was intending to settle here in New York when he was released, just so he could be close to her."

"Lucky lady," Stephanie said, shaking her head.

"Nothing like the love of a good man." Fred spit out his pick and stood. "Anything else, Nick?" he asked, looking at his watch.

"That's about it for now. Why? You got a hot date tonight?"

"Something better than a woman." Fred gave Stephanie a sideways smirk as he reached for his coat. "On the way in here, the captain told me to tell you that the search warrant for Ferguson's apartment has come through."

"You're right," Nick said. "That *is* better. Let's go."

Peter jumped up from his seat and grabbed his briefcase. "I'll come along," he said eagerly, then gathered his composure and added, "to facilitate your actions."

Marvin nodded vigorously. "Me, too."

Nick turned to Fred. "They want to facilitate us, Fred. I think that means they want to help. What do you think? Do we need help?"

Fred thought for a moment, then shook his head. *"I* don't need help. Do *you* need help?"

"Naw, not me." He gave Pete a sarcastic grin. "Sorry, guys, but me and Fred don't double date. Besides, we haven't seen much of each other lately, and we're looking forward to sharing some quality time together. Thanks anyway."

Nick picked up his jacket and backpack and headed for the door, saying goodbye to Stephanie and Ray. Then he paused and turned back to Pete. "But feel free to drop by anytime and tell us what we already know. It doesn't help much with the case, but it's great for our morale."

Eighteen

"Well, I'll be damned. I never thought I'd see the day!" Cassie exclaimed as she reached across Elizabeth's dining table and slapped her friend's shoulder. A dozen of Y.B.S.'s personnel files slid off their stacks and tumbled to the floor, but Cass ignored them. She had dropped by Elizabeth's house this evening to find her pouring over the reams of records, her eyeballs nearly burned out of her head. Enough was enough. Cass had reminded Liz that her big hunk of a cop was working on the case and she didn't have to solve it alone. That was when Cass had seen that gleam in her eye. Lust! She would have recognized it anywhere!

"Elizabeth Knight herself," she said, "bitten by the lo-o-ove bug."

"Stop it, Cass. You know I hate it when you tease me about men."

"Men are the only thing worth teasing about," Cass replied. "Lord knows, you can't take them seriously."

Cassie took a long slurp of the cappuccino which Elizabeth had just given her. Every time she came to visit Elizabeth made cappuccino for her. Cass didn't know where Liz had gotten the idea that she liked it; she didn't. Cassandra liked her coffee like her men, strong and hot, and this cappuccino crap was too sissy to be called real coffee.

But the last thing in the world Cass would ever want was to hurt Elizabeth's feelings by telling her something like that. It wasn't important. She just kept sipping the cappuccino from the phoo-phoo little cup with Bambi on it and kept quiet about the whole thing.

But when it came to love, sex, and romance . . . all bets were off. There were no such things as limits to the amount of ribbing she felt entitled—even obliged—to dish out. Cass had been waiting a long, long time for this opportunity, and she intended to make the best of it.

"How does he kiss?" she asked, puckering her Passionate Pink lips in a Marilyn pout.

Elizabeth flushed, and Cass thought how pretty she looked . . . suddenly younger and healthier. The dark circles were still under her pale blue eyes, but the blush on her cheeks didn't come from a compact or from the red glow of the Tiffany lamp that hung above them.

Nothing like a little lovin' to put the color back in your cheeks, Cass thought, and silently she blessed that good-looking cop with the cute butt who had put it there.

"Well . . . I'm waiting," she said, nudging Elizabeth's hand. "I want details. Was it soft and gentle . . . or hot and hard? Did he work into it slowly or just grab you and lay it on you?"

Elizabeth grinned and stared down at her cup.

"Come on, dammit," she said, "I don't have all night. Are we talking tongues, or what?"

"All of the above," Elizabeth said quietly. "And more."

"My God! Elizabeth, do you realize what you've got? Long, blond, wavy hair . . . broad shoulders, tight little buns, biceps from hell, he knows how to kiss . . . *and* he's got handcuffs. I have to say, I'm *very* jealous."

"I don't think we'll be getting into the handcuff scenario any time soon," Elizabeth said with a chuckle. "Not everyone is as . . . adventurous . . . as you."

"Creative is the word, dear." Cassie sighed. "Oh, well, I'll give you a tip. Heaven knows, you need some advice."

She leaned across the table, glanced left and right, then lowered her voice to a conspiratorial whisper. "You don't start off with the cuffs and leg irons, silly girl. One has to work up to these things. You begin with leg warmers."

"Leg warmers?" Elizabeth looked confused. "I don't understand."

"Good grief. Do I have to paint you a picture? Trust me, they're *wonderful* for bondage. Soft and stretchy, but strong. Easy to get out of in an emergency, but firm enough to give you that delicious feeling of helplessness, the glorious sensation of surrender, the—"

"Okay, okay, I got it. Thanks for the tip. I'll certainly file it away for future—"

"File it!" Cassie was appalled. "That was one of my better secrets. I gave it to you to be *used* not *filed* away."

They both giggled, then suddenly Elizabeth grew somber. "Cassie, I'm scared," she said.

She hadn't needed to say it. Cass could see it in her eyes. Elizabeth was no coward; in fact, she was the strongest woman Cass had ever known—other than maybe Cass's own mother. But even superwomen had secret, deep-rooted fears that floated to the surface once in awhile.

Long ago, Cass had learned that women, herself included, had certain demons that defied exorcision. Every now and then, usually when you least expected or needed it, they paid you a visit. They slipped out of their hiding places in the dark shadows of your soul and crept into your dreams, resurrecting old nightmares and pricking old wounds that you had hoped were finally healed, but never truly are.

She could see the demon's presence in Elizabeth's eyes . . . the signs of active hauntings, of old nightmares revisited.

"Don't you worry, sweetcakes." She reached for Elizabeth's hand and folded it between hers. "That gorgeous cop of yours is going to catch this bastard, and then—"

"That's not what I'm most afraid of," Elizabeth said, shaking her head. "Of course, I'm afraid of Ferguson, or whoever is doing this. I'm afraid he's going to keep doing it and more people are going to die. Sometimes I'm afraid that he's going to hurt me. But the thing I'm the most frightened of is . . ."

A light came on in Cass's understanding. Ah, the darkest demon of all. "You're afraid to love somebody, aren't you, honey?"

Elizabeth nodded. "Especially him. Cassie, he's a *cop*. It's dangerous to be a cop."

"Yes, it is. And it's dangerous to eat a hamburger at a fast food joint, and to drink water right out of the tap, and to cross the street at Fifty-fifth and Park Avenue. *Life* is dangerous. And we're all going to croak someday. Us and everybody we love. That's a given."

"It's just that . . . I've known him such a short time and already I feel so much for him." Elizabeth passed her hand over her face and Cassie could see her tremble. She needed some rest. If she continued this way, she was going to wind up in the hospital.

"That's good, honey. That's wonderful. To be able to feel love for another person is a beautiful gift. Can you just allow yourself to enjoy it? For now, anyway?"

"It seems wrong to . . . enjoy . . . anything, with so many horrible things happening to other people around me."

"Hey, let's just be grateful that something good is coming out of this mess. One thing I've learned is that life is never all black. There's always a bright spot if you look for it. Maybe a relationship with a great guy like Nick is some kind of compensation for all the hell that fate is putting you through right now."

Elizabeth looked up at her with hopeful eyes. "Maybe you're right. Thanks. I'll try to think of it that way."

Good, Cass thought, *she's got some hope.* Hope was always the strongest talisman against devils. And some of Elizabeth's demons had left . . . for the moment. It was time to go home.

She stood, walked around the table and planted a kiss on the top of Elizabeth's hair. "Gotta go. I'm gonna get hold of Bud somehow. All this dirty talkin' with you has got me horny as hell. And I guess I'll just have to take it out on him. Lucky guy."

Elizabeth laughed and walked her to the door. "Thanks," she said, as she hugged her goodbye. "I owe you one . . . again."

"Don't worry about it. Just go to bed and have pleasant dreams."

When Cass got to the end of the sidewalk, she turned and shouted over her shoulder, "Remember . . . start with leg warmers."

"He's not answering." Fred knocked on Ferguson's hotel room door for the fourth time, harder than before.

"I'm telling you, he's not in there," Nick replied. Reaching into his pocket, he pulled out the key which the clerk downstairs had given him . . . after a couple of not so thinly veiled threats. "He's out on the town, just like he was the other night when you thought he was home, tucked in beddy-bye with his flashlight and magazines."

Nick turned the key in the lock and stood to the side as he pushed the door open. A quick glance told him no one was home. In an eight by ten foot room, containing only an undersized twin bed and one rickety table, there weren't very many places to hide.

Fred hurried over to the window. "He might have gone down the fire escape."

"He didn't," Nick replied dryly, looking around the room for the object which had caused the rectangular lump he had seen earlier under the blankets.

"And how the hell do you know?" Obviously, Fred was getting irked. He still couldn't believe that someone could actually get away from him without him knowing it.

Nick chuckled quietly. Fred was a good cop, but his ego was as oversized as his paunch and the double chin he was developing. Nick suspected he was covertly stuffing his face with donuts, perpetuating the stereotype, in lieu of cigarettes.

"I know . . . ," Nick said, "because I looked out the window the other night. This room doesn't have an escape."

"That's a code violation," Fred said, slamming the window closed.

"No shit, Sherlock."

"Maybe the gal at the desk called up here and warned him we were coming."

Nick looked at Fred and shook his head. The guy was slipping; this case was apparently overloading his hard drive. "No phones," he said, "I checked that, too."

"All right, smart ass—so you checked. I'd be functioning better, too, if *I'd* had some time in the sack."

"And what's that supposed to mean?" Nick bristled. Hell, he hadn't gone to bed with Elizabeth Knight. He wouldn't do something like that; it was immoral, it was dangerous, it was completely against policy and—okay, he was too goddamned nervous to hit on her. She was a star, for heaven's sake. A celebrity of the first order. That made her off limits even if nothing else did. A lot of women went for cops, because they had a thing for the uniform. But not women like that. Ladies like Elizabeth Knight just didn't come with the territory.

"Do you mind if we get a little work done here?" he asked Fred.

"It's not like it's gonna take long to search this place."

Nick walked over to the bed, ran his hand over the blanket and found nothing. Not even wrinkles in the sheet. Ferguson got an A+ for tidiness.

There was nothing on the table except the decrepit television and a cereal box which Fred was rummaging around in.

Reaching under the mattress, Nick ran his hands the length of the bed and hit pay dirt at its foot. His fingers hit a sharp corner of something that felt like . . . yep . . . a photo album. Somehow he had known that was what the lump had been, but he hadn't wanted to think about it. And as he pulled it out and laid it on the bed, he didn't want to think about it then either, let alone look at it.

He opened the book and began turning the pages. He saw pictures. Beautiful pictures of Elizabeth. Photos taken from magazines, television guides, tabloid covers, newspapers. And then, there were the others. The candid shots which Nick was certain she had never known had been taken: Elizabeth walking in the park with her assistant, Cassandra, gardening at home in a pair of cut-off jean shorts, and some old Polaroids of her strolling the hallway of a school, her arms full of books, and the front yard of a simple Spanish-style bungalow, washing a little red Mustang. She looked so young, so innocent . . . so happy.

Good God, Ferguson had been after her for a long time.

"She was a cute kid," Fred said over his shoulder.

Nick felt his nerves tighten a couple of notches. "Yeah, wasn't she," he said. "And so was her sister," he added, pointing to a shot of Elizabeth and Martie playing with a litter of kittens on a living room floor. It had obviously been shot through a half open window.

"She's the one?" Fred asked.

"Yep." Nick slammed the book closed and returned it to its place under the mattress. Then he walked to the door and jerked it open. "Let's go," he said. "We've gotta find out how this bastard is getting away from us. We can't afford to let him out of our sight."

Elizabeth sat on her bed, smoothing lotion onto her legs and enjoying the jasmine scent. It had been a long time since she had indulged herself this way. On the table beside her sat a glass of white wine, a bowl of strawberries, a pink votive candle, and a red rose in a crystal vase. She was wearing one of her favorite nightgowns, teal blue silk jacquard with tiny straps and strategically placed lace.

For the first time in ages, she felt beautiful, she felt pampered, she felt sexy. And she wished Nick was there to share the mood, the wine, and the strawberries with her.

Would he like that sort of thing? Or was he more like Cassie, with the leg warmer tricks?

And if she ever did summon the courage to invite him here, into her private sanctuary, what would he expect? Would he want her to be "Elizabeth Knight" in bed—cool, elegant, aloof? That was a facade, a role she played. Behind closed doors, in the intimacy of her own bedroom and within her own heart, she felt she had nothing in common with that beautiful, sensuous woman on the screen.

Elizabeth Knight was the creation of makeup artists, hair stylists, costume designers . . . and, perhaps, of her own imagination. Was that the woman Nick would expect to go to bed with if they ever got that far? Was that the woman he had fallen in love with?

In love? The words flashed across her mind like a lightning bolt and jolted her back to reality. Where had she gotten the idea that he was in love with her? That was certainly presuming a lot. He had never said anything about love. Nothing at all.

She set the bottle of lotion on the table beside the wine and strawberries, which somehow no longer looked as sweet and tempting. She felt young, and stupid, and naive, and like a skinny, ostrich-legged kid with a crush on the school football captain.

Turning off the light, she pulled the crisp linen sheets up to her chin and wished they weren't always so cold when she first climbed in.

Oh well, so much for being single and going to bed alone.

As she cuddled up to her pillow, she asked herself again where she had gotten such a foolish idea that he really cared for her. Maybe it was the way his green eyes followed her when they were in a room together. Maybe it was the soft, intimate tone of his voice when they spoke about things that hurt. Maybe it was the deep huskiness of his laughter that seemed to come so easily when she said something funny.

Or maybe Detective Nicholas O'Connor was just a really nice guy, and she was misinterpreting his kindness for something more because she was lonely and incredibly vulnerable right now.

Maybe. It was possible.

But she didn't think so.

"There you go. That's it," Nick said as he played his flashlight on the loose boards in the basement wall. "Right there, behind those water pipes."

"Naw, can't be." Fred pushed at one of the boards with his forefinger and it swung loosely from side to side.

"Bet you dinner and a beer at Harry's."

"No thanks. I have a feeling this case is going to drive me back to smoking, and I'll have to hock my old saxophone to pay for that one. Besides," Fred added, swinging the board to the side, "you're right. Damn, I hate it when you're right."

Nick leaned forward and stared into the small dark tunnel which the boards had covered. "Look at that." He pointed to an odd red glow that dimly illuminated the other end of the passage. "It leads to the building next door, which is abandoned, right?"

"Yeah, I think so."

"Well, come on. Let's check it out." Nick knelt and poked his head into the opening.

"I'm not goin' into that," Fred said. "There's probably rats and spiders and shit like that crawlin' all around in that thing."

"So, you're armed. That .357 of yours should take care of any oversized rats. Just be careful not to shoot me in the ass, okay?"

"Give me a break, man . . . I'm claustrophobic."

"So am I. Get the hell in here."

Fortunately, the tunnel wasn't long, only about eight feet or so. When Nick carefully stuck his head out the other end, he found himself in a basement that was even more dismal than the last one.

At first he thought the place was full of cats. Then he realized they were enormous rats. The thick, cloying stench of decay filled his head and he tried to breathe shallowly.

"You're gonna love this, buddy," he said, as he stepped out of the tunnel and into the semi-darkness. A couple of filthy windows near the ceiling filtered the strange red light he had seen from the other end. It was the glow of the neon sign on a bar around the corner. One of the windows was ajar and a couple of crates had been placed below it.

"That's it," Nick said as Fred climbed out, groaning and casting anxious looks at the wild life inhabitants. "He's leaving this way and . . ." Nick climbed up on the crates. ". . . and he's exiting onto the street, around the corner from where you're sitting in your car."

Fred said nothing. He just sucked on his toothpick and sulked as he stood on the crates and looked out on the traffic passing by.

"Hey, don't sweat it," Nick said. "You can't be everywhere at once, you know."

The sarcastic tone was gone from Nick's voice. He could tell that Fred was genuinely upset. Being a cop had cost Fred everything, his wife, his kids, even his health. It was all he had, and he took great pride in his skills. This was a rare occurrence, a surveillance subject ditching Fred Halley. And the murder on Long Island might have been the result. Yes, for an old-timer like Fred, this was a real bite in the ass.

"Come on," Nick said, slapping him hard on the back. "Shit happens. It could happen to anybody."

"That's not what I'm worried about." Fred spit the pick onto the floor and headed back to the tunnel. "I'm wondering where the little son of a bitch is right now."

Nick hurried after him, the thought beginning to gnaw at his guts. If Ferguson had gone to a movie or down to the local liquor store, he wouldn't have had to sneak out.

The pictures in the photo album flashed through his mind: Elizabeth, her kid sister, the litter of yellow and black kittens playing on the avocado green shag carpeting that had been bright and new back then.

Maybe he'd make a quick run out to Port Madison tonight. Hell, couldn't hurt.

The killer stood beside her bed, watching as she slept. She looked like an angel. Her dark hair was spread over the white linen pillowcase and glowed blue-black in the moonlight that found its way through the lace curtains covering her bedroom windows. The floral pattern of the fabric cast delicate shadows on her skin.

Awed by her beauty, her perfection, he allowed the anger he had been feeling toward her to drift away. She wasn't evil. How could anything so lovely be evil?

Looking at her now, lying there with a touch of a smile playing on her lips, he knew he had been right to love her. He wasn't a fool, after all, for thinking she was good and worthy of his adoration.

Any man who could see her like this would love her. And not like those animals that watched her on television and mentally slid those black gowns off her body, dwelling on every voluptuous curve, imagining what it would be like to touch her, to handle her, to—

No, he didn't think of her that way. His love for her was pure, above all that. And she loved him, too. For some reason she was afraid to say the words aloud, to proclaim it to him and the world. But he saw the way she looked at him—those glances, those sly, silent messages that women send with their eyes when they want to tell a man they are thinking of him in that special way.

He took a step closer to the bed and the wooden floor creaked beneath his feet. Not daring to breathe, he watched as she shifted slightly beneath the sheet. The small strap of her nightgown fell away from her shoulder, and a small portion of her breast was bared, softly rounded, ivory satin.

It was all he could do not to reach out and touch that loveliness. After all, it *was* his, wasn't it? *She* was his. Every gorgeous inch of her.

But this wasn't the time. Not yet. He was planning many, many wonderful pleasures for the two of them to share . . . once she knew . . . once she fully understood.

For tonight, he told himself, he would have to settle for much less.

Leaning over the bed, he reached out and, oh so gently, trailed his fingertip down her cheek. It was even softer, more silky than he could have imagined. A thrill of gratitude and wonder swept over him that a creature so exquisite belonged to him.

"Goodnight, my love," he whispered. "Sleep well." Then he turned and left as silently as he had come.

Elizabeth sat on the edge of the town dock, watching the moonlight disperse into a pastel spectrum of silver, blue, and pink on the waves that washed gently at her feet. A heavy fog was closing around her, but she didn't care. For this mystical moment, deliciously snared in the silken web of a dream, she wasn't afraid . . . of the night . . . of the fog . . . or of the dark water below.

He spoke softly to her, this man with the moonlight in his golden hair and a touch of the Emerald Isle in his voice. She wasn't sure what he was saying to her as they sat there together, watching the moonlight play upon the water. It didn't matter. The emotions that were passing between them didn't need words to find expression.

You're safe, Elizabeth, her heart told her. *With this man, you really are safe.*

His hands were large, strong, and capable. She watched, anticipating their warmth, as he reached up to touch her face. Gently, with one finger he stroked her cheek.

But at the contact, a chill went through her. Something was wrong. Badly wrong.

There's no such thing as safety, another voice reminded her. *Danger is near. The evil, the darkness . . . it's very, very near.*

Elizabeth woke with a start and sat up in her bed. A chill washed over her, and she shuddered.

The room . . . the air in the room . . . it felt strange. Not empty, as it should but filled with . . . something. She couldn't quite name it, but it felt oppressive, sinister.

She didn't feel alone.

Holding her breath, she listened, straining to hear the slightest sound, but there was only the heavy, suffocating silence.

"I'm alone," she whispered, needing to hear her own words, needing so much to believe them. "There's no one here but me."

She sat, waiting, and after a long while, the presence seemed to gradually depart, like an exorcised demon spirit, and the room felt empty again, almost peaceful.

She lay back on the bed and closed her eyes. "I'm alone," she repeated. And this time, she meant it.

Alone. With only the residue of a beautiful, long anticipated dream . . . somehow gone wrong.

Nineteen

"Hey, hey, you . . ." Tap, tap, tap. "What are you trying to do, freeze yourself to death?" Tap, tap.

Nick opened his eyes and tried to figure out where he was and what was going on. Someone was talking to him—*yelling,* actually. And there was that damned, irritating rapping on—

Suddenly, he snapped to attention, fully awake. He couldn't believe he had fallen asleep in his car, parked half a block away from Elizabeth's house. He had sat there all night, watching. Just in case. But now it was dawn, and he had apparently nodded off. He glanced at his watch. Five-forty-five. The last time he had looked, it had been five-thirty. So, he hadn't been out too long.

Tap, tap, tap.

Dammit, what was that?

With a great effort he turned his head to look out his window. But he was so cold and stiff that even that small movement caused a spasm along the back of his neck.

"Nick, wake up!"

He focused and realized it was Elizabeth, standing beside the Jeep, peering into the car and clinking the fingertips of her left hand against the glass. In her right she held something that looked like—Yes, thank God!—a steaming cup of coffee. He was so thrilled that he didn't really mind the fact that it was a Pinocchio mug. Coffee was coffee. Right now he'd drink it out of Mary Poppins.

Forcing his half-frozen fingers to work, he rolled down the window and grabbed for the cup. "May the angels smile upon ye, darlin'," he said. "What a welcome sight is your bonny face this mornin'."

He took a long drink. "Ah-h-h . . . and the coffee's welcome as well."

"I do believe ye must have kissed the Blarney stone, lad," she said, mimicking his Irish lilt.

Her smile warmed him as much as the coffee. With no makeup and her hair tousled, she looked younger and more carefree than he had ever seen her. She was wearing a dark blue wool coat, but he could see the hem of an ivory satin robe peeking from beneath its hem. Dear Lord, she was still in her nightclothes.

He swallowed another gulp of the coffee, and its warmth traveled all the way down to his belly, then beyond. His body was reacting as though he were a sixteen-year-old kid in study hall and a cute girl had just walked by in a miniskirt. Only, this time he didn't have a stack of books or a notebook to cover his lap.

"Why are you here?" she asked, half scolding, half teasing.

"Why do you think?" he replied, wrapping his fingers tightly around the warm cup. "I drove out here in the middle of the night, intending to serenade you beneath your balcony . . . but I forgot my mandolin."

She laughed. "I don't have a balcony."

"Yeah, I know. That was the second obstacle."

To his surprise, she reached through the open window and lightly laid one hand on his shoulder. Her face softened and so did her smile. "You were out here keeping watch for me through the night, weren't you?" she said.

He shrugged. "I didn't have anything better to do. I told you, I lead a boring existence. No social life at all."

"Oh, I think you had something better to do . . . like maybe sleep? When is the last time you went to bed and stayed there for more than four hours?"

He thought for a moment. "Umm-m-m . . . what day is this?"

"Sunday."

"Oh, okay . . . I remember. It was two and a half weeks ago."

She reached down and pulled the handle on his car door.

"Come on," she said, swinging the door open. "If you've spent the night out here, freezing, keeping an eye on things for me, the least I can do is offer you some breakfast."

"Breakfast? Really? Come on, don't toy with me."

"I'm completely sincere. I make a mean tofu and bean sprout omelet."

He had started to climb out of the Jeep, but he halted midway. "Tofu? Bean sprouts? Oh yeah, I forgot—you're from California. I've heard they eat weird shit like that out there."

"I'm kidding, for heaven's sake." She yanked on his coat sleeve. "Come on. How about bacon and eggs?"

"Now you're talking."

She looped her arm through his as they strolled up the sidewalk toward her house. "Don't worry about the tofu," she said, giving him a sideways grin. "I understand that it's an acquired taste. I'll just blend some in with the prune juice cocktail."

"So, congratulate me," Elizabeth said, slapping a piece of paper onto the table in front of Nick's recently emptied plate. "It's legal. Ferguson has to leave me alone now, and if he doesn't, I can shoot him between the eyes, right?"

"I don't think that's the nature of a restraining order, Lizzie," he said, picking up the paper and reading the details. "But I can understand why you would feel that way."

"You can?" She turned suddenly serious as she sat down in her chair across from him. "I don't. I never thought I would say something like that about another human being, not even jokingly. I always thought I was . . . better . . . than that."

"Well, I understand it," Nick replied, remembering his first homicide case. A crazy son of a bitch had thrown his two-year-old daughter out a fourth-story window because his wife had spent his drug money on food for the kid. He had enjoyed arresting that guy. To be honest, he had been pleased that the creep had resisted. He had actually received a dark satisfaction from the amount of legal, but painful, force he and his partner had been required to use while restraining him.

And in some shadowy corner of his mind—a corner which couldn't bear the light of self-examination—Nick knew that he had actually wanted the guy to resist even more. When he thought of that baby lying there, dead and broken on the sidewalk, her young mother crazed with grief, Nick had to admit that he had wanted to have a reason, any reason, to shoot the bastard and leave him as dead as his little girl.

"I really do understand," he repeated. "It's only human. Anyone can be pushed too far. And I'd say you've just about reached your limit with Ferguson."

She sat quietly for a moment or two, as though considering his words carefully. Then the shrill ringing of the phone pierced the comfortable silence, and she jumped. *God,* he thought, *she's strung tight.*

She hurried to the phone on the kitchen wall and said, "Hello." He watched from the dining room table as she stood there, saying nothing, listening, her beautiful face was growing whiter by the second.

Nick rose from his chair and walked into the kitchen. He could see that she was trembling so badly that she could hardly hold the phone.

It was the killer. Whoever he was, he was on the phone right now. And whatever he was saying, he was scaring her to death.

Just as Nick was considering the wisdom of grabbing the phone, she slammed the receiver back onto its cradle.

"Nick. . . . ," she said, sagging against him. "Oh, God . . . Nick."

He wrapped his arms around her waist to support her and pulled her close. "What is it, Lizzie? What did he say?"

She looked up at him, and he could see the terror, as sharp and cold as shards of ice, glittering in her eyes.

"He was here . . . in my house last night. He watched me while I slept."

He gathered her against his chest and stroked her hair. "Maybe not," he said, grasping for anything to say that might offer her comfort. "Maybe he was just trying to scare you."

She reached down and pulled the edge of her robe aside, revealing her satin gown and a hint of the lace that covered her bodice. "He told me . . . he said . . . he liked my blue silky nightgown. He said he especially liked the fact that he could see my breasts through the lace."

She shivered, and he could feel her knees go weak beneath her. "He *was* here, Nick. Dear God, he was right beside my bed. He said he . . . he touched my cheek."

At the thought of that bastard invading her privacy, of him touching her as she slept, Nick felt a hot wave of fury sweep over him. The intensity of the emotion left him feeling both drained and yet charged at the same time.

"I'll get him, Lizzie, really, I will," he said. Holding her so close, he could feel the pounding of her heart. He could feel her fear.

"He touched me, Nick," she said again, as though unable to believe it. "He stroked my cheek. And the worst part is . . . I remember feeling it. But I dreamed it was you."

Brody Yarborough seldom, if ever, asked for advice or information from anyone. As for advice, he was perfectly capable of deciding what he wanted in his world, and the worlds of those around him. And information, it never occurred to him that anyone else might know something he didn't. So, what was the point in asking?

That's why it irked his butt to call this little meeting in his office with his attorney, his chief accountant, and the head of Y.B.S. public relations. He intended to make it clear at the outset that he wasn't interested in their opinions, only the facts.

"So, bottom line," he said, propping his snakeskin boots on his desk and pushing back his Stetson with his thumb. "How much is this little fiasco going to cost us in the long run, Ned?" he asked the lawyer who sat to his left in the leopard-print chair.

How appropriate, Brody thought, considering the carnivorous nature of the man. Ferraro didn't screw around. He went right for the vital organs and didn't stop until his opponent was totally eviscerated. In checking Ferraro out before retaining him, Yarborough had discovered that the guy had represented some rather prominent members of the mob. That had convinced him; what was good enough for the big boys was good enough for Brody.

"The cost will depend upon the outcome," Ferraro said. His eyes were cold, lifeless, and Brody thought—not for the first time—that the analogy between sharks and attorneys was pretty accurate. Especially with this one.

In truth, Ferraro intimidated the hell out of Yarborough, but he wasn't about to admit that, even to himself. And as always when intimidated, Brody struck out. He didn't wear rattlesnake boots for nothing.

"Don't give me some bullshit, beat-around-the-bush answer like that," he said, fixing Ferraro with his best "just before striking" stare. "You're not a goddamned politician running for office here. Tell me what it's going to cost us."

Ferraro returned his gaze without flinching—something else Brody didn't like about the guy. "A class action suit can be very costly, depending on our strategy and the outcome," he said, lowering his voice a couple of notches. Brody crossed his arms defensively over the front of his western shirt. He had never trusted anyone who got quieter, rather than louder, when they were pissed.

"I don't have a crystal ball," Ferraro continued in a condescending tone that really grated against Brody's already raw nerves. "I can only make a guess, and—"

"A *guess?* I don't pay you a fortune every month for you to be making guesses! I can do that myself. Now, I'm gonna ask you one more time, what's the most this could cost me."

"If we settle out of court—"

"Forget it. We aren't settling."

"If it goes before a jury and they win, it could be a lot." He reached into his briefcase and pulled out a sheet of paper, which he handed to Yarborough. "This is my best estimate."

"You're kidding!" Brody felt his stomach lurch. He didn't like paying three dollars for a baked potato at his favorite steakhouse, and what he saw on the paper was a sum that would knock a considerable hole in his financial boat. Maybe enough to sink it. "Why so much?"

"They've hired some very effective counsel—"

"So have *I*," Brody interjected. "Or so you keep telling me."

"And it's an extremely emotional issue. They are the suffering families, whose loved ones were murdered in cold blood; we're the big money corporation who's raking in the bucks by exploiting their deaths. It's going to be hard to appear sympathetic in a jury's eyes."

"I agree," Jim Murphy said. Brody turned to his public relation specialist, irritated that he had interrupted. But he kept silent for the moment, because Jim was pretty good at what he did. Brody had never been particularly fond of the Irish, but Jim Murphy was a big, robust Irishman with a good sense of humor and a quick wit. He really knew how to charm—the individual, or the public at large. And charm was something every corporation could use more of when dealing with society.

"I've been running a daily survey to check the tide of public opinion on this matter," Jim said. "And the vast majority feels we're being irresponsible by continuing to broadcast the show."

"Oh, really?" Brody picked up the latest ratings print out from his desk and shoved it under Jim's nose. "They may be clucking their tongues like a bunch of old hens and saying how rotten we are, they may be up on their goddamned soapboxes every day, crying about how we're causing people to get killed, and even worse, making money off it. But every Friday night, those same hypocrites are glued to their television sets along with the rest of the country, watching. They're *watching*, I tell you, and that's all that matters here."

Brody held out his hand to Tom Russell, his accountant, who had sat quietly through the entire meeting, as though hoping he wouldn't be seen. "Give me the latest figures. What are the points worth?"

For an awkward moment, Tom shuffled through his papers, before he found the appropriate forms. He pushed them across the desk to Brody.

Picking up the papers, Brody scanned the numbers with a practiced eye, and the sick feeling in his guts began to abate. The exorbitant sum that had been on Ferraro's report, the worst case scenario of what a judgment against them might cost, was only a fraction of the revenues generated by these high ratings points.

Brody grinned his best good ol' boy smirk. "Well, I guess that about settles it," he said. Tossing the paper to Ferraro, who handed it on to Jim Murphy. "It's a matter of economics, boys. Pure and simple."

The trio sat, silent, for a long time. Finally, Jim cleared his throat. "Have . . . have you thought about the impact a decision like this might make on public opinion?"

"Sure I have, Jim Bob," Brody said, lighting up a cigarette. "I think of everything. You should know that by now."

He blew a cloud of smoke in Murphy's direction. "Don't worry, I'll bump up the P.R. budget for you . . . at least twenty-five percent." He pointed at the paper in Murphy's hand. "Believe me, that kind of money can buy us a hell of a lot of good will."

It was Christmas Eve, Elizabeth realized as she stared out her office window onto the street below. Fifth Avenue had never looked more beautiful, decorated with giant snowflakes that glittered golden and silver. From her vantage point she could see shoppers hurrying from store to store, trying to make their last minute purchases.

Elizabeth had given the cache of toys she had collected all year to the Toys For Tots campaign. This annual event always brought her joy and a tremendous sense of satisfaction.

At this time of year, she couldn't help wondering how different her life might have turned out, had it not been for the success of "The Dark Mirror." Would she have been content living out her earlier goals as a research psychologist?

Somehow, she didn't think so. In most ways she liked her life as it was—or, at least she had before the murders had begun. But on nights like this one, when other women her age were tucking their children into bed with promises of a midnight visit from Santa, Elizabeth wondered how much she was missing. Her heart told her it was a lot.

Cassie was gone to Texas for several days to spend the holidays with her "kin." Elizabeth imagined what a loud, raucous scene that must be tonight, and she smiled. "Merry Christmas," she whispered to her—out of sight, but never out of mind—friend.

"Merry Christmas to you, too," said a deep voice behind her.

She whirled around and was relieved to see Nick standing in her office door. He held the end of a leash in one hand; the other end was attached to Hercules, who looked particularly festive with an enormous green and red satin bow tied to his collar. The dog wore a silly, embarrassed grin, and Elizabeth couldn't help giggling.

"Hey, don't laugh at him. It's not his fault," Nick said. "My kid sister put it on him. He couldn't help himself. But he did growl when she tried to put those damned antlers on him."

"I'm not surprised. No self-respecting British bulldog would be caught wearing anything so . . . undignified . . . in public."

Nick bent down and scratched the dog's ear. "See there, Herc. She understands these things. I told you she's cool . . . even if she *is* a girl."

"Such high praise," she said.

"Higher than you might think. Us guys have this thing about icky girls."

"So I've heard. And to what do I owe the honor of being visited by such discriminating gentlemen?" Suddenly, she tensed. "Nothing's wrong, is it?"

"Nothing new. This call is strictly social."

"You came here just to wish me a Merry Christmas?"

"No. . . ." He smiled, glanced down at his battered sneakers and shrugged. "I just wanted to invite you to the O'Connor place for the evening, if you don't have other plans, that is. I already asked Mama and Nina and they liked the idea."

Christmas Eve. With a family? With *his* family?

"I highly recommend it as a pastime," he said, his voice soft with emotion. "You haven't lived until you've had an Irish/Italian Christmas Eve."

Her elation was quickly followed by a wave of fear. This was too much, too soon, too good . . . it couldn't be the real thing. And if it was, it surely couldn't last.

Oh hell, go for it, baby cakes, said a voice in her head, a distinctive voice with a heavy Southern drawl.

"Do you have a Christmas tree? I didn't get around to putting one up this year . . . what with all that's been going on."

"An eight-footer, candy canes, tinsel, the works."

"I'd love to."

"Really?" His face brightened with a smile so wide it warmed her heart. He had really been counting on this. God bless him.

"Yes, I'd *really* love to."

"Great! Get your coat and let's go!"

As they walked down the hall toward the elevators, Hercules and giant ribbon in tow, Nick seemed distracted, lost in his thought.

When the three of them stepped inside the elevator, he said, "Do you know the difference in mistletoe and parsley?"

She gave him a suspicious look. "Is this some kind of dumb joke?"

"No, it's a perfectly serious question."

"Yes, of course I can tell the difference. Why?"

"Damn," he said, shaking his head. "How about chives, or basil?"

"Yes, Nick. I know mistletoe when I see it. What is this about?"

"I was just making a mental inventory of what I have in my refrigerator crisper. You know, anything that might work."

She laughed and shook her head. "Nick, you don't need to worry," she said, stepping closer to him so that her shoulder touched his. "I may know the difference in mistletoe and the other herbs you have in your kitchen. But I also have a marvelous imagination. I'm sure we can work something out."

"Targets," Nick said with disgust, reining in Hercules to pause before a toy store window display. "It's all I can do to keep my pistol in its holster."

Elizabeth turned to see what he was referring to. The hot pink spectacle featured the "World of Barbie" in all its glory: the dolls, the clothes, the houses, pools, hair salons, Corvettes, and ponies . . . a little girl's dream world.

"Do you mean Barbie?" she asked, shocked.

"Yeah," he replied, shaking his head. "That pukey pink is enough to turn any male's stomach. I'd like to line up the whole lot and shoot their heads off. Especially that wimpy Ken. He doesn't even have a dick. Huh, Hercules?"

She glared at him, aghast. "How do *you* know whether Ken has a dick or not?"

"I sneaked a peek at Nina's doll. And, what's just as bad . . . Barbie doesn't have a—"

"Hush!" She clamped her hand over his mouth. Several passersby were staring at them, and Elizabeth realized how loudly they were talking. She lowered her voice to a hoarse whisper. "I'll thank you to keep your opinions about Barbie and Ken to yourself, Detective O'Connor. Targets, indeed!"

Alert to her menacing tone, Hercules barked up at her.

"And that goes for you, too, Fido," she added.

"You mean you actually *like* those things?" Nick asked incredulously.

"I *love* Barbie and Ken." She stuck out her lower lip in a pout as they continued down the street. "And I don't want to hear bad things about them."

Nick laughed and put his arm around her shoulders. "Okay, I apologize. I didn't realize they were close friends of yours."

She shrugged his arm away. "Don't go kissing up now. It's too late, buddy."

He grabbed her arm and refused to let go. "So," he said, "I suppose you had a dozen of the damned things, and all the crap that goes with them."

Elizabeth looked sad for a moment. "No, actually, I didn't have any. My mom said they were frivolous and cost too much . . . three dollars, if I remember correctly."

Nick didn't reply, but his expression softened as he slid his hand down her arm to grasp her fingers.

"My cousin had dozens. I used to love to go over to her house to play with them. She had the pink case full of glittery, glamorous clothes, the works. I always wished that I could borrow one, take it home for a few days. But I was afraid my mom would get mad. So I never asked."

"That's too bad, Lizzie," Nick said, squeezing her hand. "I'm sorry you never got a Barbie of your own. I think you really needed one."

She shrugged. "Ah . . . no big deal. Every Christmas I get a kick out of buying at least a dozen of them for the Toys for Tots campaign. Living vicariously, and all that."

"I'm sure that helps, but I know how much a 'little' thing like that can hurt. I came home from college to find that Mama had thrown out my train set. I'm sure she meant well . . . you know . . . thought I had outgrown it."

"Some things we should never outgrow," Elizabeth said, realizing the truth of her words as she spoke them.

"Like walking through the snow, holding a friend's hand on Christmas Eve?" He didn't look down at her but stared straight ahead, as though uncomfortable with the sentimentality of his own words.

"Yeah," she said with equal indifference. "Even if he *is* an icky boy."

Twenty

"She seems really nice, but . . . how are we supposed to treat her?"

Elizabeth halted at the foot of the stairs that led to the O'Connor's second-story apartment when she heard the words. The shyness and anxiety in Nina's voice both touched and embarrassed her. Quietly, she waited to hear Nick's reply before she announced her presence.

"What do you mean, 'How do we treat her'?" he said. "You treat her just like anybody else. You know . . . dish out your usual dosage of verbal abuse, offend her as often as possible in the first fifteen minutes of her visit. She'll feel right at home."

"When will she get here?"

"For the third time . . . she'll be here any minute now. We were on our way here when she said she had a quick errand to run. I'm sure she—"

"Hello? Anybody home?" Elizabeth called up the stairs.

"Oops, she's here," she heard Nina say in a harsh whisper. "How does my hair look?"

"Too big, just like it always looks. Don't worry about it, kiddo. You're gorgeous."

"Don't you dare call me kiddo in front of her. If you do I'll . . ."

Elizabeth didn't hear the rest of the threat, and she decided it was just as well.

Nick appeared at the top of the stairs, a dish towel and a plate in his hands. He smiled down at her. "Hi."

"Hi."

"Sorry we didn't hear the bell. Come on up."

When he saw the packages under her arms, he shook his head. "Aw . . . you didn't need to do that, Lizzie."

"Hush. I didn't *need* to do it; I wanted to. Where can I put this stuff? It's heavy."

He tossed the towel over his shoulder and laid the dish on the top of an old table beside a collection of purses and miscellaneous bags. Holding out his hands, he said, "Here, I'll take it."

"No, you won't," she said, laughing. "Nice try."

She reached the head of the stairs and found herself in a U-shaped hallway, lined with doors. The largest one was open and through it she could see a cozy, old-fashioned parlor, dominated by an enormous Christmas tree. The pine scent of the tree, combined with the mouth-watering aroma of good food, washed over her, bringing a bittersweet wave of nostalgia.

"This is very nice. Thank you for inviting me," she said.

"We're glad you could join us. Aren't we, Nina?" He stepped aside and for the first time Elizabeth saw the girl who had been standing behind him.

She was beautiful, in a young, fresh, vibrant way. Far more lovely than she knew, judging from the awkward, self-conscious expression on her face.

"Hi," she said. She lifted her hand, as though to offer it, then stuck it behind her back. "It's nice to meet you. Nick's told me all about you . . . well, not *all* about you . . . but . . . well, you know. . . ."

"He's told me about you, too."

She gave her brother a suspicious look. "Oh, no. What has he told you about me?"

"He says you help your mom a lot in the deli, and you keep him out of trouble."

Nina laughed and Elizabeth could see her shyness slipping away.

"It would take a bigger person than me to keep my brother out of trouble," she said.

Elizabeth shifted the packages under her arm. "Nina . . . do you have a place where can I put these so that your brother won't find them for a few hours?"

"Sure," she said, pleased to be asked for a favor, "you can put them in my room. Come on."

As Elizabeth passed Nick, she shoved a box into his hand. "And would you hide this one some place where your sister won't find it?"

"Sure, I'll let Hercules guard it," he said, nodding toward the dog who had just trotted out of the living room. The satin bow was still tied around his neck, but one end was tattered and soggy, obviously well-chewed.

"No! Don't you dare let that dog near my present," Nina said. She turned to Elizabeth. "Last year Hercules 'guarded' the Christmas ham . . . if you know what I mean."

"He didn't!"

"He did."

"The whole thing?"

"There wasn't enough ham left on that bone to make split pea soup."

Elizabeth looked down at Hercules who cocked one ear and tilted his head sideways. He almost looked proud of himself.

"Hercules O'Connor," Elizabeth said. "I'm shocked!"

"Hey, he was hungry," Nick said. "The ham was there, no one was around. What do you expect a guy to do?"

He picked up the plate and headed back to the kitchen, shaking his head. "Come on, Herc. Girls . . . what good are they?" he mumbled. "They just don't understand us guys at all."

"I see you like Pegasus," Elizabeth said as she looked around Nina's bedroom at the herd of flying horses that decorated the walls, the bedspread, the curtains and the dresser. "I don't think I've ever seen so many. They're beautiful."

Nina flushed with pleasure at the compliment. "Thanks. I love horses, and I love birds, so . . ."

"I like Pegasus, too," Elizabeth said. "Did you know that he's the mythical symbol of creativity?"

"No, really?"

Elizabeth nodded.

"Neat."

A sadness stole over Elizabeth, a melancholy that she didn't want to intrude on her pleasant evening.

"Are you okay?" Nina asked, stepping closer to her, a concerned look on her pretty face.

"Yes, I'm fine. It's just . . ." She took a deep breath and decided to be honest. Obviously, Nina was very perceptive and there was no point in trying to hide her feelings. "I had a younger sister once. She loved unicorns. Had them all over her room, just like this. She was just about your age when . . . when she died."

To Elizabeth's surprise, Nina placed a comforting hand on her shoulder. Compassion seemed to run in the family.

"I'm sorry. That's really sad," she said. "I never had a sister, but I couldn't stand it if anything happened to Nick. He's a pain in the . . . ah . . . neck, sometimes, but . . ."

"But you love him."

She shrugged and nodded reluctantly. Elizabeth smiled, remembering that such admissions weren't "cool" at that age.

"I worry about him all the time," Nina said. "I'm afraid that the same thing will happen to him that happened to our dad. He was a cop, too, you know. Someone shot him."

"That must have been pretty tough for you."

"No, I was just a baby, so I don't remember. But it was awful for Nick and Mama."

"Yes, I'm sure it was." Elizabeth reached out and wrapped her arm around the girl's shoulder. "Well," she said. "Enough of this. Let's go out and join your brother and your mom. I'm eager to meet her."

As they left the bedroom and entered the hall, Elizabeth paused. She felt she needed to say something, but she wasn't sure what.

"Nina . . . about your dad and my sister. . . ."

"Yes?"

"I believe they're here with us tonight, in memory and in spirit. My sister really loved Christmas and—"

"Nicky says my dad did, too."

"Then, I believe they want us to enjoy the evening together. They would want us to remember that they lived, not that they died."

Tears welled up in Nina's coffee-colored eyes, but she smiled and nodded.

"Come on," Elizabeth said. "We'd better check and make sure that Nick and Hercules aren't 'guarding' that ham."

Nick couldn't remember a time when he had felt so at peace, so complete. And he couldn't remember ever being this scared. Before he had met Elizabeth Knight, he had been a carefree bachelor. Alone and lonely, but free from the pain of caring for someone. Someone who was in trouble, someone who might be taken from him.

He reached down and stroked Elizabeth's hair and wondered again that it was so soft, like the finest ebony silk. After eating more food than they should, drinking more than was wise, singing Irish and Italian carols, and Nick reading from Dylan Thomas's *A Child's Christmas In Wales,* they were sitting quietly in the parlor, the lamps down low, gazing at the glittering tree. Isaac Stern's violin filled the room with the beautiful strains of "Ave Maria," and a hearty fire crackled in the fireplace.

As usual, Mama and Nina sat on the opposite ends of the sofa, Nick in his father's recliner. Elizabeth had chosen to sit on the floor at his feet, her head resting against his knee, Hercules's enormous head on her lap.

Nick reached down to touch her hair again, as though the contact would convince him that this dream was reality. He glanced over at his mother and saw that she was watching him. Their eyes met and she smiled. Obviously, she approved.

Like Nina, Rosemarie had been awkward with Elizabeth at

first. But he was amazed at how quickly Elizabeth had put her at ease. The turning point had been the moment when Elizabeth had offered to help put the food on the table and had quickly loaded four bowls and a platter onto her arms in topnotch waitress style and delivered them to the table with finesse. Rosemarie O'Connor had been duly impressed, as Nick was sure Elizabeth had intended her to be.

At the dinner table, his mother was more animated than she had been in ages, as she chatted with Elizabeth about favorite holiday recipes. By the end of the meal, Elizabeth had graduated from guest to "just one of the clan." Nick couldn't believe how comfortably she fit into his family. He could easily get used to the idea of having three favorite girls, instead of two.

For a moment, David Ferguson crossed his mind, although he had promised himself the luxury of spending one evening without grinding on this case. Was he the one who had called, who had stood at Elizabeth's bed while she slept? Nick thought of the autopsy report he had read on Martie, and he shuddered inwardly.

For the hundredth time that day, he ran down the mental lists that he was juggling in his head: precautionary steps, like changing the locks on Elizabeth's doors and making sure there was no other way for the guy to get into her house, investigation procedures, who was doing what on the task force and what they had come up with so far, and, of course, the one list that was burned forever into his brain circuits—the list of suspects. Ferguson was at the top, but Nick had learned long ago to consider every option, and to suspect everyone.

Glancing down, he saw Elizabeth looking up at him, her blue eyes reaching into his thoughts.

"It's Christmas, Nick," she said softly. "Stop worrying. Everything will be okay."

He wanted to believe her. But there was something in her tone of voice that bothered him, something in those blue eyes besides the obvious desire to console him. Then, Nick realized what it was. Elizabeth wasn't just trying to convince and comfort him;

she was trying to believe her own words. But, as with him, it wasn't working. She didn't believe it either.

"Ho, ho, ho . . . Me-e-errry Christmas!" Big John, full-time deli sandwich chef and, at least for tonight, part-time Santa's helper, leaned his head out the car window and gave one more hearty hurrah. Then, as in legendary days of yore, he pulled out of sight, wishing them all a good night . . . in his new Camaro.

Every year on Christmas Eve he played Santa for his nephews and nieces, and he thoroughly enjoyed the gig. Now they were old enough to know it was their Uncle John, but they were well-behaved enough not to let on. Plus, his sister, Joanna, had told them to play along, or Santa wouldn't leave any toys. He had to admit that greed might have played as large a part in their compliance as good manners.

He didn't care; he got a kick out of it, and so did they. That was all that mattered.

The street was dark and deserted, lit only by the occasional string of multi-colored bulbs. And down on the corner, he could see the perennial "Blinking Nativity" as he called it. This monstrosity was the pride and joy of the dear old lady who lived there, but it was the butt of many cruel jokes around the neighborhood, garnering some rather rude chuckles from passersby and a few outright guffaws.

The huge, life-size figures were molded of white plastic and lit from inside with various brightly colored lights which blinked off and on. Mary was lavender, Joseph red, the manger and infant green, and the wise men were assorted shades of blue and pink.

A devout Christian himself, John couldn't help being a little appalled by this display which was at best, tasteless and at worst, blasphemous. But his faith had also inspired him to be forgiving and charitable to others. He realized the scene had been placed there as a symbol of devotion. And all of God's creatures had the right to worship Him in their own manner.

He nodded to one of the wise men as he passed and sang a line of "Silent Night."

Halfway down the block, he could see Elizabeth Knight's Victorian house, tucked away among the pines. If it had been earlier, he might have dropped by and wished her good cheer, but the lights were off and she had probably gone to bed.

He thought of how scared she had been the other night, and he wondered how anyone could want to frighten anyone so nice. Or even hurt them. That was unthinkable. John couldn't stand the thought of anything bad happening to Elizabeth. He whispered a quick prayer for her safety.

As he drove by, he was surprised to see a man walking around the side of the house. John slowed the car and peered through the dark pine boughs that partially obscured his vision. The man was wearing a uniform . . . from the local power company, John decided when he saw the lightning bolt insignia on the sleeve. He was carrying a small black case and appeared to be on a service call.

Weird, John thought as he drove on down the block. *Who does service calls this late on Christmas Eve?*

He shrugged it off. The power company would come out any time if it were an emergency. And as cold as it was tonight, Elizabeth wouldn't want to be without electricity if she had developed a problem.

But by the time John had rounded the next corner, he had shot down his own theory. Her house lights had been off, but the porch lamp was on. She had electricity, so what was that guy doing there? And, come to think of it, there hadn't been any sign of a power company van parked out front. Those guys always drove those big gray vans.

Feeling a cold jolt of adrenalin hit his bloodstream, he did a U-turn in the road and drove back down the block. This wasn't right. He had to check it out, for Elizabeth's sake.

But when he arrived at the house, he saw no one at all. Up and down the street, in her yard, all was deserted, dark and quiet.

Still feeling uneasy, he climbed out of the Camaro and walked cautiously up the sidewalk toward the house. For a moment he had a vision of himself tackling the guy, wearing this Santa suit. Wouldn't that be cute? He could just see the picture on the front cover of the *Port Madison Weekly Review*. And the headline: "Local Deli Man Captures Mirror Killer."

He climbed the stairs and walked up onto the porch. Still, he couldn't see anyone or anything moving. No sounds came from the house.

After knocking on the door, ringing the bell, calling out for Elizabeth, and then repeating the process at the back door, he determined that no one was home.

With the aid of the porch lamp and the street light, he could also see that the "repair man" was gone.

Not a creature was stirring, he thought, *not even a mouse.*

He wasn't sure what to do. Somehow he didn't feel right about just leaving and doing nothing but. . . .

Then he got an idea.

A moment later he was wedging a note between the door and the jamb. He had thought carefully about what he should write on it. There was no point in alarming her by explaining what he had seen on paper. So, he had made the message short and sweet.

> *Dear Elizabeth,*
> *Hi! It's your buddy from the deli. I dropped by to say Merry Christmas. Give me a call as soon as you get home.*
> *God bless,*
> *John*

There, that should do it, he thought as he walked back down the steps toward his car. He felt much better, having done what he could to help. Elizabeth was a good person, a friend. And Big John stood by his friends, even if it meant traipsing around like an oversized elf in the middle of the night, wearing a red suit and white beard, and stuffing notes in their doors.

Now he could go home with a clear conscience and get some sleep. Sooner or later, even Santa's helpers and Good Samaritans had to grab a little shuteye.

About the time John arrived at his own home across town, a figure stepped out of the shadows behind Elizabeth's house and walked toward the front of the property. Only the small lightning bolt emblem on his sleeve shone in the darkness as he walked with silent steps onto the porch and up to the door.

Two seconds later, he was hurrying down the sidewalk away from the house. With John's carefully written, sensitively worded note crumpled in his pocket.

"Thank you for bringing me home, Nick," Elizabeth said as they pulled up in front of her house. "You didn't have to do that, but I'm glad you did."

"I wanted to," he said. "There's still a few hours left of Christmas Day and I wanted to spend it here with you. Besides, if I had stayed home Mama would have kept plying me with food and drink until I passed out."

Elizabeth laid her hand on her abdomen and groaned. "I know what you mean. I don't remember when I've eaten that much. It was delicious."

"We were all glad you were with us. Herc, too. He told me so."

"He did?" She turned around and patted the bulldog's head. He was sulking in the back, obviously peeved about having to give up his front seat. "I don't think he's too happy with me at the moment."

"Ah, he'll get over it. He'll forgive anything for a piece of pastrami."

"I'll remember that." She reached into the back floorboard for her bag of "loot" which consisted of the latest glittering Barbie and a hot pink carrying case full of clothes.

"I still can't believe you bought me a doll," she said, feeling a rush of warmth for this man who seemed to be able to touch that wounded child inside her with his kindness.

"Hey, you needed it," he said teasingly, but she heard the truth behind his words.

"Yes, I did," she admitted, "far more than I could have imagined." She thought of the tears that had sprung to her eyes when she had opened the package which he had so carefully wrapped for her. She *did* need to play more. Life had become so serious, so dark. She silently thanked Nick and his family for shining some light and warmth into her night.

"I really like the electric train," he said. "Thanks. Nina and I had a lot of fun playing with it this afternoon."

"I don't think we'd better talk about that right now," she said, pouting. "I'm still very upset about what happened."

He laughed, wrapped one arm around her shoulders and planted a kiss on her forehead.

"No, no," she said. "Don't try kissing up to me now."

Earlier that afternoon, Elizabeth and Rosemarie had been in the kitchen, assembling platefuls of the leftovers for the rescue mission, when they had heard peals of laughter coming from the kitchen. Agreeing that the cackles were much too sinister in tone, they had decided to investigate.

Elizabeth had been appalled to find that her new Barbie doll—only an hour out of her box—had been tied to Nick's train track. Neither Nick nor his sister would confess to the crime. They kept babbling on about a one-armed G.I. Joe, whom they had seen running from the scene of the crime, wearing a long black cloak and twirling his handlebar mustache. Supposedly, he had been muttering something about unpaid rent.

Remembering, Elizabeth allowed her pout to turn into a smile. It really had been a fun day. She glanced back at Hercules. "We might as well get it over with," she said. "It's time for Hercules O'Connor to meet Katie Kat. Prepare for the worst."

"Have you ever read 'The Duel,' you know, that poem about the gingham dog and the calico cat?" he asked with a chuckle.

"Dear Lord, let's hope it doesn't come to that!"

"Come on, Herc, ol' boy," Nick said, crawling out of the Jeep. "It's time to eat—excuse me, I mean *meet*—a kitty cat. And if she's half as feisty as her mistress, you're in for some fun."

* * *

His plan wasn't working. After four Dark Mirror killings, nothing was going the way he had intended. And it was beginning to really wear on him.

He lay on his bed, staring up at the ceiling, as though the answer could be found on its white, plastered surface.

He couldn't eat, couldn't sleep, and with so many damned cops on the case, keeping an eye on him and everyone else near Elizabeth Knight, it was getting harder to even get out and do anything.

It wasn't easy, pulling these murders off. He wished people would realize that. Not just any dummy could do it. First he had to study the script and decide how he was going to copy it. Then he had to do all that damned research at various libraries—he didn't dare go to the same one twice for fear of being remembered by one of the librarians—going through old newspapers until he was nauseous from looking at blurry microfiche. And finally, after he knew who he was going to kill, he had to work it out so that he and they were in the right place at the right time, as soon as the show had aired.

It was quite an accomplishment, and he couldn't help being proud of himself. Sometimes, he thought the hardest part of all was not being able to tell anyone about it, to brag about his intricate, well-executed plans.

The whole world knew about him now. They called him the Mirror Killer. He had his own name, just like the Son of Sam, the Hillside Strangler, and the Night Stalker. Stories, describing in gory detail what he had done and predicting what he might do next, were splashed all over every newspaper front page and tabloid cover in the country. But he couldn't even take credit for what he had done.

Yes, it was definitely getting to the point where this wasn't fun anymore. It was tough being a celebrity, when nobody knew who you were.

Something had to change. He was going to have to do something differently. This just wasn't working.

Twenty-one

"I can't tell you how sorry I am about this, Nick," Elizabeth said as she ran out of the bathroom with peroxide, cortisone cream, and cotton swabs in hand. "I really had no idea that she would—"

"It's all right," Nick replied. "He'll live, and it'll be a good lesson to him."

Nick sat in the middle of the living room floor, holding a wounded and sulking Hercules in his arms. The dog's dewlaps bore the bleeding scratches of a combatant who had lost "the duel."

"Bad cat," Elizabeth told Katie as she passed her on the stairs. The calico hovered near the top steps and peered down into the living room at the devastation she had wrought. She looked pleased. "Ba-a-a-ad cat!"

Elizabeth knelt beside Nick and his mangled canine and placed the medications on the floor.

"Poor Hercules," she said, opening the peroxide. "And he was only trying to say hello."

The dog rolled mournful eyes up at her and whimpered pathetically.

"Oh, for Pete's sake, Herc," Nick said. "You're really playing this one for all it's worth."

He held the bulldog's head as she gently cleansed and medicated the wounds. "Where did that cat of yours learn to punch like that? She's a hell of a boxer."

Now that the shock of the attack had passed, Elizabeth felt a giggle welling up inside. It was all she could do not to laugh aloud when she thought about it.

When they had first entered the house, the dog and cat had ignored each other, casting only furtive glances around the furniture as Nick and Elizabeth had shared a cup of coffee and a sandwich. But later, Hercules had made the overture by sidling up to Katie and sniffing her rear. Katie took affront, whirled around and grabbed his dangling dewlap with her left claws. Having a firm hold, she began to box him furiously with her right. Her hooks and jabs would have been considered remarkable at a championship bout.

"Well, at least we don't have to worry about him eating her alive," Nick said as they finished their first aid. "After that, it will probably be months before he'll even *look* her direction."

Months? Elizabeth wondered if he had meant that literally, or if it had been nothing more than a passing figure of speech. Did he really intend to be around months from now? When this case was solved and the murderer was behind bars—God, let it be soon—would he still have a reason to come around? She wanted so badly to know, but she couldn't think of any graceful, subtle way to ask.

In fact, she wanted a lot of things from him . . . and was afraid to ask for any of them. For once, she wished she were as brazen as Cassie and a little less ladylike. Ladies spent a lot of lonely nights without companionship, and tonight she was really hoping she wouldn't have to be alone.

Last night as she slept in the O'Connors' spare bedroom, she had longed to get up in the middle of the night and cross the hall to Nick's apartment. But she hadn't been able to summon the courage. Besides, she told herself that as long as she was beneath Mrs. O'Connor's roof, she should behave as a proper Irish/Italian Catholic out of respect.

But how about tonight? It was already nearly midnight, and he would need to be leaving soon. The thought of being without his warm, masculine presence after enjoying him for so many hours made her loneliness even more acute.

"Well, I should get going," he said. "Tomorrow's going to be a long day."

"Yes, of course," she said half-heartedly. "I understand."

Walking from window to window, he checked the new locks they had installed the other day after she had received the disturbing phone call.

"It looks like you're pretty secure here," he said, examining the new dead bolt. "I'd offer to leave Hercules for protection, but obviously, with the Katie Kat from hell, you don't need a guard dog."

Would he stay if she asked? she wondered. Other than a few breath-stealing kisses, he hadn't made a move toward anything more. Maybe he didn't want more. And yet . . .

Do it, Elizabeth! she told herself. *Just take the chance and do it!* If she didn't at least ask, she would hate herself later when she was lying in that big, cold bed all alone.

"Nick," she said, her voice shaking. *Oh no.* She had taken the first step and now there was no turning back.

"Yes?" he said, turning to her. He seemed expectant, but not surprised.

"I . . . ah . . . I was wondering. . . . Do you really have to leave?"

His eyes searched hers, looking for the message behind her question.

"No," he said slowly. "Not really. Why? Are you afraid to be alone?"

"No, I'm more afraid to be with you. But I'm so tired of always being alone. I want . . ."

He walked over to her and placed his hands on her shoulders. His touch was warm, as always, and she could feel his vitality even with such casual contact.

"Would you like me to stay the night?" he asked softly. "I'd be glad to sleep here on the sofa and just keep an eye on things, if that would make you feel better."

Her fear rose in her throat and nearly choked her. If she did it, if she made love with him and never saw him again, she didn't think she could stand it. Not another loss.

And yet, if he walked out that door without knowing how she felt, wouldn't that be an even greater loss? She couldn't control what happened to him, to them, in the future. Fate could be cruel and send along a criminal's bullet, a runaway bus, a malignant cancer cell, and there would be nothing she could do about it.

But for tonight, in this present moment, she did have the power to make a choice. If she could only find the courage.

She looked up into his green eyes and saw that he understood what was going on inside her. He was also going to let the decision be hers.

Slowly, she lifted her hand and stroked his cheek. The stubble of his beard grazed her palm, and she found she liked the male roughness, the complimentary contrast to her feminine softness.

"Is that what you want . . . to sleep on the sofa?" she asked, running her fingertips over his lips. Just remembering how they had felt against hers made her weak with wanting.

He smiled and kissed her palm. "It wouldn't be my first choice, but . . ."

"Mine either," she said. She drew a deep breath and plunged ahead. "I want you to sleep with me, Nick. I want to make love with you all night long and wake up and have breakfast together tomorrow morning. I want . . ." Her courage and breath spent, she paused to regroup. "I want so much and I can't find the words to express it," she said.

He stood, silently staring down at her with an incredulous look on his face, puzzled and somewhat amused. Then he laughed and pulled her to him in a tight bear hug. "Ah, Lizzie, you're so funny." He kissed the top of her head. "I think you expressed yourself quite well for someone who's speechless. God help us when you break out of your shell."

"Then you want it, too?" she asked, pulling back and looking up at him.

"Do I want to spend the night making love to the most exquisitely beautiful and sensual woman I've ever known?" He sighed and donned an Irish brogue. "Well, 'tis a hardship to be sure, but I'll bear up."

He slid his hand up her back, pressing her closer to him. She could feel his heart beating at the same accelerated pace as her own. Reaching up, she ran her fingers through the golden curls that she remembered so fondly from before. They were as soft as she recalled.

Dipping his head, he kissed her. It was a leisurely gentle kiss of affection which was exactly what she needed to put her fears to rest. The only barrier left was her own awkward shyness.

"Nick," she said, as his lips traveled from her mouth to her throat. "How do we get . . . from here . . . to there?" she asked pointing upstairs.

He smiled and she knew he understood.

"That's easy," he said, guiding her to the foot of the staircase. "We just take one step at a time."

Nick had been lying beside her, watching her sleep for the past hour and a half, and he still couldn't quite believe it had happened.

Nina had known. As he and Elizabeth had left his apartment, she had pulled him aside and slipped him a packet of condoms.

"I know you're a good boy, Nicky," she had whispered with a smirk. "But if you decide not to be good, at least be careful."

He smiled at the memory. Nina was a great kid . . . and a nosy one. She would be waiting eagerly to hear if he had been "good." And even though he wouldn't answer her, she would know. Women always knew.

Funny, he hadn't known. Men were rather dense that way. At least, he was. He had certainly thought about going to bed with her. Hell, he had thought about it constantly. But he had never dreamed that it would happen, and that the reality would be far more satisfying than his fantasies.

Strangely enough, it wasn't the fact that he had made love to a world-famous television personality that astounded him. He had gotten over that starstruck routine the first time he had kissed her. At that moment he had known that she was flesh and blood . . . warm, soft, tender, and passionate.

She wasn't that one dimensional, ten-inch high figure dressed in glistening black gowns on the television screen. The woman he had just spent the night making love to had been real, more real than anyone he had ever known. And the level of intimacy they had reached had been a wonderful surprise for Nick, and he suspected it was for her, as well.

He knew he should get up and head back to the city. The task force meeting he had called was supposed to begin in two hours, and he needed to prepare. But he couldn't pull himself away just yet.

He reached over and picked up a strand of her hair which lay on the pillow beside him. Rolling it between his fingers, he marveled again at how silky it felt. He liked the way the end of it curled around his thumb.

"What are you thinking?"

Her words startled him. He hadn't noticed that she was awake.

"What am *I* thinking?" he asked. "Oh, just mushy stuff. You wouldn't want to hear any of it."

She laid her hand against his chest, and the heat of her touch went through him as he recalled her caresses the night before.

"Were you . . . were you disappointed?" she asked, her blue eyes registering her vulnerability.

He laughed softly. "Disappointed? No, disappointed is definitely *not* the word that comes to mind. Why? Did I act disappointed last night?"

She blushed and shook her head, grinning shyly. "No."

"Then why do you ask?"

"I thought maybe you were expecting something different . . . someone different. I was afraid maybe you thought I was . . . her."

"Her?"

"You know, Elizabeth Knight."

He raised one eyebrow and drew away from her. "My God, you mean you aren't? You're her evil twin or—"

"Oh, stop it. You know what I mean," she said, punching his shoulder.

His smile faded and he reached for her, pulling her tightly against him. "Yes, I do. And that's silly. You *are* Elizabeth Knight."

"But I'm not that woman on the screen. I was afraid you would expect me to be elegant and graceful and worldly like her and—"

"You *were* all those things," he said, "and more to me last night. That woman on the screen *is* you; you dreamed her into being and she's one facet of who you are. But you aren't her. You're so much more than Elizabeth Knight. You're Liz, the young woman who worked her way through school by serving Guinness in an Irish pub. You're Elizabeth the wonderfully creative writer, whose work entertains millions every week."

He leaned down and kissed her lightly on the cheek. "And you're my Lizzie, a delightful child who loves Barbie dolls and makes great angels in the snow . . . and, most importantly . . . who appreciates the beauty of a bulldog."

She ducked her head and pressed her face against his chest. Obviously, she was embarrassed, but pleased, and that was all that mattered to him. Remarkably, it seemed that no one had told her these things about herself before, and it was high time someone did. Nick was enormously grateful that he could be the one.

"I . . . ah . . . hate to have to be practical at a moment like this," he said, stroking her shoulder. "But I was wondering—are you going into the city today?"

She rolled onto her back and stared up at the ceiling. "Yes, I have some ends to tie up at the studio. I guess it's back to the 'real' world, huh?"

"I'm afraid so. Why don't we go together?"

"Are you doing this so that you can keep an eye on me?"

"Me? Naw, not a chance. I just thought maybe I could talk you into buying me one of those fantastic bagels in the Y.B.S. cafeteria."

She sighed wearily. "And I suppose you'll want cream cheese on it, too, even though that costs extra." She climbed out of bed and slipped into an emerald satin robe.

"Lox cream cheese," he said.

"Men! And I thought you were only after my delectable body. But it's my money, lox, and bagels, that you want. I should have—"

Her words were ripped away by an explosion that rocked the house like a seven point earthquake. She was thrown back onto the bed. Above the ear-ringing roar of the blast, he heard her scream.

"Holy shit!" he yelled as he jumped out of bed and ran to the window. "What the hell was that?"

From the back of the house he saw billows of dust and debris still falling. The rear section of the veranda was lying strewn across the back yard.

He ran back to the bed and grabbed Elizabeth, running his hands over her to check for injuries.

"I'm okay," she said breathlessly. "Are you?"

"Yeah, I'm fine."

"What happened?"

"Well, I think we'd better consider getting out of here. Either you just had a gas explosion or . . ."

He didn't want to say it. God knows, she had enough to worry about already. But he knew it wasn't a gas leak.

"Or what?" she asked.

"Or a bomb just took off the back of your house."

Twenty-two

"We can be thankful for one thing . . . the guy was a lousy bomb builder," Nick told the members of the Mirror Killer task force who sat around the long table, holding coffee mugs and photos of what had—until recently—been Elizabeth Knight's rear veranda. "In shot number six, you can see the other two sticks of dynamite that didn't detonate. They were found where you see them there, on top of the garage."

Fred Halley picked up his copy of the arson squad's preliminary report and shook his head. "The guy has no imagination either," he said. "Plain old demolition site dynamite and a wind-up clock. You can't get much more basic than that."

"Apparently he doesn't have a connection to any well-organized terrorist groups," Ray said, "or he could have put his hands on some good plastics and done the job right."

Nick turned to Stephanie. "How does this compare with the clinic bombings that our favorite reverend was suspected of in Florida?"

Stephanie thumbed through her notebook, which was tidy, but not so colorful as Ray's. Pulling out a sheet of paper, she read, "Dynamite, electrical sparking device wired to cheap wristwatch, placed beneath building. Three sticks used, only two detonated."

"Practice doesn't always make perfect," Fred said with a toothpick smirk. "Clue number one, boys and girls—Our guy's not a quick study."

"Was Ms. Knight hurt?" Ray asked.

"No, she's all right," Nick said, being careful not to look at Stephanie. "She's a bit shaken up and more than a little pissed, but she'll be okay. They've already started the repairs on her house."

"She doesn't intend to keep living there, does she?" Stephanie asked.

"Yes, I believe she does. She's determined that this guy isn't going to disrupt her life any more than he already has."

"Then we'll have to keep a close eye on her and make sure she stays out of trouble," Fred said. "I can handle it if you want, Nick."

"Thanks for the offer, Fred," he replied dryly, "but I've already taken care of it."

"Imagine that," Stephanie muttered into her coffee mug.

Nick decided to ignore the comment. He looked down at his notes. "So, I'm in the process of getting a search warrant for the reverend's house. I'd like you to come along with me, Fred. We'll be looking for the usual: tools that match the markings on the evidence we found still intact, copper wire, twine, the kind of brown butcher paper that he had wrapped everything in. Stuff like that."

Folding up his notes and shoving them into his backpack, Nick said, "Taggerty has been a secondary suspect all along. If it's him, maybe we can nail him today. Then we can all resume our normal lives—you know, the simple things like eating, sleeping, taking long showers."

As they were beginning to file out of the room, Stephanie said in a weary tone, "Even if Reverend Taggerty did set that bomb, it doesn't necessarily prove that he's our Mirror Killer."

Nick silently cursed her for speaking the words that had been nagging at him from the corner of his brain where he had shoved them. "Thanks, Steph," he said. *"That"* is why you've never been elected head cheerleader."

When Nick returned to his office, he found Pete waiting for him. He looked like hell. His face was an odd shade of gray, the only color being the bright crimson on the end of his nose. His eyes were equally irritated and red. He was sniffling into one of his monogrammed kerchiefs.

"I thought you'd be at the meeting," Nick said as he walked to his desk and sat down. He busied himself with shuffling the papers on his desk so that he wouldn't have to look at him. "It isn't like you to miss a golden opportunity like that."

"I'm sick; can't you see that?" Pete said, dabbing at his eyes. "I've contacted a malignant sinus infection that is making my life wretched."

"You mean you've got a cold?"

"Well, yes . . . only worse than that."

Nick gathered up a collection of the papers which had been distributed at the briefing and shoved them at him. "Here you go . . . homework. I want the pictures back, so don't get snot on them."

Pete snatched them out of his hand and tossed them into his briefcase. "Thanks," he said, as he stood and headed for the door.

Nick watched him, a puzzled and suspicious look on his face. "Hey, buddy," he said.

Pete turned around. "What?"

Nick hesitated for a second, then decided to go ahead and step in it. "That *is* just a cold you've got, right?"

Pete's red eyes turned redder, along with the rest of his face. "What are you saying, O'Connor?"

"You've had that cold and the runny nose for most of the fall and winter now."

"Yeah . . . so?"

"If I didn't know better, I'd think you'd been burying your snout in the blow."

The startled look on Pete's face confirmed Nick's worst suspicions. Damn, he had been hoping he was wrong.

"Then it's a good thing that you know better, huh?" Pete said, recovering his composure. But Nick could see the muscles in his jaws twitching as he fought to control his anger.

"Be careful, buddy," Nick said softly. "That stuff will get you in the end. You know it."

Without another word or a backward glance, Pete jerked the door open and marched out of the office, slamming it behind him.

Nick sat, stunned by his own revelation. Pete? Old "Climb Every Mountain, Follow Every Rule in the Book Until You Find Your Dream" Peter J. MacDonald?

Suddenly it made sense. The pallor, the hyperactivity followed by periods of lethargy, the paranoia, and the cold that wouldn't go away.

Well, he didn't care what happened to Peter MacDonald, not anymore. Pete had seen what cocaine could do to a person. He had witnessed its devastation over and over again on the streets, so he had no excuse. If he was stupid enough to shove that shit up his nose—and under his eyelids, judging from the redness— then he deserved whatever was coming to him.

Of course you don't care, said a sarcastic voice inside as Nick gathered up his pack and his coat to leave. *You don't care at all. That's why you feel like you're about to puke.*

Well, it ain't because of you, Peter ol' boy, he silently told his friend as he pulled on his jacket and took his keys from the pocket. *It's the burrito I had for lunch, so don't flatter yourself. It sure ain't because I give a tinker's damn about you anymore.*

As Elizabeth sat at her dining room table and sipped her cappuccino, she thought, not for the first time, how blessed she was to have a friend like Cassandra. She had teasingly accused Cassie of coming over to her house just for the cappuccino, but Cass had insisted it was the stimulating conversation, not the refreshments.

Today, Elizabeth knew very well why Cass was here; it was to offer comfort and support. God bless her.

"You didn't need to cut your vacation short and fly back here like that," Elizabeth told her.

"No problem. I'd enjoyed my relatives about as much as I could stand. It's good to be back. Besides, it isn't every day my best friend gets her back porch blown to kingdom come."

"It could have been worse," Elizabeth said, pulling her robe more tightly around her. Just the thought of what might have happened gave her icy shivers that no amount of warm chenille or hot cappuccino could thaw. "The arson squad detective said the guy had intended to blow up the whole house. If the bomb had worked properly and if he'd placed it a little further under the house, we would be 'red mist' as the detective not so delicately put it."

"We?"

Damn. Cassie never missed a thing. Elizabeth hadn't intended to tell her about her night with Nick. She wasn't emotionally prepared for the teasing that was inevitable.

"We?" Cass repeated, leaning across the table and wearing the alert expression of a hound dog that has just detected an interesting scent. "I assume you mean—you and the cat."

"Ah . . . yeah. Me and Katie, that's what I meant. Yep, you got it." She buried her face and her telltale grin in her mug.

"You're lying to me, babycakes," Cassie said. "I can always tell when you're—"

"I'm not exactly lying; I'm just withholding information that might tend to incriminate me."

"My God! He spent the night. You slept with that gorgeous cop! I knew it! I knew you looked different—in spite of your porch, you look more . . . relaxed, more . . . fulfilled. Elizabeth, you got laid! I'm so happy for you!"

"Good grief, Cassie, why don't you just tell the whole world while you're at it? There might be somebody on the block who didn't hear you."

"I told you he'd be good. You can tell just by looking at some guys, and the minute I saw him, I thought—"

"Cass, please. It was more than that. He's a wonderful, skilled lover, but it wasn't just . . . good. It was really special. *He's* really special."

Cassandra sat back in her chair and the teasing, lascivious look left her eyes. "My goodness, Liz," she said solemnly. "You didn't get laid; honey, you made love. No wonder you don't want to talk about it."

"At first it was scary. But then he kissed me, and the rest was so natural."

"Scary? You've got a serial killer after you, your house was bombed, and you call that scary?"

Elizabeth nodded.

"Wow, you *must* be in love." Cassandra reached across the table and took Elizabeth's hand. "I'm happy for you, honey. Really happy. Do you think he's in love, too?"

Elizabeth allowed herself to drift back for a moment, remembering the way he had looked down at her and gently brushed the hair away from her face. Several times during the night, she had seen her own feelings mirrored in his eyes. "Yes, I think so," she said.

"And after he's caught the killer and the case is over, do you think you'll still be seeing him?"

"One step at a time," she said with a smile. "One step at a time."

Cassie stood and took her cup to the kitchen sink where she rinsed it and hung it on the rack. "I need to get going," she said. "Are you sure you won't come home with me? I don't like the idea of you staying here alone after what happened."

"I'm sure," she said. "I'm more mad than scared right now. I'll be damned if I'll let him chase me out of my own home. He's invaded my life enough already. I have to draw a line somewhere. Besides, Nick has posted a guard outside the house, and he'll be spending the nights with me . . . I think."

"Hm-m-m, a good sign." She walked over to the table and picked up her purse. "Okay, then I'm going to give you something. Or maybe I should say *loan* because it isn't mine and its owner doesn't know I've got it."

She reached into her purse and pulled out a tiny pistol. It was beautiful, an antique, with a pearl handle and French filigree. She dropped it into Elizabeth's hand.

"A gun?" Elizabeth promptly laid it on the table. "Cassie, where did you get a gun?"

"Brody's cabinet."

"Brody's! Good heavens, you take that back this minute!"

"No way. He's got a zillion. He'll never miss it. Here . . ." She reached into her purse again. ". . . I brought you a bunch of bullets, too. It's a dueling pistol and it only holds two shots, so you'd better get in some target practice."

"You're crazy. I don't want a gun. I don't even know how to use one."

"I didn't figure you did, you bleeding heart, California liberal. But, lucky for you, I do. In fact, I can shoot the right eye out of a squirrel at sixty feet."

Elizabeth gave her a long, scrutinizing look. "You're full of it, Cass. As soft hearted as you are, you've never shot a squirrel in your life."

"All right, that's true. But I'm hell on soup cans. I can get the Campbell kids every time."

Elizabeth looked down at the gun and wondered. In the past few weeks, she had entertained a plethora of homicidal fantasies. But if it really came down to it, could she kill another human being, even in self defense?

She thought of the bomb planted under her porch, of how it could have killed her, or Nick, or even Katie or Hercules.

She had done nothing to warrant this sick individual's hatred, and yet, he wanted to turn her and those she loved into "red mist."

Slowly, she picked up the gun and tested how it felt in her palm. Cold, impersonal . . . powerful.

The momentary sense of power felt better than she wanted it to. Much better.

"Okay?" Cass asked.

Elizabeth nodded and, by doing so, felt the last vestige of her innocence die. "Okay," she said.

* * *

When Nick and Fred pulled into the herringbone brick drive-way that led to the antebellum plantation-style mansion, Nick double checked his notebook to make certain of the address. Yes, this was it . . . 35 Thornbury Drive.

"Looks like you and I are in the wrong line of work, buddy," Nick said as they approached the sprawling edifice with its towering white pillars and lacy wrought iron balconies.

"Yeah, have you ever 'heard the call' to go into the service of the Lord?" Fred asked, sucking furiously on his toothpick.

"I think I'm hearing it now. Either that, or it's the theme from *Gone With the Wind* playing in my head."

They parked the Jeep and walked up onto the enormous porch which was lined with white wrought iron tables and chairs which matched the metal work on the house. Ornate stained glass side-lights flanked the double doors. Nick grabbed the heavy brass knocker and pounded several times.

"Seriously," Fred said, "these guys really burn my butt. They give the honest, sincere ministers a bad name. The preacher in the little Baptist church were I grew up . . . he was as humble as you please. He'd give his last dollar to anyone in need."

"Yeah, well, what goes around comes around, as they say," Nick said, knocking again. "And if we find what we're looking for here, the reverend is going to reap some of that divine retribution he keeps talking about."

"Amen."

The door swung open and a small woman in traditional black and white maid's garb offered them a broad smile. "Good morning, gentlemen. How may I help you?"

Nick pulled out his badge and held it up for her inspection. "I'm Detective Nicholas O'Connor and this is Detective Fred Halley. We'd like to speak to Reverend Taggerty."

The brilliance of her smile dimmed a bit, and she took a step backward. "The reverend isn't home right now," she said. "I'm expecting him any minute. Would you like to speak to his son, Christopher?"

"Yes, thank you," Nick replied. As she scurried away down the black and white tiled foyer, he turned to Fred. "Do you suppose we'll be invited in for a mint julep?"

"I doubt it. Besides, right now I'd rather have a cigar and brandy in the parlor."

"You gonna light that cigar . . . and *smoke* it?" Nick asked with a grin.

"No, I was just going to roll it on my thighs and sniff it, asshole."

"You know, Fred, since we made this little wager, I've come to realize that you have a very wide competitive streak in your character."

"I do not."

"Do, too."

"Do not."

Nick decided to give him this round, rather than be caught doing the, "Do not—to infinity," routine like a couple of kids while serving a search warrant. It didn't matter, he was going to win the big smoke out, anyway.

Christopher Taggerty appeared at the door, looking as gaunt and peaked as Nick had seen him on the picket line. He was one of those guys who looked old for his years, as though the life had been drained out of him, and maybe he hadn't started with much to begin with. Unfortunately, Christopher hadn't inherited his father's ruddy complexion, triple thick pompadour, or forceful personality. But, on the other hand, he would probably inherit this mansion and the Bentley sitting in the driveway, so, Nick decided, the guy hadn't exactly struck out in all innings.

"Good morning, detectives," Taggerty said. "I understand you're here to see my father."

"That's right," Nick replied.

"May I ask what this is regarding?"

Nick hesitated, then decided to go ahead and tell him so that he could gauge his reaction. "The Dark Mirror killings."

Christopher looked only mildly surprised. "An awful thing," he said, shaking his head. "I'm sure my father would want to help you in any way he could. Unfortunately, he isn't here right now. Would you like to come in and wait?"

Nick reached into his pocket and pulled out the warrant. "Actually, we didn't come here to talk to the reverend. At least, not initially. We have a warrant here to search the premises."

This time Christopher registered unmistakable shock. His mouth dropped open and his eyes widened as he peered at the document in Nick's hand. "A search warrant? But why? You can't think that my father would have anything to do with something like that!"

"Let's just say we're investigating all possibilities," Nick said.

"But this *isn't* a possibility. My father would never, *never* hurt anyone, let alone go around killing innocent people. I mean, he's a little outspoken sometimes, and he isn't always very diplomatic, but he's a good man."

"I'm sure he is," Nick said evenly. "And the sooner we do our job here, the sooner we'll all be certain of that."

Christopher opened and closed his mouth several times, like a landed perch, then said, "Yes, of course. Come on in, officers."

He stepped back and beckoned them inside.

"Thank you," Nick said.

"Yeah, thanks," Fred echoed, wiping his muddy sneakers carefully on the welcome mat before entering.

"If I knew what you were looking for," Christopher said, twisting his hands in front of him, "maybe I could help you find it."

"Oh, that's all right," Nick said. "I'm sure we'll find everything we need."

As Nick and Fred descended the steep staircase into the basement, it became increasingly clear that the reverend hadn't intended his cellar to be open for viewing by his guests. The opulence ended abruptly at the door and the atmosphere became more oppressive with every downward step.

The place was dimly lit with a few sickly yellow fluorescent bulbs that flickered and sputtered, giving the room an eery, strobe effect. Battered, Mediterranean-style furniture from the "gold and avocado green crushed velvet era" was stacked haphazardly against the unpainted walls, which were stained with rusty water marks.

Miscellaneous boxes were stacked to the ceiling against the far wall. They had been there so long that the bottom ones were caving in on the top and bulging at the sides.

Nick looked around for the obligatory dart board, ping pong table, or shuffleboard lines on the floor which would signal that this had once been enjoyed as a recreational space. But the room was void of amusements.

"Any minute now . . . ," he told Fred, ". . . we're going to see a giant pendulum come swinging down from the ceiling. Be prepared to duck."

"No kidding," Fred agreed, looking over his shoulder. "There's no telling what we'll uncover down here. Hell, we might even find Jimmy Hoffa."

Nick laughed, then sobered as he peered behind a small mountain of shag carpet scraps and around a stack of light fixtures made of red plastic and wrought iron. "Never mind Hoffa," he said. "Right now, I'd just settle for a skeleton or two from Taggerty's proverbial closet."

"You really think it's him?"

"One can only hope. Some busts I enjoy making a lot more than others. This one . . ." He smiled to himself. "This one would be *extremely* satisfying."

Fred disappeared for a moment behind some crates, then he said, "Hey, we got a door over here." Nick heard it squeak open. "Hey, we got a *workroom* in here."

"A la-*bor*-a-toory?" Nick asked.

"Everything but the boiling beakers and lightning rods."

Nick picked his way between the leaning towers of crates and entered the small room which was little more than an oversized closet. "Looks like the reverend or Christopher does the 'handyman' bit," he said, pointing to the workbench, which was strewn with assorted tools, wire, and tape.

"I'll bet he's not very good at it," Fred commented, perusing the table and its contents. "This is pretty run-of-the-mill stuff."

"And no self-respecting handyman would leave his bench in a mess like this. My highschool shop teacher would have definitely flunked him."

Nick reached into his pocket and pulled out a photocopy of the bomb squad detective's report. "Okay," he said, looking at the crude drawing in the lower right corner of the paper. "We're looking for a pair of pliers that have a distinctive gouge out of one of the jaws."

"Pliers . . ." Fred examined the pile on the table without touching anything. "We have a claw hammer, several screw drivers, wire cutters, copper wire—"

"Copper wire?" Nick perked up. "Copper wire is good, very good," he said, looking at the report.

"A soldering gun, a watch band—"

"Just the band?"

"Yep. Black leather. It looks like new."

"I'll bet it is." Nick's smile grew broader. "The sun is breaking through the clouds, Fred, my man. Now if we can only find those . . ."

He squatted and searched the floor, which was littered with bits of wire, splats of solder, crumpled candy wrappers, and several decades of filth.

"Bingo," he said, as he retrieved a surgical glove from his inside jacket pocket and pulled it over his right hand. Leaning over, he lifted something from a pile of dust in the corner.

Fred produced a flashlight and pointed the beam at the pliers as Nick opened them wide.

This was it, the part Nick loved . . . the moment when it came together. Adrenalin surged through his bloodstream as he held the tool under Fred's light and searched for what he instinctively knew was there.

A serration in the metal, a diagonal scoring across the gripping treads on the inside jaws. The scar had left its reverse image on the copper piping which they had found at the scene.

"We've got him," Nick said with an almost reverent whisper. He looked up and saw the same elation he was feeling, registered on Fred's homely face. "That lousy son of a bitch . . . we've got him!"

They heard a scraping sound and turned around to see Christopher Taggerty watching them, his pale face three shades lighter. He looked down at the pliers in Nick's gloved hand.

"What do you mean?" he said in a shaking voice. "What's going on here?"

"A bomb exploded under Elizabeth Knight's house earlier this morning," Nick said, watching his expression carefully. He saw an unmistakable quantity of genuine shock, mixed with sadness.

"No . . . no . . . ," Christopher said, shaking his head. He wiped his hand across his eyes and stumbled backwards a few steps before recovering himself. "This is all my fault. Oh, God. Is she dead? Did he kill her?"

"She's alive," Nick said.

Christopher closed his eyes and moved his lips in a brief prayer of thanks.

"Why did you say it was your fault?" Nick asked quietly.

"My dad has been really upset about the situation—the show, the killings—and he said he was going to do something about it. But I had no idea he would actually try to hurt Ms. Knight. If I'd known, I would have found a way to stop him."

Nick glanced at Fred, who raised one eyebrow slightly. The guy hadn't even given them a chance to accuse his father of anything. This sort of thing happened frequently when he questioned people. They were like emotional reservoirs, full and ready to burst their dams with little or no encouragement. Sometimes they just had to spew.

"I have a lot of respect for Ms. Knight," Christopher continued, his voice shaking. "I don't agree with what they put on her show, but I think she's a really special lady, and I would never have let my dad hurt her."

Nick's eyes locked with the young man's as he evaluated his words and the truthfulness behind them. As a cop, Nick was lied to ten times a day and twice as often on Sunday. He always got a particular gut reaction when someone was jerking him around.

He walked over and laid a hand on the young man's shoulder. "I believe you," Nick said, "if that makes you feel any better."

"Thanks." He seemed genuinely relieved. It always amazed Nick how much stock people placed in a total stranger's opinion of them. "And my dad," he said, "he's not really a bad person. I'm sure he thought he was doing the right thing."

Nick chuckled and shook his head. "Sorry," he said, "that one, I *don't* buy."

Twenty-three

"Wait just a minute, Brody!" Elizabeth called across the empty set. "I have to talk to you!" Someone had left an outside door open in the studio and a cold wind whistled around the sets, rattling lights over her head as she hurried up a half flight of stairs to one of the control rooms. She shivered inside her Mets jacket; it was definitely time to open the cedar chest at home and take out the more substantial winter apparel.

But she knew, even as she made the mental note, that the brisk wind wasn't the reason she felt cold. The news she had just heard in the hall outside post-production had been far more chilling than the weather.

She could see the top of Brody's cowboy hat through the tinted window across the front of the booth, and she could also see that he was starting to head out the back way to avoid her.

"No, you don't!" she shouted. "You stay right there! We have to talk, now!"

Run away from me, will you? she thought. It wouldn't help him. She was prepared to chase him to hell and back if that's what it took.

She burst through the door and entered the small room with its blinking panels, digital readouts, multi-screens and control boards that stretched from one wall to the other. Brody stood at the door opposite the one she had entered, his hand on the knob, and a perturbed frown on his face.

"I'm on my way out, sugar," he said with a nonchalant drawl

:hat didn't match his scowl. "Sorry, but I don't have time right
now. I'll make it up to you later, promise."

She stomped over to him and braced her arm against the door,
preventing him from leaving. "Brody, if you air that adultery
episode tomorrow night . . . ," she said, dispensing with the over-
ure, ". . . I swear I'll sue your ass off."

His frown turned to something much darker as he stared down
at her, his eyes narrowed and his lips tightened. She could see a
muscle in his right cheek twitch. It occurred to her that he could
certainly turn ugly in an instant.

"Is that right, Miss Priss?" he said. "And what legal grounds
are you going to use to sue me for airing a show that *I* produced,
on a network that *I* still own?"

"I don't know. But I'll spend whatever I have to and hire a
topnotch lawyer who *will* know what legal grounds."

"You'd spend the money that *I* gave you to sue me? You un-
grateful little bitch."

"You *gave* me?" She shook her head and smiled bitterly.
"You've never given anyone anything in your life, Yarborough.
I earned every cent your company ever paid me . . . the hard
way . . . by putting up with you week after week."

He moved closer to her and she could smell the odor of alcohol
on his breath. Lately, he always smelled like booze. Strange that
his success seemed to be taking an unexpected toll on him. "Listen to me, you little over-priced, over-rated piece of ass. I gave
you your start in this business, an opportunity other girls would
have given anything for. *Anything* . . . ," he added with a leisurely
perusal of her chest. "You owe me, sugar."

"And *I* gave *you* your first hit series," she said. " 'The Dark
Mirror'—my creation—put your floundering network on the
map. That's a substantial return on your investment in me, many
times over. So, the way I see it, we're even. I don't owe you
squat."

They stood, glaring at each other, the only sound that of their
accelerated breathing. Elizabeth could taste the bitterness of her
own fear and anger. Her mouth was so dry she could hardly

speak. Yarborough was a formidable enemy, to be sure, but too
much was at stake. She couldn't afford the luxury of backing
down now.

"Brody, don't air that episode. I know I can't stop you; it's
already in the can and all you've got to do is roll it. But if you
do, someone, somewhere will die. Don't do it, please."

Shoving her anger down for a moment, she had softened her
tone, hoping to appeal to his gentler, more humane side. She had
forgotten that he didn't have one.

"Look," he said, "it's not like *I'm* the one killing these people.
Some nut's doing it, and I can't help that. I happen to believe in
freedom of speech, and I'm not going to let some bleeding heart
liberals tell me to censor my programming just to suit them. It
just ain't the American way," he added, resuming his lazy drawl.

"Bull shit! You don't care about freedom of speech or oppos-
ing censorship. The truth is, you're willing to let an innocent
person be murdered so that you'll rake in your advertising reve-
nue."

She paused, breathless from her outburst, expecting him to
deny her accusation. But he didn't. Instead, he grinned down at
her.

"Innocent person?" he said mockingly. "This episode is about
a woman who gets killed because she's foolin' around with another woman's husband. If the murderer stays true to form, he'll
knock off some slut somewhere . . . so, what's the problem?" He
pushed her aside and yanked the door open. "Hell, any broad
who's screwin' around deserves what she gets, right?"

As she watched him walk through the door, her anger flared.
How could anyone be so callous? How could she have ever entered into a partnership with this man?

"Brody," she said, following him out of the booth and down
the steps to the main floor. "I mean it. If you go through with
this, I'll make your life a living hell, I swear I will."

Whirling around, he grabbed her arm and twisted it so hard
that she cried out. "I told you," he said, "don't threaten me!"

won't take that off another man, and I certainly won't take it from a broad. Got me?"

He squeezed even harder, until she was afraid he would break her wrist. Sharp pains shot up her arm and into her shoulder as he yanked her toward him.

"Let go of me," she said, matching his tone. Instead, he dug his fingertips deeper into her flesh. She could feel a warm trickle of her own blood running down her arm as his nails pierced her skin. "I mean it, Brody. Let go!"

From the corner of her eye, Elizabeth saw a movement at the edge of the stage. A second later, Bud appeared from behind some props. "Are you all right, Ms. Knight?" he asked quietly, without looking at Yarborough.

"Yes, I'm fine," she lied. "Thank you, Bud. I was just saying goodbye to Mr. Yarborough, then I'm on my way out."

She turned back to Brody and fixed him with her best dead-level stare. "Goodbye, Mr. Yarborough," she said pointedly.

He squeezed even harder for a moment, then flung her arm away from him and marched across the stage, the thudding of his boot heels echoing from wall to wall of the enormous room.

Bud hurried over to her and gently lifted her arm to examine it. Her wrist was already beginning to swell and turn blue. Four red, bloody crescents marked where his nails had dug into her skin.

"He *did* hurt you," he said, cradling her wrist in his rough and calloused hands. "I ought to go after him and stomp a mud hole in his hide."

Elizabeth laughed softly. "Oh, Bud, listen to you. You've been hanging out with Cass too long. Next thing I know, you'll be telling me that you're going to kick bohunkus."

"Yep, Cassie has corrupted me," he said, nodding his head. "That's for sure." His eyes gleamed with affection as he spoke Cass's name, and the thought crossed Elizabeth's mind for the first time that maybe their relationship was more than just a casual affair for Bud. Maybe he really did care for Cass. Maybe he even loved her.

"Come on," he said, taking her hand. "I'll smear some antibiotic ointment on that for you. And, considering it was Brody, I'll slap on some rattlesnake anti-venom, too."

"Exactly what have you got?" Ryerson asked. He stood with his nose all but pressed against the glass of his window which gave him an overview of the station from his office. From here he had a front row seat to watch the large and small dramas being played out in his domain.

More than once, Nick had thought that Captain Bob Ryerson would have been a lot happier if he hadn't been bumped up that political ladder. Nick could see a longing in Ryerson's eyes as he watched his people jostling elbows with the community's most colorful citizenry.

Not that it was particularly pleasant, being on the street, but Nick could see how a guy would miss it if he were stuck behind a desk.

Nick reached into his backpack and pulled out some papers. "The arson lab went through his cellar workroom a couple of hours ago. They have positive matches on several items: the copper wire, electricians' tape, traces of powder, and best of all, the pliers he used for crimping. They're scarred and make a distinctive pattern."

"Good," Ryerson said, nodding thoughtfully. "Very good." He turned away from the window and walked back to his desk. Nick could see his mental wheels turning. "And where is Reverend Taggerty right now?"

Glancing down at his watch, Nick said, "For the next hour and fifteen minutes he'll be preaching at his Divine Light Tabernacle downtown. Stephanie's been watching him for us. She's one of his faithful followers."

Ryerson lit a cigarette and blew the smoke in Nick's direction. "You stuck Steph on that? She's right, you guys *are* pigs."

"Hey, she looked a lot more like a Sunday schoolteacher than Fred."

"True."

"I sent a couple of guys over to 'mingle' with the flock, just in case he gets tipped off and tries to run."

Leaning back in his chair, Ryerson sighed and shook his head. "Taggerty wouldn't run. He's not the type."

"What do you mean?"

"We can bust him, we can even put him away for a while . . . but in the end, he'll win."

Nick was confused, but he didn't argue. Experience had shown him that Ryerson had a sixth sense about people. It usually went down exactly the way he had called it.

"How do you figure?" Nick asked.

"We'll arrest him for the two-bit punk he is, but he's a smarter than average punk. By now his people will have told him that you've been to his house and what you found. He's already figured out how he's going to play it. You wait and see, we'll be doin' the guy a favor. By the end of today he won't just be a loud-mouthed, controversial preacher with a fanatical following. Thanks to us, he'll be a martyred saint."

With far more care than usual, Elizabeth laid her purse on her dining room table, acutely aware of its unnatural and disturbing heaviness. *Strange how a little gun and a box of bullets can weigh you down,* she thought, *in more ways than one.* She couldn't remember when she felt this low.

Yes, you do, she reminded herself. *Feeling helpless is a lot worse than this.*

If she were honest with herself, she had to admit that the thought of killing another human being—as revolting as that might be—was preferable to the idea of being murdered, or standing by impotently while someone she loved was killed.

Maybe she wasn't as highly evolved as she had thought . . . as she had hoped. Now that push had come to shove, she had to admit she simply wasn't that altruistic. At a time like this, it seemed that idealism flew the coop and gut-level survival instincts took over.

"You were a pretty good shot, kid," Cass said. "Much better than I'd expected."

Elizabeth turned around and saw Cassie watching her from the kitchen door. The worried look on her face didn't match her complimentary words.

"Yeah, wasn't I though," Elizabeth replied dryly. "A real Annie Hickok."

Cassie grimaced. "I think you'd better bone up on your Western history, California girl."

Elizabeth shrugged and walked past her into the kitchen. "Almond tea and chocolate-mint cookies?"

"Sure."

Elizabeth set the copper kettle on the stove and turned the flame on under it. "If I'm such a great shot, why do you look so worried?" she said.

Cass hesitated, as though deciding whether to answer her honestly.

"Out with it," Elizabeth said.

"Okay, I am a little worried," Cass admitted as she opened the cupboard and took out a box of their favorite cookies. "My daddy was the one who taught me to shoot when I was a kid. Took me out in the woods and had me shoot at a piece of paper tacked to a tree, just like I showed you today."

"Yes . . . and . . . ?"

"But the most important lesson he taught me that day wasn't how to load, or aim, or how to keep from blowing my foot off. It was something else. He told me this and I'll never forget it: He said, 'Cassandra, don't you *ever, ever* pull a gun on somebody, unless you fully intend to use it. Because, if you do, you've just decided how you're going to die. You've handed them the weapon that's going to kill you. Looking down the barrel of a gun makes a guy mighty mad, and if he wasn't intending to kill you before you pulled it on him, he sure will afterwards.' "

"So, as Donahue would say, 'What's your point, caller?' "

Elizabeth said, refusing to look Cass in the eye as she poured water into the tea pot.

"When the chips are down, I'm afraid you won't be able to do it."

Elizabeth bristled, mostly because it angered her to hear her own concerns voiced by someone else. "Do you think I'm a coward?" she snapped. "Are you saying I'm too big a chicken-shit to pull the trigger and take a bad guy out?"

Expecting Cass to retaliate in anger, she was surprised when Cass walked over to her and put her arms around her, hugging her tightly. "No, sweetie. I don't think you're a coward. Far from it. I think you're the bravest person I've ever known. It's just that you and I are different. Me, I'm just a shit-kicker from Texas. I'd blow his balls off and go right out and eat a fried oyster dinner, 'cause I'd figure he had it coming. Wouldn't bother me a bit. But you're better than me. And I'm afraid that you're too good to kill, even if your own life was in danger."

Elizabeth returned her hug, burying her face on Cass's shoulder. She breathed in the familiar comforting smells that she always associated with Cassie: tobacco smoke, musk perfume, and an underlying hint of Jack Daniels.

"I love you, Cass," she said, realizing that she had never actually said the words. It was high time. "I really do. You've been a good friend to me."

"Aw, pooh," Cass said as she gently pushed her away. "Don't go getting gushy on me now."

Elizabeth smiled. This was the first time she could ever remember seeing Cassie blush. Then Elizabeth's smile faded and she shook her head. "I think you have too high an opinion of me, Cass," she said. "I think I've answered my own question . . . the one I asked every week on 'The Dark Mirror.' What does a normal person do when confronted with abnormal circumstances? The answer is pretty simple, after all. They do whatever they have to do to survive."

* * *

When Nick and Fred stepped inside the Divine Light Tabernacle, Nick thought he had walked into a Las Vegas casino. From the plush red carpeting to the huge crystal chandeliers and stained glass windows, the building was a living testimony to Reverend Taggerty's knack for turning a buck.

The foyer was empty, but they could hear the echo of a fiery sermon which was being delivered just beyond the three sets of oak and inlaid ebony doors that lined the other side of the ornate lobby.

"Can you believe this?" Nick asked Fred, who stood beside him, looking just as amazed. "A more appropriate name might be the Church of the Presumptuous Assumption."

"No kidding. What bothers me is that there are old ladies eating dog food, so they can give ten percent of their welfare check to 'the Lord's work.' They hand it over to Taggerty and he spends it like this."

"Yeah," Nick said. "The Baptist church around the corner from our house can't afford an elaborate sanctuary, but when my dad was killed, they brought us food, helped with his burial costs and offered to pay my mom's rent for six months until she got on her feet. And we didn't even belong to their congregation."

"Well . . . cops, teachers, preachers . . . there's good ones and bad ones in every bunch, huh?"

"Seems so."

"What's next?" Fred asked. "You wanna just go in and get him now?"

"No way. We aren't going to let him make a production out of this. He'll turn it into a media circus if we let him. We can wait until he's finished and leaves the sanctuary. Then we'll take him."

Nick heard a slight sound behind him and turned to see Christopher Taggerty standing there, a sick look on his pale face. He crossed his arms over his chest, sticking his hands in his armpits as though warming them.

"I . . . ah . . . I'm sorry, detectives," he stammered. "But, you know, he's my dad. I had to come over here and warn him."

Nick didn't reply; he just stood quietly, watching the misery play across the young man's face.

"He's not going to give you any trouble. He won't try to get away or anything like that," Christopher continued. "But I had to tell him, to prepare him a little."

Nick nodded slightly. "I understand," he said.

"You're not going to go in there now and arrest him in front of his congregation, are you? I mean, even if you think he deserves to be embarrassed like that, the congregation shouldn't have to go through it." Christopher shifted his feet and stared down at the carpet. "They're really good folks, and they think the world of my dad. It would kill them to see him—"

"No," Nick said, holding up one hand to stop his pleading. "We can wait."

Nick glanced over at Fred and could tell by his puzzled expression that he was thinking the same thing—How could a man like Taggerty engender such loyalty in the hearts of so many decent people?

Turning to Fred, Nick said, "Hang around out here for a minute, while I go inside and check it out."

Fred nodded, and Christopher walked slowly across the foyer and out the front door. "Good," Nick said, "he doesn't need to see it either."

Nick chose the pair of doors to his far left and opened one as quietly as possible. He found himself at the back of a cavernous auditorium that was as opulent as the vestibule. In the front of the room, beneath an enormous wooden cross bedecked with lilies, stood Taggerty. He was clothed in a shining white satin robe with a purple sash around his waist.

All eyes were transfixed on him as his authoritative voice boomed from wall to wall. The effect was aided—Nick noticed—by a reverb in the sound system. *Nice touch,* he thought, thinking of Bill Cosby's "Noah" skit.

Nick searched the crowd until he spotted Stephanie. She was sitting only a few rows ahead with some ladies her own age, and she appeared to be as spellbound by the reverend's message as they were.

For a brief moment, she glanced his direction, but she looked away just as quickly, showing no indication that she had seen or recognized him. Stephanie was good, he thought with that familiar feeling of respect tinged with regret.

He took a seat in the back row, intending to listen for a moment and consider the best way to handle the arrest. At first, he didn't think the reverend had noticed him. But then, Taggerty locked eyes with him and changed the entire message and tone of his speech.

"Today . . . ," he said with great gravity, ". . . today is the day when we will be *severely* tested. I have wrestled with the Devil himself. I have done what the Lord commanded me and battled the Prince of Darkness. But the laws of this land, laws made and enforced by those who don't know God . . . they disagree with what I've done. And like the disciples, the saints, and the blessed martyrs before me, I am to be persecuted by Caesar."

A soft rumbling of voices washed through the crowd. One by one, various individuals turned to look at Nick with frightened, hostile eyes.

Damn, he's gonna do it, Nick thought. *He's gonna do it now.*

"I'm to be led away in shackles," Taggerty intoned, lifting his hands to the heavens. "And thrown into a cold, dark prison cell, like Saint Peter. But just as that blessed disciple was delivered from his chains, so shall I be delivered. If the Lord *Himself* has to send an angel to do it . . . *I will be set free!* So, do not lose faith in me or in God, my flock. For this, too, shall pass. Pray for me . . . as I will pray for each and every one of you."

He's good, Nick thought, feeling a sinking weight in his stomach. *I'm definitely out-classed here.*

He turned and saw Fred standing in the doorway, wearing the same sick look that he was sure was on his own face.

"And now . . . ," Taggerty said, holding out his hands in front of him, wrists together, and staring straight at Nick, ". . . I give myself over to you, oh tribune of Rome, to do with as you will."

Nick sat there, feeling like someone had poured lead into his shoes, as every eye in the place turned on him. He glanced at Stephanie and was irritated to see her staring down at her lap, a rather irksome grin on her face. He looked back at Fred, who simply shrugged and lifted one eyebrow.

Nick stood and began to walk down the aisle that looked at least ten miles long. Along with everyone else in the auditorium, Nick felt as though his father were staring at him, gazing down from heaven's portals this very minute. And Nick just knew that retired N.Y.P.D. officer, Ryan O'Connor, was wearing the same grin as Stephanie.

Twenty-four

Nick sat down at his desk and realized for the first time all day how bone-tired he was. Everything ached from his hair to the soles of his feet. But it wasn't anything that a few cups of coffee, a hamburger, and a couple of hours of sleep wouldn't cure.

Besides, it was worth it all just to place this call. He glanced at his watch—two minutes to five. Grimacing from the pain in his lower back, he leaned over and flipped on a small, black and white television that sat on top of his file cabinet. It would probably be the lead story . . . or at least in the top three. God knows, it was sensational enough.

He reached for the phone and dialed her number. It only rang twice before Cassie's twangy voice answered.

"Hi, Cass," he said, "this is Nick O'Connor. Is your boss lady around?"

"She sure is, Detective O'Connor," she replied in a sultry voice that reminded him of hot Southern nights, moonlight, and magnolia blossoms.

He grinned. "Then how's about you let me talk to her?"

"Hang on. . . ."

Nick shook his head and chuckled. Cass could recite the stock market report and make it sound dirty. She was quite a character, the kind he enjoyed.

His pulse quickened as he waited. God, he had it bad. Just the thought of talking to her on the phone got his body juices flowing south. And the thought of being with her last night . . . no, that wasn't something he'd better contemplate right now, because in a couple of minutes he was going to have to walk through the station and—

"Hello, Nick," she said in that famous voice that sounded the way fine cognac tasted.

He made a quick mental note to carry his backpack in front of him on the way out. "Hello, yourself," he replied. Memories of the night before came rolling in like breakers: the warm silkiness of her skin, the feel of her hair on his chest, the soft sounds of pleasure she had made, the way she had . . .

"I've been thinking about you all day," he heard himself say. Damn it, he hadn't intended to wax sentimental. That wasn't why he had called. Why was it he had called? Oh, yes—

"I've got a present for you," he said, glancing at the television. Yes, they were announcing the story.

"I would have thought last night was present enough," she said in a low, intimate tone that made those juices flow even faster. "I don't need anything else, except maybe another night like that one."

"I'm sure that can be arranged, but trust me, you're going to like this present. Turn on your television. Channel seven."

"My television? Why?"

"Just do it and I'll talk to you later. Maybe we could . . . get together . . . later this evening?"

"I'm sure it can be arranged," she said teasingly. "And thanks for the present, whatever it is."

"Oh, you're welcome, Lizzie," he said, unable to keep the softness and affection out of his voice. "You're very welcome."

Later this evening, he mused as he hung up the phone. *Hmm-mm.*

Glancing down at his lap, he groaned. Hell, he'd have to sit here awhile before venturing out in public. For *quite* awhile.

At least until after the weather report. Maybe even the sports.

"What did he say? What did he want?" Cassie exclaimed as she burst into Elizabeth's office. "Does he want to do it again

tonight? Tomorrow night? Saturday? Does he, huh? Don't keep
me in suspense, girl."

"Good grief, Cass. Roll your tongue back into your head before you trip over it." Elizabeth shook her head as she walked
over to a turn of the century Italian armoire and opened the door,
revealing an entertainment center. "He told me to turn on the
television because he has a present for me."

"A present? On T.V.?" Cassie hurried over to a wing backed chair
and plopped down on it. "How intriguing. How ro-m-a-ntic."

Elizabeth laughed as she flipped to the appropriate station.
"You are incorrigible."

"Somebody around here has to be, and since you're not keeping up your end, I guess it has to be me."

A sly smile played across Elizabeth's face. "I did my part last
night. Even *you* would have been proud of me. Wait, here we
go. . . ."

She stood back and stared at the screen, trying to make sense
of the chaos being played out there. A crowd, an *enormous* crowd
of angry and upset people were mobbing a trio of people who
were hurrying down the steps of a large building.

"I recognize that place," Cassie said, leaning forward in her
chair. "That's the Divine Light Tabernacle, that blowhard Taggerty's church."

Elizabeth peered at the three men and identified the snowy
white hair first. "That's him, there in the middle and . . . oh . . .
look!" Her heart pounded against her ribs. "It's Nick!"

"And he's handcuffed!" Cass said. "The reverend, that is, not
Nick."

"Sh-h-h, listen," Elizabeth said, sitting in a chair next to
Cassie's.

The announcer's voice could barely be heard above the crowd's
angry shouts. ". . . Arrested today for the attempted murder of
T.V. personality, Elizabeth Knight. Investigating officers say they
uncovered evidence at Reverend Taggerty's Westchester mansion
which links him to the bombing of Elizabeth Knight's Long Island home this morning. Taggerty was taken into custody during

a worship service here at the Divine Light Tabernacle, and his followers are outraged at what they consider a sacrilegious invasion on the part of the police."

Elizabeth sat, stunned, hearing only half of the remainder of the broadcast. "Reverend Taggerty?" she whispered. "I can't believe it. I mean, he's made no bones about how much he hates my program, but to bomb my house?"

"Well, I believe it," Cass said with a sniff. "I was raised in Sunday School along with the best of 'em, and I know a real stand-up Christian when I see one . . . and *he* ain't one. Never was, for that matter. I could tell he was fishy a mile off, and I didn't need to be downwind of him either."

"He tried to *kill* me . . . and Nick," Elizabeth said, shaking her head, a glazed look in her eyes as she watched the threesome on the screen get into a car and drive away. The crowd roared its disapproval, and even the newscaster appeared uneasy.

"This is Charlene Madrid reporting from the steps of the Divine Light Tabernacle," she said, glancing over her shoulder at a group of women who were crying and screaming at the departing car. "And now, back to our studio."

Elizabeth got up and walked woodenly over to the television. Switching it off, she felt a strange numbness flowing through her mind and body. It hadn't been David Ferguson, after all. It had been someone she had never thought would hurt her. Confront her, condescend to her, and insult her, maybe, but try to murder her?

If Taggerty had been better at bomb construction, she would be dead right now. And so would Nick, and Katie, and Hercules . . . and her house would be a pile of firewood.

He didn't even know her, but he hated her enough to want her dead.

"Why, Cass?" she asked, fighting back the tears that had threatened to fall since she had been jarred by the explosion that morning. "What does he think I've done that would justify him killing me?"

"I don't know if a bastard like that needs any justification, honey," Cass said as she stood and walked over to Elizabeth. "Come on, it's been a rotten day. Let's go have a bite to eat at Donahue's."

Elizabeth allowed herself to be guided from the office and down the hall toward the elevators. One small part of her brain was alert enough to be grateful for Cassie's comforting presence, but the rest was too tired and too numb to think or feel anything.

She didn't know when she had been this exhausted, this completely drained. But maybe . . . just maybe . . . Nick's "gift" to her had put an end to the nightmare.

All she could do was hope.

When Elizabeth and Cassie exited the building onto the street, they found an even larger and more volatile group of protesters. The pickets quickly surrounded them, shouting and pushing from every side.

Accusations flew; clearly the crowd considered Elizabeth personally responsible for their leader's arrest.

"Get away!" Cass shouted, waving her suitcase-sized purse at the nearest ones. "Get away from us or we'll call the cops on you, too!"

"Cassie! Please!" Elizabeth said, laying a restraining hand on her arm. "You're making it worse," she whispered out the side of her mouth. "Stop it."

Suddenly, the crowd quieted and parted to allow someone to pass through their ranks. Elizabeth was somewhat relieved to see that it was Christopher Taggerty.

"I'm sorry, Ms. Knight," he said, as he waved his fellow picketers aside. "They're just really worried about my dad. We all are," he added quietly.

"I'm sure it's very difficult for you," Elizabeth said in a tone that was less than warm. She felt a little sorry for the young man, but his father *had* tried to kill her. "It's a hard time for all of you. And I regret the fact that this happened at all. Believe me, I would have preferred that none of it had occurred. Then your father wouldn't be in jail and the back of my house wouldn't be in shambles."

"I know why he did that," Christopher said, "and I know he thought it was the right thing to do." At Elizabeth's side, Cassie snorted, but she caught the warning look from Elizabeth and said nothing.

"I want you to know," he continued, "that *I* don't believe it was right. I want to apologize to you on his behalf and tell you that I'm really glad you weren't hurt."

Elizabeth felt the tears burning her eyelids again, and she had a desperate need to get away before any of these people could see her crying.

"Thank you, Christopher," she said. "I appreciate what you've said, and I don't hold anything against you personally." She looked out over the mob that was somewhat subdued now, and she saw the pain and devastation in their faces. "I don't have a complaint with any of you. I know that you're good people who believe in what you're doing out here. I, too, am praying that this will be over for us all . . . very soon."

Christopher nodded and seemed both pleased and embarrassed by her words.

Turning to Cass, Elizabeth took her arm and said, "Let's get going. All of a sudden, I'm hungry."

"Me, too," Cassie said, but she wasn't looking at Elizabeth. She had just spotted Bud, who was pushing his way through the crowd toward them. "In fact, I'm famished," Cass added, rolling her eyes in a fair impression of Mae West. "And there's my lover boy, now. I think I might just have dessert first, if you know what I mean. . . ."

Her meaning was all too clear, and Elizabeth cringed at her lack of discretion. This wasn't the first time Cass and Bud had flaunted their affair in public. In fact, it was a regular occurrence. Elizabeth doubted the wisdom of this, considering that almost everyone knew that Bud was married. Every morning his wife dropped him off at work with a quick kiss and a black, industrial-sized lunch pail.

"I guess this means I'm on my own for dinner tonight," Elizabeth mumbled in her ear.

Cass grinned apologetically and shrugged. "Do you mind very much? I'd forgotten that I promised Bud and—"

"No, I don't mind very much," Elizabeth replied, shaking her head. "Never let it be said that I stood in the way of true love."

"Love?" Cassie said as she grabbed Bud and pulled him to her. "I keep telling you, babycakes, this ain't love. Just a red-hot, sizzling case of ol' fashioned lust."

Cass winked at Christopher and a couple of ladies standing next to him. "Ya'll should try it sometime. It would cure what ails ya, guaranteed."

"Bud," Elizabeth said, nudging him, "get her out of here. Now!"

Bud laughed, grabbed Cass around the waist and propelled her back into the building.

So, alone for dinner . . . again, Elizabeth thought as she left the studio and the pickets behind. Then she spotted a pay phone in a cubicle beside the bus stop. *Or, maybe not.*

She deposited some coins, dialed a number and waited, her pulse quickening with every ring.

"O'Connor here," said a curt, brusque voice that sent tendrils of warm desire through her body.

"Knight here," she replied just as gruffly.

"Liz-z-zie." The voice softened considerably. "What a nice surprise."

"For me, too. Thank you for my present."

"It was my pleasure . . . well, sort of. I'll have to tell you all about it."

"When?" she said, shocked at her own eagerness.

"As soon as possible. Maybe sooner," he replied with equal enthusiasm.

She silently blessed him for not leaving her out on a limb, feeling awkward and unrequited.

"Have you had dinner yet?" she asked.

"Nope."

"Donahue's?"

"Twenty minutes?"

"Unless you can make it in fifteen."

"I'll try," he said. She could hear the smile in his voice. "God knows, I'll try."

He made it in ten.

Elizabeth watched as Nick hurried through the door and quickly scanned the room, looking for her. She loved the way his eyes lit up when he spotted her sitting in the corner booth. It was satisfying to know that he was as happy to see her as she was to lay eyes on him after . . . well, it hadn't been that many hours, but . . .

He leaned over and gave her a peck on the cheek before sliding into the opposite seat.

"I have to tell you," he said, "seeing your pretty face, after looking at all those ugly mugs at the station, is a welcome experience."

"Why, thank you, sir," she said in her best Georgian drawl as she batted her lashes at him. "You aren't so bad on the eyes yourself."

She leaned across the table and squeezed his hand, aware that dozens of Donahue's faithful patrons were watching their every move. For once, she didn't give a hoot. Let 'em look.

"Thank you again," she said. "I've never had my own knight in shining armor before. I could get used to this."

"Shining? Armor?" He glanced down at his battered bomber jacket. "I'm not sure I'm dressed for the part."

"No problem," she said, looking him over with a gleam in her eye. "Contrary to popular opinion, the armor doesn't make the knight."

"I'm glad to hear that."

They sat quietly as the momentary exhilaration of seeing each other began to subside and reality reasserted itself.

"Do you really think it was him?" she asked somberly, staring down at the beer in front of her.

"He did it. No doubt about it. We found all the evidence we needed."

"We're talking about the bombing, right."

Nick nodded. "Right."

Elizabeth hesitated, not wanting to ask the question that was echoing in her brain. Somehow, she was afraid that by speaking the words she would bring something terrible into being. But she had to know. She had to ask.

"Is there any reason to think that he's the Mirror Killer? Did you find anything to lead you to believe. . . ?"

He folded her hand inside both of his and gave her a comforting look that went straight to her heart, but it didn't relieve her anxiety.

"We can always hope," he said.

She lowered her voice to a whisper. "But is there any real reason to hope?"

"We'll have to wait and see, Lizzie," he said. "Time will tell."

She glanced down at her watch and over at the television set in the corner of the pub, where "The Dark Mirror" episode was just beginning to air. "Yes," she said wearily, "time will tell."

The killer stood, gazing at his reflection in the mirror, amazed at the transformation. A waist-length, brunette wig, a generous application of makeup, and a dress with the proper amount of padding in all the right places had changed him into a woman—who was at least six months pregnant.

Not bad, he thought as he turned sideways and studied his enlarged belly in the mirror. *Not bad at all.*

For a second or two, it occurred to him that maybe he shouldn't be enjoying this experience, not even a little bit. It wasn't like he was one of those queers who got their kicks dressing up like drag queens. No, he had never doubted *his* masculinity. Not at all. He was just enjoying his own ingenuity, his creativity in putting this outfit together.

And, of course, most of the excitement he was feeling was from the anticipation of what was next. He was going to get to do it again, after all. For a while there it had looked as though there weren't going to be any more "Dark Mirror" shows. But there was another one on tonight. Which meant that *he* was on, too.

He looked in the mirror again and adjusted his bulky abdomen to what he thought was just the right height. Yes . . . this one was going to be fun.

Nick sat, studying Elizabeth as she watched the television in the corner. He had considered asking Michael Donahue to turn the thing off. But he knew it wouldn't make any difference in the long run. No matter what was on the screen, no matter what topic of conversation Nick chose, she was only going to be thinking of one thing . . . who was going to die tonight.

"We were never going to air this episode," she said quietly, her eyes still on the screen. "I wrote it from an idea that Brody came up with. I never liked it and it just didn't work. In the end he agreed with me and we'd decided to just put it away for a rainy day."

Nick glanced quickly out the window over the bar. A fairly heavy rain was falling, glistening silver streaks in the light of the street lamp. Looking back at her, he saw that she, too, had noticed the irony of her statement.

"Or a rainy winter's night," she said with a bitter tone.

Nick moved his leg under the table so that it rested against hers and nudged her knee gently. "Let me tell you something," he said. "I don't tell just everybody this, so listen up."

"Okay, I'm all ears," she said, giving him her full attention.

Good, he thought, *at least she isn't looking at the television anymore.*

"My dad, Ryan O'Connor, was the greatest guy on earth, but he had a problem. He battled alcoholism for most of his life. When I was about eight years old, he took his last drink, started going to A.A. meetings, and stayed dry until the day he died. So I don't remember a lot about the 'bad times' as my mom used to call them. But I do remember one thing, and I'm very grateful to my dad for sharing that with me, because it carries me through my own bad times."

"What did he say?" she asked. He was touched by the alert interest in her eyes as she leaned across the table toward him. Most women he had known weren't that curious about a guy's battle stories. But he and Elizabeth seemed to connect, no matter what they talked about.

"It isn't very original," he said, "but effective. It's the prayer about having the serenity to accept the things you can't change, the courage to change the things you can, and—"

"And the wisdom to know the difference," Elizabeth added. "Yes, I've used that one myself many times. It's the last part that's tricky."

"It sure is."

Elizabeth turned and looked up at the television. Nick followed her line of vision. On the screen a pregnant woman with long, dark hair was pouring a liquid into a soft drink bottle, rescrewing the lid, and replacing it in a refrigerator. Then she walked over to a broom closet, opened the door, and hid inside.

"She's going to poison her husband's mistress," Elizabeth said. "She's under a lot of stress, with the baby coming and all. Finding out that her husband was having another affair—after he had promised it would never happen again—sent her over the edge. She didn't want it to end that way, but she didn't know what to—"

"You can't change it, Lizzie," he said, gently interrupting her. "Whatever is going to happen tonight . . . you can't change it. It isn't in your hands."

She sat quietly for a long time, considering his words. Then she said, "Serenity . . . right?"

"That's right, Elizabeth. Serenity."

She closed her eyes and nodded. "I'll try."

"That's all any of us can do." He reached out and stroked her cheek, wishing they were somewhere else, a private place where he could kiss her, hold her and be close. "You just keep trying. It'll all work out. You'll see."

Her smile told him that some part of her believed his words. That was good, at least one of them felt better.

Serenity, courage, he prayed, sending his own supplication heavenward. *And wisdom—more than anything else, please, give me wisdom.*

As the killer crawled through the shrubbery, then over the wrought iron balcony, catching his skirt on every branch and iron bolt along the way, he cursed himself for dressing up for the occasion. At the time it had seemed like a good idea. But having this pillow, that felt more like a bowling ball, strapped to his belly was a major nuisance.

No wonder pregnant women walked funny and looked tired all the time. He decided, as he straddled the balcony railing, that in the future he would always give up his seat to an expectant mother on a subway or bus.

He was relieved to find the sliding door unlocked, as it had been for the last two nights when he had checked it. She probably didn't think anyone would be determined enough to crawl through all that damned prickly shrubbery or over the high railing. Wrong. And that mistake would cost the woman her life.

Carefully, he slid the door open and stepped inside. One lamp burned on the end table beside the sofa, illuminating a large poster-sized picture of Elvis. The apartment had a definite Western motif with its cowboy prints, rope-trimmed lamp shades and saloon-style bar, complete with spittoon and etched mirror. It wasn't fashionable enough to be called "Southwestern." The place was just plain old western.

He took off the warm wool gloves he was wearing and shoved them in his coat pocket. Underneath the woolen gloves were surgical ones . . . just to make sure he left no prints.

Walking over to the bar, he pulled a small bottle of pills from inside his jacket. It wasn't the same poison as they had used on the show tonight, and that irked him. He took pride in being as similar as possible with what he liked to think of as his "reproductions." But, this time, his own prescription sleeping pills would have to do. He'd have to suffer through some sleepless nights. He couldn't go back to his doctor for a refill without arousing suspicion. But that was the price a devoted man paid to fulfill his mission.

Carefully, he removed the top of the Jack Daniels bottle and began to break open the capsules, pouring the powder into the whiskey. It was a challenge to get enough in to do the trick, but not so much that she would detect it.

For the last two nights he had snuck in here, before she had returned home, and hid in the kitchen closet with the vacuum cleaner and washer/dryer machine, then watched through the louvered doors as she came in. As soon as she had hung up her coat and flipped on her answering machine, she had poured herself a shot and bolted it. He was betting on the fact that she would do the same thing again tonight.

If not, he would just wait until she was asleep, smother her, then pour the poison into her mouth. It didn't really matter whether she died from the stuff or not, as long as it "looked" like she had.

He glanced at his watch . . . actually, it was a woman's watch which he had bought at the thrift store with the dress and wig. She would be home pretty soon. Time to get ready.

Although he wasn't looking forward to being in that miserable cramped space again, he squeezed himself into the closet and closed the door.

He had been wrong. This wasn't a particularly fun one. In fact, it was rather miserable, with the scratchy, hot wig making his head sweat, the bundle of joy strapped to his waist, and this stupid dress that was too tight through the shoulders.

Oh, well, he told himself, *nobody said it would be easy.* Things would liven up once she arrived.

Now all he had to do was wait.

Twenty-five

Elizabeth didn't want to look at the screen in the corner. She didn't need to look; she knew, all too well, what was there. But she couldn't stop herself.

In spite of Nick's steady stream of conversation, which changed from light banter to words of comfort and back to banter every few minutes, she couldn't concentrate on what he was saying.

The woman on the screen was about to die.

"Why don't I ask Michael to slug in a Makem and Clancy video?" he asked, trying to distract her.

She shook her head. "Thanks, but it wouldn't help. It isn't as though I don't know what's happening next."

She knew every action, every word of dialogue. She knew it because she had imagined it and brought it into being. Her thoughts, her fantasy, right there on the screen for millions of people to see.

Once the idea had thrilled her, filled her with the excitement of high level success. But now, the joy was overshadowed by the thought that, in a few minutes, some woman out there might have to suffer the same fate.

The victim on the screen stumbled across her living room, growing weaker and weaker as the poison raced through her bloodstream. Her murderess stood over her, crying, pointing to her belly where she carried *his* child. As the dying woman fell forward, she reached for her tormentor, grabbing her long, dark hair in her fist. The pregnant woman screamed in pain and pushed her away. Losing her balance, the mistress tumbled to the floor with strands of the wife's hair still tangled in her fingers.

With one arm wrapped around her swollen belly, the murderer bent over her victim and shoved a picture at her face. It was a photo of two small children . . . *his* children. She told her to look at the family she had destroyed with her selfishness. Then the wife ripped the photo into tiny pieces and threw them at her. The bits of paper fluttered downward like the white flakes in a glass snow ball, settling on the woman's face as she slipped into unconsciousness.

The expectant mother stood, staring down on her enemy, a glazed look in her eyes. Finally, she knelt and pressed one finger to the woman's jugular.

Woodenly, she walked to the phone on the end table, picked up the receiver and pushed some numbers. "Hello honey, it's me," she said quietly. "I just called to let you know . . . you should come over here to your 'home away from home' and check on your girlfriend. She doesn't seem to be feeling very well."

Elizabeth turned away from the set. She had seen enough . . . far more than enough. She found Nick watching her with a thoughtful, worried look on his handsome face.

"I'm all right," she said, reading his thoughts. "But thanks for asking."

"You're welcome," he replied. "Anytime."

As Cassie climbed the stairs out of the subway tunnel, she tried to pull her collar as tightly around her neck as possible to keep out the cold rain. Her throat was already sore and she was getting a nasty cough. *There's nothing like adding insult to injury,* she thought, feeling more miserable than she had in ages.

She was catching a cold, torrents of icy rain were pouring down on her head, and she had had a fight with Bud. What more could happen?

Superstitious, she quickly abandoned that train of thought. *Never ask what else can happen,* she reminded herself. There was no point in tempting those pesky, mischievous critters who lurked about, unseen, but forever causing trouble for mortals. "The Little People" the Irish called them. Of course, she didn't really believe in the wee folk. But she wasn't stupid enough to let them know she didn't believe in them, either.

This really had been a cursed day, Cass decided, and she was eager for it to be over. She hated it when she and Bud fought. Well, they hadn't exactly *fought* tonight or any other night, but lately their special times together were becoming less and less special. In fact, she had decided tonight, after leaving him at the studio, that it was over. At least the sex part.

He was feeling guilty. She could tell by the way he looked at her—or *didn't* look at her, by the way he touched her and made love to her. Recently, things had been going better between him and his wife, and the old guilt booga-boo had crept in.

Bud had been the first married man Cass had ever been involved with. She had broken one of her top five rules when she had succumbed to his seductions—okay, she had done her share of seducing, too—and now she was sorry she had. It had been exciting, sure, and she loved Bud. She wasn't "in love" with him, but she would always love him. He was funny, tender, sweet, and damned good in the sack.

But she couldn't go on with this if he was feeling bad about it. If he felt guilty, she felt guilty . . . it ruined everything.

As she turned the corner, heading toward her apartment building, a particularly strong gust of cold, wet wind hit her in the face. She began coughing again, only this time deeper in her chest. The wracking spasm made her sore throat hurt even more.

Reaching into her jacket pocket, she pulled out a menthol cough drop, unwrapped it and popped it into her mouth. The strong vapors filled her sinuses and temporarily numbed her throat.

"Tastes like hell," she mumbled, quickening her pace as the rain began to fall harder.

One more block to go, she thought. *And then it's a couple of stiff drinks, a hot bubble bath, and a candle. Oh, yes . . . and Kenny Rogers crooning in the background.*

Ah, yes, Cass knew how to treat herself when she was down. *Just roll with the punches, ol' girl,* she told herself, feeling better already, *and come up swingin'.*

"Is something wrong?" Nick asked.

Elizabeth looked around her living room, searching for any evidence of an intruder; nothing was disturbed . . . other than Katie Kat. She sat at the top of the stairs, peering down, her tail bushed out like a raccoon's. But Elizabeth attributed the cat's distress to the bulldog that had entered with her and Nick.

"No, I guess not," Elizabeth replied as she laid her purse and gloves on a small piecrust table beside the door. "I'm just paranoid these days. Sometimes when I come home it feels like . . ."

She hesitated, afraid she would sound like an idiot, but he coaxed her to continue. "It feels like what?"

"Like somebody's been here. More specifically, like *he's* been here. But I'm willing to chalk it up to an over-active imagination. It's an occupational hazard for a writer."

"Maybe, maybe not," he said, as he walked from window to window, examining the locks they had installed. "For myself, I've always been a strong believer in intuition."

"Women's?"

He grinned at her over his shoulder. "Anybody's."

She followed him through the dining room, kitchen, and downstairs guest room as he checked every window and door on the ground floor. Hercules trotted along behind, wagging his corkscrew tail, along with his entire rearend, and looking perfectly at home. After one night's occupancy, he appeared to think he owned the place.

"Everything looks fine down here." Nick headed back to the living room. "Let's check upstairs."

"Oh, yeah . . . subtle," she said, lifting one eyebrow. "You just want to get me up there so that you can take advantage of me again."

He assumed an expression that was more saccharin than innocent and said, "Actually, I was only going to check your windows and under your bed. But if you really want me to check your drawers . . ."

"Fun-n-ny," she said dryly.

"Hey, give me a break; I'm ad-libbing here. On a cop's salary, I can't afford professional writers."

He started up the stairs, but when he reached the fourth step, he turned around and looked down at her, his eyes soft with laughter and affection. Elizabeth couldn't remember when a man had looked at her like that. For a moment it felt as though her heart had stopped, but her rapid pulse that pounded in her ears convinced her that it hadn't.

"Why don't you make us some coffee, Lizzie?" he said in an intimate tone that reminded her of the way he had talked to her in bed last night. She felt her face growing warm . . . along with other, less conspicuous but rather predictable, parts of her anatomy. "I think I'll have mine in the Pinocchio mug this time."

"Okay," she said, only slightly disappointed that he hadn't gone through with the seduction.

"I'll just make sure everything's clear up here and I'll be right down." He continued up the stairs and disappeared at the top with Hercules struggling to haul his own massive bulk up the steep steps after his master.

Elizabeth walked back to the kitchen and pulled the coffee pot from the cupboard. A quick glance at the stove clock told her that it was eleven-thirty.

She mentally scolded herself for even thinking about sex at a time like this. For all she knew some woman out there was being killed, right this minute . . . because of a television show that *she* had written.

But then, making love symbolized life, procreation, continuation, and renewal.

Maybe—she decided—just maybe, in the face of death love was the best thing to think about, after all.

The closet was becoming more and more cramped. And that damned bundle he had tied around his middle was making his back ache.

Where was she, anyway?

The last two nights she had been home before this. Long before.

A thought occurred to him and it made him feel sick to his stomach. What if she didn't come home in time for him to do it before midnight? What if she didn't come home at all?

It would be ruined. Everything would be ruined. After all the precautions he had taken, all the attention to detail, the thought that a woman like that would wreck it made him shiver with fury.

She'd better get here soon, that was all he had to say about it. She was going to die before twelve o'clock tonight, if he had to go out and hunt her down. And it didn't have to be an easy death, like poison, either.

Just when he was beginning to really get into the fantasy of an alternative plan, he thought he heard the doorknob rattle. His glands reacted on cue, and adrenalin flooded his bloodstream.

Ground zero, he thought. *And away we go!*

As Elizabeth sat down at her desk and Nick lowered himself onto a chair beside her, she thought how much smaller this little room looked with him filling it.

"Cozy," he said, looking around at the publicity memorabilia from "The Dark Mirror," which she had framed and hung on the walls. "And right next to your bedroom," he added with a sexy smile that made her blush.

"It used to be the nursery, in the olden days," she replied with a twinge of sadness. She had often thought it was unfortunate that she didn't need to use this room for its intended purpose. If she were honest, Elizabeth had to admit that she would prefer to convert the downstairs guest room into an office and use this for—

She pushed the thought away. It was always an uncomfortable line of thinking, but somehow even more so with Nick sitting beside her.

"Maybe it will be again someday," he said quietly in a tone that surprised her. Surely he didn't mean . . .

She turned quickly to the computer on her desk and flipped the power switch. "This will only take a minute," she said. "I'll just call it up and print it out."

"Take your time. There's no hurry. I've got all night."

Again the intimate tone of his voice made her pleasantly uneasy. Suddenly, her chair seemed too warm to sit on comfortably and she squirmed a bit.

Trying to distract her thoughts, she watched the monitor screen carefully as the miscellaneous boot-up data streamed past. Then she typed the code to engage her word processing program.

"What do you hope to find in the 'adultery' script?" she asked, afraid she didn't really want to know.

"I'm not sure, yet," he replied.

The "yet" bothered her. What he wasn't saying—out of consideration for her feelings—was that the script would be useful once they identified the person who had been murdered tonight. He would compare the similarities in the script to the details of the murder scene. As always.

An unusual message flashed on the screen, and she stared at it, puzzled, for a few seconds. "What . . . ?" she mumbled, reading the words:

Old backup document exists. 1—Rename, 2—Delete

"Old backup? Why would it say that?" she said, turning to Nick. "It only shows that when the system was turned off in the middle of the program . . . like a power outage, or something. I always close the program down before turning off the computer."

"Always?" he asked, leaning forward and staring at the screen.

"Always." She chose to rename the file and see what it was.

Pulling it up onto the screen, she was again surprised by what she saw. "It's the 'adultery' script. I haven't worked on that file for ages. Why would that be—?"

The realization hit her like a blow to the stomach that nearly knocked her breath out.

"What is it?" Nick asked, placing his hand on her forearm. "Liz, what's wrong?"

"He was here . . . recently," she said. She turned to Nick, her face pale as she felt all her strength drain down her legs and arms and out of her body. "My God, Nick. I don't know how he got into the house, but he *was* here. And he accessed my computer. *This* file. Either he forgot to close the program down before turning the computer off, or . . ."

She couldn't say the words, so Nick spoke them for her. "Or maybe he was here when we arrived. We interrupted him, and he had to shut down in a hurry." He saw the alarmed look on her face. "Or maybe not. Who knows? Either way, we have to figure out how he's getting in here. Let's check everything again.

As Elizabeth closed the program and turned the computer off, she had another disturbing thought. "You know . . . ," she said, ". . . we thought it had to be somebody at the studio, someone who had access to copies of the scripts."

"Yeah, I've already thought of that," Nick said, suddenly sounding very tired. "If he's getting the information right out of your computer here at home . . . hell, he could be anybody."

Home again, home again, jiggidy jig, Cassie thought as she twisted the key in the lock and pushed her front door open. With a considerable mental effort, she had dispelled the gloomy thoughts of Bud and the transgressed-against Mrs. Bud. Never one to dwell on the negative side of a matter, Cass was determined not to let it ruin the rest of her evening.

The idea of a bubble bath and Kenny Rogers had never been so appealing. Her throat was getting worse by the moment, and so was her cough. As she closed and locked the door behind her, another series of wracking spasms shook her body, nearly taking her breath away.

"You gotta give up those cigars, kid," she muttered, tossing her purse onto the bar and slipping off her fringed suede jacket.

She punched the button on her answering machine and listened to a couple of messages, one from the dry cleaners—her square dancing outfit was ready—and another from her nine-and-a-half-months pregnant youngest sister. Apparently the baby still wasn't ready. The last time Cass had talked to Sylvia, Cass had offered to come back to Texas and chase her around the farm a few times, holding a dead rat by its tail. Sylvia hadn't thought that particularly witty; in fact, she had broken down and bawled hysterically.

Cass decided she would return her call tomorrow morning, if she could still talk. If she couldn't, it would make a great excuse.

With a sigh of fatigue and satisfaction, Cass settled herself on one of the bar stools and poured herself a shot of Jack Daniels. She swirled it in the glass, then smiled. Things were starting to look up.

A second before she brought the glass to her mouth, a strange feeling crept over her. A slight shiver tickled its way from the back of her neck all the way down to her tailbone. The sensation was as brief as it was unpleasant, and she attributed it to one of her mother's time-worn theories: Somewhere a goose had just walked over her grave.

With an expert flick of her wrist, she downed the shot of whiskey, then grimaced at the taste. Drinking booze after a menthol cough drop was about as appealing as orange juice after toothpaste. Maybe a little less.

Undaunted, she poured the second drink and bolted it as well. After all, Kenny was a two drink sorta guy, and he deserved to have her at her best.

The liquid fire traced her throat, her esophagus and on down to settle warmly in her belly. Ah . . . in a few minutes she wouldn't even mind being sick.

Slowly she sauntered over to the stereo and popped in an old tape of "The Gambler." Kenny's raspy-sweet voice washed over her, warming her as effectively as the whiskey. She sang along . . . loudly. Cass was completely tone-deaf, a fact that was obvious to anyone within earshot when she sang. But she had never let that dampen her enthusiasm for the pastime. She was convinced that any music was good music—if it were only loud enough.

As she rose from her squatting position in front of the stereo, Cass felt a weak trembling in her thigh muscles. The shakiness traveled downward to her calves as she took a few steps.

Apparently, she was sicker than she had thought.

Maybe this wasn't a cold at all. Perhaps she had the flu. That was just what she needed, a virus that would keep her cooped up here at home for the next week or so. Cass prided herself on the fact that, when others around her were dropping like flies, she always managed to battle off any impending flu-bugs.

Unable to keep her balance, she stumbled over to the sofa and lay down on it, nearly falling over her coffee table on the way.

A weariness, more profound than any she could remember, stole over her, blurring her vision and dulling her senses. Even Kenny seemed to be drifting away into some sort of tunnel . . . far, far away.

Since when did whiskey hit her this hard? she wondered. Even with the flu, she shouldn't be going down this fast.

She thought of the cold shiver, the goose, her grave. It didn't seem like a harmless little folktale now.

"Help me," she whispered. Her voice sounded strange and high in her own ears. "Somebody . . . I think I'm . . . sick. . . ."

There's no one here, she told herself. It was useless to call out for assistance, but she heard herself trying again. "Please, somebody . . ."

Then, through the fog that was swirling through her head, she saw someone. A woman. She *wasn't* alone. Someone had heard and come to help.

Squinting her eyes, Cass stared up at the figure that stood beside the sofa, looking down at her. She could see the long dark hair, the flower-print dress, the large bulge in the abdomen.

"Sylvia?" she whispered. "Is that you?"

The figure said nothing, but just continued to stand there, staring down at her. Cass fought to remain conscious; her instincts told her that her life depended on it.

"Sylvie, honey . . ." She was losing it. She couldn't remember why Sylvia was here. Or how she had gotten here from Texas. "Is it time?" she asked. "Is the baby coming?"

The silent figure bent over her. Cass reached up to grasp her sister's sleeve, but grabbed a handful of her long dark hair instead. To her horror, Sylvia's entire scalp slid off her head. Cassie was holding it in her hand. With a cry of alarm she dropped it to the floor.

Sylvia was holding a photograph in her hand; she was showing it to her. Cass tried to see it, tried as hard as she could, because it seemed important to her sister. She was shoving it right under her nose.

From far away, Cass could hear another voice besides Kenny's. The voice was saying something about a family . . . a family that she had destroyed.

"What . . . what do you mean?" Cassie whispered.

She was dimly aware of Sylvia ripping the picture into pieces and throwing them at her. They fell, one by one, onto her face, but she could hardly feel them. She was sleepy. So very tired and so sleepy.

Sylvia needed her. She couldn't go to sleep now. The baby was coming.

The woman leaned over her, much closer now, until they were almost face to face. Even in her diminished mental state, Cass could clearly see now that it wasn't her sister's face before her.

"You're not . . . not Sylv—"

"No, I'm not." The voice was a man's, not a woman's. This wasn't her sister, but the face, the voice . . . they were somehow familiar.

"You're a slut, a home-wrecker," he said. "And now, you're going to die for it."

Suddenly, in a brief, but brilliant moment of clarity, Cass remembered. She remembered the pregnant woman, the long dark hair, the torn picture. . . .

And she remembered the face.

"Oh, God," she whispered, realizing at last what was happening to her. "It's . . . it's you."

A heartbeat later, Cassie's eyes closed. Her fear was gone. The fleeting memory was gone.

All memories were gone.

He sat in an armchair beneath the picture of Elvis, watching her. She hadn't moved for a long time.

Glancing at his watch, he saw it was five minutes until midnight. He needed to make the call soon, but he wanted to be sure she was dead. Her chest was no longer rising and falling. That was a good sign.

Three minutes until twelve. He had to do it now.

Clumsily, he rose from the chair, still hampered by the bulk strapped to his belly. He walked over to the sofa and squatted beside her. With his fingers pressed to her throat, he searched for a pulse but found none. He checked her wrist. The same.

He held his palm in front of her nose and mouth and couldn't detect any breathing.

Yep, she's dead. The thought gave him a grim sense of satisfaction. A job well done . . . again.

Reaching for the phone on the endtable, he pulled a piece of paper from inside his stuffed bra and dialed the number. A woman answered. He asked to speak to her husband.

"Hello honey, it's me," he said. "I just called to let you know—you should come over here to your 'home away from home' and check on your girlfriend." He glanced at the still figure on the sofa; she had turned a rather nice shade of blue. "She doesn't seem to be feeling very well."

Twenty-six

"This cellar is what I, not so fondly, call 'The Catacombs,' " Elizabeth told Nick as she led him down the stairs into her basement. She stopped and turned around so abruptly that he nearly ran into her. "Be sure to shut the door behind you," she said. "We can't let Katie down here."

"Why not? Isn't it the *cat*-a-combs."

"Chuckle, chuckle," she replied dryly. "I can't let her play in the cellar, because she'll catch the mice."

Nick studied her with a puzzled and slightly wary look in his eyes. "Isn't that what a cat is supposed to do? I thought it was part of their job description or something."

"No! I don't want her to catch them; she might kill them."

"O-o-kay," Nick said, shaking his head. "Sometimes I don't know about you, Lizzie. I think you must have overdosed on Disney movies when you were a kid."

"When I was a kid? I went to see *Beauty and the Beast* six times when I was . . . well . . . thirty-something."

"Figures." He pointed to the bottom of the stairs. "Let's get on with it. I'll try not to step on any of your pet mice."

"Thank you. I appreciate that."

Nick wondered as he followed her down the stairs how she could discuss something as light and upbeat as Disney when a multiple killer was slipping in and out of her house at will. He suspected it was her way of coping, one she had learned long ago, and he admired her for it. Disney movies and guarding the mice in one's cellar were preferable to many of the coping mecha-

nisms out there: booze, dope, numbing your brain in front of the
television night after night . . . and worse.

When they reached the bottom of the staircase, she said,
"Please remember that this house was built pre-Civil War, and
the basement has never been renovated. Cassie is convinced there
are bodies buried down here somewhere."

"She could be right," Nick said, trying not to breathe in the
stale, musty air. It seemed like he was spending most of his life
in basements lately. *One of the job perks,* he thought, right up
there with crawling under houses, examining bodies that were
old and very ripe, having to wrestle criminals who hadn't bathed
or changed clothes in months. All in all, he decided, this wasn't
so bad.

A single bulb hung from the center of the ceiling, and did little
to chase away the gloom. It reminded him of the swinging light
in *Psycho.* The walls were primitive, haphazard layers of blocks
partly covered by wooden panels. Some of the planks hung di-
agonally, held by one nail at the top corner. Old yellowed newspapers were plastered here and there to take up the slack. Reading
the date on one, he was surprised to find it a turn-of-the-century
account of post-war politics.

"To be honest, I haven't done anything with this cellar because
I kinda like it the way it is," Elizabeth said. "I feel like Nancy
Drew when I come down here."

"I can see why. I feel a bit like one of the Hardy Boys myself,
searching for treasure chests full of pieces of eight."

She smiled. "Exactly. Ambiance."

Nick pulled his flashlight from inside his jacket and turned
the beam on the walls. "Well, let's see what 'treasure' we can
find."

Carefully, he passed the circle of light along the walls, looking . . . for what, he wasn't sure. There was no outside door; she
had already told him that when they had installed all the new
locks.

No windows either. For a guy to get in this way, he'd need to
be half gopher.

"I don't see any—" The shrill ringing of the phone upstairs interrupted him.

"I should probably get that," Elizabeth said, heading for the stairs.

He saw the worried look on her face. Things were pretty grim when a simple phone call was a source of high anxiety. She was a decent person, and she didn't deserve to live like this. Not after all she had already been through.

For at least the hundredth time that day, Nick felt a deep, hot wash of anger toward the bastard who was causing this.

Damn, but he really wanted to nail him.

He had decided there was nothing down here of interest and had turned to follow her upstairs, when he heard a familiar snuffling sound. Hercules.

He had turned the dog out a few minutes ago to "make yellow snow" and hadn't let him back in yet. But he could hear him clearly, as though he were in the same room with him.

"Herc?" he said, shining his light around the room. "Where are you, fella?"

Again, the snuffling, along with a whine.

It was coming from the wall in the other end of the room, the wall at the front of the house.

Nick hurried toward the noise. As he approached the wall, the dog barked twice, sounding even closer. "Atta boy, Hercules. Come here. Come on."

Carefully, Nick moved one of the loose panels aside and saw a small beam of light . . . street lamp light . . . filtered through the lattice woodwork that skirted the front of Elizabeth's porch. But there was a hole in the lattice and when he shined his flashlight on it, he illuminated Hercules's broad grinning mug.

"Hey there, big boy. Can you come through here?" he asked.

In answer to his question, the dog began to crawl beneath the porch with ease, heading straight toward him.

"Wait," Nick said, holding up one hand like a traffic cop. "Sit, Herc. Sit and stay."

The dog halted about fifteen feet away. Nick was surprised;

aristocratic, British bulldogs—even ones as well-behaved as Hercules—seldom obeyed commands. They were simply above all that nonsense.

"Stay right there for me while I look around here," Nick said as he shone his light around the tunnel.

Tunnel, he thought . . . *déjà vu. Ferguson likes to come and go through tunnels.*

His light played off the myriad cobwebs that crisscrossed from the bottom of the porch to the ground and back, over a century's accumulation. But when he shined his beam on Hercules, there were no webs between them, as though someone had pulled a gauze stage curtain half way open and left it.

"Stay, Herc," he repeated as he studied the hard-packed dirt floor of the crawlspace. Sure enough, there they were . . . fresh lines in the soil. Narrow, parallel lines that twisted from side to side. The same kind of lines left in the sand by a slithering snake.

A rather deadly snake, Nick thought.

The nagging sense of helplessness that had been weighing Nick down lifted a bit. At least now he knew how the guy got in, and he could stop it. Some sturdy boards and some nails the size of railroad spikes would keep the bloody bastard out.

He smiled, hearing his father's voice in his head. Nick didn't use the curse "bloody." That was Ryan O'Connor's word. It seemed to pop up at times like this . . . when he felt like a successful cop. In reality, he had long ago risen above his father's rank, but for Nick, feeling like a successful cop had little to do with rank. Unlike Pete MacDonald.

Nick believed there were only two things a policeman could do in the line of duty that really mattered. One—help innocent people who were in trouble, such as: deliver a baby when there was no one else to do it, show a senile old lady the way home when she couldn't remember what planet she was on, or find a three-year-old, alive and healthy, who had wandered away from his mom in the park.

Those were the sort of things that made you warm inside and

put a smile on a cop's face. A sappy, sentimental smile . . . maybe . . . but definitely a feel good smile.

Then there was the other side of the job, other moments that put a smile on your face. But it wasn't a sappy, *Leave It to Beaver* smile. It was more of a grim smirk that didn't make it from your mouth up to your eyes. The sort of grin you had when you knew you'd gotten one up on a bad guy—one of those egotistic, cocky punks who thought they could take someone else's property, safety, peace of mind, sexuality, even their life from them, just because *they* wanted to.

Nick enjoyed showing them that nobody was that damned important, not even them. He had seen the devastation they carelessly left behind, the broken bodies, the ruined dreams, the shattered hearts. If he could catch them and throw their asses in jail, frankly, he loved it.

But he had never wanted one of them the way he wanted this one. The killer was close, so close that Nick could smell him; he could feel his stinking vibes right there in that tunnel. And the fantasy of busting him had never played so sweet.

"Stay put for a minute, Herc," he said. "I'll come up and get you."

The dog whined, but obeyed.

As Nick turned and hurried up the stairs, the thought occurred to him that Elizabeth had been on the phone quite a while. He hoped it wasn't bad news. He really wanted to be able to give her good news for a change. She would be relieved to hear what he had discovered.

He walked through the living room to the front door, opened it and let the shivering bulldog inside. "A little nippy out there, boy?" he asked, rubbing the animal's broad back.

Hercules gave him a drop-dead look that said, "You're damned right it's nippy out there, pal. Thanks for leaving me out so long."

"Listen . . ." Nick kneeled in front of the dog, put his hands on either side of his head and lowered his face to his until they were nose to nose. ". . . If you want to be a trusty K-9, you have to endure a certain amount of discomfort in the pursuit of justice. It's a price we all have to—"

Nick glanced up to see Elizabeth standing in the kitchen doorway. One look at her face told him that his good news wasn't going to help very much.

He quickly rose and walked over to her. Placing his hands on her shoulder, he could feel her body shaking, and he didn't have to ask; he knew.

"He did it again," Nick said, looking into her eyes. He had seen a lot of pain, but never more than he saw registered there.

"Yes." The word was little more than a breath. She leaned toward him, her face a ghastly shade of gray-white. Then she crumpled and would have fallen if he hadn't caught her before she hit the floor.

With his arms around her waist, he helped her over to the sofa and gently sat her down. Placing his hand on her cheek, he thought he had never felt anyone so cold . . . at least, not a *live* someone. She was well on her way to going into shock.

"Lizzie, come on, sweetheart. Look up at me." He slid his hand beneath her chin and forced her to raise her face to his. "Talk to me. Tell me about it."

She didn't reply, but stared at him with eyes empty of everything except the pain.

"Who was that on the phone?" he asked. "What happened?"

"Bud," she said, so softly that he could barely hear her.

"Bud, who? The Bud who works at your station?"

She nodded. Then she began to sob, harsh, dry, racking sobs that frightened him more than her pallor or low body temperature.

"Nick . . . ," she cried, burying her face against his shirt.

"Yes, honey. What is it?"

He knew it was something more than that the killer had struck again. She had been expecting that; she wouldn't have been this shocked, this devastated, by news that she had been anticipating.

"He did it again."

"I know, sweetheart. I know he did, but—"

"Cassie," she said, drawing back and looking up at him with an expression that went straight to his heart.

No, he thought. *No. She doesn't mean. . . .*

"This time he . . . he . . ." She was sobbing so hard she could hardly speak. "Oh, Nick . . . it's my Cassie."

As Elizabeth stood and stared down at the still figure which had been her lively friend, a hardness began to creep over her heart. Cass's face, which had once been so animated, showed no signs of the spirited person who had added so much joy to Elizabeth's life.

Over Cassie's hospital bed, half a dozen monitors beeped and blinked, tracing green lines that were, thankfully, jagged. But Elizabeth didn't need a medical degree to know that those feeble readings meant little, other than the fact that he hadn't completely killed her . . . not yet.

Nick's hand on her shoulder gave Elizabeth some of the comfort that he, no doubt, intended to impart. But no amount of consolation from a friend was going to lessen the pain.

"They're doing everything they can for her, Liz," he said. Standing behind her, he slipped his arms around her waist and kissed the top of her head.

She didn't reply. She couldn't trust herself to speak, not knowing if she would begin to cry again, or if she would start screaming her rage. It was difficult to tell which emotion, pain or fury, was uppermost at the moment.

"I'm so sorry, sweetheart," he said, drawing her against him. "I—"

They both jumped as the door opened, and the doctor stepped into the room. He nodded to them, then bent over his patient to examine her briefly. After glancing over her chart, he motioned to Nick and Elizabeth to follow him out into the hall.

Once the door was closed behind them, Elizabeth couldn't wait any longer to know. "Is she going to live?" she asked, surprised at how hard and angry her voice sounded in her own ears.

The middle-aged doctor gave her his best, soothe-the-loved-ones, benevolent smile that lifted the ends of his long, silver mustache. When Elizabeth didn't return the smile, he rearranged his wire-framed glasses on his nose and said brusquely, "I'm not sure at this point, Ms. Knight. She's a very sick girl. We haven't been able to determine what substance she was given. Apparently, it was a sedative of some kind, probably a sleep aid, but we aren't sure which one."

"Has she had an E.E.G. yet?" Nick asked.

"Yes. She has brain wave activity. We can be thankful for that. But her coma is very deep. I don't know when or if she'll come out of it."

"Has she said anything?" Nick sounded hopeful.

"No, I'm sorry. She was unconscious when the paramedics arrived. They couldn't even detect vital signs at first."

"Is there anything we can do for her?" Elizabeth asked, knowing the answer. There was only one thing she could do for her friend right now, and the burning desire to do it was growing inside her by the minute.

"No, nothing at all, Ms. Knight," the doctor said, offering another of his bedside smiles. "The nurses say you two have been here for hours. Why don't you go on home and get some sleep. We'll call you if there's any change in her condition."

If. He had said if, not when, she noticed. The flame burned hotter.

"Thank you, doctor," Nick said, taking Elizabeth's hand in his. "That's a good idea."

Gently, he led her away and down the hall toward the exit. She submitted to his direction, lost in her own thoughts . . . a dark, convoluted maze of ideas that both frightened and excited her.

He paused when they reached the door and looked down at her, his green eyes probing hers. "What are you thinking about, Elizabeth?" he asked with more than a hint of concern in his voice.

"Why do you ask?" she replied.

"You just look like . . . like you're thinking something you shouldn't . . . or . . ."

She smiled, a bitter wry smile. "Maybe, maybe not," she said. "Either way, you don't need to worry. It isn't yours."

"What do you mean?" He gave her a suspicious look.

"I mean, that when he hurt Cassie . . . *my* friend . . . he became mine to deal with."

"That's what I was afraid you meant," he said, shaking his head. "Lizzie, talk like that could get you in trouble. Am I going to have to sit on you to make you behave?"

She knew he was trying to lift her spirits, but it didn't help.

Turning, she saw her reflection in the glass door. No wonder he had been concerned. She had seen many faces like the one she wore right now . . . in "The Dark Mirror."

They were ordinary people, caught in extraordinary circumstances, who wanted to kill another human being.

Just ordinary people . . . like her.

As Nick maneuvered his Jeep through the early morning, midtown traffic, he kept glancing sideways at Elizabeth, trying to read her mood. She sat beside him in the passenger's seat, staring straight ahead, unnaturally quiet, even for someone who's best friend was critically ill.

"Are you sure you don't want to go straight to my apartment?" he asked.

She shook her head.

"It's four-thirty in the morning, Liz." He reached over and placed his hand on her knee. "You've been up all night. You need to get some sleep."

"And how about you?" she asked, speaking for the first time since they had left the hospital. "You've been awake as long as I have. When are you going to sleep?"

He hesitated, then said, "Soon."

"Soon, when?"

"As soon as I take care of a few things."

"Cop things?"

"Yeah, cop things. I need to brief the task force on . . . the latest."

She sighed. "The latest being: He's struck again, and we have even less idea who he is than before. He, or she, for that matter, could be anyone who doesn't mind crawling under my house to get to the information."

"It's pretty tight under there, and it appears to be infested with spiders. So, we can rule out anybody who's claustrophobic or arachnophobic."

It was a feeble attempt at humor, he knew, but it was worth a try.

She didn't laugh, but she did turn and look at him. That was an improvement, even if the look was a bit condescending.

He shrugged. "Hey, I thought I'd try out some of my new material on you."

Her expression softened. "Thanks, Nick," she said quietly.

"For the bad jokes?"

"For caring enough to make any kind of joke at a time like this." Leaning back on the headrest, she closed her eyes. "I don't want you to think that I don't appreciate all you're doing for me."

"It's my job, ma'am," he said, giving her knee a squeeze.

She covered his hand with hers. "You're going way beyond duty, and we both know it."

"Well, kid, I sorta like you. For a broad, you're not too bad."

Her eyes flew open and she gave him a semi-hostile glare. "Watch who you're calling a broad." Then she smiled. "I kinda like you, too. But don't tell anybody."

"I wouldn't dream of it."

As they approached Fifty-fifth Street, she pointed right. "Just drop me off up here at the studio."

"The studio?" He almost asked why, then he realized it wasn't any of his business.

"Yeah. I have things to do, too."

He couldn't resist. "What kind of things?" he asked as he pulled over to the curb.

She opened the door and stepped out. With her hand on the handle, she paused, as though debating whether or not to tell him something important. His attempt at humor had worked, but only briefly. That strange, haunted but determined, look had returned to her face.

"Writer things," she said at last.

Instinctively, he knew she had decided not to tell him.

"You're not really going to write at a time like this, are you?" he asked.

"Hey, a pro can write any time. See you later?"

"Yeah. I'll drop by in a few hours."

"I'll be in my office."

As she turned to walk away, the uneasy feeling in his gut compounded. She was up to something, something she didn't want to share with him . . . probably because she knew he wouldn't approve.

And she was right. He wouldn't approve of anything that might get her hurt.

He watched as she climbed the few stairs to the front of the building and recorded every graceful movement for playback later.

Yeah . . . he sorta liked Elizabeth Knight, all right.

He sorta loved her.

Twenty-seven

Elizabeth sat in her studio office, unaware of the fact that a new day was dawning, as gray and somber as the last, outside her window. Her eyes hadn't left her monitor screen since she had sat down, two hours before. But on the screen was the evidence of her intense concentration, and her ability to create under pressure. She had written and polished the synopsis for the next episode of "The Dark Mirror."

She smiled grimly as her eyes ran over the words. The story was good; it held together. And, best of all, it would serve her purpose. At least, she hoped so.

Reaching for her telephone, she punched a couple of numbers. The phone on the other end rang . . . several times . . . but no answer. She hadn't really expected Brody to be in his office so early, but it had been worth a chance.

She hung up and dialed his home number. After a couple of rings, he answered, sounding groggy and more than a little hungover.

"Good morning, Brody," she said in a too-cheery voice.

"What do *you* want?"

"How good a producer are you?" she asked, knowing that a question like that would shock him awake. Blows to Brody's vanity always got his attention.

"The best," he snapped. "But you know that, so why wake me up at this ungodly hour?"

She noticed his drawl was gone; he must still be peeved at her.

His bad moods had never bothered her that much before, and, besides, she knew it wasn't going to last long.

"Are you good enough to produce an episode of 'Dark Mirror' in less than a week?"

There was a long pause on the other end. She could practically feel his adrenaline flood into the telephone line. If there was anything Brody liked, it was a challenge.

"Well, I'd consider it, darlin', if I had someone to write one for me." The drawl was back, she noted, a good sign.

"Is your computer up?" she asked.

"It's always up."

"Then I'm sending a synopsis over to you. Read it and call me back here at the studio."

Again, a long pause.

" 'Lizbeth . . . are you all right?"

She couldn't tell if it was genuine concern or simple curiosity behind his inquiry. It didn't matter. The answer was the same either way.

"I'm fine. In fact, I'm better than I've been in weeks. Read it and tell me what you think."

She replaced the phone, stood up and walked over to the window. The traffic was beginning to thicken on the avenue below. Another day . . . but not just any day.

She needed to go to the ladies' room, she needed a cup of coffee, she needed a donut or two. But she couldn't bring herself to leave the room. It would take Brody only three minutes to read the synopsis.

Which meant—he would call back in three and a half.

"You're kidding. You're screwing with me, right?"

Elizabeth chuckled, leaned back in her desk chair, and wedged the phone receiver between her ear and shoulder. "I've told you, Brody . . . that will *never, never* happen. It's just wishful thinking on your part."

"You're serious," he said. She could hear the breathless excitement in his voice. For Brody Yarborough, this was better than a five-star orgasm. "You really want to do this. I can't believe it."

"Then, am I to assume that you think it's a good idea?" she said smoothly, running her fingers over her computer keyboard.

"It's a *fantastic* idea. The ratings will go sky high. But have you thought about the fact that you'll be—"

"Of course, I've thought about it, Brody. But it's the only way."

"Yes, yes, I agree." She could almost see him bobbing his "reputed to be half bald" head vigorously, and she wondered briefly if he wore his Stetson to bed, too. "I think it's the only way," he said, "We *have* to do it!"

"I thought you'd feel that way," she replied, knowing that his determination had more to do with ratings points and cold cash than civic duty. "Can you do it on such short notice?"

"I can if you can."

"Then we're on. I'll get things rolling on my end and we can have a meeting this afternoon with the rest of the crew."

"Fine with me."

"Brody . . . I . . ." She paused, hesitating. For a moment she felt very afraid. Then she swallowed the fear and plunged ahead. "After the airing . . ."

"Yes?"

"I want to broadcast a special one hour interview, from eleven until midnight. Live from here in the studio."

"You want one of the news anchors to interview you about the show?"

She nodded and took a deep breath. "That's right."

She heard him take one, too. "I gotta say one thing for you, sugar," he said, spreading it on thick, "you sure got balls."

"Why, thank you, Brody. I think that's the nicest thing you've ever said to me."

"You're welcome. So, we're on?"

She glanced at the screen, at the words she had just written, and felt a heavy sense of inevitability descend on her, thick and suffocating. Too late. The ball was rolling. No turning back.

"We're on."

Elizabeth hung up the phone, waited only a second, then dialed her own home computer modem. With a few strokes on the keyboard, she sent the information to her office on Long Island.

She thought of the crawl space under her house, of the silent figure that had crept through her home and defiled its sanctity with his dark presence, of him standing over her, watching her as she slept, of his hands playing across *her* keyboard, accessing *her* files, reading *her* private thoughts and creations.

A bright red square lit up the center of her monitor screen, signalling that the information had been sent, transmission was complete.

She pushed away from her desk and knotted her hands into fists in her lap. "There you go, you rotten son-of-a-bitch," she said. "Read that one. . . . I wrote it just for you."

As Nick stood at Pete MacDonald's office door, he stared at his friend through the window and thought, *Good God, Pete's getting old . . . fast.* Of course, they were the same age—actually, Nick was six months older—a thought that didn't bear thinking about at the moment.

Pete sat at his desk, unaware that he was being observed, his face drawn and gray as he thumbed through the enormous pile of papers before him. Nick could sympathize; he had a stack just as high on his. This damned case was getting the best of everyone involved.

He rapped a "shave and a haircut" on the glass with his knuckles and walked in. The knocking was a new thing between them. Even a year ago it would never have occurred to Nick to knock on Pete's door—office or apartment. They were certainly getting formal with each other these days.

When Pete looked up, Nick couldn't help noticing that he wasn't particularly glad to see him. His expression said that Nick's visit was clearly a nuisance rather than a pleasure.

No problem, Nick told himself. *This is gonna be short and sweet anyway.* He was supposed to pick up Elizabeth at her office in a couple of hours, and Pete's bug repellent scented aftershave couldn't hold a candle to her perfume. He closed the door behind him and plopped down on a chair beside the desk.

"To what do I owe this pleasure?" Pete asked, pushing the papers away and leaning back in his chair. His eyes looked anything but curious. Not even mildly interested.

"Just a tidbit of news I thought you downtown jerk-offs should know."

"Let me guess, you and Doctor Watson have solved the case and have the villain in custody?" he said, not bothering to dilute the caustic sarcasm in his voice.

Nick took a deep breath and pulled in the reins on his temper. He was too damned tired to get mad; it required more energy than he could spare right now.

"We found out how he's getting access to the script prematurely," Nick said in a monotone, as though doing a predictable Southern California weather report—"The skies will be clear and the highs in the low eighties . . . again."

Pete perked up perceptibly. "Oh? How?"

"He's been getting into Elizabeth's Long Island house through the crawlspace which leads into the basement. She realized that someone has been getting into her computer when she wasn't at home. He's been reading the scripts as she's working on them."

"Then we've probably been squandering our human resources going through all these damned profiles on everybody who works at the studio," Pete said, pointing to the paper mountain on his desk. "Shit, that means it could be anybody."

"Hey, I didn't say it was *good* news." Nick stood. He had enjoyed Pete's company as much as he could stomach for the moment. "That's it, that's all. I'm outta here." He walked to the door and pulled it open.

"Nick . . ."

He paused and turned. "Yeah?"

"What kind of word processing program does Elizabeth use when she writes?"

Nick thought back, trying to remember the logo that had flashed across the screen when she had gone into her program. "Maximum Word? Something like that."

Pete shuffled through his files, picked one, and scanned the information inside. Flipping it closed he said, "Then there's something you midtown assholes might want to know."

"What's that?"

"David Ferguson worked in the prison library for five years and—"

"Yeah, we've been privy to that information already, remember?"

Pete ignored the jab. "The library files were computerized," he said evenly. "And the program he used was Maximum Word."

"How's it comin', sugar?" Brody asked as he strode into Elizabeth's office. His face was flushed all the way up to his Stetson. A money-making project, thrown together under pressure—Brody Yarborough was in his element and enjoying every minute of it.

"It's coming," Elizabeth said without looking up from her monitor to acknowledge his presence. "I'll have the first thirty pages finished before I leave tonight."

"You're kidding!"

"It's just a matter of putting it down." She continued to type and watch the screen. "I worked it all out in my head last night, while I was standing beside Cassie's bed."

"Oh . . . yeah . . . how is the old girl doin'?"

"I just called the hospital. Again. They won't say much, except that her condition isn't changing."

He walked around her desk and looked over her shoulder at the monitor where line after line of words were appearing in neat, white rows on a dark blue screen. "How does it look?"

"Don't worry; it'll do the job."

He reached down and patted her shoulder, and for once, she

didn't shrug him away. "Good. That's all we need . . . to get the job done."

"So, lady and gents, that's about it." Nick shoved his notes into his backpack and stood, signalling that this worthless meeting of the Dark Mirror Task Force was now closed. "Anybody got anything else to add to the nothing we've got so far?"

They all shook their heads.

"Great. Then, we are adjourned. Ray, keep going over that paperwork, particularly the background checks. Steph, keep your ears open at the tabernacle. And you, Fred—"

"Yeah, yeah, I know, surveillance. Did you tell the captain we need a few more bodies on the job? I can't watch everybody all the time. Even superheroes have to take a pee once in a while."

"I asked," Nick said. "I begged. I wrung my hands and squeezed out a couple of tears."

"But . . . ?"

"As high profile as this case is, we've only got four dead and one comatose, and only two occurred here in midtown. I've been told in no uncertain terms that we're lucky to have a task force . . . such as it is. The boys with the calculators are already bitching about the bill on this one."

He looked around the room and felt a pang of sympathy for his fellow exhaustees. This was the last thing he should be telling them right now. He should be giving the old one-two pep talk, the "Buck up, little beavers, everything's gonna be fine," routine.

"I've got a lab team out at Elizabeth's house right now," he said, "combing the place for fingerprints, spit out hangnails, lone pubic hairs, etc. Maybe we'll get lucky."

They gave him a unison, drop-dead look that clearly said, "Yeah, right."

So much for pep talks.

"O-kay. Then let's get going. If you need me, buzz me," he said, patting the pager on his hip and being careful not to look in Stephanie's direction.

They filed out of the room, one by one, a much less energetic team than a week ago. *We'd better solve this one fast,* Nick thought as he threw his backpack over his shoulder. *This engine is running out of steam, and we ain't even close to the station yet.*

Nick found David Ferguson with his head in a toilet. At first he thought he was throwing up, then he realized the guy was cleaning it—up close and personal.

"Don't they give you gloves for that job?" he asked when Ferguson pulled his bare hand out of the john, holding a dripping piece of steel wool.

Ferguson shot him a look, grumbled, and returned to his task. "This isn't exactly a five-star hotel, detective," he said. "They don't spend a lot on the extras . . . like gloves or toilet brushes."

"You don't sound like a man who's happy at his work." Nick looked around the bathroom that might have been charming in an art deco way, back in the Ice Age, before the lavender and black tiles were broken and sprouting a thriving crop of mold and mildew, back when the broken stained glass window was intact and looked out onto something nicer than a graffiti-scarred ghetto.

"Work's work," Ferguson said, groaning as he stood up and stretched his back. "Ex-cons can't exactly be choosy."

Nick leaned against the doorjamb and crossed his arms over his chest. "So . . . been doin' any word processing lately? Maybe a little computer work when you aren't scrubbing crappers?" His tone was as casual as his stance, but his eyes were sharp and probing as he watched for any reaction: a shifting of the eyes, a change in breathing, dilation of the pupils.

Damn. Nothing of notable consequence.

Ferguson met his stare briefly, then turned and squirted some foul-smelling, lime-green disinfectant into the shower stall. "If you want to know my social schedule, why don't you check with your boy out there in the old Chevelle? He knows every time I take a leak and what color it is."

Nick grinned, satisfied that Ferguson appeared to be sufficiently pissed about the surveillance. Lucky he didn't know how much of the time he *wasn't* being covered. Fred could only pull about eighteen hours a day, and he could keep an eye on only one of the hotel entrances at a time. That left quite a bit of unsupervised, recreational opportunities for Ferguson. Hopefully, he wasn't aware of the cracks in their security system.

"I don't know why you guys are on my ass," Ferguson said, scrubbing the shower with the same hunk of steel wool. "You caught the killer . . . that preacher dude, right?"

Preacher *dude?* Oh, yeah, Ferguson was from California.

"Let's just say, we like to keep our options open." Nick uncrossed his arms and took a step toward the shower. He saw Ferguson cut him a quick, worried, sideways glance. Good, he still had his bluff in on the guy. "I just wanted you to know that I'm still *very* interested in you and that 'social schedule' of yours. I like knowing the color of your piss. It gives me a warm, cozy feeling, being informed." He leaned over him and lowered his voice. "Let's just say, I sleep a lot better if I know when and where *you're* sleeping."

Ferguson gave a snort but didn't look up. "Gee, I'm touched."

"Don't be. It ain't exactly love and concern. I'm just looking for an opportunity to hang your ass in a sling . . . about forty stories up somewhere. I want to dangle you over, let go, and watch you splat."

Tentatively, Ferguson ventured a glance up, then quickly averted his eyes. "I think this . . ." He choked on the words and Nick smirked. "I think this might be bordering on police harassment."

Nick leaned lower closer to him. "Naw, this isn't harassment. Not the real thing, anyway. Believe me, Dave, if I decide to harass you, you'll know right away. You won't have to stop and think about it."

As Nick turned around and walked out of the lavatory, he had an uneasy feeling—one he didn't welcome.

Ferguson was a killer; his gut would have told him that, even if the records hadn't. But was he the Mirror Killer?

God, how he wished he was. It was always easier when your enemy had a face, a name, and best of all, a location.

But Nick couldn't get rid of the rotten, sick feeling that, this time around, David Ferguson wasn't the enemy.

Elizabeth realized that she had "hit the wall" when her fingers refused to obey her and her eyes would no longer focus on the screen. Glancing at her watch, she couldn't believe that it was eight o'clock in the evening. She hadn't taken a break to eat, or even take a deep breath since she had sat down sixteen hours before. Her periodic calls to the hospital had been her only diversion.

Slowly she became more aware of her surroundings as her mind left the time and place she had created in the script and readjusted to the "real world." The building was quiet without the usual hum of voices, telephones, and miscellaneous computer noises. Most of the staff had left for the day. The outer office was dark, and Elizabeth had to remind herself that Cassie wasn't out there, waiting for her to quit so that she could go home herself.

Would she ever return to that office? And if she did, would she still be the same Cass Elizabeth loved? Sometimes, Elizabeth desperately wanted a crystal ball, so that she could answer an equally desperate question. But she wasn't sure this was one of those times. For tonight, it felt good to hold onto that bit of hope. Even potentially false hope was better than none at all.

"Hey, beautiful," said a soft, deep voice. "You wanna come home with me tonight?"

She turned and saw Nick standing in her doorway. He was certainly quiet on his feet for such a large man.

Her weary spirit heartened at the sight of him. His blond hair was tousled, his jeans and leather jacket a bit scuffed, and he definitely needed a shave. But his smile was warm and the affectionate light in his eyes made her want to get up from her desk, run to him, and hold him close.

So, she did.

"Wow," he said, pulling back a bit and looking down into her face. "What did I do to deserve that? Tell me so I can do it again."

"You stayed up with me all night, while I was keeping watch over my friend," she said, gratitude softening her voice.

He didn't reply for a moment as he looked down at her, his eyes mirroring the affection she felt toward him. Then he chuckled. "Damn. I was hoping to get a little shuteye tonight, but if you promise to throw yourself at me like that again, I'll—"

She reached up and placed her fingertips over his lips. "Sh-h-h. I wouldn't ask you to spend the night there again. The hospital staff probably wouldn't allow it. Maybe just a ten minutes stop to see how she's really doing?"

"That could be arranged. Anything else?"

"Yes . . . what was that you were saying about me going home with you?"

"Would you?" he asked. "I'd feel a lot better if you were lying safe in bed next to me tonight."

"I'd like that, too," she said. With a grin she added, "Although I don't know how 'safe' I'll be, lying in a bed beside you."

"Before I forget . . . here are your keys back," Nick said as he dug the keyring out of his jacket pocket and handed it to Elizabeth.

The light changed from red to green and traffic surged forward. Nick turned his attention back to his driving. Conversation between them had been minimal since they had left the hospital. Cassie's condition remained the same. Not encouraging.

Reaching over the back of the seat, Elizabeth felt a cold, wet nose nuzzle her palm. "Hello, Hercules," she said, finding the magic spot behind his ear that he loved to have scratched. Often she had found that giving comfort and affection to an animal made her feel better herself. She thought of Katie, alone in the house, waiting for her mistress to return, and silently promised that she would return first thing tomorrow morning to pick her up and bring her and her litter box to the office for a little "vacation."

"Are they finished at my house?" she asked. "The lab guys, that is."

"Yep, finished two hours ago."

"Did they find anything?"

He hesitated long enough that she knew it wasn't great news. Probably, not even good.

"Not sure yet . . . but I don't think so. I'd bet that he wears gloves when he 'visits' you, just like at his crime scenes. He's not stupid. Most murderers are, and that's why we catch them. But this one . . . he's a cut above."

"Did you ask them to clean off that black stuff when they finished dusting for prints?" she asked, trying not to sound too anxious.

"Yes, I did. Don't worry. They assured me they left everything neat and tidy." He gave her a curious look. "Are you really that meticulous of a housekeeper?"

"It isn't that. I just . . . well, it's hard to explain."

He laughed. "I hope you won't decide to end this friendship when you get a look at my apartment. There was a good reason I didn't take you in there Christmas Day. It's a little . . . rustic . . . to say the least. And I haven't had time to do any cleaning at all before I picked you up."

"I'm sure it's fine," she said absentmindedly. "Right now, a few dust bunnies are the least of my concern."

He didn't say anything for a long time, but she could feel him studying her. Finally, he said, "What *is* your concern right now, Lizzie? What's going on in that pretty head of yours?"

"I'll tell you . . . ," she replied, staring out the window at nothing in particular. In her mind's eye she could see the scenes she had written today, placing herself in that fantasy world she had created, a world which would soon merge with the "real world."

"When?" he asked. "When are you going to tell me?"

She could hear the worry in his voice, but she couldn't bring herself to tell him yet.

"Later. I promise."

Twenty-eight

"Like I said, I haven't had time to clean at all," Nick said as he ushered Elizabeth into his apartment. "So, please excuse the dirt and clutter."

Elizabeth looked around at what appeared to be rather carefully organized chaos. At first glance, the piles of books which covered every horizontal surface seemed to be haphazardly strewn. But a closer inspection revealed some peculiar method of groupings by genre and author. The Dewey Decimal System, it wasn't; but Elizabeth was impressed.

"Have you read all of these?" she asked.

"Naw, I just buy every book I can get my hands on at garage sales in Queens and use them to prop up the furniture."

Being a book lover all her life, she was mortified—but only for a moment, then she realized by his grin that he was teasing her.

"I really like to read," he said. "If I don't keep a lot of books around, I find myself perusing the cereal boxes or shampoo bottles."

"And if you've read one good box of corn flakes, you've read them all."

He nodded soberly. "True, and most shampoo bottle labels are written by hacks; entertaining, but they'll rot your brain."

"Absolutely. I avoid them whenever possible."

He waved his hand toward the sofa. "Have a seat, and I'll make us a cup of coffee."

"Don't mind if I do." As she sank into the deep, comfy cushons, a shudder of fatigue went down her back and through her legs, leaving her weak and shaky. The difficulties of the past twenty-four hours were beginning to exact a hefty toll on her. She knew she would need to take better care of herself or she would wind up in the hospital along with Cassie. And, with all she had planned for the next seven days, she couldn't allow that to happen. Too much depended on her holding it together for a while longer.

Then you can fall apart, she promised herself. *Hang in there until next Friday night, kid, and then we'll come unglued at the seams.*

Hercules trotted over to sit at her feet and cocked his head to one side, giving her a beguiling crooked-toothed smile. She was too tired to administer the usual "behind the ear scratch," but he looked so hopeful that she couldn't refuse. Her reward was his look of ecstatic pleasure as he closed his eyes and leaned against her hand.

"Do you like your coffee strong . . . or are you a pansy?" Nick asked from the tiny alcove that served as a kitchenette.

"High octane. Maybe it'll kickstart my motor," she said. "I don't think I even have a pulse right now."

A loud knocking on the door made her jump, twanging her taut nerves like the highest "C" string on a grand piano. *Well,* she thought as she pressed her hand over her pounding heart, *at least I have a pulse now.*

"Come in, Nina," Nick called. "What took you so long?"

The door opened and Nina peeked around it. A bright smile lit her face when she saw Elizabeth. "Hi," she said with only a touch of the shyness she had shown when they had first met.

"Hi yourself," Elizabeth said, warming at the sight of her. Nina had that same spark as Martie. The same enthusiastic outlook on life, the same refreshing, youthful optimism.

"Are you guys . . . busy?" the girl asked, wriggling one eyebrow.

"Not yet," Nick growled. "Feel free to sit down and make a nuisance of yourself."

"Thanks!" She bounced into the room, sat beside Elizabeth on the sofa, and took over the task of satisfying Hercules's perpetual itch.

Elizabeth noticed the fresh, carefully applied makeup, the "big" hair, and the attractive oversized sweater, leggings and boots. "Are you ready for a date?" she asked.

"Uh . . . no," Nina said with a shrug and an awkward smile. "I just . . . you know . . . it's nothing special."

Realizing the girl had dressed up for her visit, Elizabeth was touched, but she knew enough about teenagers not to make a big deal of it.

Nina glanced around the room and gave a low whistle. "Wow, Nicky! The place looks great! You must have brought a bulldozer and a street sweeper in here this afternoon."

Sticking his head around the corner, Nick shot her a warning look, but it was too late.

Elizabeth snickered and said, "Gee . . . really? He said he didn't have time to do any housecleaning at all."

"Thanks, kid," he said. "Sell me out, why don't ya?" He turned to Elizabeth and shrugged, looking deeply humiliated. "Actually, I think it was the firehose that made the most difference."

He disappeared momentarily then came back into the room, carrying a tray with three mugs and some biscotti. He handed Elizabeth a cup which bore the grimacing face of a bulldog. "Now *that's* a cup," he said, "not those sissy, Cinderella things you've got at home."

Elizabeth stared at the wrinkled face, the sprouting fangs, the drooping dewlaps. "He's a rough-looking character," she said. "Like those cartoon bulldogs that are always beating up the cats and smoking cigars."

"Sh-h-h!" Nina pressed her finger to her lips and nodded toward Hercules. "It's not a 'he.' It's a girl . . . Herc's girlfriend. You'll hurt his feelings saying something like that."

"Oh, sorry." Elizabeth looked at the mug again. "How could I have been so foolish? Of course, she's a lovely, lovely . . . ah . . . example of canine pulchritude."

"That's better," Nina said, then added suspiciously, ". . . I think."

"How's Mama tonight?" Nick asked, sitting in his father's recliner. Hercules immediately left the women and took his usual place, chin across the toes of Nick's sneakers.

"Went to bed early," Nina said. She gave Elizabeth a sideways glance. "Lucky thing, too, considering. . . ."

"What are you implying?" he said, sipping his coffee. "That Mama wouldn't approve of my overnight guest?"

Nina sighed. "She probably wouldn't care . . . since it's you. But if she caught me even kissing my boyfriend in the house, she'd ground me for a month."

"Elizabeth is staying with me tonight because her own house isn't safe," Nick said.

"Yeah, right." Nina rolled her eyes and pursed her lips in a way that Elizabeth had seen Martie do a thousand times.

"Which reminds me," he said, turning to Elizabeth. "Have you arranged for someone to close up that wall for you? I know a couple of good carpenters on the island, if you need a reference. One's a retired cop. He'd do a good job for you."

Elizabeth hesitated and chewed her bottom lip. Here it was—time to tell him and listen to all the objections.

"I'm not going to have it boarded up," she said carefully. "At least, not yet."

He gave her a searching look. "Really?"

"Yes. That's what I've decided."

"I see." For several seconds he stared at her, and she felt like a bug under a powerful microscope. "No, I don't," he said suddenly. "I don't see. What's going on, Lizzie?"

The tension in the room thickened by the moment, filling the silence. Nina looked from Elizabeth to Nick and back, instantly alert to the prospect of conflict.

Finally, Nick broke the stalemate. "I think you'd better go now, Ninuzza," he said gently. "I'm afraid Elizabeth and I are going to get 'busy' soon."

She looked disappointed, but she stood and walked to the door.

"No problem. Are you going to be here tomorrow morning Elizabeth?" she asked hopefully.

"I . . ." Elizabeth looked at Nick. "I think so."

"She'll be here," Nick said. "I'll take us all out for breakfast."

"Mama, too?"

"Mama, too."

After Nina had closed the door behind her, they sat quietly saying nothing. Elizabeth could feel her stomach tightening into a knot. She wasn't afraid of what Nick was going to say when he heard her idea. She was afraid of what he would feel. The last thing she wanted was to hurt or worry him right now. She knew that he had all he could handle already.

But she had no choice.

He rose from his chair and walked over to her. Sitting beside her on the sofa, he took her hand in his and squeezed it.

"You promised you'd tell me, Liz," he said, his eyes searching hers. "Now, what's going on?"

Brody Yarborough had gone home three hours before, but he had taken the job with him. Long ago, that tenuous dividing line between personal life and career had blurred, then disappeared altogether. An evolution aided by the simple fact that Brody Yarborough had no personal life, and that was the way he liked it.

He sat at his kitchen table which hadn't enjoyed a close encounter with a plate since he had turned it into a desk five years prior. His mood was rapidly deteriorating; the voice that was coming from his speaker phone wasn't saying what he wanted to hear.

"Don't tell me you can't do it!" he shouted, pronouncing the word "can't" like "c'ain't." "You just keep working on it. 'Can't never did nothing!"

"We're doing the best we can here, Mr. Yarborough." Francois sounded weary, frustrated, and grandly pissed. "You must admit this was rather short notice."

"I'm not gonna admit anything of the sort. You get that damned promo ready for the eleven o'clock news tonight or don't bother coming to work tomorrow . . . you or any of those peabrains you call a crew. Got it?"

"Yeah. I got it. And you'll get it. Don't worry."

Brody didn't notice the edge to Francois's words that might have implied a secondary meaning.

"Good. I'll be watching and it damn well better be there. This could be our biggest audience yet, but we've gotta let them know it's on. We don't want any of our faithful viewers out there in T.V. land to miss the big showdown. Elizabeth Knight herself vs. 'The Mirror Killer.' Live and in person."

He poked a button, punctuating his speech and getting rid of Francois. Pulling another beer out of the cooler on the floor beside him, he felt a rush and a buzz that had nothing to do with the other five he had drunk in the last hour. This was a high induced by the powerful narcotic, Natural Adrenalin, the most addictive substance known to humankind. And—his numerous other vices not withstanding—Brody Yarborough was a primo junkie.

Elizabeth Knight, Miss Priss herself, goes one on one with a serial killer.

Beauty and the beast.

It was all just too, too sweet.

"There will be one more episode of "The Dark Mirror." I wrote the first act today," Elizabeth said, her eyes soft, almost apologetic as they met Nick's.

He was afraid to ask, but he had to. "Okay . . . what's it about?"

"The story line is pretty straightforward." She paused and took a deep breath. "It's about a female television personality, the host of a mystery show. Someone is committing copycat murders, mirroring her television show."

"Gee, what a novel idea," he said dryly, trying not to think about the flood of acid that had just hit his stomach. She couldn't be serious.

She was serious; he knew it.

"I'm going to play the part," she continued. "And right after the show airs, between eleven and midnight, I'll be at the studio, doing a live interview with one of the news anchors. We haven't decided who gets the honor," she added, looking down at her hands which were folded in her lap.

"You mean, you haven't found anybody on your staff who's willing to commit suicide with you," he said, far more sarcastically than he had intended.

"I wouldn't put it like that . . . exactly."

"And what would you call a stupid stunt like that?" His temper flared, a hot, bitter fury that she would endanger herself that way. Goddamn, didn't she know how much she meant to—

"I'd call it . . . ," she said, lifting her chin defiantly and glaring at him with eyes the color of blue ice, ". . . an incredibly brilliant plan to catch a killer."

"Don't think much of yourself, do you, lady." He glared back at her, giving her his best stare-down fix, but she didn't budge. Why had he thought he actually liked feisty females?

Suddenly, her expression softened, and he thought with alarm that she might start crying. "Please, Nick," she said. "Try to understand. He's using *my* show, *my* creation as an excuse to slaughter innocent people. I *have* to do anything and everything I can to stop him. I couldn't live with myself if I didn't."

She reached up and stroked his cheek once with her fingertips, a gesture he sincerely wished she hadn't made. The last thing he needed was to feel right now. It wasn't a good time to evoke emotion, because once the flood started, it wasn't likely to stop.

Who was he kidding? he asked himself. She didn't need to touch his cheek to touch his heart. Sitting here beside her on his beat-up sofa, looking into her beautiful eyes and seeing her pain, her fear, her courage . . . and yes, her love for him . . . he was already feeling more than he could stand.

She didn't know. She was a civilian, and civilians never knew what it was like. *He* knew—far more than he wanted to—about the stark reality of death and dying. He had seen firsthand what a bullet, knife, or even a fist clenched in rage could do to a human being. In a matter of seconds a person . . . a living, loving, thinking, laughing, alive person . . . could be changed into a pile of meat. And hours later, a putrid pile of meat. The love, the thoughts, the laughter gone forever.

It was reality. It happened every day, over and over, in this city alone. Civilians didn't know how vulnerable, how fragile they were. They thought that all they had to do was dial 911 and Captain James T. Kirk himself would arrive with a convoy of shining emergency vehicles, flashing lights and sirens, accompanied by a team of concerned and highly trained paramedics who knew exactly what to do to set everything right.

But that wasn't the way it usually happened. Nick knew, because he had been present many, many times when there hadn't been a television-style happy ending. He knew, all too well, that once you were dead, it didn't matter who loved you or how much; you were still meat. And you weren't coming back.

"Elizabeth," he said, choosing his words carefully. "Is there anything I can say to convince you that you don't have to do this?" He reached over and placed his hands on her shoulders. "Sweetheart, we'll catch him, *I'll* catch him for you. I promise. Don't let some misplaced sense of guilt about these deaths goad you into sacrificing your life. There has to be another way, and we'll find it."

For a long moment, she didn't say anything, and he began to hope that maybe he had gotten through to her. Maybe . . .

No. She shook her head emphatically. "I appreciate what you're saying, Nick, and I know you're worried about me, but—"

"Worried?" The dam overflowed. He pulled her to him and buried his face in her soft, fragrant hair. "Hell, Lizzie, you have no idea how I'm feeling right now. Dammit, I love you. I'm ass over teakettle—"

"Tea cup," she interrupting, smiling.

"Whatever—in love with you, and I don't want to lose you.

You're a pain sometimes, but you're also very, very special, and I could never replace you. I don't want a hole that big and that empty in my life."

He paused, surprised by his own words. Whatever he had meant to say, it certainly hadn't been a declaration of love.

"You love me?" she asked, looking up at him with wide, incredulous, little girl eyes. "Really?"

He slowly nodded, the same wonder in his own eyes. "Seems so," he said. He shrugged and looked away, embarrassed. "I guess this wasn't the best time or circumstances to mention it."

She threw her arms around his neck and gave him a long, passionate kiss that made him forget everything and everyone for its duration. Unfortunately, it had to end.

"I'm so glad," she said breathlessly, coming up for air.

"You are?"

"Oh, yes. Because I love you, too."

He had known it all along. At least, his heart had known it. His head had been busy telling him that cops didn't get to fall in love with television stars . . . or, if they did, it wasn't going to be reciprocated. But somewhere deep down inside, he knew that they hadn't just had sex that first night. He had found himself making love to her, and she to him. He'd experienced plenty of lust along the way, enough to know that this was different.

"So, I love you, you love me," he said with a weary sigh, "and you're going to set yourself up as a target for a serial killer next Friday night. Is there anything else you'd like to tell me tonight to make this situation a little more complicated?"

She laughed and the deep, husky sound of it went through his body like a liquid heat, warming and igniting. "Oh, Nick," she said, kissing his cheeks, his chin, and finally his mouth. "Thank you for understanding."

"Who said I understand?" he asked gruffly against her lips as he returned and escalated the kiss.

But he did. He understood that she had to do this, just as his conscience had forced him to do certain things in the past. It *was* a good plan. Hell, it was the only plan they had. And it just might work.

Now all he had to do was figure out how to keep her alive.

Until recently, the killer had never been particularly interested in television news. As far as he was concerned, the world which revolved around his own was more of a irksome nuisance than a matter of importance to him. Who gave a damn about the price of rice in China, as long as it didn't upset his own personal apple cart?

But since he had undertaken his "mission," he couldn't wait for the eleven o'clock news and the reports of his latest exploits. He rated his success by whether or not he was the lead story. Often he was, especially the day after a murder. As the week wore on, he would drop back to the third or fourth, but come Friday, he'd be right up there on top again.

He glanced at the clock on top of the television. Ten fifty-eight. Eyes riveted on the screen, he cursed the lengthy car commercial, as though his blasphemy could somehow "fast forward" the broadcast. One more stinking commercial, and then the headlines.

But as the station promotional spot unfolded before him, his face turned a sick shade of gray and his mouth dropped open. He couldn't believe what he was seeing and hearing. The shock to his system was so great that he only comprehended snatches of the broadcaster's words.

" 'The Dark Mirror' explodes across on the screen . . . for the first time, Elizabeth Knight in the starring role . . . beautiful television show hostess murdered by the serial killer who has been stalking her . . . a demon obsessed with . . ."

What the hell did they think they were doing? He jumped up and began to pace the room. What kind of bullshit was this?

Fear and excitement raced through him as every muscle in his body constricted, raising his blood pressure to stroke-potential levels.

A blatant challenge. A glove thrown right in his face. *She* was taking him on, forcing him into hand-to-hand combat with *her*. Of all the moves he might have expected she would make, this wasn't one of them. And that thought bothered him as much as any other. What else had she thought of that he hadn't?

"Following the show will be a one hour, live interview with Elizabeth Knight," the announcer continued, "as she talks candidly about the pain and trauma the Mirror Killer's spree has cost her personally."

Live? She was going to be there in the studio from eleven to twelve, being interviewed in front of the whole nation . . . waiting for him, asking for him to kill her.

Mixed emotions and thoughts warred inside his brain. On one hand, he couldn't stand the thought of actually killing her. Oh, sure, he had threatened to many times before, fantasized about it, even planned it in detail. But even when he knew she was being unfaithful to him, he had found it in his heart to forgive her.

Killing *for* her was one thing. Killing *her* was quite another.

And yet, she was forcing his hand. He was furious to think that she would set him up like this, put him in such a dangerous position. If he intended to continue his mission—and he had to—he would have to walk right into the police's hands, and just hope he could figure out a way not to get grabbed.

He had thought that maybe she loved him, maybe those gentle, slightly flirtatious looks had been subtle messages, saying that she cared. But, if she truly loved him, she would never have done this.

The T.V. news came and went, but he wasn't watching or listening. Moment by moment, as he paced from one side of the room to the other, his anger grew, supplanting the love he had felt for her. The gentler emotion died a quick and brutal demise, and the rage that replaced it was more intense than any love he had ever experienced.

She had declared war. So be it.

The final conflict. Fine. He had wanted her to be his eternal love. But she had chosen to be his enemy.

He thought of the way he had felt when he'd killed before. The sense of power that surpassed any other on earth. A moment to feel like God, Himself, or a great Caesar, giving or taking life on a whim.

He would feel that again. Only this time it would be *her*. This time it would be even better.

Twenty-nine

It's just a reading, Elizabeth thought as she stood outside the room where the actors, actresses, the director, and assorted crew members were assembled and waiting for her. *Calm down . . . no big deal.*

But as she opened the door and walked into the room, she knew that her headache and queasy stomach were caused by something much more substantial than simple stagefright.

When she saw their faces, eager and looking as nervous as she felt, she realized why she had such a heavy, oppressive feeling about this reading. In a conversation yesterday with the casting director, she had found out that it had been difficult to find actors willing to accept the roles. Apparently, contrary to popular opinion, there *were* actors and actresses in Hollywood who valued their hides more than the "big break."

But as she scanned the rows on either side of the table, she saw courage as well as fear in their eyes. Thankfully, there had been enough who were willing to take the risk.

"Good morning," she said, as she sat in the empty chair at the end of the table beside Francois. Since they had begun this project, three days ago, he had been avoiding her. Even now, he wouldn't meet her eyes.

"I'm sorry I was late," she said. "But I want to thank each of you for being here, for accepting this challenge. I truly believe that it's a good thing we're doing here, an important thing, or I wouldn't ask you to do it."

"Why are you asking *yourself* to do it?" Francois asked, his voice high and tight with tension. "I don't understand, Liz. Nothing is worth getting yourself or someone else killed over. Let the cops catch this guy. It's their job, not yours."

Shocked at his outburst, Elizabeth turned to him and saw genuine pain and concern in his eyes. His affection for her was the root of his anger, and she couldn't blame him for feeling the way he did.

Leaning over to him, she placed her hand on his forearm. She felt him flinch, as though she had struck him. "Francois," she said softly. "You've been a good friend to me for years. But I have to do this, and I haven't acted since I was in college. I don't need you to be my friend . . . not *this* week. For the next six days I need you to be my director. Help me do this. Help do it right. Please."

He stared at her through his tortoise shell rimmed glasses for a long moment, his brown eyes softening. Taking a deep breath of resignation, he shook his head and picked up the script from the table in front of him.

"All right, boys and girls," he said. "You heard the lady. . . . Let's go."

"And you're going to let her do this? You're crazy, Nick. I won't allow it."

Nick stood in front of captain Bob Ryerson's desk, having a brief flashback of a similar situation in fourth grade . . . only then it had been Principal Harry Nelson. He half expected Ryerson to take a board out of his desk drawer and whack him across the ass with it.

"You don't understand, Captain," he said. "Elizabeth Knight isn't exactly someone you 'let' do this or that. Whether you or I will 'allow' her to do something doesn't mean diddly squat to her. She does whatever she damn well wants. And she's made it very clear to me that she wants to do this."

Ryerson groaned and leaned back in his chair, propping his feet on his desk. "Why?" he said. "Why does she want to go out on a limb like this? What's in it for her?"

Nick shrugged. "I guess she just wants to get the bad guy. Simple as that."

"How refreshing. Maybe you can get her to give up acting and become a cop."

Ryerson wiped his hand across his forehead, then rubbed his eyes wearily. "All right. We'll put as many bodies as we can spare around her that night. We've gotta make sure a fine, upstanding citizen like that doesn't get herself killed on our watch."

Nick turned and headed for the door.

"Nick . . ."

"Yes?"

Ryerson had a funny look on his face, and Nick braced himself, knowing he wasn't going to like what he was about to hear.

"Have you heard about your buddy, Pete MacDonald?"

Nick's throat tightened. "No, what about him?"

"He was taken to the hospital about an hour ago."

"Why? What—?"

Ryerson sighed. "Just between you and me, let's say he had a severe sinus infection."

An O.D. Well, Nick couldn't say he hadn't seen it coming.

"He's been put on indefinite leave. I think he'll be vacationing someplace where he can . . . get over his cold."

Nick nodded. "Thanks for telling me."

"Did you know anything about this problem of his, Nick?"

Nick shrugged. "Not for sure."

"Okay." Ryerson waved him on. "Get outta here. I've got things to do and so do you. Nail that guy before Friday night, okay?"

Nick turned and walked to the door. "I'm trying, captain. Believe me, I'm trying."

Nick entered the jail cell with a spark of hope glimmering somewhere in the region of his heart. Thirty minutes ago, he had received the message: Reverend Taggerty wants to talk to you.

Maybe . . . probably not . . . but maybe. A little hope never hurt.

"You asked to see me?" he said, surprised at the difference a short stay in the Midtown Homicide Hilton had made in the man. The reverend sat, stoop shouldered on the cot. His halo of silver hair was bedraggled and his face gaunt and pale. His eyes had a strange, vacant look, reflecting none of the charisma that had attracted so many followers.

"Reverend?" Nick asked, stepping into his line of vision.

The man seemed to shake himself out of his trance and notice Nick for the first time. "You are . . . ? Oh, yes . . . I know you."

"I'm Detective Nicholas O'Connor. You asked to speak to me."

"That's true. I told them I had something important to tell you."

Nick took a step closer and sank to one knee in front of him, bringing himself down to his eye level. "What is it? What do you want to say?"

"I want you to understand why I did it."

"The bombing?"

"Yes."

Nick nodded encouragingly. "Okay. Why did you do it?"

"I'm in a battle against the Devil himself."

Nick's glimmer of hope flickered. "So you said when I arrested you. You told the entire world that, in a very loud voice, as I remember," he said dryly, recalling Taggerty's spectacular tantrum in front of the media cameras.

"But it's true. We wrestle not against flesh and blood, but—"

"Against principalities," Nick interrupted. "Yeah, I know. I read the Bible, too. But what does that have to do with you trying to blow up Elizabeth Knight's house?"

"The Lord spoke to me in a dream. He told me that she had to die. It was the only way to win the victory over Satan."

Nick felt like his little glimmer had just been doused by a bucket of ice water. Damn. "Is this what you brought me down here for? That's what you wanted to tell me?"

"Yes, it's very important that you understand." He reached out and grabbed Nick's jacket sleeve. "I tried, but Lucifer defeated me. Now *you* have to take up arms against him. You must succeed where I failed. The Lord has spoken."

Nick rose and shook his head. "You know, reverend," he said, feeling suddenly about twenty years older, "I believe the Lord *has* spoken to me a few times. He told me to duck a bullet once, and He's helped me catch a couple of particularly nasty guys who really needed to get caught. But He's never told me to plant a bomb under somebody's house."

He walked back to the cell door and signaled to the guard to let him out.

Before leaving, he turned around and saw the reverend who seemed to be, once again, lost in his trance. "Maybe the next time that voice speaks to you in a dream," he told him, "you'd better find out for sure who you're talking to. With directions like that, it might be the old boogie man himself who's giving the orders."

They had saved the worst for last. But the day and hour had arrived, and it was time to shoot the final scene of the episode.

Elizabeth walked out of makeup, wearing a black, slinky beaded gown of the style that had become her trademark. She could feel the perspiration breaking out all over her body, damp and cold, and she wasn't even under the lights yet. The makeup personnel were going to have a tough time keeping the shine off her face.

When she walked onto the stage, she felt everyone freeze up and heard a considerable drop in the conversation volume. Cast and crew watched as she walked onto the news set and took her place in the interviewee's chair beside the anchor's desk.

A couple of the grips carried the large oval mirror, the symbol of the series, onto the stage and positioned it beside her. She thought it rather awkward looking, but declined to say so. Bud was a great prop master, and she wasn't going to starting telling him how to do his job.

"Gees, this thing weighs a ton," one of the grips said, grimacing as he rubbed his lower back. "I don't remember it being that heavy."

"You're just gettin' soft, Tom," Bud said, slapping the young man on the back and giving Elizabeth a wink.

She offered him a weak smile in return, trying not to show how nervous she was about doing this scene. It wasn't every day that one had to act out their own murder . . . especially when that scene could easily become reality in forty-eight hours.

During the course of this "interview," a shadowy figure, whose face would never be revealed, would step onto the set, point a gun at the television hostess, and kill her while her stunned fans watched in horror.

As she waited for Francois to begin, Elizabeth felt as though she were sitting on an electric chair at two minutes until execution time, instead of on one of the sets in her own familiar studio. But she had no one to blame for her situation but herself. She had written this scene. Every movement, every word spoken was straight from her own imagination . . . a mirror image that reflected the dark side of her own soul.

Francois appeared on the set, gave her a compassionate look, enhanced by an encouraging smile, and said, "Okay, let's get this puppy in the can. Just this one last scene and then we can all go out and get snookered!"

A cheer echoed across the stage, breaking some of the tension. But the respite was short-lived. No amount of humor or good will on Francois's part, or anyone else's, was going to make this any easier for Elizabeth.

It has to be done, kid, she told herself, steeling for the moment she would have to tumble, seemingly lifeless, from this chair onto the floor. If this worked, it would be worth it all. Elizabeth was determined to take back her freedom from this unknown enemy who had stolen it. She would save her own life . . . even if it meant plotting her own death.

* * *

Nick stood in the back of the sound stage, watching the taping. The sick feeling in his gut intensified every time he saw the woman he loved fall onto the floor and die, over and over again until, thank God, they finally got it right.

He had been apprehensive before, but after speaking to the head of security at the studio for the past hour, he was deeply concerned about the lack of protection they provided. Nick had worked with security personnel at network studios before and had always found them highly professional and dedicated. But Brody Yarborough seemed to have hired a gang of thugs with more muscle than intellect.

Unfortunately, brawn alone wasn't going to be enough to combat an enemy as cunning and resourceful as the one they were up against this time.

Nick thought of how few officers the captain had promised him for Friday night and fought down the feelings that were much closer to panic than he would care to admit.

Elizabeth needed him. She needed someone who was cool, objective, and logical on her side if she were going to live through this.

Was he logical? *Yeah,* he decided, *on a good day.*

Cool? Objective? No way.

Seeing a woman he was crazy about lying on the stage, blood staining the front of her gown and hearing someone pronounce her dead on the scene, took a harsh toll on his cool. All traces of objectivity evaporated.

You're a damned fool, Nicholas O'Connor, he thought as he forced himself to turn and walk away. He had known better than to put himself in a jam like this. He should have waited until after he had solved the case to fall in love.

On second thought, he decided maybe he wasn't all that logical either.

* * *

Elizabeth knocked on Nick's apartment door for the third time, but still no one answered. He had extended an indefinite invitation to her, offering his apartment as her home away from home, until this ordeal was over. Both agreed that her house on the island presented a distinct health threat as long as a serial killer was coming and going as he pleased.

All day long she had looked forward to coming here to this cozy place and sliding into a hot bath, a warm bed, and his arms . . . though not necessarily in that order. Now she didn't know exactly what to do. The door was probably unlocked, but she didn't feel it would be appropriate for her to just go on in and make herself at home.

The door behind her opened, and Rosemarie O'Connor stuck her head out to look around. When she saw Elizabeth standing there, she gave her a warm smile.

"I'm sorry, dear, but Nick hasn't come home yet," she said, stepping into the hall. She wore a pink chenille robe over a white, lacy nightgown. Her hair, which Elizabeth had only seen pulled back into a bun at the nape of her neck, was loose and floated in soft curls around her face, softening the age lines. Elizabeth thought how pretty she was and how kind. It was little wonder that Nick adored her.

"He invited me to come by," Elizabeth said uneasily, not knowing how Rosemarie felt about her spending the night with her son, here in her own house.

"Oh, yes, I know. He called half an hour ago and told me to expect you. He sends his apologies and said he'd be home as soon as possible."

"Thank you, Mrs. O'Connor," Elizabeth replied sincerely, feeling no condemnation from the woman, only warmth and unqualified acceptance.

"I'm having a cup of coffee and some coffee cake," Rosemarie said. "I'd love to have your company, if you'd like to wait with me."

At the simple gesture of kindness, Elizabeth felt a knot form in her throat and tears sting her eyes. *I'm more tired than I*

thought, she decided. Usually an invitation for coffee—no matter
how pleasantly delivered—didn't threaten to send her into a crying jag. Unfortunately, she was almost drunk with exhaustion
and it frightened her to realize how fragile she was, emotionally
and physically.

"I'd love to have a cup of coffee with you," she said, fighting
back the tears. "Thank you so much for asking."

"Nick, why don't you just bring a sleeping bag along with
you next time and move in permanently?" Officer Patricia Sullivan leaned over the half wall which separated her desk area
from the evidence room. This was Pat Sullivan's domain and she
ran the operation with the casual abandon of a Marine Drill Sergeant.

Nick had spent hours combing through the drawers that held
the physical evidence associated with the murders: personal ef-
fects found on the victims' bodies, miscellaneous debris—which
might or might not be significant—collected from the crime
scenes, documents taken from the victims' homes, including address books, letters, phone bills.

He had memorized the contents in each drawer. At night he
lay awake and ran every item through his mental computer, looking for pertinent data. Hell, he even dreamed about these drawers.
But nothing had clicked. Nothing at all.

"Ha, ha," he said dryly, looking up from Larry Burtrum's "little black book," which was complete with one-to-five star ratings
in the margins. Maybe one of his bimbos had croaked him for
giving her a "one."

With a sigh he tossed the book back into the drawer and
slammed it closed.

"Coming up dry?" Pat said. She gave him a heavy-lidded look
which suggested that her interest went beyond the scope of his
investigation.

"It's the Sahara, Officer Sullivan, and I just sucked the last
drop from the old canteen."

"That bad?" she said, her voice dripping with sympathy.

"And gettin' worse." He headed for the door. "The buzzards are a'circlin', sugar. Wings a'flappin' right over my head."

"Are you in love with my son?"

Rosemarie O'Connor's question caught Elizabeth completely off guard. A moment ago they had been discussing their favorite potato salad recipes; then came this abrupt change of topic.

"I . . . um . . ." Elizabeth stalled for time by leaning forward on the sofa and pouring a bit more cream into her coffee. It wasn't as though she hadn't considered the concept before. But she hadn't heard it voiced so bluntly.

"You don't have to tell me," Rosemarie said, grinning at her over the rim of her cup. "I know you are."

"Is it that obvious?" Elizabeth felt her cheeks growing hot, and it had nothing to do with the cozy blaze that crackled in the fireplace.

"About as obvious as the fact that he's in love with you." She chuckled and propped her feet on the overstuffed ottoman in front of her chair. Her house slippers were as pink and fluffy as her robe with the emphasis on comfort rather than style.

Elizabeth felt her embarrassment fading away. The woman wasn't trying to put her on the spot. Quite the contrary. Rosemarie was just one of those refreshing individuals who said what they thought at any given time with very little mental censorship beforehand.

"I suppose it's one of those things that everyone knows except the principals involved," Elizabeth said as she inhaled the fragrance of the rich, amaretto-laced coffee.

"Not everyone," Rosemarie replied, soothingly. "Just anybody who happens to have eyes, or ears, or . . ."

"Oh, please," Elizabeth said, choking on her coffee.

Rosemarie laughed. "Or anyone who's ever been in love themselves," she added tenderly. "Don't be embarrassed, dear. You're going to have to get used to me teasing you. It's a sign of affection."

Surprised and touched, Elizabeth looked into her eyes and saw the same gentle intimacy that she had seen in Nick's. "Thank you," she said softly.

"You're welcome. I just want you to know that I think you're very good for Nicky. I can see that you've brought him a lot of happiness in a short time."

Elizabeth sighed. "I'm glad that you think so, but I'm afraid I've brought him a lot of grief, too. He's really worried about . . you know. . . ."

"Yes, of course I know. Anyone who watches television or reads a newspaper knows what you're intending to do this Friday night. I think you're very courageous."

"Your son thinks I'm foolish for trying it."

Rosemarie shook her head. "No, he doesn't. He's just afraid. He's terrified that he's going to lose you."

"I'm sorry to be putting him through this. I wish there was some other way."

Rosemarie stood and walked over to the coffee table where she refilled her cup. Then she sat on the sofa beside Elizabeth and covered her hand with her own.

"I'm sorry, too, dear," she said. "But in the long run, it'll be good for Nick."

Elizabeth was confused. "What do you mean?"

"The anxiety that he's feeling now . . . the sleepless nights . . the nightmares he's having when he does go to sleep . . . those are all miseries that you'll be going through, year after year, if you're in love with a policeman."

Rosemarie looked away and gazed into the fire, as though seeing something, someone else, far away in time and distance. "It's good for Nicky to know what it's like to worry about your mate. My Ryan thought he was invincible. When others walked into danger, he ran . . . and he died because of it. If he had only known that he wasn't immortal, if he'd only realized how much we all would suffer when we lost him, he would have been more careful with his life. I know he would have, because he loved his family dearly."

"I'm sure he was a very good man," Elizabeth said, touched by the woman's openness. "I wish I had known him."

"So do I." Rosemarie smiled and squeezed her hand. "Oh, he would have adored you. Ryan O'Connor was a faithful and devoted husband, but he did enjoy the sight of a pretty lass."

The tears that had been threatening to fall welled up again, and this time Elizabeth didn't bother to choke them back. On impulse, she leaned over and placed a quick peck on Rosemarie's cheek.

It was the older woman's turn to be surprised. "Why, thank you, dear," she said, obviously pleased as well as a little flustered.

Tears of gratitude spilled down Elizabeth's face. It felt good to have another woman to talk to. She missed Cassie so badly. "No, Mrs. O'Connor," she said, "thank *you*."

"Burning the midnight oil again, eh, O'Connor?" Captain Bob Ryerson stood in Nick's office doorway, wearing his "Let's keep down the overtime around here; this city isn't made out of money" look.

Blurry eyed, Nick tried to focus on him, but his eyes wouldn't adjust after staring at white paper half of the night.

"How about you?" Nick said, looking at the clock on his desk. It was one-thirty A.M. "Why haven't you gone home yet?"

Ryerson hesitated. "I had some paperwork to catch up on. Quarterly report to the chief."

"I see." Nick nodded knowingly. "So, you and the old lady had a fight, she kicked you out, and your favorite bar's closed. Gonna sleep on the sofa in your office?"

Even with fuzzy vision, Nick could see that he had scored the shot.

"The bill you and your terrible threesome have been racking up on this case is ridiculous. My wife can't even spend that much

money. Get the hell out of here. Go home," Ryerson said, flipping
the light switch and leaving Nick in the dark.

"Okay," Nick muttered, feeling for his backpack and jacket
"I can take a hint."

As he left the office and closed the door behind him, he saw
Ryerson hanging around, pretending to be busy at the water
cooler. If Nick hadn't known better, he would have thought the
guy was lonely.

"Wanna beer?" Ryerson asked. "I've got a couple stashed in
the cooler in my office."

"Thanks, but I've got to get on home," Nick replied, thinking
of Elizabeth, who was hopefully waiting for him.

"Are you saying you prefer that damned bulldog for company
than your commanding officer?"

Nick grinned as he turned to leave. "Hell, yeah!" he said over
his shoulder. "Hercules tells better jokes, serves better booze
he's cuter . . . and, most importantly, his breath is a hell of a lot
better."

Elizabeth was thankful for the gentle hand and kindly voice
that coaxed her out of her nightmare.

"Lizzie, wake up, sweetheart. You're having a bad dream."

For a moment she couldn't remember where she was. The
room was unfamiliar, the bed she was lying on felt strange, and
the shirt she was wearing wasn't her own.

But the voice and the hands she recognized.

"Nick . . . ," she murmured sleepily.

"Yes, love. I'm right here."

He slid into bed beside her, and she luxuriated in the warm
masculine hardness of his body against hers. Putting his arm
around her, he pulled her closer to him. Again, she marvelled at
how well they fit together, every feminine curve and masculine
contour finding its complement.

"I'm sorry I'm so late," he said, brushing his lips against her
cheek.

"Working on my case?" she mumbled.

"Of course. It's what I live for."

"Mm-m-m . . . then I forgive you."

"Thank you." His lips grew more insistent as he kissed her mouth, her throat and traced a path down to the deep vee in the flannel shirt she had borrowed from his closet.

Something about his caresses made her uneasy, and at first, she wasn't sure why. He had been deeply passionate with her before, and she had delighted in his attentions. But tonight, as his hands moved beneath the shirt, stroking her, pulling her so close that she could hardly breathe, she sensed something much more desperate than passion. He wasn't enjoying her; he was holding on for dear life . . . for *her* life. This wasn't desire she felt radiating from him. It was fear.

His mother had been right. He was terrified of losing her.

"Nick, please . . . ," she said, gently pushing him away.

He raised himself up on one elbow and looked down at her. Even in the semi-darkness, she could see that he was hurt by her rejection.

"I'm sorry," he said. "I thought you would want to—"

"Make love?" she asked, smoothing his tousled hair away from his forehead.

"Ah . . . yeah."

"I do. But I want to talk first."

"Oh, sorry. I guess I got carried away." He took her hand in his, turned it over and pressed his lips into her palm. "Do I have to buy you dinner first, too?" he said teasingly.

She pulled her hand away and slapped his shoulder. "No, thanks. I had a plate of your mother's famous ziti." She paused. "I also had a long talk with her."

"Huh oh." He plopped back onto the bed and stared at the ceiling. "I guess I'm busted. Did she tell you everything?"

"Everything."

"About the wife in Jersey, the nine kids, and the mistress in Queens?"

She nodded. "And the time in prison, the drug problem, the gambling addiction, and the overdue library books."

Sighing, he shook his head. "I'm sorry you had to find out that way."

"It *was* a shock." She ran her fingertips over his cheeks and chin, delighting in the masculine texture of his "stakeout shave."

"What else did she tell you?"

Laying her head on his shoulder, she wrapped her arm around his waist and snuggled close. "She said that everything is going to turn out all right in the end . . . that she has a 'good feeling' about it."

"Really . . . ?" he said thoughtfully. "She said that?"

"Yep. And she said she's pretty accurate about that sort of thing."

"That's true; she is."

"Then, you don't have to worry so much about me . . . right?"

He didn't say anything for a long moment, then he slid his hand beneath her chin and lifted her face to his. Again, he kissed her, but this time it was loving and soft, not so desperate.

"Just promise me one thing, Lizzie," he said. "Promise me that this time tomorrow night, we'll be lying right here together. And you'll feel just as good as you do tonight."

"Sure. It's a promise."

"Well . . . if you promise, and if Mama O'Connor says everything is going to turn out all right . . . I guess I won't worry."

"Good." She wriggled against him, pressing the softness of her breasts against the hardness of his chest, and delighting in their differences. "Then whatever are you waiting for?" she said in her best melodramatic, silverscreen voice. "There's no time for hesitation. Take me, you fool."

But he did worry. Hours later, he lay, holding her in his arms as she slept. Through his window he could see the dawn turning the black sky to a dull gray over the buildings across the street.

Ordinarily, Mama's "good feelings" were enough to put his mind at ease. But this time, there was so much at stake.

He looked down at Elizabeth, her face relaxed and free from worry for the first time in weeks. Her glossy black hair was splayed across his chest, and her soft body warm against his.

"I love you, Liz," he whispered, wondering if some part of her subconscious would hear and remember.

How could a man not worry . . . when he had so very, very much to lose?

From the bushes across the street, the killer watched the house and the gray sedan parked down the block. He was getting impatient. The cop inside the car had been drinking coffee from a Thermos bottle for the past two hours. Wasn't it about time for him to leave and go take a pee somewhere? Usually, the guy couldn't hold out this long.

Sure enough, as though the driver of the car had sensed his thoughts, the sedan's engine coughed, sputtered, then roared to life. The headlights came on, and he ducked lower behind the shrubs.

As the car pulled away, he glanced down at his watch, squinting to see it in the pale, murky, morning light. The cop in the sedan was pretty predictable. It would take him about twelve minutes to go to the nearest gas station—or wherever he went to relieve himself—and return with a full Thermos and a box of Dunkin' Donuts.

Twelve minutes wasn't long, he thought as he hurried across the street and around the side of her house. But it was all the time he needed.

Thirty

"This is a tricky situation, people. It certainly isn't your run of the mill security challenge," Nick said as he studied the members of his team, a hodge-podge consisting of: patrolmen and detectives from the three precincts involved, and a scruffy assortment of recently transplanted pool hall bouncers which Y.B.S. studios called security personnel.

He missed Pete. Peter should have been here, instead of vegetating in that damned drug rehab clinic. But he couldn't think about Pete right now. Pete had made his own way, and Nick had a job to do.

"The problem is . . . ," he continued, ". . . we have to keep him from killing anyone—Ms. Knight in particular—and yet, we don't want to do our jobs so well that he can't even get near the building. We want him to find a way in; we just want to know it the moment he sets foot in the place."

Nick picked up a stack of photos and began handing them out. "As though you haven't all memorized the face, this is David Ferguson, a convicted murderer who's been stalking Ms. Knight off and on for years. He's our number one suspect. Needless to say, if anyone sees anyone who even sort of looks like him, we all want to know about it. But we don't know for sure that he's our man, so keep your eyes open for anyone who looks out of place."

He turned around and tacked a sheet of paper to the wall. "This is a list of who's partnered with whom, and which area you're to watch. I've divided you into teams of two: one security person to one cop. I did this for a couple of reasons. First, the Y.B.S. people can tell us who is a familiar face on the set and who isn't. And second, the cops have guns."

Several of the Y.B.S. thugs chuckled and gave each other sideways looks. *Okay,* Nick thought, *some of them have guns, too.* Whether that was a good idea or a pain in the ass, only time would tell.

"Any questions?"

There were none. That always made Nick nervous. Did their silence mean that they understood everything and all was under control, or were they half-asleep?

"Then let's get to it. Showtime is in a couple of hours. Everybody be careful. I want to get this guy, but I don't want any more dead bodies in the process. This has gone far enough. The son of a bitch doesn't get any more."

As the man turned left from Second Avenue and headed toward the waterfront, he realized this wasn't the best time or place to be out and about. But the guy on the phone had insisted that he meet him here, and he didn't have time to argue the issue.

He needed the gun, and he needed it tonight. A call to a friend's brother's step-cousin, and the two one hundred dollar bills in his jeans pocket would buy him what he needed.

The wind off the East River cut through his thin jacket and set his teeth on edge. The pungent, musty smell of the waterfront filled his head and made him think of death. Understandable, under the circumstances, he assumed.

He looked at his watch. He was here on time, too bad the other guy wasn't. With places to go and people to see, he couldn't wait around all night.

The Desert Winds Restaurant was expecting him to put in an appearance in little over an hour, and as a responsible and time-conscious representative of Elite Temporary Services, Inc., he couldn't be late.

Besides, he had to get home in time to mess with his hair and that damned fake mustache. He'd already got a flat-top cut and dyed the remaining fuzz a shade which the seductive ad on the box had called Copper Sunshine Satin. But the stupid, bristling mess wouldn't stand up like it was supposed to, and his previous experiments with that gel goop had been disastrous. He needed all the time he could get.

"Hurry up," he whispered through chattering teeth to his tardy, and as yet still invisible contact. He hopped from foot to foot and—ever the optimist—rubbed his hands together, as if it would help.

It didn't.

He thought of what he had to accomplish tonight, of all the things that had to go just as he had planned, and he began to shiver even harder. The emotion of fear could be more chilling than the coldest river wind.

Hearing a noise behind him, he whirled around and saw a young kid standing there, looking like he had just stepped off the honors list of a prestigious prep school. "Hey," the boy said, "you waiting for me?"

The man shook his head; they just didn't make criminals the way they used to, he observed. It was getting harder and harder to tell the good guys from the punks.

"That depends," he said. "Are you Terry?"

"I am tonight." The kid grinned. "I hear you're in need of a little personal protection."

"No, you're wrong," he replied. "I need a lot. Show me what you've got."

Elizabeth sat, staring into the brightly lit mirror in front of her as Francie applied her makeup. In the chair next to hers, also receiving a liberal dusting of powder, sat Charlene, Y.B.S. late night news anchor and occasional prime-time reporter.

"I can't tell you how much I appreciate you volunteering to do this interview for me," Elizabeth said to Charlene's reflection. "I understand that no one from the six o'clock team could be bribed or threatened into doing it. You're a *real* reporter, not just another gorgeous talking head."

Charlene glowed under the compliment, then she sobered. "Thanks, but I'm not doing this to uplift the cause of journalism. As much as I like you, Liz, I'm not even doing it for you. It's for Cassandra. Every time I think of her lying there in that hospital bed I . . ."

"I know. Me, too."

"Cassie's a good-hearted person and tough when she needs to be. She'd do it for any of us."

Elizabeth nodded. "That's true. She would."

A knock sounded at the door. "Ten minutes, Ms. Knight."

"Thanks," she called back.

Looking in the mirror again at her own reflection, she liked what she saw. Her satisfaction had little to do with Francie's expertly applied makeup. It was the determined gleam in the woman's eyes who looked back at her. No more helplessness, no "lay-down-play-dead" routine.

She was fighting back . . . and it felt great.

"Come on, Charlene," she said, as she stood and removed the protective draping that covered her evening gown. "Let's do it. This one's for Cass."

They'll be checking everybody who comes through the doors tonight, he thought with a high degree of satisfaction. They would be oh, so careful to make sure that he didn't sneak in, disguised as a nun, boy scout, or a vampire.

No, Halloween was over. He took pleasure in the fact that his techniques were a little more sophisticated than that.

His legs ached from being all cramped up in such a tight space. Stabbing pains jabbed his lower back, like a dozen tiny ice picks. The pistol which he had tucked into the waistband of his jeans was cutting into the tender flesh of his belly. But the physical misery would pay off . . . soon.

While it wasn't a particularly "comfortable" plan, it had

worked beautifully, and he was obnoxiously proud of himself for thinking of it.

Knowing that security would be heavy today, he had made certain that he had gotten into the building yesterday morning. It hadn't been that difficult. Where there was a will, there was always a way, as the old saying went.

His way had been in the form of a large metal cabinet, half-filled with video tape—and better yet, half-empty.

Every morning, bright and early, the guys in charge of the props transferred furniture from the warehouse to the sets. Enough to stock a large department store. He knew, because he had watched. From his hiding place in the shrubs across the road, he had noted that the larger pieces of furniture often sat, unattended, on a loading pad until someone came along with a forklift to move them inside.

He recognized opportunity when he saw it. And opportunity had knocked loud and clear that morning. In his wildest dreams he had been hoping for a storage chest, an armoire, even a refrigerator—he'd figure out how to get out when the time came—but luck had been on his side. This large metal cabinet with two vertical doors and the left side empty had proven to be the perfect hiding place.

Well, almost perfect.

When the fellow with the forklift had come along and scooped it up, half of the tapes slid to the side and smacked him in the head. The landing had been a little rough, too. After being slammed against the back of the cabinet, he wasn't sure his ribs weren't broken.

Then it had been silent. Completely silent. After an hour or so, the air began to get a little thick, and the smell of his own nervous sweat was making him nauseous. Carefully, he opened the door a crack but saw only more darkness. Where the hell had they put him?

Looking around, he saw that he was in a small, dark room, filled with intricate electronic panels. The boards were studded with scores of toggle switches, levers, sliders, and miscellaneous buttons. A large window across the front of the room looked down on . . . the unlit set of "The Dark Mirror."

This was a control booth. He laughed aloud. How appropriate!

From this window he could see three other similar windows, other booths. Apparently, they used this one only for storage at the moment.

He couldn't have been more pleased with what Fate, in her kindness had dealt him.

Until now.

Having crawled back into the cabinet, just in case someone unexpectedly popped in, he was anxious to be getting on with it. He wasn't going to be much good under fire if his arms and legs were too numb to work. He was hungry and thirsty, and, even though he had had the foresight not to drink fluids for several hours before stowing away, his bladder felt like it was about to burst.

But that was okay. Everything was okay, because it was worth it. He was a man with a mission, and the mission was the most important thing in the universe.

After tonight, he thought, *after tonight, I'll be immortal. Everyone, everywhere will know my face, my name. And they'll know that I was a man who accomplished what he set out to do.*

You may be dead, too, whispered the quiet voice of doubt, of fear. *If you're dead and buried in the ground somewhere, how are you going to enjoy being famous?*

He shook his head, refusing to listen. This was no time to let cowardice ruin everything.

Long ago, he had chosen this path. And now, with his destination within sight, was no time to turn back.

"We've got ten minutes to air, folks. Get ready," Francois said as he walked across the set, headphones in place, a microphone attached to his collar.

The crew was minimal . . . only two cameras and one boom. It was only an interview, and nothing more was needed. Besides,

Brody had been coerced into paying quadruple time for the few crew members who did show. Apparently, even in periods of deep economic recession, few people could be bribed to risk their lives for the almighty dollar.

Charlene sat behind a desk, Elizabeth in a chair beside her, a mirror image of the scene being played out on the studio monitors. The final scene of "The Dark Mirror": shots exploding across the stage, Elizabeth slumping to the floor, a dark figure disappearing into the shadows.

At the last moment, Brody had cut the part where the director had announced that she was dead. "Don't need to kill off our star on screen," he had said. "We'll just leave 'em wonderin'."

Elizabeth watched the scene, refusing to recognize that feeling which was probably raw panic, welling up inside her. This was it. This was real. But it didn't feel like it, and that was the only thing that saved her. It played before her eyes like a surrealistic fantasy, a dream from which she would awake, alive and safe.

"It will all turn out okay," she remembered Mama O'Connor saying with such certainty. "I just have a feeling."

"Don't let anyone else be hurt, please," she whispered, thinking of Nick, his fellow officers, and her crew. "Please, God. No one else."

"What did you say?" Charlene asked, leaning toward her with a worried look on her pretty face.

"Just saying a little prayer," she admitted.

"Yeah, really. That's all I've been doing since I volunteered to anchor this show."

A movement to her right caught Elizabeth's attention. Her heart thudding against her ribs, she turned to see that it was only Bud. He walked up to her and knelt on one knee beside her chair.

"How ya doin', kid?" he asked with a paternal look on his wrinkled, sun-leathered face.

"Peachy," she said. "Just . . . peachy."

He leaned closer and whispered in her ear. "You know why that mirror was so heavy when the boys hauled it up here?" he asked, nodding toward the gilt oval mirror beside her.

"No," she replied in a hushed, conspiratorial tone to match his. "Why?"

"Because I . . . doctored it up . . . a bit."

Her eyes searched his, but all she saw was a mischievous twinkle. "What did you do to it?"

"Let's just say it's reinforced. As in—steel plating."

"Steel?" She studied the mirror from top to bottom, but saw no changes. "You're kidding."

"Nope. I thought that if . . . you know . . . it starts to go down the crapper, you might appreciate having something substantial to dive behind."

Touched by the gesture, Elizabeth reached out and grasped his hand. "Thanks, Bud. You're a doll."

Embarrassed, he yanked his hand out of hers. "Aw, no big deal. I just wanted to help in some way. I mean, you're doing this to help Cassie, and I feel responsible for—"

"One minute," Francois announced. "Quiet on the set."

Elizabeth gave Bud a smile and a wave as he retreated.

Her mouth went dry and she could taste her fear like bitter copper, welling up from her stomach. Cold sweat covered her palms, making them feel wet and clammy.

Francois walked onto the set. "Okay, this is it. Good luck, everybody," he said. He held out one hand, fingers spread, and counted down. "Five, four, three . . ."

Showtime.

Fred Halley stood guard on the left side of the set. On the right Nick watched . . . and listened. He couldn't believe how cool Elizabeth had been, sitting there for the past forty-five minutes, answering Charlene's questions, opening up and telling the world what it was like to live in a hell created by a stalker.

To Nick's surprise, they had even touched on the subject of Martie's death. He knew how painful that had to be for her, and he knew she was sharing it in hopes of helping someone else out there, some unseen, unknown stranger in television land.

Several times, he had seen her seek him out with her eyes, and he saw the comfort his presence gave her, registered on that classically beautiful face. He would have adored her if she had been homely as the side of an unpainted barn. But he had to admit that just looking at her made him happy.

Forty-five minutes into the interview. Only fifteen left. He wanted to feel relieved, to let down and hope that the killer wouldn't show at all. But he knew better. The guy was coming. He could feel him getting closer and closer.

"Any time now, boys and girls," he whispered into his walkie-talkie as he scanned the set and surrounding space for the thousandth time. His eyes met Fred's, and Nick knew that he felt it too. "Heads up," he said. "Everybody keep sharp."

Stephanie stood at her post near the service entrance, trying to ignore her boorish companion. The two-hundred pound, fifty-point intelligence quotient Godzilla-from-hell had already made six passes at her.

"If you 'accidently' touch my butt again," she said in a low menacing whisper, "I'm going to shoot your hand off. Got it?"

He stared at her, wide-eyed for a moment, then grinned. "Playing hard to get, huh?" he said, thick saliva stretching from his crooked uppers to stained lowers.

She watched as the parade of caterers passed, bearing elegant trays of delicacies from the van outside to the kitchen and dining area behind the sets. Having missed her dinner—lunch and breakfast, too, for that matter—she was starving. Besides, she was P.M.S.ing and desperately needed a chocolate fix. She had to summon every ounce of her willpower not to grab a Napoleon as it and its buddies floated by on a silver tray.

Briefly she turned to her companion-in-arms, only to catch him oogling her butt. "Do you mind?" she snapped. "You're supposed to be watching for unfamiliar faces."

"I'm watching, I'm watching," he said, spit stringing.

"Oh, God," she mumbled, "Nick, you owe me for this one."

* * *

Unfolding himself from the metal cabinet, he stretched and felt a thousand pins and needles pricking his limbs. The gun, tucked in his waistband, seemed to have left a permanent impression on his belly.

He didn't feel as if he had any blood at all from his waist down. The only fluid there was the ten gallons or so of urine he had been saving since eternity.

But all awareness of physical discomfort vanished the moment he looked out the window and down on the set below. There she was, looking as beautiful . . . no, more beautiful . . . than ever before.

How unfortunate for them both that she had decided to betray him.

"Come and get me, sucker," she had said in so many words.

Okay, he had come. Never let it be said that he was a man who refused a challenge . . . no matter what the ultimate cost.

Silently, his expression fixed, his mission clear, he left the control booth . . . and melted into the shadows.

Elizabeth could feel the tension mounting on the set as the end of the interview drew near. Francois stood, just out of camera shot, his face red and flushed beneath his headset. He held up six fingers to them.

Feeling a sense of relief, mixed with a generous dosage of bitter disappointment, she tried to concentrate on Charlene's latest question. What had it been? Oh, yes, she remembered.

"What have I learned from this experience?" she said. "Many things. I've learned what it is to fear, to hate, on a level I'd never thought I was capable of before. I'm not sure that could be considered personal growth, but it is self-knowledge, however dark."

She looked over at Nick, feeling his concern and drawing strength and encouragement from it.

"I've also learned some more positive things," she continued.

"I've learned that we don't have to go through our own private hell alone. There are people who are worthy of our trust and our love . . . if we can find the courage to believe in their basic goodness, if we can take a step of faith and open our hearts to them."

Across the set, Nick heard and felt her words. This wasn't the time to feel, he told himself, trying to shut off the emotions that were building inside him. He'd save the feelings, push them away and take them out later, when they were lying in bed together. Then he'd be able to savor this strange, new experience and think about what it meant in their lives, but for now—

"Nick!" the urgency in Stephanie's voice snapped him to attention.

"Yes, Steph," he said into the walkie-talkie.

"Ferguson. We've got him here in the back!" Her voice crackled with excitement in the tiny speaker.

"Hold him," he said, motioning to Fred. "We're coming."

He left the set, Fred right behind him, and ran as quickly as he could through the maze of plywood walls, facades, and half-rooms, toward the back of the building where he had placed Stephanie.

"Nick!" Stephanie's voice sounded even more charged than before. He could hear some noises that sounded like a scuffle. "Oh, shit, he's—"

"What? What's going on?" Nick yelled as he ran, one hand holding the walkie-talkie, the other on his gun. He could hear Fred pounding along behind him.

"We lost him! He's running."

"Which way?"

"Straight toward you. Watch yourselves. He's armed."

When Elizabeth saw Nick and Fred run from the set, she knew. The killer was in the building.

The thought gave her throat a squeeze, making it difficult for her to breathe, but some part of her was relieved. One way or the other, it was finally going to be over.

She glanced at Charlene, who had turned several shades lighter, in spite of her thick stage makeup. She was frozen, unable to speak.

Francois held up three fingers, trying to get her attention.

"I want to thank you, Charlene," Elizabeth said, improvising to fill up the dead space, "for allowing me this opportunity to—"

"Elizabeth!" The shout echoed across the stage as a figure stepped from behind the set wall and advanced toward her.

Charlene dropped to the floor behind her desk. The crew scattered or hit the deck, except for Francois, who took over the camera. Even Bud had disappeared. Elizabeth sat, stoically facing the phantom of her nightmares. Stepping into the light, he was a phantom no longer.

"David," she said. He looked different, something about his hair, but his face was all too familiar.

"Why?" he shouted as he ran up to her. "Why did you do this?"

She started to reach for the pistol inside her skirt, but at that moment she saw the gun in his hand . . . already drawn, already pointing in her direction.

"I didn't want to have to come here," he said. She was shocked to see tears in his eyes. His hand which held the gun was shaking violently.

"Why did you?" she asked, afraid of the answer.

"Because I had to. Don't you understand? I love you. I always have. I had to show you this one last time."

He began to sob openly, and Elizabeth's mind raced down a dozen paths, trying to decide the best way to handle him. She looked around the set, hoping to see someone who was making a move to help her. But they remained motionless on the floor. Even one of the security guards had decided to act like a rug. Looking up at the control booth, she could see Brody's wide-eyed face pressed against the glass. Like everyone else, watching, but doing nothing.

Frantically, she looked around for the one person she knew would help her.

Nick. . . . Where the hell was Nick?

As soon as he had heard Stephanie's last transmission, Nick stopped running and began to pick his way cautiously around every shadowed nook and cranny.

"See anything?" Fred said, practically breathing down his neck.

"No," he whispered. "Not a thing. It's so damned dark in here."

Suddenly, they heard footsteps ahead. Loud, fast, running toward them. Nick pulled his gun and assumed a Weaver stance, bracing the pistol with both hands.

A body slammed into the three-quarter plywood wall in front of him, then careened around a corner. Nick cursed the dim light. He couldn't see if the person was holding a gun or not.

"Stop!" he shouted. "Or I swear, I'll blow your head off!"

"David, please," Elizabeth said as she slowly rose from her chair and took a step toward him. "There's no reason for anyone to be hurt here. We can work this out. Let's talk about it."

He looked at her blankly, as though not comprehending what she was saying. "But that's . . . that's why I came here," he stammered. "You don't understand."

In her periphery Elizabeth saw another movement to her right. Thank God, she thought. Maybe Nick had returned or Brody had decided to get one of those guns out of the cupboard and act like a true Texan. Either way, help had arrived, but she didn't dare look around for fear of alerting Ferguson to her rescuer's presence.

"I'm trying to understand, David," she said soothingly. "Really, I am."

The person to her right moved closer, and she began to fear

for his safety. If Ferguson saw him, he would probably turn and kill him in a heartbeat.

The man took one more step, and Elizabeth cringed, knowing the showdown was imminent.

"Please, put the gun down, David," she said. "I don't want you to get hurt. And I don't want you to hurt anyone else."

"What?" David looked at her as though she were crazy. "What do you think I'm—"

The man stepped closer, and David whirled around to face him. Elizabeth recognized him instantly, although he was the last person she had expected to see. Her avenging knight was the shy, red-faced Christopher Taggerty.

Not him, she thought. *Please, not him.* She couldn't stand the thought that this gentle young man might be Ferguson's next victim.

"Christopher," she said. "Stand back, please. Everything is all right. David and I can work this out between the two of us."

But Christopher didn't move. He just stood there, staring at her.

He's frozen, too, she thought. *He's come to my rescue and as a result, he's going to lose his life.*

"Don't come any closer!" David shouted, pointing the gun at Christopher. "Take another step and I'll kill you. I will!"

But Christopher didn't seem to hear him. His attention was fixed fully on Elizabeth. "I am Michael," he murmured. "Michael."

"Michael?" Elizabeth said. "What are you talking about?"

"Michael the Archangel," he replied. He lifted his arm and she saw a flash of metal. Another gun. "And I come with the avenging rod, to strike down evil, to accomplish what my father couldn't. He thought that if he killed you, I would stop. But I can't stop. Not until it's finished."

For a moment Elizabeth couldn't comprehend what was happening. Christopher. David. Both of them? She glanced from one to the other. What was going on?

"The Whore of Babylon must die." Christopher lifted his hand, pointed the gun at Elizabeth and fired.

Nick heard the shot, then another, and for a moment thought he and Fred had been fired on. But the sound had been muffled and behind him. And the person in front of him wasn't the enemy, after all. Stephanie stood there, gun in hand.

"That shot was on the set!" Nick yelled, whirling around and running back through the maze he had just negotiated.

Somehow Ferguson had gotten past them. A shot on the set. That could only mean one thing.

No! his mind screamed as he ran. *No! It doesn't mean that!*

The shot had missed Elizabeth and struck the gilt-framed mirror. The glass exploded, spraying silver shards across the stage.

Charlene screamed. Several of the crew shouted something . . . but remained on the floor. Elizabeth dived behind the mirror, whose back was still intact. Desperately she hoped that Bud had been right about its protection.

The roar of another shot shook the stage, then another.

Elizabeth reached for the pistol beneath her skirt and took a quick look around the edge of the mirror. David Ferguson lay on the floor, a dark crimson spot spreading rapidly across the front of his white uniform.

Christopher was walking slowly toward the mirror, his expression strangely blank, as though he were in some sort of trance. He still held the gun in his hand, though it was pointed at the floor.

As he neared the mirror, he saw her hiding behind it and his vagueness disappeared. His eyes locked with hers, and Elizabeth could see the depth of his insanity, an intense hatred that she couldn't comprehend.

Again, time seemed to slow as her mind readjusted to the truth of her situation. The Mirror Killer hadn't been David Ferguson, after all. David had just been shot, trying to defend her . . . from Christopher Taggerty. Her heart refused to believe what her mind knew was fact.

Christopher fully intended to murder her. The strange glow in his eyes left no doubt. He was a man completely obsessed. He would kill her . . . unless she killed him first.

Elizabeth lifted the dueling pistol and aimed, bracing herself the way Cassie had shown her. "Stop," she said. "Stop right there, or I'll shoot."

Her heart pounded and her ears rang from the close-range gunshots as she waited for him to respond.

Finally, he took another step toward her and said, "It doesn't matter. I've shown them." He nodded toward the camera. Francois was still rolling. "I've shown them all. I've accomplished more in the last few seconds than my father has in his whole life. So, it really doesn't matter what you do now."

As though in slow motion, she saw him lifting the gun to take aim at her again. She wasn't aware of pulling the trigger, but she felt the pistol kick, stinging her palm.

His body jerked, and he stumbled backward a step or two. But he recovered quickly and continued toward her.

The dueling pistol only held one more bullet.

Better make it count, she told herself. Time slowed to a crawl, giving her a moment to consider how willing and ready she was to take a human life. The choice was: Kill or be killed. But that was no choice. Determined to live, she didn't even consider the alternative.

She fired her final bullet, but the shot went wild, striking one of the large lighting fixtures that hung from the ceiling. Again, glass exploded across the set, spraying everyone in a twenty foot radius.

Elizabeth ducked and covered her face with her arm. But a dozen tiny shards pierced her bare arms, shoulders and back, stinging, burning, as the glass rained down on her.

When she looked up, she saw Christopher standing directly

in front of her. His gun was pointing to the middle of her forehead, the barrel tip only inches away.

"It didn't have to end this way, Elizabeth," he said. "I didn't want it to end this way. I had wonderful things planned for the two of us."

"Christopher, please don't," she said, trying to appeal to the dedicated young man she had seen every morning, standing in the rain and snow, supporting a cause he was devoted to. "I can't believe you would want to hurt me. I've never done anything to hurt you. Why would you—?"

"Never done anything?" he said, his jaw tight, his eyes blazing like a person with a high fever. "You've hurt me so many times. I thought you were wonderful. I thought you were a good woman who would be a good wife to me. But you're a whore, just like my father said you were. You aren't worthy of my love."

Elizabeth didn't dare make a move, toward or away from him. She could see his finger tightening on the trigger. With painful clarity, she realized she only had seconds to live.

"I didn't know you loved me, Christopher," she said gently. "I wish you had told me."

"It wouldn't have made any difference. You wouldn't have wanted me. You wanted that cop. You slept with that cop. But it isn't going to happen again. Never again. You won't be mine, but you're not going to be his, either, Because you're going to be dead, Elizabeth. Very dead."

She saw it in his eyes. He was going to do it. She watched as his finger tightened on the trigger, but there was no place to go. Nothing to do.

She thought of Nick, that she would never see him again, touch him again. And a terrible sadness swept over her.

Closing her eyes, she waited for the inevitable.

Nick stood at the edge of the set, gun drawn and trained on Taggerty. Stephanie, Fred, and two Y.B.S. security guards did the same from various vantage points around the set. But no one dared to make a move. Not with him holding the gun to Elizabeth's head. It was too risky.

Nick was the closest . . . close enough to hear everything that Taggerty was saying. He saw the look in Elizabeth's eyes just before she closed them. And Nick knew, as she did, that Taggerty was getting ready to do it.

Nick had often wondered what he would do in this nightmare situation. Someone he cared about, a partner, a loved one . . . at the wrong end of a gun.

Elizabeth and Taggerty were standing so close. If he missed, he could kill her. If he missed, Taggerty could kill her. Nick could hit his target, and Taggerty would still have the ability to pull the trigger and kill her.

Nick weighed each possibility for a split second each. That was all he had time for. Because, all the "coulds" aside, one fact still remained. If he didn't take the shot, Taggerty *would* kill her.

Now, O'Connor, he told himself. *Do it now.*

Nick took a deep breath, held it, and did what he had hoped and prayed he would never have to do in the course of his career.

He pulled the trigger . . . and took a human life.

Elizabeth sat on the edge of the examining table in the hospital emergency room, waiting for the nurse to finish bandaging the last of her cuts. The slivers of glass had been picked out, a few stitches taken, and the painkiller they had given her was finally beginning to take effect, giving her a woozy feeling.

She wished they could give her something to numb her mind and heart as well. But only time, a lot of it, would bring the healing she needed.

And maybe the love of a good man, she added mentally, as she looked across at Nick, who hadn't left her side since the moment he had—

She couldn't stand to think about that yet. The horrible bloodstains that covered the front of her gown were reminder enough of what had happened. Christopher Taggerty, the Mirror Killer, was dead. Cleanly shot with one bullet, fired by Detective Nicholas O'Connor.

Elizabeth couldn't say that she was sorry he was dead; if Nick hadn't killed him, *she* would be the one lying in the morgue right now. But she certainly couldn't say that she was glad. It seemed such a waste of a young life. A haunted, troubled life maybe, but a life, nevertheless.

She would never understand what had driven Christopher to do what he had. What components were necessary to create a psychopath? A repressive, abusive environment, emotional neglect and deprivation, low self-esteem, a desperate craving for control? Perhaps it was just a matter of having a screw loose in the mental machinery. Who knew?

But for now, for tonight, it was over, and that was all Elizabeth cared about. That and to go home, have a long, hot shower, and maybe, if she were fortunate, to sleep for days with Nick's arms around her.

"There you go, Ms. Knight," the nurse said as she snipped the last bit of surgical tape. "All done."

"Thank you." Elizabeth stood, slowly and carefully, as her legs were still too shaky to be reliable.

Nick hurried to assist her with an arm around her waist. "Let's take you home, Lizzie," he said, "before you fall down."

"Sounds wonderful."

But as he was helping her walk from the emergency ward into the hallway, Stephanie came running up to them. The look on her face told Elizabeth that, for some reason, they weren't finished for the night. Not yet.

"It's David Ferguson," Stephanie said breathlessly. "The doctor sent me to get you, Elizabeth. He said that Ferguson is asking for you."

Elizabeth felt as though she were sinking into a deep, dark pool of stagnant water. And she was beginning to think she was never going to hit the bottom.

Looking up at Nick, she said, "I don't think I can do it. I just don't have anything left inside me. I . . ."

"It's all right, Liz," he replied. "You don't have to see him. You don't owe him anything."

"He took a bullet for me."

"That was his choice. If you ask me, it was the least he could do, considering what he's put you through over the years."

Stephanie cleared her throat and looked uncomfortable. "Ah . . . I don't know if this would make any difference in your decision, Ms. Knight, but I think I should tell you—the doctor says that David Ferguson is dying."

"I did it for you, Elizabeth. I did it *all* for you."

David Ferguson *was* dying. Elizabeth wouldn't have needed a doctor to tell her that as she stood next to his hospital bed, Nick beside her, and listened to his final words.

She didn't know what to say. So, she said nothing and just let him talk. For the last two minutes he had been telling her how his actions had been a result of his devotion to her.

Even in death, David Ferguson wasn't going to take responsibility for killing her sister. "Love" had made him do it. His love for her. Somehow, in his crooked rationale, this made *her* responsible.

Nice try. But she wasn't buying it. Not anymore. For years she had shouldered the guilt, but no more. The guilt was going to die along with David Ferguson.

"Elizabeth, please," he said, reaching for her hand.

She cringed as his fingers closed around hers, but she didn't pull away. "Please what?" she asked warily.

"Please . . . say that you understand. Say that you love me."

That was the reason he had given for killing Martie. He had been trying to get her to say she loved him.

No, he was asking far too much. She couldn't bring to herself to speak the lie, not even for a dying man.

"I can't say that, David." She looked down into those brown, doe eyes and knew that she hated him with every ounce of her being. Strange . . . the hate didn't give her strength any longer. It had turned bitter and was poisoning her spirit.

Did she intend to live with this bitterness for the rest of her life? Was she going to carry this heaviness, day after day, year after year, allowing it to sap her energy and drain her dry?

No. This was the time to release it. This was the time to bury the hate along with the guilt, neither of which served her any longer.

"I can't tell you that I love you, David," she said. "It simply isn't true. But I will tell you one thing. . . . on my porch that night, you asked for my forgiveness, and I told you I couldn't give it. Well, I couldn't then, but I can now."

A look of disappointment, quickly followed by wonder crossed his face. "Really?" he asked.

"Yes, David. I forgive you. I have to, if I'm ever going to find peace."

She felt his grip on her fingers lessen, then his hand dropped to the sheet beside him. He gazed up at her, but he seemed to be having difficulty focusing. "Thank you," he whispered. "I took her life . . . but I saved yours. Are we even?"

Elizabeth nodded. "Yes, David. We're even."

He closed his eyes, and Elizabeth knew instinctively that he was never going to open them again. Her nightmare, which had started ten years ago, was over, finished at last.

"May your soul find its own peace, David," she said. "In the next world, if not in this one."

She turned to Nick and held out her hand to him. "Let's go home," she said. "I really need to go home."

Epilogue

A cold beer, a good steak on the grill, his dog snoring at his feet, and three days off—three in a row. What more could a guy ask for on the Fourth of July? Nick thought as he stretched out on the chaise lounge and breathed in the hickory-scented smoke that wafted toward him. His stomach growled in anticipation. The aroma of the barbecue, and everyone else's in the neighborhood, filled the hot, humid air, along with the smell of newly mown grass and the occasional pop of firecrackers from merrymakers who couldn't wait until sundown.

As he watched his mom puttering in the flower bed at the edge of the small yard, he congratulated himself once again for talking her into buying this house, moving to the island and retiring. God knows, she deserved it. She looked up from her rose cutting for a moment and their eyes met. Her smile and her slightly sunburned nose and cheeks said it all. She looked at least ten years younger, healthier and happier than he could ever remember seeing her.

She's doin' good, Papa. Silently he sent the message heavenward. *Just look at her. What a beauty! No wonder you were so in love with her.*

He could have sworn he heard the silent answer, "And still am, Nicky my lad, still am."

From inside his mother's small house, he could hear laughter and it occurred to him that he should go in and play the host. But the beer and heat had made him deliciously lazy, and they sounded like they were having a great time without him.

A moment later, the back door opened and Elizabeth emerged, carrying a platter of assorted chips and dips. Ah, Elizabeth's homemade salsa . . . a good thing was getting even better. She sashayed over to him and placed the plate on the T.V. tray beside his chair. Her white shorts and halter top set off her golden tan to perfection. As she bent over, his eyes followed the line of her nicely rounded bottom and Nick decided to amend his list of things that made a perfect Fourth of July afternoon.

"What are you thinking?" she asked with a mischievous grin as she sat beside him on the edge of the chaise.

"The word 'hot' was uppermost in my mind," he said, running his hand along her bare midriff below the halter. After seven months of being her steady lover, he still couldn't get over how soft her skin was.

"The weather?" she asked. "The salsa?"

He growled softly, glanced at his mother to see that she was occupied, then moved his hand down to cup her bottom. "Guess again."

Before she could reply, the party spilled out of the house and into the yard, Nina and her new boyfriend, Tony—a punk if Nick had ever seen one—Fred and his latest squeeze, a still recuperating, but feisty as ever Cassandra.

Her recovery had been slow, and sometimes painful, but she was nearly herself again. Nick was happy for her; he only wished he could say the same for Pete. Last he had heard, Peter was in rehab . . . again. Maybe one of these days it would take, but Nick wasn't holding his breath.

The teenagers walked over to Rosemarie, and Nick could see that Tony was doing his best to charm Mama. Nick shook his head, remembering the routine all too well. Boys . . . always horny as hell. Not like men, of course. His hand moved across Elizabeth's hip and he made a mental note that she didn't seem to be wearing panties.

"Stop that this instant, you two!" Cassie said as she walked over to where they sat, Fred in tow. "We're the only ones allowed to do stuff like that."

Nick looked at Fred and lifted one eyebrow. Fred blushed beneath his sunburn and shrugged. Privately, he had told Nick that Cassie was going to kill him for sure. But he had decided to just up his life insurance and hope for the best. Actually, their five-month romance had been great for them both. Fred had proved a faithful friend, standing beside Cassie as she had endured the rigors of physical therapy.

And Fred Halley, whose only regular exercise for years had been hefting an extra large Dunkin' Donuts coffee, had been spending a lot of time in the gym. Over the months, Nick and Elizabeth had noted how the bulk around his waist had gradually migrated upward, turning into chest and shoulders.

Cassie might kill him, Nick thought, but at least he'd die a happy man.

He and Cass plopped down on the grass beside the sleeping bulldog. Cassie tweaked his ear, tickling the tiny hairs inside. He snorted, then resumed his snoring. She leaned down and sniffed his breath. "You've got him soused again," she told Nick with an accusing tone. "He's not asleep; he's passed out."

"Ah, you're just jealous now that you're on the wagon," Nick replied, toasting her with his beer bottle.

"You're damned right. Can't drink, can't dance, yet, but I'm working on it. If it weren't for babycakes here . . ." She nodded toward Fred. ". . . life wouldn't be worth living."

Fred flushed a darker shade of red, Elizabeth giggled and Nick snickered. "Babycakes, huh? Gee, wait 'til the guys at the station hear that one."

Shooting him a deadly look, Fred wrapped his arm around Cass's shoulder and said, "I thought you were going to . . . you know . . . ask Elizabeth something."

"Oh, yeah." Cass glanced over at Rosemarie and the kids and lowered her voice. "We were wondering if we could walk over to your house and . . . well, I forgot to take my medicine and it's in my purse there on your coffee table and . . ."

"Yeah, yeah." Elizabeth reached in her pocket and pulled out a key. "But stay off the furniture," she whispered.

"All of it?"

"All. Since when have you gotten picky? I thought any horizontal surface would do."

Cassie looked at Fred and laughed. "Or even vertical. You get creative during physical therapy."

"You've always been creative," Elizabeth muttered under her breath.

"Yeah, thanks for the leg warmer tip," Nick added, then winced as Elizabeth gouged him in the ribs.

"That reminds me." Cass leaned closer to Elizabeth. "Do you have any—"

"Third dresser drawer on the right," she whispered. "Throw them in the laundry when you're done."

"Red ones?"

"All colors. Take your pick."

"Wow, let's go, babycakes. Time's a wastin'." She rose and hauled Fred to his feet.

He gave Nick one of those, "Life's hell, but what can you do?" looks and followed obediently.

As soon as they had left, Nina and Tony sauntered over. "Tony's going to take Mama and me out for ice cream. Wanna come?" she asked, looking up at Tony with what Nick disgustedly called "cow eyes." This punk was such a suck up. Taking the family out for ice cream—what an original idea. Nick had used it for years.

"No, thanks," he said. "You guys go along and have fun. Us oldtimers will just hang out here."

Nina gave him a suspicious grin. "You oldtimers just want to be alone, huh? Gonna set off some fireworks a little early?"

"Go." Nick waved them away. "Now."

Nina slipped her arm through Tony's and they returned to Rosemarie.

"Fireworks, humph. . . ." Nick said. "That kid's got a smart mouth. Wonder where she got it?"

They watched the threesome pile into Tony's old beater and drive away. "Yeah, I wonder," Elizabeth replied.

She leaned over and gave him a long, lazy kiss. Her hair fell around her face and his, tickling his cheeks and neck. His hand moved from her hip upward to cup her breast. Breathing in her warm, female scent, he promptly forgot the barbecue.

"Wanna set off some premature fireworks, toots?" he asked, nodding toward the house.

She nodded. "Sure. Tell me, big boy . . . how do you feel about . . . cherry bombs?"

Sitting at the end of the dock, her feet dangling over the edge, Elizabeth looked out across the moonlit water which glistened in sparkling shades of pink, silver, and blue . . . and she remembered.

"I dreamed this once," she said, turning to Nick who sat beside her, playing with a strand of her hair. As he lifted it off her neck, his fingertips brushed her skin and gave her a delicious shiver. "It was a beautiful dream. I had it the night that . . ."

The night that the killer had crept into her house and touched her as she slept. Christopher Taggerty. At least now, her midnight phantom had a name and a face. Slowly, month after month, his name and face and touch were fading, losing their power over her emotions.

"I'm healing, Nick," she said, feeling the wonder of the realization. "It doesn't hurt so much now. I still remember everything, but it's somehow becoming removed, distant."

"I know," he said, leaning over and kissing her forehead. "I've seen the difference. I'm really happy for you . . . for both of us."

He paused and looked out over the water where the last of the Independence Day boat parties were winding down. She wondered what was on his mind. He seemed preoccupied. "It will be dawn soon," he said thoughtfully. He turned to face her and took both her hands in his. "I've been waiting, Liz," he said.

"For what?"

"For you to start healing, to get your life back in order, to know where you're going and what you want."

She laughed. "My life has never been in order, Nick, and I've never been sure what I want. I hope you aren't waiting for that."

He lifted her left hand and kissed her fingers. "You know what I mean," he said solemnly.

She sobered. He really was serious about something. "I have my book deal," she said. "I'm very excited about that. I've always wanted to try writing a novel. Is that what you mean?"

"Yeah, kinda." His grip on her hands tightened and the look on his face frightened her.

"Nick, what is it? What's wrong?"

"Nothing." He dropped her hands into her lap and took her into his arms. "It's just that . . . I enjoy being your friend and your lover, but I need—"

"Oh, Nick!" She pushed away from him, her heart pounding as tears sprang to her eyes. "Are you trying to break up with me? Is this the 'I need my freedom' routine?"

He stared at her and slowly shook his head. Then he began to laugh. "Lizzie, you're a nut, you know that? Why do you always assume the worst?"

Cupping her face with both his hands, he lifted her chin and kissed her lips, her cheeks, and the end of her nose. "I was going to say that I love being your boyfriend, but I need more."

"More? You need more, not less?" Her mouth dropped open.

He pushed up with his thumb, closing her mouth. "Watch it, kid. You're going to catch fireflies. Yes, I don't want to just be your boyfriend. I want to be your husband."

"Husband?" The word felt strange on her lips. Strange, but very nice. And natural when applied to Nick. "I . . . I. . . ."

"You . . . you . . . ?"

"I never had one of those before."

"Neither have I . . . a wife, that is." His eyes searched hers and she could tell by the smile that spread across his face that he had found his answer. "But I want to try it. Marry me, Lizzie, and maybe we can start doing something about changing that office of yours back into a nursery. What do you say?"

"I say . . . yes," she whispered.

In an instant, Nick tackled her, pushing her onto her back and throwing himself on top of her. Growling, he began to kiss her, nipping at her lips and neck, while she squealed and wriggled beneath him.

Finally, he came up for air. "Yes?" he said breathlessly. "Did you really say yes?"

She nodded. He threw back his head and laughed loudly, the sound echoing across the water. "She said yes!" he yelled to the boats and their, by now, badly hungover occupants. "Did you hear that? She said she'd marry me!"

"Yeah, yeah, we hear you, asshole," a grouchy voice echoed in return. "We *a-a-ll* hear you. Congratulations and shut up already!"

A few seconds later, a flare rose from the boat, raining red stars onto the water.

"Now look at that," Nick said as he put his arms around Elizabeth and kissed her again. "And they say New Yorkers are rude."